PRAISE FOR *THE IRISHMAN*

"The Irishman is rich with emotion that tugs the heart-strings, warm with humor and characters who enchant. . . ."
—Bestselling author Raine Cantrell

"The Irishman is every woman's dream fulfilled, a warm and charming story to engage your heart. Ms. McGowan brings turn-of-the-century Minnesota to life with the detailed skill of a seasoned artist."
—Bestselling author Shirl Henke

PRAISE FOR WYNEMA MCGOWAN

"Unique, refreshing, heartwarming—Wynema McGowan is a wonderful new talent."

—Kathe Robin

* * *

The last thing Ella Mae Botts Hermann needed was a good dose of love. She already had more trouble than she could handle! Her mother was crazy, her uncle was worse, her baby was teething, and her husband long-gone. If something could go wrong with her life in the last year, it had—and now she had Sean McGloin to deal with. The man claimed to be looking for work. She claimed she couldn't afford to pay him. He stayed and worked anyway. Nothing she, or her crazy family, or her even crazier life threw at him drove him away. What held him in Otter Tail, Minnesota? As she struggled to cope, she vowed to find out—and love was only part of the answer!

Turn the page and see why everyone loves this author!

SHE KNEW HE WAS TROUBLE THE MINUTE SHE LAID EYES ON HIM. . . .

"Can I give you a hand, ma'am?"

"Aah!" Mae whirled around. Heart pumping, her eyes searched a dark silhouette less than five feet away. A man—no, a giant—stood in her yard!

"Yes? Can I . . . Can I help you with something?" As she asked the question, a hundred thoughts ran through her mind. *. . . The rifle . . . was it by the front door? . . . was it loaded? . . . where was her Uncle Ed? . . . what good would Uncle Ed do? . . . this was the biggest man she'd ever seen! . . . Oh my God!*

"I'm looking for work." Courteously, he removed his hat, revealing shiny hair that was as black as an iron skillet. She wasn't reassured by seeing his eyes clearly. The color of breath in February, they seemed to penetrate her soul like forty-below winds.

She walked the few steps to the screen door, reached out and latched it. Those eyes of steel followed every move she made. She pressed her fingers to her lips. *Oh, God, what were you thinking? That piddling latch wouldn't stop him from opening the door!*

Some people, she had read once, have a predator's sense. They can smell fear like a wolf pack scents blood. This man was one of those people. She knew it like she knew her name—which she couldn't recall right now for the life of her. Sweat gathered between her breasts.

"I don't need . . ." Her throat felt like she had an apricot pit wedged in it. "I mean, we . . ." It wouldn't do for him to think she was alone. ". . . don't need help. But thank you anyway." The silence stretched to an uncomfortable length. The man looked over at the chicken coop with the wire on one side hanging open, then at the cows and chickens sharing a pasture.

"Looks to me like you could use a hand."

"I . . . we have no money, mister." Her voice rose pleadingly. "Really. None."

As if he hadn't heard he commenced working. He knew that there wasn't a woman alive immune to the charms of Sean McGloin. Not even one . . .

THE IRISHMAN

WYNEMA McGOWAN

PINNACLE BOOKS
KENSINGTON PUBLISHING CORP.

PINNACLE BOOKS are published by

Kensington Publishing Corp.
850 Third Avenue
New York, NY 10022

First Printing: April, 1995

Printed in the United States of America

Thanks to everybody who had a hand in this. You know who you are, and I couldn't have done it without you.

Prologue

Otter Tail, Minnesota
Fall, 1895

The most junior conductor for the Chicago Northwestern Railway paused in front of the solitary traveler. The man looked like he was asleep with his arms folded across his chest and his denim-encased legs skewed into the aisle. The conductor hesitated. He hated to wake the guy but then again, he *had* asked about the next fuel stop. He cleared his throat. "Mister? We're gonna lay over in Otter Tail for a bit. Not much to see there, but you said to let you know."

The hat brim lifted, revealing a lynx-eyed stare that wasn't a bit sleepy. "Thanks." The man rolled up out of his seat and resettled his hat.

Holy moly! the conductor thought. Tall as he was, he was only eye level with the guy's collar. He took in the width of the man's shoulders and a score of small facial scars and his interest kindled. He was an avid sports enthusiast. "Been around these parts before, mister?"

"No."

The man was peering out the soot flecked window where steep, heavily forested bluffs lined a glassy river of awe-inspiring dimensions.

"Traveling to the Cities, I'll bet?"

The man nodded toward the impressive scene. "What river's that?"

The conductor looked outside where two fishermen rowed a small dinghy past a long-legged waterfowl majestically poised at the end of a sandbar. "Oh, that's the St. Croix. Runs between part of Wisconsin and Minnesota. Pretty, ain't it?"

"Yeah," the man replied as he moved toward the end of the car. He lit a smoke first then he stepped through the door.

The young conductor snapped his fingers. *Yeah! Why that's Jake Kilrain! The great bareknuckle fighter! I'd know him anywhere! Holy moly! Wait'll I tell the gang.*

Sean McGloin straddled the coupler and braced a hand on each car. Cool air tugged at his hat and flapped his jacket behind him. He inhaled deeply. *Ah, but it smells fine. Clean. Fertile. Unused.* It was nearly dusk. The rugged terrain had smoothed to rolling hills and tidy farms with brush-skirted windmills.

Soon signs of a denser population flashed by. A weather worn livery and stable. A slaughterhouse with a holding pen. Three dray wagons in front of a clapboard building with "Oberlin Creamery" painted on its roof. When the train slowed enough, Sean swung off. Turning his collar against the wind, he looked down the ribbon of road that led to Otter Tail. He didn't have to see the faded sign on the depot wall— Otter Tail. Pop. 402—to tell it wasn't much of a town.

He'd just propped a boot sole back on the station house wall when the girl got off. Shadowed beneath the brim of his hat, his eyes tracked her across the platform. She was carrying a baby! He hadn't noticed a kid before. He had, however, noticed the girl. Indeed he had. She'd been seated several rows ahead of him. About two hours earlier she'd stood and bent and reached under her seat—which resulted in a nicely rounded derriere being pointed right at him—and after tucking a small battered case under her arm, she'd walked his way.

Now there, he'd thought, is a pretty gel. No, he'd amended as she neared, pretty's too tame. Beautiful's more like it. Reed slender yet voluptuous. Long thoroughbred legs. Hair like silver. No, more like moonlight.

Ah, t' hell with the hair, man! The gel's better endowed than a railroad baron's trust.

As she passed, her wide-spaced blue eyes—red-rimmed and underscored with crescent-shaped shadows of purple—briefly met his, then looked away.

For the next two hours, the knowledge that she had been crying had bothered him, and it continued to bother him like a pebble in a boot on a ten-mile march. Now why was she crying, do you suppose?

From his vantage point by the station wall, he watched her get a bear hug from an older man—her father, by the looks of him—then she nodded shyly to two big farm boys who were standing off to one side. The old man bent down to the baby who had its face hidden in the girl's neck. She coaxed the child in a soft voice and jiggled it a little. The baggage car door slid open with a loud clang. She flinched. A couple of train workers eased a coffin over to the opening.

Ah, Sean thought, so there's the rub.

The old man and the two boys started wrestling with the coffin. It tilted. The girl groaned and covered her mouth. Sean tossed aside his smoke and went over. "Give you a hand?"

The old man nodded. "Mighty nice of you, mister."

"No' atall." He helped carry the coffin to a flatbed wagon that had been pulled parallel to the platform. The old man nodded again.

As he strolled back toward the train, he encountered the girl. He stopped and pulled on his hat. She improves with scrutiny, he thought. Except that right now she's got the kind of glassy-eyed stare one sees right after delivering a knockout punch. When she smiled slightly he experienced a vague feeling of . . . recognition. There was something about her eyes or maybe it was the shape of her face. A memory eluded him.

It seemed they stood there for quite a time before she whispered, "Thank you," and walked away.

Sean pushed back his jacket and just stood there.

Like an idiot. Like somebody'd nailed yer bloody boots to the platform.

With his hands on his hips in a wide-legged, unconsciously contentious stance, he watched the wagon disappear around the corner. A piercing whistle and he turned. The blasted train was pulling out! He spat a word and raced alongside and made a flying leap for the narrow iron stairs.

A feeling knifed through him as he watched the picturesque depot vanish from sight. It was a feeling not unlike the one he had when a comrade fell in battle.

One

Sean sprawled across the narrow bed with one arm curved under his head and a thin, black cheroot clamped between his teeth. Through an open window came the patter of rain and a brisk breeze that fluttered the curtains.

No wonder Minnesota has ten thousand lakes, he thought. If it wasn't for the temperature, a person would mistake the place for Ranchipoor in the rainy season. He'd been here a week and it had rained every day.

As O'Brien had promised, he'd been met at the train station in Minneapolis. "Look for a man with liver-spotted hands and two-tone hair the color of gull droppings," O'Brien had said. "He'll ask you if you've heard the score of the Drogheda game and then he'll escort you to a safe house."

An escort. The thought brought a quirk to grim lips. Sean was used to being escorted to the edge of town. Not to a soft bed and hot water.

"You'll be safe here," Special Agent Hanson had told him as the driver slowed to a stop. Sean leaned up and parted the curtain. 7TH AVENUE HOTEL, the rain smeared sign read, HOUSEKEEPING ROOMS BY THE WEEK. He opened the door and started to get out.

"You'll be . . ."

Hanson stopped speaking abruptly and looked beyond Sean to the street. A man pulling a two-wheeled ash can had stopped to pick up a pile of horse manure. Sean watched the old man and then looked back at Hanson. *Surely he didn't think . . .*

Apparently he did, because Hanson waited until the man had stowed his shovel and moved on before he continued. "Like I was saying. You'll be fine. Everything's been paid for. Just tell the guy at the desk if you need anything. He's one of ours. He knows how to get in touch with us if need be."

Sean grabbed his grip from the back. "We'll be in contact weekly," Hanson added and then pulled the door closed and snapped the lines over the horse's flank.

Abruptly Sean stubbed out his cheroot. Weekly? He picked up his timepiece and turned it into the light and then cursed and flung it across the bed. Weekly! He rolled up and buried all ten fingers in his hair. He wasn't sure he could last another day.

He should be sleeping like the dead. He'd walked a hundred miles in the last week, his footfalls echoing off the slick cobblestones like hobnail boots in church. But every time he closed his eyes he saw the creaking sign. The tiny depot. The casket on the wagon. And the girl.

There was something about that girl! Why did she strike such a chord in him? He knew he'd never seen her before.

He got up, walked to the window and braced both hands on the sill. The streetlamp's spotlight-shaped cone gave the slick pavement a warm amber glow but the predawn sky promised yet another dismally cold and rainy day.

"Bloody hell!" He stalked to the dresser and poured himself a hefty drink. His muscular shoulders gleamed like teak in the rain-diffused light. His torso tapered to a narrow waist, tight buttocks and legs that were very long and quite hairy. He tossed down the drink. Then, as if testing the perimeters of a cage, he started pacing.

Stay put, Hanson had said.

And run the risk of bein' taken like an animal in a snare? his unerring inner voice cautioned. *Moreover, 'tis worse than jail.*

Worse than Cuba? Worse than Marrakech? He snorted. In a pig's eye. Besides, I've sort of given me word.

A few more weeks of this an' ye'll be a blitherin' idiot, the voice warned.

'Tis true, he allowed. He was not a man to take confinement easy. He had to find something to do. There must be some way he could pass the time until O'Brien was ready. He was not a stranger to work. Mentally he catalogued his "jobs" over the years—sailor, pugilist, patriot for hire—and snorted again. Wonder if they have much callin' for soldiers of fortune in . . . what was it? Otter Tail?

He froze in midstride, like he'd just heard a gun cocked.

Well? Why not? He'd agreed to stay somewhere for the duration but he had not specified where exactly.

It was raining in earnest now. Rivulets of water ran off the pane and splashed onto the sill. Gray fingers of dawn streaked the sky.

Why not, indeed, he thought as he started emptying the bureau, tossing items on the bed, rolling them sailor-style and stuffing them in his grip. He worked silently and efficiently. In minutes, except for a neat pile of clothes on the chair, all evidence of his pres-

ence had been removed. *I'm long past justifying me
actions. To meself or anyone else.*

Next to his skin he strapped a leather money belt,
followed by an oriental scabbard holding a jade-
handled stiletto, and then he shrugged into his shirt.

He'd send O'Brien a wire. Tell him he was of a
mind to see a bit o' the country. As his tree-trunk
sized thighs disappeared into well-worn blue denim
pants, he muttered, "See a bi' o' the country, me arse.
A bi' o' silver haired fluff is more like it."

Two

Chilly gusts of wind carried the scent of wood smoke from the farmhouse below. Overhead, a noisy flock of Canada geese stretched their black necks against the taupe-colored sky as if reaching for a finish line. Unfortunately their grand passage went completely unacclaimed.

Mae huddled at the foot of her father's grave with his old coat slung over her shoulders. A tear rolled down the curve of her cheek. She struggled to rein in her emotions, but minutes passed before she could dry her eyes on her skirt hem.

She looked over her rounded shoulder at the isolated farm in the valley. She was feeling sorry for herself again. In spite of all her resolve, her attitude remained as poor as her purse. She was determined to overcome her poor spirits but she couldn't seem to think clearly any more. Everything was happening so fast!

She'd left Chicago in a daze. She just wanted to go home! Home to be coddled and fussed over, home to heal, home to her mama and papa. Her mama and papa, she told herself as the train pulled into Otter Tail, would make everything all right.

She knew something was wrong with her mother immediately. They had been sitting at the kitchen table when her father made a comment about Peter's funeral.

"Wait a minute, dear," her mother interrupted. "I'm not sure I know him. Peter who?"

Mae gave her mother a slightly-strained smile. "You know, Mama. My . . ." she choked on the word husband. ". . . You know. Peter!"

Her mother pointed a finger at her. "Don't use that tone with me, young lady." She huffed. "Trying to rush me! I will not stand for being rushed."

Shocked speechless, Mae watched her mother tap the table.

"Peter. Peter. Peter." Tap. Tap. Tap.

Her mother's lips were pursed, her eyes narrowed in thought. Mae looked up at her father. He patted the air then cocked his head toward the barn in a silent signal.

"Peter. Peter. Peter." The lantern sputtered. Tap. Tap. Tap.

Mae about jumped a foot when her mother snapped her fingers, "Oh, I know who you mean now. That fella works at the creamery." She smiled from Mae to her father, as if she expected to be congratulated.

Soon as dinner was finished Mae followed her father to the barn, walking as if she had a sack of potatoes tied to each ankle. The clement night, star-spangled and brightly moonlit, suddenly seemed bleak and ominous. Warily she hesitated in the door. "Here I am, Papa."

"Good. Come, then." He motioned her to him, but then he was silent. He held a cigar can under the edge of the work table and brushed some rusty nails into it. Two fork-tailed barn swallows flew around the ceiling beams, disturbed by the late night visit.

She turned her father toward her and put a hand on his arm, "Please, tell me what's wrong with Mama."

He rubbed his horny hand over his brow. "Your mama's very sick."

"Why didn't you write me about it? Why didn't you . . ."

"There was nothing you could do. Way down there and just having the baby. You'd just worry yourself sick, too."

Mae looked at her father then. Really looked. How had she missed the anguish in his face? "Is it . . . serious?" *Saynosaynosaynosayno,* she chanted inwardly.

"I . . . yes, I guess so." He hooked an arm around her shoulder and pulled her close. She felt him drop a kiss on her parted hair.

"Doc says it's senile dem . . . demetoria . . . Well, something like that. Hardening of the arteries anyway. Started out, she couldn't remember little things. Then it got to be big things too. Sometimes she don't even remember me." He inhaled raggedly and then fell silent.

She waited a long time, eyes riveted on his face. His Adam's apple jerked and moisture was gathered in the corners of his sky blue eyes. Papa wasn't going to cry, was he? Not Papa!

"One day, couple of months back, I said, 'Here's a letter from Mae Ella, just come at the post office'— and your Mama says—'Mae Ella who?' "

She pressed her face into his shirt. "Oh, God, Papa!"

"Shush," he murmured against her hair. "Crying don't help." He hugged her tighter. "Now you're here. With God's help, we'll manage somehow."

Two days later she walked into the barn and found her father sprawled spread-eagle by the loft ladder. Sandy was pawing him and whining pitifully. She dropped to her knees beside him. "Papa?" Only seconds before, he had grabbed his battered hat off the peg, kissed her cheek and walked out of the kitchen. She heard his sharp whistle to his dog, like always.

Like always. Like a thousand times before.

Mae blew her nose and her father's dog rolled his eyes in her direction. The old hound lay on top of her father's grave with his hind legs splayed like a leap frog. "Darn you, Sandy!" She stood, but the hound only rippled his brow and followed her movements with moist, sad eyes.

Best leave him be, she decided. He might stop eating again. The first couple of days after the funeral, the dog had almost grieved himself to death! Papa would never forgive her if she let that happen. For as long as she could remember, she had seen the two of them together, coming in from the fields, going hunting or, as if the dog were as human as her father thought him to be, sitting side by side on the wagon seat.

That darn dog depresses me. The grave. The raw ground. The bleak weather. . . .

All right, it's true. Everything depresses me.

The other morning she'd been collecting eggs and dropped one. She sat down on the hard packed dirt—right in the chicken poop—and bawled like a baby.

"I've had no time!" she cried. "No time to heal, to grieve."

That was another thing. She'd started talking to herself. But that wasn't all. Somebody answered. Well, not just somebody. She'd started hearing her grandmother's voice.

"Ve kom from strong stock." (That was Granny talking now.) "Ve get knocked down, ve get up again. Strong stock, liebchen."

"You do, maybe. My stock must've gotten diluted."

Mae's fingers skimmed the wood and wire fence, absentmindedly noting that the north side sure needed shoring up. She walked on to the crest of the hill where her grandfather and grandmother's graves were designated by almost illegible wood markers. Above them, like a child's drawing of the sunshine, were their babies' graves. Their names were written in the Bible in Grandfather's bold, back-slanting scrawl.

> *Kris Wilhelm, aged four. Of the cold.*
> *Alexandra, six days. Never well.*
> *Sophia Louise, two years. The fever.*

So sad, she thought and shivered as she slid down the tree. Poor Granny. How had she ever done it?

All her life people had told her, "Mae Ella, you sure do remind me of your grandmother." Oh, she loved hearing that. Good, she used to think, I'm going to be just like Granny when I grow up.

She leaned against the knurled oak. Those people were wrong. I'm not a bit like Granny. Granny had grit and gumption. She would never wallow in self-pity. Faced with calamity and misfortune, Granny had not only survived, she had flourished. Her grand-mother had possessed a zest for living Mae had never seen duplicated. Right up until the day she died.

What she wouldn't give for some of Granny's grit! Tucking her chin onto her chest and rocking rhyth-mically, she whispered, "Are you still there, Granny? It's me again, Mae Ella."

Nothing but the sigh of the wind.

"I don't know what to do. I could sure use some help, Granny."

A long pause, and then, "Alvays put on clean apron. Alvays add more oats to egg basket. You vil be fine, liebchen. You yust hav' to get your face straight."

Mae smirked. Granny always got her words mixed up. "It's get your head straight, Granny."

"Ask und you vil receive."

"Ask?"

"Ask for help, liebchen. It vil not hurt."

"Well, all right." Pushing her legs straight out, holding the leaf in both hands between her breasts, Mae closed her eyes tight.

Her mind went blank. She panicked. Oh, God, that's how her mother's illness had started. One day she could no longer remember everyday things like her prayers. Long seconds passed, but for the life of her Mae could only recall the prayer she used to say as a child. "Now I lay me down to sleep, I pray . . ."

She sat there a long time. Finally, only just remembering where she was, she glanced around. She sighed. Her mother would be awake by now.

"Come on, Sandy." The dog surprised her by standing up and trotting to her side.

"Let's go home."

Three

Whores. Barbers. Bartenders. The best sources of information in any town in the world. Sean was willing to bet that Otter Tail was no exception. He dropped his grip inside the door of the barbershop; curtains—red and white to match the symbolic candy-striped pole outside—parted in the rear of the shop. A small man who could've been anywhere from fifty to eighty years old hurried out. "Ya! Kumin. Ya caught me yust afore I vas ta close . . ."

Norwegian as galdhopiggin, Sean thought, and reached for his bag. "I can come back tomorrow."

"Heck, I sure got no place ta hurry ta." He tossed a magazine on the counter, then dusted off the worn leather chair with a towel from his back pocket. He swiveled the chair toward Sean invitingly. "Yust sit down right here an' velkomin t'yew, Mister . . . ?"

"McGloin. Sean McGloin."

"Einar Torkelson here." He held out his hand and they shook. "Pleased t'make yewr acquaintance, Mr. McGloin." He pointed to the magazine. "I vas only readin' dat story dere."

A dime novel. *Frank Merriwell's Great Victory— Or The Effort of His Life*. The book's cover had a caricature of a pomaded blond man running. "How is it?" Sean asked.

"Oh, dat's good stuff! It's a serial, yew know? By

golly, dat Merriwell fella gets himself inta more pickles. I could save it for yew ven I'm done, if yew like?"

"I, er . . . think I've read it." The little man was almost Sean's height now that he was sitting down. Over half glasses the barber's fjord-colored eyes twinkled with friendliness and honest curiosity.

"Shave an' a cut taday or yust vun uf 'em?"

"Might as well do both." Sean loosened a couple of buttons on his blue twill shirt, leaned up and flipped his collar inside.

"I see yew like t'wear yewr hair kinda longish." Einar draped a protective smock made of a shiny black material over him.

"Yeah."

"Whew, by golly! Yew sure got yewrself a fine moustache." He bustled around, selecting certain bottles, arraying the tools of his trade. He snapped a towel, then fastened it around Sean's neck.

"I'd better still have it when you're done." Sean softened his words with a slight smile but he meant every word. He was very partial to his 'stache.

"Yew bet! I don't vant ta get on da wrong side uf a man yewr size. What are yew? Six-five?"

"Four." Sean hooked his bootheel on the chair's metal rung and laid an ankle on the opposite knee. His eyes rimmed the rectangular mirror in front of him. Ads stuck between the glass and wood frame cut its size considerably. Hair Cut & Shave—25 cents . . . Herman's Pomade—5 cents . . . White's Elixir and Tonic. "Say, that elixir there, are you supposed to drink it or smear it on your head?"

"Heh, heh, heh! Dat's a good vun!"

Sean gave the barber a narrow-eyed look. He hadn't been joking.

Torkelson ran a rat-tail comb through Sean's hair.

"Yew won't never need ta do either vun. Yew'll never be bald. But yew probably already knew dat. Bet yew don't have vun bald relation, do yew?"

"I don't have one relation, period."

"Oh? Vell . . ." The barber, ill at ease, quickly changed the subject. "Before I start to trim, should I touch up dis gray right here?"

"Gray? No shit!" Like it was the first time he'd noticed, Sean turned his head right to left. "Nah. Guess not."

"Kinda gives yew a distinguished look, heh?" The barber disappeared through the candy-stripe curtains. He returned shortly, flipping a steaming towel back and forth in his hands, "I like ta do da shave first. Okay by yew?"

"Suit your mmpft . . ."

"Yust passin' through, Mr. McGloin?"

"Mmpft!"

"How long yew figure on stayin'?"

The towel growled.

"Dis is a nice little town, growin' every day since da train started stoppin' on a regular basis. An', bein' as we're close ta da river, we get quite a lot uf people down from da Cities. For da fishin', don't yew know." Einar removed the towel.

Sean smiled. Fishing! God, he used to love to fish! Trout, salmon. When he was a kid. About a thousand years ago.

"We got da saugers—some call 'em sand pike— Muskies an' da northern. Striped bass, but yew come too late in da season for da fishin'. Now yew gotta wait for da ice. Heh, heh, heh. Won't be a long wait either." Einar ran a finger down Sean's jaw then slapped the towel back on, pressing with surprising strength into his face. "By golly, yew got yourself a toughie dere. Ever grow it out?"

"Mmpft."

"Vell, yew sure don't have ta, not vid dat yaw uf yewrs. Some fellas need a beard ta hide da fact dat dey don't got no yaw. Yew sure don't got dat problem!"

Torkelson started stropping the hell out of a straight razor. The man was very close to Sean's mental picture of what a leprechaun should look like. With a little peaked hat and a green jacket and some big buckled shoes . . . 'Course, he'd have to keep his mouth shut. Probably an impossible task.

"Lookin' for da work?" Einar twirled the chair. It protested Sean's weight with a strident squeal.

"Maybe. First thing I'm looking for is a good meal."

"Ya? Vell, by golly, I vas yust gonna grab a bite myself at da cafe. Best eats in town." He paused in lathering Sean's jaw with a soft bristled brush and met his eye in the mirror. "Would yew care ta yoin me?"

"I would."

"Say, if yewr in town long enough, maybe yew'd like ta do a little ice fishin'? Dere's a little lake not far from here. It's real shallow so it freezes early. Last year I had a bite dat yust about yerked my arm outa da socket! My cork vent down like a shot an' . . ."

Sean knew exactly where he'd stick a cork if he had one but, seeing as how the man had a razor to his neck, he listened up.

". . . Yumpin' Yimminy, I sez. Must be Ol' Yewelry Mouth. I got a quick looksee an, by golly, dere he vas. Ol' Yewelry Mouth, the killer muskie. Vel, I figured I vas ready for him, yew betcha. But I no sooner got set ven he bit off my line. An off he vent vid my favorite lure! Dat's how he got his name, from all dem lures in his mouth.

"Not a veek later some fella from Iowa vas campin' yust below the falls. He had his bull terrier vid him. Dog vaded too deep an' Ol' Yewelry Mouth got a holt uf him. Dat fella from Iowa pulled an' Ol' Yewelry Mouth pulled. An' anyvay, finally the guy from Iowa got dat dog loose an' dere vas my lure caught in da dog's fur . . ."

Later, Einar locked up, rattling the doorknob several times. "Da cafe's yust on da udder side uf town." He pointed.

Sean looked down the road. As if conforming to an ordinance about lack of movement after sundown, the streets were deserted. Even the previously brisk wind had died at dusk.

One last rattle of the knob and they started out. In order to reach the restaurant, they would apparently be passing through all of downtown Otter Tail. Three blocks.

Lining the wide planked boardwalk were narrow frame buildings painted either white with brown trim or brown with white trim. Dr. B. C. Neimark—Physician, Watson & Son General Store, Village Hall, and across the street C. O. Hecktner—Dentist, Hoff's Fine Furniture and Fixtures.

At the cafe they were served an excellent meal of pheasant and wild rice by a ruddy-cheeked girl with mustard-colored pigtails.

Sean asked Einar about the early settlers, a leading question.

"Along da river some Norwegians, ya, an' a few Irish, but mostly Yermans." Einar replied. "By da vay, if yew hadn't tole me, I'd've never guessed yew vere da Irish. Yew don't have a bit uf an accent."

That was no accident. Sean spoke several languages fluently and was adept at copying nuances of speech.

"When I came through town before, I got off the

train for a minute to have a smoke and stretch my legs. A young girl with a baby got off. I . . . thought for a minute I had met her before. I was about to ask her when a couple of men removed a coffin . . ."

Einar tapped a finger on the table and rubbed his jaw thoughtfully. "By golly, I'll betcha dat vas Mae Ella Botts. Vell, she's a Herrmann now. He shook his head sadly, tsking. "Now dere's a real tragedy. An' since she got home, it's gone from bad ta vorse!"

"Why? What happened?"

"Vell, da poor girl's no more dan a baby herself an' got a little boy tew. Her husband died in a construction accident, I heard, in Chicago, so she an' da little vun come back ta live vid her family. She wasn't back but a few days ven her fadder up an' had a heart attack. Good man he vas, too, her fadder. I know all dat family pretty good an' . . ."

"Chicago, you say?"

"Yeah, dey vent down dere right after dey got married. Five boys in Peter Herrmann's family an' Peter right in the middle. Not enough land for all of 'em, I guess. I vas talkin' ta her fadder right after dey left. He sez dey were hopin' ta save enough ta buy some land down southern Minnesota. Around Rochester maybe. I thought dat vas funny, dem livin' so far away from family like dat.

"Anyway, he vas vorking construction down dere in Chicago, fell offa some scaffoldin' an' died. Yust like dat!" Einar removed his glasses and rubbed at the red indentations on the bridge of his nose. "Now, I heard from somebody dat her mudder is sick too. Poor girl. She's havin' nothin' but bad luck."

"She's alone with a sick mother and a baby?"

"No. Her uncle lives out dere vid her. But he's got vat dey call da tunnel disease. Can't see diddl-lee squat on either side uf him—yust smack in front, an'

den only if he gets right down on top uf sometin'."
Scratching his head, Einar frowned in thought. "I forget vat they call dat. Mette's aunt had da same ting.
Mette vas my wife. Slipped on da ice, right in front
uf da store . . ."

"Glaucoma."

"Ya! By golly, I think dat is vat dey call it." Einar's
expression showed surprise and admiration.

"A person starts to lose their peripheral vision until
they have a smaller and smaller field of sight. I, uh . . .
read something about it once." Another time when his
encyclopedic mind supplied some obscure fact.

Perplexed, Einar nodded. "Ya? Vell, if yew say so.
Say, vhy do yew ask? About Mae Herrmann, I mean?"

He shrugged. "Maybe she's hiring."

"I doubt she's got money ta hire help."

"I work cheap."

Einar dug in his pocket but the big man had already tossed sufficient coins on the table saying,
"This is on me."

"Vell, tank yew." Einar neglected to ponder the in-
congruity of a man who was looking to hire out for
farm work picking up the tab.

"Juz go that direction." The hefty farmer flung his
arm in an arc big enough to encompass half the state.
"It's about six, seven miles. The last place before the
river." Sean lifted his grip off the back of the wagon.
"Sorry I can't bring you no closer," the farmer added
over his shoulder as his wagon bounced down the
badly rutted dirt road.

Well, as his mam used to say, 'twas a soft morning
for a walk. After a mile or so, Sean took off his jacket
and tied it around his waist.

The weed-tufted road led him past an old farmhouse where a cat hunkered by the front door, then across a trestle bridging a crystalline clear brook. Sean propped his elbows on a railing, his boot on his bag and lit a smoke. Cattails, fringed gentian and purple loosestrife grew in unruly profusion on the banks of the stream. Overhead a flock of prairie marsh-mallards winged their way south. As he picked up his grip, a small black bird with red epaulets sang "O-K-a-leee" from a nearby pine bough.

He called "Same t' ye, mate!" and felt a bit of a fool for it.

He reached the top of a hill and the farm was below him, cradled in a rippling patchwork of dun and tan and framed by woods aflame with the colors of autumn. On the north, mature red oaks provided a windbreak and shade for the two-story home. To the south, jack pines towered like vigilant sentinels. In the muddy pasture, half a dozen cows grazed companionably with a score of pecking chickens. The outbuildings—the sway-backed barn with a lean-to shed, the adjacent chicken coop and the lop-doored head—were weather-worn to a dull gray. There was a silo, a corn crib and a pig pen. A sagging line of laundry stretched from a T-shaped post in the backyard to the edge of the house but there wasn't a soul in sight.

He hefted his bag and started down the hill. The nearer he got, the less tranquil the setting was. Somewhere a door slapped constantly. The windmill, trying to keep pace with a rising breeze, twirled in a high-pitched squeal. Through an open window, he heard a woman repeatedly call someone's name. "Bloody hell!" he muttered, as the yellow hound lying in a patch of sun near the front porch raised his head and started barking.

* * *

"Mae Ella?

"Coming, Mama." Mae set the bowl on a plate, added a spoon, a slice of buttered bread and a napkin.

"Mae Ella?"

"Coming." She ladled the broth into the bowl.

"Mae Ella!"

Mae lifted the tray, walked to the bedroom and pushed the door open with her hip.

"Here I am, Mama." She set down the tray. "And I've brought you some soup."

"I don't want any soup." Her mother folded her arms and pressed her lips together.

"Please, Mama. It's bean soup."

"I hate bean soup."

"Mama, you do not! It's your very own recipe."

"I hate bean soup."

Mae held the bowl, spoon poised but her mother pushed it away.

"Is your father back yet?"

Mae didn't answer. She simply didn't know what to say anymore. She'd said it all so many, many times before. But her mother could not comprehend that Papa was dead. She had even taken her mother up to the grave once. Her mother had sat in the sun, humming "Buffalo Gal" and plucking at her dress while Mae tried to straighten the fence. At one point her mother asked, "Did I tell you about when I was in the circus, Frannie?" She sometimes thought Mae was Uncle Ed's deceased wife Frannie.

"Mama, you know you were never in the circus."

"Why, I most certainly was." Insulted. "I rode bareback and sang 'Buffalo Gal.' At all the intermissions I collected the coins in my tambourine."

"Oh, Mama!" Mae didn't know whether to laugh or cry. Some of the things she said were so strange, especially if a person knew how straitlaced her mother had been before she got sick.

Mae held up the spoon again and almost said "MmmMmm," like she did when she wanted Johnny to eat. "This is really good soup, Mama."

"There were some whores in here before. Three of them."

"Oh, Mama! For heaven's sake!"

"I saw them with my own eyes. Shocked! I was shocked that they would have the unmitigated gall to come right into a person's home. One was sneaking down the hall . . ."

"Mama, that was Uncle Ed, going out to see to the stock. You about scared his socks off, jumping out at him like that."

"I don't want Ed," her mother whined. "I want my Bill." She cupped her mouth and bellowed, "Bill!"

"Hush, Mama, you'll wake the baby."

"What baby?"

Mae rebuttoned a few buttons on her mother's nightgown. If only there was something someone could do to bring her peace. Doc Neimark was a good doctor but his bedside manner was as bad as his hearing. "You can either put her away in an institution, keep her sedated or run yourself ragged with her," he had boomed during his last house call. "She'll never improve one lick."

"Bill? Bill!"

Mae had neither the money nor the heart for an institution. She smoothed her mother's hair, then pulled up the blanket bunched at the foot of the bed. It instantly started marching downward. Her mother rarely got out of bed on her own but her blue-veined legs walked about a hundred miles a day within it.

"Mama, I have to get back to the wash. Today's Monday, you know. Please eat some soup."

"Is it beef?"

"No. Bean."

"Beef?"

"Bean."

"I hate bean soup."

Mae walked to the dresser where she kept a pitcher of cool water and a basin. She never put anything liquid near her mother. Last week her mother had tossed the contents of a glass of water in Mae's face, then covered her mouth and giggled like a schoolgirl. Mae had started out laughing with her, but in the end she'd started to cry and then, well, there went her mood for another day.

She dampened a cloth, returned to the bedside and pressed it to her mother's brow. And avoided looking into her eyes.

Mae told herself she was being ridiculous. She told herself that growing up on a remote farm with busy adults and a much older brother, she had evidently developed an overactive imagination. Evidently.

Mae turned aside and pressed the cloth to her eyes.

She'd had that nightmare again last night. It was always the same. She and an evil demon were fighting over her mother. Her mother stood to one side, complacent, waiting to see who won. Hard as Mae fought, coming back at the demon again and again, scratching and biting and kicking and clawing, the demon always won in the end. Just before she woke up, she would look in her mother's eyes and the demon would be inside, looking out. "Here I am, Mae Ella, in here." He would smile wickedly and twiddle his fingers. "I've got your mama now, Mae Ella! And I'm keepin' her!"

She'd wake up then, wringing wet, her lips open in a silent cry.

After coaxing her mother into swallowing a thimbleful of soup, she tiptoed into her bedroom. Johnny was sleeping peacefully in his crib, oblivious to the mayhem around him. She checked his diaper, adjusted his covers, then kissed her fingers and laid them on his brow. She oftentimes wished for more hours in the day—it was probably the only way she would ever get caught up with her chores—but if she had more time, she would squander it with her boy.

After softly closing the door, she went onto the screened porch where the wooden laundry tubs sat. One tub was full of laundry that was ready to be hung. Nearby was a tub full of diapers soaking in strong solution prior to being washed. And the wash she had hung out earlier wasn't even close to dry yet. She sighed, grabbed the edge of the first heavy tub and started to drag it across the plank floor toward the pump outside.

"Can I give you a hand, ma'am?"

"Aah!" Mae whirled around. Heart pumping, her eyes searched a dark silhouette less than five feet away. A man—no, a giant—stood in the yard! Too late she recalled she had heard Sandy barking earlier.

A wide-brimmed felt hat was canted over the man's face leaving exposed a prominent, beard-roughened jaw. His upturned collar only partially enclosed a bull neck that was dark as an Indian's. . . .

An Indian! Oh, God! Fear arrowed through her. In '76, the same year her brother John was born, the Indians and General George Armstrong Custer had met at the Little Big Horn. There the Sioux and Cheyenne wiped out all two hundred and twenty-five men of the 7th Cavalry.

People around Otter Tail still talked about it as if it was yesterday.

"Yes? Can I . . . Can I help you with something?" A hundred thoughts ran through her mind. . . . *The rifle was by the front door . . . was it loaded? . . .*

*where was Uncle Ed? . . . what good would Uncle
Ed do! . . . this was the biggest man she'd ever
seen! . . . Oh my God!*

"I'm looking for work." Courteously, he removed
his hat, revealing shiny hair that was black as an iron
skillet. She relaxed a little, for although his cheeks
were high and broad, he was no Indian. His features
were too defined, too chiseled. She wasn't, however,
reassured by seeing his eyes clearly. They were the
color of breath in February and penetrated like a
forty-below wind.

With a cylindrical bag slung over one broad shoulder, the man looked like a landlocked sailor. It's his
stance, she thought, motionless, but with his muscular
legs slightly apart as if bracing himself against the
pitch of a ship.

Those eyes of steel watched her walk the few steps
to the screen door and latch it. She pressed her fingers to her lips. *Mae Ella, what on earth are you
doing?* That piddling latch wouldn't stop him from
opening the door!

She'd read that some people have a predator's
sense, that they can smell fear like a wolf pack scents
blood. This man was one of them. She knew it like
she knew her name—which she couldn't recall for
the life of her. Sweat gathered between her breasts.

"I don't need . . ." Her throat felt like she had an
apricot pit wedged in it. "I mean *we . . .*"—it wouldn't
do for him to think she was alone—" . . . *we* aren't
hiring help."

The silence stretched to an uncomfortable length.
She fingered her collar and looked behind him for a
horse or a wagon. Had he walked here? All the way
from town? "Uh, but thank you anyway." Abruptly,
he swung his head toward the broken gate, held
closed by the two-by-four propped against it, then he

looked over at the chicken coop with the wire on one side hanging open, and then at the cows and chickens sharing one pasture.

"Looks to me like you could use some help, ma'am."

"I don't . . ."

"I could at least fix your gate there. And the coop . . ."

"I . . . we have no money, mister." Her voice rose pleadingly. "Really. None."

". . . in return for a meal." He spoke as if she hadn't.

"Whores!"

Mae flinched as if she'd been slapped on the back.

"There they are! Mae Ellllla?" her mother bawled like a calf. "Where is that girl? Those whores are back. Frannnnnie?"

"Ma'am?" He held his hat in hands folded respectfully in front of him. "All right if I do those things?"

"There they go! You'll never catch them."

She chewed her lower lip. She had to get him away from the house. She never knew what Mama was going to do. Last week, she'd come to the door with only her drawers on. Uncle Ed was working on a harness right in front of the barn. Mae had thrown down the hoe and hurried her mother back into her room. God forgive her, but she'd been thankful, just for a minute, that her uncle was blind as a bat.

"Yes." Nodding, she started to back across the porch. "All right. For a meal. All right."

He nodded toward the tub. "If you'll leave the screen unlatched, I'll carry out that tub."

She *knew* he had seen her latch the screen! "Oh no!" She heard a giggle and was horrified to realize it was her own. "That's all right." She continued backing toward the door to the house. "Thanks very much anyway. Ah . . . I can get it later." She turned and scurried inside, closing the door to the porch behind her. She listened a moment, then threw the bolt.

Sean stared at the door. The deep shadows had prevented him from seeing her distinctly, but it was the same girl. Paler and thinner, but it was her.

He walked to the barn, propped his bag against the trough and pumped a handful of water from the rusty pump. After quenching his thirst, he pumped more and splashed the water with cupped hands onto his face. He wiped his face on his jacket sleeve, then leaned a shoulder against the pump and lit a smoke.

So, his inner voice began to chide sarcastically, *what exactly did ye expect? That she would say "Oh, mister! I remember you from the train that day. I've thought of you so many times. I've prayed I would see you again."*

Fool! He flicked the spent match aside. *She dinna even recognize ye.*

Now what?

He glanced around him. One side of his mouth turned up. She was still one of the best lookers he'd ever seen, and she still intrigued the hell outa him.

So?

So, now we kill some time and maybe while we're doin' that we see exactly what it'll take to bring a smile to those ruby lips. There's nae a woman alive immune to the McGloin. He rolled his shoulders like a boxer warming up, then picked up his bag.

Nae a woman alive.

Four

She caught glimpses of the man throughout the afternoon. It took him less than a minute to fix the gate—the one that only the day before she and her uncle had wrestled with for hours. They'd taken turns standing on the end of a board but neither of them were strong enough to lift the gate. The man simply picked up the gate with one hand and dropped the cotter pin in with the other. A few swings and a quick adjustment to the latch to make sure it worked properly and then he was restringing the wire around the chicken coop. He shooed the squawking chickens in, moving his arms like a giant pinwheel. He even piled rocks up around the bottom of the wire. That should fix that old wily fox, she thought approvingly.

By the time she had another tub of laundry finished, it was almost dusk. She was struggling with a strong wind, trying to finish hanging the clothes when she peeped over the line. The man was about to put the repaired wagon wheel back on the axle. He lifted one side of the wagon. His shirt bulged like it held a bunch of rocks and Mae held her breath expecting to hear a big rip.

Just at that second, her uncle came around the side of the barn leading the plow horse, Jocko, and walked right into the man's rear end. The man staggered four or five long steps off balance while the wheel rolled drunkenly away. The wagon fell back to its original position with a big *whump* and a cloud of dust. "Who the devil are you?" her uncle said and then walked within an inch of the man. Behind the flapping sheet, she covered a giggle. What a sight they made! Chin tucked into his chest, the big man was looking down at her little Uncle Ed like a hawk at a mole.

She couldn't hear their words but it was obvious the man had justified his presence when he took the bridle from her uncle and led the horse into the barn. Her uncle was a picture of perplexity, one hand on his hip, the other scratching his marmalade-colored hair. He resettled his hat and then walked toward the house. Still smiling, she stabbed a split wood clothespin on the end of the last sheet and hurried after him. She got to the screen door just as he slammed it in her face.

"Mae Ella?" Opening the door to the house, he leaned in, hollering. "Hoo hoo?"

"Behind you, Uncle Ed."

He jumped a foot. "Shit-house mouse!" He held a hand over his heart dramatically. "Don't sneak up behind me like that. Between you and your mother . . . !"

She overturned the empty laundry tub on the porch and patted his arm as she passed. "Sorry about Mama, Uncle Ed."

"Never mind that now." He followed her down the hallway. "There was a big monster man in the yard! Ran right into him. Thought I might've hurt him, but he said he was okay."

"He's working for his supper." It tickled her to think of her little uncle hurting that Goliath. "Which reminds me, I better get a move on dinner," she said, as she walked into the kitchen.

"If'n what he said is true, he's been busier than a

cat coverin' shit on a tin roof. Did he fix that blamed gate?"

"Yes, I saw him myself. Cursed thing! Took him less than a minute!"

"Well, I'll be!" Uncle Ed looked in the direction of the barn and sucked his eyetooth thoughtfully.

Her uncle was a man of habits. Snapping his suspenders, tugging his hat, sucking his tooth. That tooth-sucking habit was Mae's least favorite.

"It'd be nice if he'd hang around a bit longer than just an afternoon," he added.

"I think he's one of those road bums, down on his luck. You know, here today, gone tomorrow." She washed her hands, dried them on a dishtowel, then flung it over her shoulder.

"I don't know. He's pretty well dressed for a bum. He ain't all that anxious to get back on the road. He said he noticed the plow blade needed sharpening. Which it does. And I was thinking that you need to have a couple of your knives done too." When he sat down at the table, Mae automatically poured coffee into the mug in front of him.

"I figured he would be leaving right after supper." Sitting across from him, she toyed with the doily centerpiece, straightening its edges and positioning the glass salt and pepper shakers just so.

He whipped off his hat. It was his favorite and had been known to draw flies. "Speaking of supper, what are we having?" He intended to hang his hat on the ladder-back chair, but missed the wooden knob completely.

"Roast chicken, cornbread stuffing and acorn squash." Mae picked the hat up.

"Mmm! You gonna fix the squash like I like 'em? With cinnamon and honey?"

"Yes." She hung his hat on the back of his chair.

"Exactly like you like them." She smiled. "And there's your favorite for dessert."

"Raisin bread puddin'?"

"Yes."

"Mmm. Mmm."

She stretched to reach an oblong platter on the high shelf above the cast-iron cooking range. "I'll fix up the man's plate if you'll take it out to him." She opened the oven door and poked a fork in the chicken leg. Done. The squash looked done too, with golden meat and shriveled skin.

"Maybe I better not, Mae Ella. 'Member when I tripped last week? All that slop flew straight up in the air and come down right on top of me."

Mae rubbed a finger under her nose. "Hmm. Yes . . ."

It hadn't seemed a bit funny at the time it happened. Seconds after Uncle Ed'd taken the slop pail out to the hogs she'd had heard a loud "Shit-house mouse!" and went running. Arms out like a scarecrow, he had walked back to the screen door where she stood. "Look what I done, Mae Ella!" At the time her spirits and shoulders had sagged simultaneously. She had just washed and ironed his shirt and pants the day before. If there was one thing that wasn't funny, it was more laundry!

Until today. If it had happened today, she'd be splitting her sides.

"Maybe you're right." She hung the dishtowel on the back of a chair. "I . . . I'll just . . . ah, I'll be right back."

She slipped into her bedroom. Johnny gave her a wet, ragged grin. "You're awake, hmm?" She scooped him up and kissed his smooth cheek. Johnny clutched a carved wooden toy in his small fist. "You're such a good boy," she whispered. The baby had added several tooth marks to the toy that Granddad had made for her when she was his age. Even teething, a stage she had always heard could make the best of babies irritable, Johnny was placid and happy. She checked his diaper, then—reluctantly—laid him back in the crib. She sat on the end of the bed in front of the mirror.

Oh my god! She turned her head. How long since she had looked at herself? When she got up in the morning she cleaned her teeth with baking soda, brushed and rebraided her hair then washed her face. She supposed she must glance at her image at some point during the ritual but she couldn't remember the last time she had. She splayed her hands over her ribs. She was so thin! She brushed a hand over her cheek and ran her tongue over her teeth, then leaned close to study her reflection. She didn't see high cheekbones, full lips and dark-winged brows. She saw a face too thin, lips too thick and brows too dark to match her hair.

"And a tomato nose," she added under her breath. She had been outside less than an hour yesterday without a hat, tilling some fertilizer into the garden. She could, as her mother always used to say, sunburn in the house. She looked at her hair. "Blasted wind!" Her part had disappeared, covered by wisps of hair going every which way. Long hanks hung in front of her ears, calling to mind a lop-eared rabbit. She ran a comb through her hair, following the curve of her scalp, then turned her head sideways. She had only succeeded in moving the mess farther out of reach. Takes care of any hope of a quick fix, she thought, studying the rat's nest she'd built on the back of her head. It looked like she had a growth! "A waste of time, Mae Ella," she said, as she tossed the brush on the dresser.

She returned to the kitchen and started dishing up food with a vengeance. She would give the man his decent meal. It was part of the deal and he deserved it. And more. She portioned out the lion's share of the chicken and pretty near half a loaf of fresh-baked wheat bread. She slathered butter on a whole squash and sprinkled it with cinnamon. She put the honey on the side—in case he didn't care for honey on his squash like her uncle. Lastly, she added a smaller plate with a generous helping of raisin bread pudding. "There!" she said, "that ought to hold you, mister."

Mae was proud of her cooking skills. Growing up with two good cooks such as Granny and Mama had been somewhat intimidating. There had been a time when she couldn't even make hard-boiled eggs. The eggs she cooked had either grown spongy tumors or lost great gouges of white when peeled. Miraculously, one day when she was about nine, her deviled eggs came out perfect. She'd loved to cook ever since.

She filled the biggest mug she had with coffee and set it on the tray. On impulse, she searched through the neatly folded linens in Granny's ornate cabinet. "Here they are." She folded a blue-and-white-checked-cotton napkin with fringed edges under the knife and fork.

Holding the tray carefully, she walked to the door and nudged it open. The wind slammed the screen door behind her. Skirts billowing around her legs, she walked quickly across the yard.

She leaned into the barn's cool interior. Empty! Did the man leave without his meal? She felt a stab of disappointment. "Mister?"

He stepped out of one of the stalls, shovel in hand. Now she noticed the manure piled in front of each stall. A necessary but a menial chore. And one that hadn't been done for too long. She blushed. It wasn't like he'd found a cockroach in the pudding, she told herself, but she was still embarrassed. "I have your supper here, mister."

He paused first to hang the shovel on a spike on the wall and then walked down the length of the barn. He moved like he'd been well oiled, she thought, and then realized she was staring. She directed her gaze to the dung in front of the nearest stall.

He took the tray. She raised her eyes slowly, acutely aware of her dress, her hair and her nose and him. But not in that order. He smiled at her. Their eyes locked and her ability to inhale left her. Something seemed to pass from his eyes to hers. Whatever it was, it slithered around, spreading warmth and weakness, and then tried to get out through her toes, which were curled tight as a sow's tail inside her boots.

A year passed. Or at least it felt like a year.

Finally she tore her eyes away. Slightly breathless, she looked back at the pile of dung and rubbed her collar bone. She had an almost painful tightness in her chest and throat, like . . . like congestion!

Oh, no! Wonder if I'm getting a chest cold? Darn! I can't afford to get sick now! She swallowed a few times to test her throat.

". . . food looks great. Thank you, ma'am."

Mae nodded and murmured something, still testing her throat.

She had assumed he would take the plates off the tray and give her back the tray. Instead, he set it down on the long bench inside the barn door and walked to the pump. Awkwardly she followed and stood a few feet away. Affecting a nonchalance she didn't feel, she alternately studied her apron hem and him.

After working the handle just the right number of times (Now, how do you suppose he knew that?), he stuck his hands under it. Using the tiny sliver of soap from the rim of the trough, he built up a lather. With care he scrubbed up to his elbows, then leaned over and soaped his face and neck.

Propped against the barn door like a door-stop—her feet seemed to have taken root—she watched him throw the frigid well water up on his face. The droplets of water that flew behind him glistened like shooting stars in the lantern light. He ran all ten fingers through his hair then pulled a handkerchief from his pocket to wipe his face and neck. When he leaned down to pick up the tray, Mae examined the planes and angles of his face, the set of his hair where it curled around his ears and on his neck. A thin scar intersected his right eyebrow, quirking it and giving him a sardonic look. Why, he's unusually handsome, she thought. For an older man.

"There's enough for two men here . . ." His voice was deep and resonant. ". . . but I'll bet I can do it justice."

She wiped moist palms on her apron. "It's the least . . ." Her voice sounded odd to her, like she had gone swimming in the river and still had water in her ears. She stuck a finger in her ear and opened her mouth. She'd have to get the tray later. She was definitely coming down with something! She'd better make herself a pot of Granny's herbal tea straight off. ". . . we could do."

She hurried away, then stopped and looked back at him over her shoulder. "Just leave the tray right there when you're done, mister." He was sitting on the bench, easily balancing the tray on his massive thighs. She walked briskly toward the porch.

Her steps slowed halfway to the house. Granny would say "Not so nice, liebchen." She'd be right.

He probably he thinks I am the most inhospitable person he has ever met, not to even offer him a seat at the kitchen table. She retraced her steps. He looked up at her and raised that thick brow with the kink in it.

"Thanks for doing what you did today, mister. We, uh, my Uncle Ed and I, appreciate your fine ah . . . work." She flipped up her apron hem and ran her finger along its length. "Ah, I haven't asked you to share our table because my mother is . . . ah, very sick."

"Sean." He smiled up at her and broke off a piece of bread.

"Excuse me?" She tilted her head.

"That's my name. Sean. Sean McGloin."

"Oh? Yes. Well . . . That's sure an . . . an unusual name. Thank you, Mr. McGloin." She nodded. "Good-bye then and . . . good luck." She turned and headed toward the house again. With his eyes on her every single step of the way, she felt like a three-year-old wearing her papa's boots.

Why? she wondered.

Sean bit into a crispy piece of excellent baked chicken and admired the way she held herself—as ramrod straight as a Prussian soldier. The tip of a silvery braid—about as thick around as the anchor rope on a four-masted schooner—bounced against her gorgeous rear end as she swayed up the steps. He ogled her over the rim of his coffee cup. Sassy little snip!

"You better start eatin' more, girlie, or you're gonna get sick too."

Her uncle carried his plates to the basin. Mae held her breath as he leaned way down to make sure they were over the counter. *Poor old guy!* "I'm not hungry right now." She mashed the meat of an acorn squash with a fork, then got a jar of apple sauce from the storage room. Mama and her baby were on the same diet—which, looking on the bright side of things, certainly made meal preparation a lot easier.

There, that wasn't hard, she told herself. A better state of mind was just a matter of how you looked at things. That talk she had with herself up at the cemetery must've finally sunk in, she thought. She hadn't felt blue all day.

"I'm gonna go out to the barn and jaw with that Irishman. He seems real interestin' to me." Uncle Ed unscrewed his tin of Copenhagen, tucked a pinch in his lower lip and ambled out.

So, that's what he is! Mae thought. Irish! Not many Irish lived in Otter Tail, but there were lots in Chicago. Their neighbors across the hall had been Irish, Timothy and Moira O'Toole. Mae had liked Moira right off the bat. She was one of those people who looked like they were smiling even when they weren't. Left alone all day by their mates, the two girls had struck up a friendship immediately. The exact same age, both married to their childhood sweethearts, both lovely and lonely, they had much in common. They started meeting for tea, or doing their marketing together or taking a walk in Fullerton Park. Mae was surprised at the ease with which they could talk.

When Peter found out, he was furious. "She's a common shanty Irish. Coarse and vulgar." He forbade Mae to talk to her. She would have argued with him and would have defended their friendship, but because of the problems she and Peter were having, it had seemed easier just to acquiesce.

How wrong Peter was! When Mae had been stiff with shock about Peter, it was Moira who had slept over for two days straight. She'd taken care of Johnny and Mae as if they were both the same age.

Mae sat at the table, wondering how Timothy and Moira were getting along these days.

Oh, that Moira had a temper. Mae whewed and shook her head. Nobody would dispute that. Not if they were within ten blocks when Moira got into one of her snits about Tim drinking with his buddies from work. But they always made up.

Did they ever! Mae blushed, recalling the time she had been late getting home from the market.

She'd hurried up the stairs, turned the corner and there were Timothy and Moira, standing right in the hallway, kissing to beat the band. They didn't even hear her. She didn't know what on earth to do! She stood there, cradling her groceries and trying not to gawk.

In her entire life she had never seen people kiss like that. Moira's back was to the wall. Tim's arms were bracketing her head, his knee bent and wedged between her legs. They were twisting and turning their faces, smearing their lips all over. Tim looked like he was trying to eat her alive! And Moira! Her freckled hands were wide on Tim's rear, pulling, tugging him closer. Mae turned and very, very quietly crept back down the stairs to the vestibule.

She stood there, seemed like forever, studying the slime-green wall tiles and feeling vaguely foolish. There were eight, she recalled, chipped tiles on the south wall alone. After at least an hour, she slammed the heavy door hard enough to rattle its glass pane, and clomped up the stairs like a herd of elephants. Luckily they had gone inside their apartment. She scurried past their closed door but not before she heard Moira's giggle and Tim's deep laugh. The sounds had danced up and down her spine like icy fingers.

Months afterwards, Mae could still feel her face

flush. She realized she was fanning herself with a dishtowel. Well, it's hot!

I'm hot!

Oh, no!

She felt her forehead. Damp! *Oh, no!* She covered her pounding heart. *Drat! I am getting sick!* She started the water to boil and stretched for a canister above the stove.

Half an hour later, she was sitting in the kitchen trying to decide which chore to tackle next. Mama had been asleep when she went in to feed her. Rather than wake her—she slept so poorly of late—Mae was keeping food warm on the back of the stove.

Johnny had been fed, washed, loved up, then rocked to sleep. She would have liked to have spent more time with him but she had mending to do, clothes to fold and put away, and the ironing. The house could use a good cleaning. Last season's vegetables downstairs in the root cellar were going to spoil if she didn't finish the canning soon. She needed to dry some apples or there'd be no dried apple cobbler this winter. No strudel. No red cabbage for sauerbraten. No spaetzels. Granny would be appalled.

Her uncle walked in and tossed a couple of knives on the counter. "You be awful careful with those knives, Mae Ella."

"Are they sharp?" They looked it, with edges that gleamed like new silver.

"Boy, I'll say. Whew! The foot pedals on that old grindstone were squealin' like a stuck hog."

"Has he . . . gone?" Some part of her held totally still and waited.

"Well, Mae Ella, that's the thing." Uncle Ed sat down heavily. "He says he'd be willing to stay on for a time." He shook his head. "Don't ask me why, 'cause a man as handy as him could do lots better . . ."

"Better tell him no, Uncle Ed."

"Now, why, for Pete's sake?" He squinted rheumy eyes at her, trying to bring her face into focus.

Mae hunched her shoulders then expelled a big breath. She had spoken impulsively. Yet there was something about the way she felt around the stranger. Was it an omen? Yes, that's it. A bad omen. She was never wrong about these things.

"I think I have a premonition. I think he could be . . . bad luck."

Uncle Ed let out a big hoot and slapped his leg. "Mae Ella, you're a card!"

She didn't see what was so funny.

He wiped his eyes on a train-conductor red handkerchief, then honked in it. He could rattle the window panes when he blew his nose. And often did. "You're an eighteen-year-old girl . . ."

"Nineteen." She interjected testily. "Excuse me, Uncle Ed, but I am nineteen."

"O.K., nineteen then. A nineteen-year-old girl . . ."

"Woman."

"Shit-house mouse! Will you let me finish?"

She gave a regal nod.

"A nineteen-year-old woman . . ." He dragged out the word. ". . . with a babe in arms, no husband, no father, a mother in diapers and a half-blind old man who's not worth spit. Hell, your taxes are gonna be due . . ."

"Not worth spit! Uncle Ed! What would I do without you?" She patted his bony knee. "What taxes?"

"Hush up and listen to me. I could croak any minute. Why, I'm just a year younger than your father! And I can't hardly see the hand in front of my face." As if proving his point, he searched for her hand on the table. She moved it into his path. He patted it. "Why not have a talk with the man? What's the harm of letting him stay for a few days? I don't think you have to worry about him being, uh . . . you know . . . uh, funny or nothing." He shook his head in amazement . . . "The places he's been!" and then with regret. . . . "Damned shame about that bug."

"What bug?"

"Nothing to be concerned about. Not catchy or nothing. Just something his doctor told him he'd get rid of a lot faster if he spent some time in the fresh country air. See, that's why he'd like to stay. For his health." He snorted in disbelief. "Hell, if he's sick I'd sure hate to see him when he's healthy. Anyhow, I ain't about to look a gift horse in the mouth. I think we ought to count our lucky stars!"

"But where is he going to stay? We don't have accommodations for hired help."

"He says he'll bunk down on that cot in the tack room for the time being."

"Oh, Uncle Ed!" She curled her lip in exasperation. "We're coming on winter soon!"

"He knows that. Didn't I just say that I pointed it out?"

"No, you didn't, and if you did, he can't have understood." She stood impatiently raking her chair across the wood floor. "I better go talk to him."

He was backlit by the glow of the kerosene lantern, leaning in the doorway with one booted ankle crossed over the other. The size of him amazed her once again. He had a forearm braced on the crossbar above the door. Why, she didn't even have to duck her head when she went through that door on horseback!

For a minute she posed on the porch step like a dancer. He was looking her way. She was almost breathless with anticipation. Her heartbeat drummed frantically against her ribs. She slipped off the step— moving, she thought, with particular grace and agility.

Until the porch door caught the wind and slammed. She shot forward like she'd been goosed.

"Wrong foot, liebchen." She heard a voice say. As if she had forgotten something, she turned and went back inside.

She paced the shadows on the porch, muttering to herself, "It's when you let a dog know you're afraid of him that he'll bite your butt off for sure. Be confident. Con-fi-dent! This is your home, Mae Ella. *Your* home. Conduct yourself like a woman of refinement." Mentally recharged and backbone stiffened, she opened the door and started across the yard again.

She knew the instant his rain-colored eyes homed in on her but she kept going. Somebody, she thought as she walked, has added a hundred yards to the backyard. Finally she stopped in the orange patch of lantern light spilling out of the barn.

He straightened respectfully and threw down his cheroot and ground the butt beneath his heel. "Ma'am?" He folded his arms across his chest and stood with his legs slightly apart.

Now, there's attitude, she thought. Just look at him. Confident, arrogant, cocky. "Mr. Mc . . . McGloin, is it?"

"Yes, ma'am, Sean." There was a flash of white teeth in a predator's grin. "Sean McGloin."

"Mr. McGloin." With an air of serious consideration, she paced a few steps away and then returned. She stopped in front of him. "My uncle says you would be willing to stay on for awhile." She folded her arms across her chest also. "Why, Mr. McGloin? Since I still can't pay you?"

"The pay'd be room and board."

"I don't even have a decent room to give you."

He shrugged and hitched his thumb toward the tack room. "That's enough."

She waited for him to say more, but apparently that was it! Exasperating man. "That's not a real good deal for you, Mr. McGloin."

"I'll be the judge of that, ma'am."

"What are you?" She flung her hands out. "Some wandering good Samaritan?" He smiled—a diabolical slash beneath a midnight moustache—and cold fingers played her spine like a piano.

It was funny that she hadn't noticed the diamond shaped cleft in his chin before. She used to be fascinated by them. Her old schoolteacher, Mrs. Dinwiddie'd had a chin hole just like the man's. Mama'd told her it was because before Mrs. Dinwiddie was born God had poked her with his finger.

She would bet Granny's sapphire earrings that whoever had poked this man, it sure wasn't God.

A cloud drifted over the moon. The wind swept through the branches and made an eerie crackling sound. A rustling came from the shadowy depths of the barn. Her eyes returned to him and stuck like over-cooked oats.

She should have trusted her intuition! She'd been right. Evil was as plain as the hawk nose on his face. All he had to do was stretch out one long arm and . . .

An owl hoo'ed and there was an inch of air between her soles and the ground.

"That was just an old snowy owl." He pointed. "He's sitting on that tree over there."

"I know that." She replied testily, but moved so she stood more in the feeble light. He smiled again. Was he laughing at her? Fear receded and annoyance rose.

". . . was thinking maybe we could do each other a service. You could use some help and I need a place to stay. On a temporary basis, of course."

"All right, Mr. McGloin." Why are you saying this, she asked herself. Tell him to go! Tell him no!

"All right. But only for as long as the weather holds." She held up two fingers in a V-sign. "Two meals a day—breakfast and supper—and the use of the tack room in the barn." She walked a few feet then stopped. "And one more thing, Mr. McGloin . . ."

"Yes, ma'am?"

"Please don't . . . ah . . . come into the house. My mother . . ."

"No, ma'am."

"And, Mr. McGloin?"

He looked up expectantly. "Yes, ma'am?" He had cupped a match to one of his little black cigars. The match's flare revealed the tilt to his lips. That hint of a smile irked her no end! "No liquor on the premises."

"No, ma'am." Sean watched her walk stiffly away and grinned. *Sassy little snip! I canno' wait to get me hands on ye!*

Five

Hoary old man winter hovered just around the corner, waiting to take the ill-prepared literally by storm, but when Indian summer brought the daytime temperature into the seventies, it was easy for human beings to think the cold weather was a long way away. The wild critters knew better.

Squirrels bounded about in a renewed quest for stores, and found plenty since the bur and red oak acorns had ripened and fallen. In the pond, muskrats and beavers refurbished their lodges. Young deer grew winter coats and lost their dappled camouflage. Snowshoe hares and ermines started turning white. Flies woke up and, to Mae's consternation, joined the field mice in a last-ditch effort to get into the house.

The clement weather had other consequences. Mae could continue to hang the laundry outside. During an earlier rainy spell she'd draped diapers over every chair in the house and even hung a line in Granny's parlor. Better yet, once the sun warmed the air, she could put Johnny on a blanket outside. Sometimes she felt walleyed, one eye on the baby and one on her work, but her spirits stayed high, like the temperature.

That day was particularly nice. She set her tub under the laundry line and walked to the melon patch. Sitting on her haunches and wrapping one arm around her legs, she thumped her middle finger against each of the four pumpkins in turn. Time soon to make use of them. Careful not to break their stems, she rotated them all so their lighter, flat parts faced the warm sun. She should've done it earlier. It made their color more uniform and their shape rounder. She looked at her son, flailing his arms and legs like a turtle on its back. She wished Johnny was old enough to cut out a jack-o'-lantern. When she was little there was a contest at Halloween. Everybody did their own jack-o'-lantern—Granny, Papa, Mama, John and herself. The competition was stiff, with a lot of griping between contestants that so-and-so had snuck a peek and stolen their idea.

Her uncle was partial to pumpkin pies and she had a good recipe for pumpkin bars with raisins and crushed hazelnuts. Maybe she'd save more seeds and start her garden in the house, like her grandmother used to do. Come spring there'd be dirt-filled tin cans containing tiny thin-stemmed seedlings in every window in the house. Each night Granny would go around and set the cans on the floor where they'd stay warm. She planted two seeds to a can initially. When the plants were a couple of inches high, she'd hold each up to the light. "Dis von is strongest, liebchen, see?" Holding the can at Mae's level, she'd indicate one.

Mae would feel sorry for the less vital-looking plant. "Well, maybe. I don't know, Granny," she said, hoping to delay what she imagined was an agonizing death.

"Nein, liebchen," Granny'd say, "veak vons must go." Then she'd viciously tear the fledgling seedling from the dirt and toss it in a compost can filled with eggshells and coffee grounds. "Der!" Granny'd say and brush her palms together like cymbals. "Dat is dat!"

But Mae would hook her nose on the rim of the can and whisper, "Sorry, sorry," to the little plants that already looked limp and lifeless.

Brushing some dirt off a pumpkin, she decided she would put some cans on the windowsills, but she would plant only one seed to a can. She caught herself and thought, now that's surprising. Me. Planning for the future like that. She hadn't done that in a while.

A black-and-gray chickadee landed on the split-rail fence bordering the garden, cocked his head, then started preening his feathers. Suddenly, a deer fly flew by and the bird flipped upside down and dangled like a trapeze artist. She chuckled, stopped abruptly and looked around.

She'd caught herself doing that lately—chuckling. And this morning she'd been humming.

It struck her then that something inexplicable had happened: In spite of the fact that there was no change in her workload, her mother's illness or the fullness of her purse, her life seemed less bleak.

Better than less bleak, she amended, it seemed . . . worth enjoying. She'd noticed a matching improvement in her uncle's attitude as well.

It's the weather, she told herself. It wasn't. Perhaps it was that Johnny had said *Mama* as clear as a bell. But she knew it wasn't that, either. She and her uncle were leaves caught in an incredible whirlwind of limitless energy—it was the Irishman.

She heard Uncle Ed's voice from behind the barn but not his words. Resting her cheek on her knees, she looked in that direction. A minute later, she heard the Irishman's deep voice in reply. Shortly thereafter, they both sauntered around the side of the barn. The Irishman, sleeves rolled up as far as his muscular arms would allow, wielded a wheelbarrow containing three bales of hay. Uncle Ed walked alongside, gesturing. Their precise words were carried away on the wind.

She smiled again. Another of their heated discussions. Uncle Ed loved "discussing." Papa used to tease, saying he had caught Uncle Ed discussing with Jocko once. But the Irishman, her uncle had claimed only the night before, was one of the most interesting men he'd ever "jawed" with.

But insofar as revelations about his personal life were concerned, Mr. McGloin was as stoic as a Norwegian and as sober as a Calvinist. Except for "Thank you, ma'am" or "Can I help you with that, ma'am?" he hadn't said much to her at all. Well, she was accustomed to quiet men. Papa had been a man of few words and Peter had, toward the end at least, never talked to her at all, but the Irishman was different somehow. An enigmatic man with a compelling manner. No doubt about it.

"Didya ever look into his eyes, Mae Ella?" her uncle had asked her.

"No," she had replied. But she had, and thought of the sea—gray and turbulent, deep and mysterious.

"They've kinda got a seen-everything, done-everything and don't-give-a-damn look to 'em, don't ya think? You know, he said . . ."

She had just smiled at her uncle while he ran on about . . . "The Irishman this . . . and the Irishman that . . ."

Her uncle was known for his salty talk. He said damn and hell and Shit-house mouse all the time. Her mother used to admonish him, but Mae didn't bother. She simply closed her ears and saved her breath to cool her coffee. For all her mother's efforts, and Frannie's too for that matter, her uncle hadn't changed a lick.

Mae rested her chin on her knees and her thoughts

returned to the Irishman. There wasn't much the man couldn't do. Mind reading included, Mae thought. It seemed she would just walk by the dwindling pile of firewood and Uncle Ed would say, "Sean and me is goin' out to the river bluff and find some dry blow-downs to chop up." Or he'd glance at the stain on the ceiling and say "I told Sean about that place where we had the bad ice back up under those old shingles last winter. He said he's gonna build up that area good. Slop on some more tar."

Even if she didn't hear the sound of the hammer or the ring of the axe, or his booming voice—"Hold that right there for me, Ed, me man. That's good!"— the results of his sure hands were all around.

It was funny, but she had never noticed how noisy the windmill was until its groaning and squealing had ceased. The back screen no longer flapped with every gust of wind, but shut quietly and tight as a drum.

He was too good to be true. Why, Mae asked her-self, would a man like that hang around a place like this? The Fagers, one of their nearest neighbors, hired three or four extra men on their place this time of year, not only feeding them but paying them too! Course, Uncle Ed said why look a gift horse in the mouth? but she wondered . . . did he have a family someplace? How did he know so much about farm-ing? Did he own a farm once? How did he learn to fix just about anything that was broken and improve on things that weren't?

Without letting on that she did so, Mae watched him. All the while she wondered why she felt so com-pelled to do so.

And she was pretty sure—not positive, mind you— but pretty sure, that he watched her with equal if not greater intensity.

Sometimes—like when he was working in the yard

and she was hanging clothes or when he was on the roof and she was walking to the chicken coop with her egg basket—she would swear to it. That sure knowledge gave her two left feet. She felt like the back of her skirt was tucked into her bloomers or she was dragging some privy paper on her shoe. She became so flustered the other day, she stumbled over her own feet and almost pole-vaulted headfirst into the chicken coop!

She watched the chickadee hop along the rail, then groaned and buried her face in her hands. Yesterday! Oh, after yesterday she hoped she would never lay eyes on him again.

She always performed her ablutions quickly in the morning. While braiding her hair it was her habit to pull up the window shade to check the status of the weather. (She had always, always done that, even as a child! Certainly, she was *not* looking for the Irishman!)

The last few days, when she did as she had always, always done—for her entire life (she consoled herself again with the reminder of that fact), invariably the Irishman would be standing just outside the barn door, having a smoke.

That morning she had opened the shade, as usual, and continued to brush her hair. No laundry today, she recalled thinking. It was drizzling and the ground was blanketed with a thick gray mist.

Suddenly, the fog parted like Moses' sea and there he was. One foot propped on the fence rail, he was bent over tucking his pant leg into his boot. Mae stepped to one side of the window and peered around the edge. He straightened and faced the house.

Tall. Lean. Fiercely masculine. Magnificent.

Naked!

She came close to swallowing her hairpins! His

belt was hanging open with one, no, no, two! It was two, buttons undone on his pants! The breeze caught his shirt and blew it back behind him. She got a glimpse of dark hair spanning a tanned chest before she pulled the window shade down. She stood there a minute. Her hand spread wide over her heart but then she had to let go of the shade in order to blot her suddenly hot face.

The shade flew up with a loud flutter. She was framed, mouth agape, in the window.

He was looking straight at her.

She dropped as if she'd been felled by a rifle!

She had lain there, holding her breath, for a long time. Then cautiously, she gathered her feet beneath her. Crouched, she allowed one eyeball—and nothing else—to appear over the ledge.

Nothing! Thank God! There was nothing between her and the barn but misty fog.

The memory alone was enough to turn her into the color of her uncle's union suit. She pulled at a clump of weeds with vigor.

"Frannnnnie?"

She turned. "Mama?"

Her mother stood at the back door clad only in her nightie. Her face was blotched and tear-streaked.

"What is it? What's wrong?" Torn, Mae looked from the baby, who was prone to crawl off, then back at her mother.

"Go to your mother," the Irishman said, walking quietly up behind her. "I'll watch the lad for you."

"Well . . ."

"It's all right."

After getting her mother back into bed and calmed, Mae went looking for Johnny. He was no longer on the blanket. She headed toward the barn. A few feet from the door she heard the deep rumble of the Irishman's voice. She couldn't make sense of his words but it sounded like he was conversing with a grown man. Maybe Uncle Ed was inside too. She tiptoed to the barn door and peered around its edge.

The Irishman and Johnny were sitting on a bale of hay. The Irishman leaned against a post with Johnny on his lap. The baby's back was supported by a thick thigh. His eyes, wide with delight, were riveted on the Irishman's face.

"It happened in Algiers. The bloody Casbah. I'd been drugged. Couldn't remember a bloody thing. I woke up. First thing I thought is: me mouth tastes like a ship's head after a week's layover in Cuernavaca!"

The baby blew a few spit bubbles. "Ye've been there, eh? So, I open me eyes. About a foot away from me throbbin' head is a guy wearing a turban, trying to coax a cobra out of a little wicker basket. Now, you can believe this for a fact, Jack, me boyo, the Casbah 'tis nae the place to be with nae money and nae gun . . ."

Although Mae was practically holding her breath, she must have made some slight movement. The Irishman rolled his head toward her. Without a bit of a brogue, he said, "Hello. Is your mother all right?"

"Yes, fine, thank you. And thank you for taking care of Jack . . . I mean Johnny."

"No' atall."

Johnny, the little traitor, actually screwed up his face and cried when she collected him.

Days passed, a week, then two. Still, the weather held. Sean went to bed at night bone-tired but with a contentment he had never known before. He would lay on the small cot in the tack room—a rack which he knew had been used successfully during the Spanish Inquisition—and organize his day.

He had already turned all the fields and made the most pressing miscellaneous repairs. Now he was worried about the wood supply. Having heard of Minnesota winters he asked Ed how much was enough. "There's never too much," he'd replied succinctly. It was the only time Ed had ever been succinct in Sean's hearing. So he'd decided to cut and haul more wood tomorrow. Then he should head back to Minneapolis.

Course, there was the problem of where to store the wood so it was handy to the house and the barn. Between those two big oaks would be perfect. He could make a three-sided shed with the slats wide enough apart to let the air in but close enough to keep the snow out.

Now, if the roof were sharply slanted . . .

Sean was chopping wood and listening with one ear. Ed was loading the wood on the wagon and talking, it seemed, with two mouths. Sean had wondered out loud whether anyone in the area bred cattle for slaughter.

". . . be a damned good idea. Providing a person had the money for a good bull. Ol' Bill was always gonna save up enough for another bull. Before his bull died, he used to do pretty good, selling a couple of heifers every season . . ."

It was a simple matter, Sean had discovered, to find out about the family. A leading question got the ball rolling. To keep it spinning, an occasional "Ah?" or "Y' don't say?" was all it took.

It was midday and the sun was warm. Sean had taken off his shirt.

"Bill put a couple of cows to Herrmann's bull a

few years back but he wanted a pretty penny. Then there was the ill will about Mae Ella and Peter getting married and . . ."

They were working on the edge of the woods where there were several dead trees. Once split, it wouldn't take the wood long to season. Suddenly Sean tuned in to the old man's rambling.

". . . fell off a ten story building. Ten stories! What a way to go, heh? Snapped his back like a wishbone. Now, I never much cared for Peter—the Herrmanns are a cold bunch—but I didn't wish him any harm, especially being Mae's husband."

"Cold, y'say?"

"Yeah, and old beyond his years, you know? A person would look in his eyes and see an old man like me looking back."

Sean stood the axe on the stump and rested his hands on the handle. Mae was walking across the field toward them. The bairn was straddling one hip, and she carried lunch in a covered basket over one arm.

". . . Johnny, Mae's brother what died in Bolivia? He went to school with one of the older sisters. Said she was oddest person he'd ever met. I never . . ."

I love to watch her walk.

". . . expected Mae to marry Peter, them being the same age and all. I thought they was just school chums, you know?"

The wind blew against her, flattening her dress and outlining her legs and a hot feeling snaked through Sean.

"Mae Ella was always close to her family. The day Mae Ella and Peter left for Chicago I knew she was gonna be miserable. Nothin' I could do. Man, I sure felt for her."

Sean pulled his shirt out of his belt, wiped his chest

then shrugged into it. Ed stopped chucking wood onto the wagon and looked at him. "We done?"

"Mae . . . Mrs. Herrmann's coming."

"Oh?" The old man turned, shaded his eyes and squinted.

It was then, when Sean started down the hill toward her, that he remembered. It hit him with such impact he almost staggered.

The brother! The kid in prison in Bolivia was her brother John.

He'd never known the boy's last name. The kid, laying in a corner of the cell, delirious and burning with fever, hadn't even been aware of their presence in the beginning. Sean and another guy—a Maltese he knew only as Lupa—had been captured, tried as seditionaries (which they most assuredly were) and summarily sentenced to execution by firing squad the following morning. They were thrown into a bug-infested cell crowded with men who faced a like fate. Provided they lived through the night.

"You're just wasting water, *mon ami*." Lupa had said as Sean gave the kid a swallow. "He's gut shot. An' from the smell of him, he's got jungle rot already."

Privately Sean agreed, but gave the kid small amounts of water anyway.

While he and Lupa made their wild, one-chance-in-a-hundred plan to escape, the kid mumbled . . . crazy, fever-induced ramblings about how cold the snow was and about a deer he shot. Later, hoarse but strangely rational-sounding, the kid started pleading, "Take me!" "Take me!"

"Sure," Sean'd lied, "Sure, kid," and wiped the kid's face with a piece of his shirt. He couldn't see much. Only a little moonlight came in through a tiny window high on the cell wall.

"Promise me. Promise." The kid rasped.

"Sure, kid. When we go, you go with us."

"Thanks." He'd finally quieted down and slept fitfully. The next morning there'd been no need for Sean to feel guilty when he and Lupa made their break. The kid was dead.

Mae looked up to the top of the hill and hoisted Johnny higher up on her hip. They hadn't seen her yet. Uncle Ed was bent at the waist, picking up logs, tossing them in the wagon. The Irishman was chopping. He'd apparently worked up a sweat. His shirt hung from his belt like a loincloth. Except for gloves and a bandanna tied around his head, he was nude from the waist up. Her eyes were drawn to his broad back like metal shavings to a magnet.

He stopped and turned. Mae looked down at the path, then snuck a look from beneath her lashes. He was using his shirt to wipe his broad, hairy chest. She concentrated on not tripping on any blades of grass.

Suddenly he was beside her. He took the basket. "Ma'am." He would probably tip his hat, if he had one. Which he didn't. His hair curled wetly around the bandanna like fat black snakes.

"Mr. McGloin." Gray eyes met blue ones and clung.

"What's for lunch, Mae Ella? I was about to take a bite outa Jocko there."

Mae smiled at her uncle. "You, Uncle Ed? Hungry?"

She brought lunch the next day and found her uncle working alone.

"I told the Irishman to take the wagon into town

for that feed we need. No reason for me to go along, I said."

"Oh," Mae said and looked down the road to town with foreboding.

That afternoon her work took her to the front of the house where the road to town was clearly visible. As the day waned and her chores brought her inside, she found all sorts of reasons to work in the front parlor.

Finally, giving up all pretexts, she brought Johnny into the parlor. Pulling Granny's rocker up to the window, she sat, rocked and watched the road. Her stomach was in knots, her hands and face were clammy. She recognized the feelings because she'd experienced them before. She'd forgotten about that time— maybe on purpose—but now she remembered it with stark clarity, like it was yesterday. It was the day her brother left.

She was crying and hanging on Johnny's arm. Mama was crying too, only much more delicately. Even Papa, standing with his arm around Mama, had red splotches on his cheeks. John leaned down—Mae remembered how his huge shoulders had blocked out the entire sky—and whispered in her ear. "Any kids give you trouble, write down their names. I'll get 'em when I get back."

She knew then that her brother loved her. She hadn't been sure because of that time when he had tried to swap her at school. She was too little to remember, but everytime there was a family gathering, somebody would tell about when John tried to swap Mae Ella for a yo-yo and everyone would laugh.

Mae didn't think it was a bit funny. "Oh, Johnny was just joking," Papa would say when he saw her crestfallen face. But she hadn't been a hundred percent convinced until that day at the train station.

John took his handkerchief out and dried her face like a plate. Then he picked up his suitcase and, with big giant leaps, he ran to the train. On the steps he turned and pointed at her. "Okay?" he mouthed.

She nodded. Tried to smile. Then he was gone!

On the ride home Papa tried to joke her out of her mood telling her how her wail had been louder than the train whistle. But the feelings—stomach in knots, hands and face clammy—stayed and stayed.

A few days after John left, because she was so glum and "moping around like a wilted wildflower," Papa took her with him to the field to work. He let her ride Jocko home. All their horses were Belgians and all were named Jocko. The first one Mae remembered had died of old age. Full of oats, warm and content in its stall. Jocko Two stepped in a gopher hole that day and broke his leg while she was riding him.

Tears streaming down her face, she had screamed, "Hurry, Papa! Hurry!" Pressing her slight weight on Jocko's lathered neck while he rolled his eyes and tried valiantly to stand, she watched her father run down the hill. It seemed to take him forever to reach the house, get his rifle then run back. Turning away, she had covered her face with her hands and stuck her thumbs in her ears, unable to watch, unwilling to hear.

The feelings got worse. She nearly drove her mother crazy. "Where's Papa?" She would ask the same thing every day at the same time.

"He's in the field, sweetling. He'll be back by suppertime."

But she was compelled to *see* him. Right that second. So, skinny legs flying and knobby arms pumping, she would run to the hill above the pasture.

There! There was her Papa, plowing or digging around an old stump. Resting her hands on her knees, she would watch him.

She finally got better but it took a long, long time.

Mae, rocking, rubbing Johnny's back, looked down the road.

He's never coming back.

The Irishman probably decided once he got as far as town that he might as well just keep right on going. I'll bet the horse and wagon are tied up at the train station right now.

Still empty.

Well, it doesn't matter. He was going to be moving on sooner or later anyway. We got along without him fine before. Just fine.

Empty. Empty. Empty. Never coming back.

Finally, a wagon appeared at the crest of the hill. Outlined against the setting sun, it was growing steadily larger as it came closer to the house.

Mae stood.

It was a man at ease with himself and his surroundings, a man who sat with his arms resting on his knees and his hat brim down and his collar up. A man confident and self-assured.

Mae laid the baby on the couch and went to the window and pressed her hands on the glass.

No mistaking, it was him. The Irishman.

She pulled the heavy curtains over the long window and sat on the settee in the darkened parlor until she heard the rattle of the wagon in the yard. And until her heartbeat slowed to normal.

Had the Irishman taken the place of her father,

coming as soon as he had after Papa's death? Had he?

"Oh, Granny, Granny! You'll never believe this, Granny . . ."

Hanging clothes the next day, she was still thinking on it. Snapping a towel before pinning it, she shook her head. *If that's not crazy, Mae Ella, I don't know what is.*

"Ma'am?"

Removing the wooden clothespin from between her lips, she stuck it on the towel before she turned. "Hello, Mr. McGloin." She smiled. He flashed a winsome smile in return. Her eyes, after a long minute, dropped from his white teeth and black gleaming moustache and that cute little hole in his chin to . . . the mass of tangled rope, tarp and part of a board he was holding. "Why, whatever is that, Mr. McGloin?" She came closer, intrigued.

"I . . . well, I made this swing for your boy."

Carrying the apparatus and unwinding it as he went, he stood under the gnarled red oak near the laundry line. There were two mismatched hooks on the underside of one limb.

Why, I've never noticed those hooks being there before.

He fastened the flat piece of two-by-four to the hooks and let the ropes hang free. Dangling from them was a little canvas pouch with tiny leg holes. "Why, Mr. McGloin," she smiled up at him. "What a wonderful idea!"

He dug deep into one of his pockets and held out a big hand. Lying in his callused palm were two more hooks—matching ones. "I could put these in your

kitchen ceiling, ma'am, and this winter, the lad could
be in there, close to the heat with . . ."

Sean's voice trailed off when she lifted her face
and really, truly smiled at him. 'Twas the most spectacular smile he'd ever seen! Warmth radiated from
her, sizzling his innards like a Caribe pepper pot.
Sweet Jesu, but she was a gorgeous woman! Hungrily,
he ran his eyes over her face and hair before settling,
like a bee on a morning glory, on her lips. Wha' a
nice full mouth . . . He thought about tasting it—
kissing, nibbling, sucking . . . She reached out and
touched one of the hooks in his hand with her finger
and he sucked in his stomach muscles. Her finger on
his palm brought as much reaction to his groin as if
she had just caressed his privates! His mouth went
dry as a Libyan sirocco. He almost dropped the hooks
and grabbed her.

"Oh! Mr. McGloin! Thank you! I spend so much
time away from Johnny, in the kitchen and out here,
hanging clothes and working in the yard. This way,
as long as it's nice outside, Johnny can get fresh air
and I can keep an eye on him. He's starting to crawl,
you know . . ."

You're babbling, liebchen.

She pressed her lips together. Whirling away, she
tossed a clothespin down on top of the laundry basket. "Just you wait right there, Mr. McGloin!" The
screen door slammed behind her.

Sean grinned and folding his arms across his chest,
rocked on his heels. *Well, 'tis workin' for ye again.
The ol' McGloin charm. Course, the bairn's swing
was a stroke of genius. Sheer genius! Next thin' ye
know, ye'll have her right where ye want her! On her
back and in the feathers! Now, if ye can keep yer
nose clean and yer hands to yerself and yer fly buttoned for a wee bit . . . Only a wee bit, mind . . . !*

She came out with the bundled-up baby in her arms, walking quickly. "Here we are, Mr. McGloin."

When the baby turned toward Sean, his crocheted cap covered part of his face and one eye. Sean hooked a long finger in its fold and tugged it around straight and grinned at the baby's alert face. He was a takin' little mite. He saw her features in the child's dark, finely curved eyebrows, in his pointed chin and his wide-set, Wedgwood eyes. Ah, twenty years and the boy's eyes will get him more . . . Sean's perusal dropped. The baby's fist was clasping her dress in a death grip, puckering the material and stretching it tighter than a sailor on shore leave. Clearly defined below his hand was her lovely breast, perfectly rounded, upthrust and tipped with a hard, thimble-sized nipple.

He trained his eyes skyward for a ten count before speaking. At that, his throat was gravel-coated. "He's a . . . a foin lookin' lad, ma'am."

"Oh, thank you! I think so. And so good." She smiled at the baby, nuzzling him. "Very good."

Walking together toward the slowly swaying swing, Sean tried to keep his eyes off her bosom. Unsuccessfully. "Let me put him . . ." Sean put his hands under the baby's arms, lifting him.

"Uh, just a minute, Mr. McGloin." She snatched the baby back. "Are you quite certain it's secure?" With one hand, she pulled down on one of the ropes as hard as possible. "Well, it . . . it seems to be."

"I tested it with my own weight, ma'am, which is considerably more than the boy's," he advised dryly. "I wouldn't be puttin' the bairn in somethin' unsafe."

"Oh, well . . . I didn't mean to imply . . ."

Taking the baby from her, Sean held him at eye level and grinned at him. The baby grinned back and produced a long thready string of drool. "Hello,

Jack!" The baby smiled even wider. "Hey! He's got a tooth already!" Sean turned back to her. "Did you notice that . . ."

"Of course, I noticed, Mr. McGloin." She rolled her eyes.

Sean stood the baby in the swing and carefully fed his legs through the cutouts in the canvas, lowering him. Then, he pushed the swing slightly.

Johnny's eyes and mouth rounded to O's. His bootie-covered toes barely reached the dirt below but he pressed up hard, working his legs up and down several times. He giggled.

Sean leaned against the tree and lit a smoke. "He's got a lot of strength in his legs, ma'am. Make for a good rugger, he would."

"A rugger? Oh, good! He's terribly smart. I mean, I know every mother says that about her child but truly he's exceptionally . . ." Mae's ear-to-ear grin changed to a frown. "Uh, what exactly is a rugger, Mr. McGloin?"

"A rugby player. Probably don't play rugby here. It's sort of like that new sport you've got. Football, I think it's called. They just had that big football game in Boston a few weeks back."

"Oh." Mae lost interest immediately. If he had said Johnny showed promise to be president or something, she'd have been thrilled, but ballplayers didn't make any money.

Leaning down, Sean ran a finger around the leg holes. "I can put some more padding here if you notice any chafing."

The baby smiled and pushed up again.

Mae jumped in front of the baby, clapping her hands. "Johnny! Do like Mommy!" She crouched down then hopped up, flinging her hands up high. *"Whee!"* Crouching, she jumped again. *"Whee!"*

Sean looked at her, shaking his head. "Ma'am?" He put a hand on her shoulder just prior to another jump. She looked up at him then blushed vividly. "Ah, yes?" She smoothed her hair back.

"Can I put these other hooks in the kitchen?" He showed her the hooks again.

Mae debated quickly. Her mother had just gone to sleep and she usually slept for an hour or so at a stretch. She hated to have him go inside, but what fun it would be to have the swing in the warm kitchen tonight! "Yes, Mr. McGloin. Please do, but my mother's sleeping . . ."

"I won't make a sound." He lifted the clothesline and ducked under it and noticed how it sagged when he let go. *She could use another one anyway. I could string one.*

"Look! Johnny! *Whee!*"

When Sean entered the warm confines of the house, the smells of breakfast bacon and maple syrup were still trapped within. The heavy wooden door to the back porch closed with difficulty.

Grease the hinges, shave off the bottom.

A row of pegs just inside the door held the old coat she sometimes wore, a man's yellow rain slicker and a woman's threadbare, dove-gray cloak. A pair of black, high-top galoshes with a few missing metal buckles sat in a wooden crate under the coats. A long, runner-style hook rug covered the hallway floor leading to the kitchen. There were four doors leading off from the hall.

Intuitively he knew which bedroom was her mother's and passed its slightly ajar door quietly. He pushed open the second door, leaning into it with one hand on the knob and the other on the jamb. It was small and simply furnished, a room barren of all but the necessities. One of Ed's shirts was tossed negligently on the dresser. The single bed, pushed up under the window, was covered with a patchwork quilt. A shaving mug and oval bowl sat on a stand under a silvered mirror with a strap conveniently hung on a nail on the wall nearby.

The little squint must have to shave by feel, Sean thought and experienced a feeling of affection the strength of which surprised him.

Opposite Ed's room was a narrow pantry. Wide shelves on two opposing walls were filled with canned goods, sacks of flour, coffee beans and sugar. A broom and a mop stood in an empty metal pail, their handles propped in the corner. At the end of the room, one set of rickety-looking stairs led down to the root cellar. Another set led up to a square trap door. Probably the attic, he thought and pulled the storage door closed. He went into the room he knew was hers.

How he knew had become a bone of contention with his conscience.

The first night he'd arrived, he was standing in the shadows of the barn having a last smoke when a new light in the farmhouse had drawn his attention. Without conscious thought, he had stepped deeper into the shadows. The gel was framed in the amber window. She held the pajama-clad baby up, shaking him and doing a little dance. Then, she sat, apparently in a rocking chair because her upper body began to sway rhythmically back and forth. From the tilt of her chin, the boy lay on her lap. She gestured, smiling down at the baby. Sean had remained fixed to the spot, unable to force himself either to look away or to turn and go into the tack room. Enthralled, he drank in the sight of her softened face and silvery hair glowing in the light like the shaft of a moonbeam.

He'd become physically aroused by the sight of her innocently playing with her child.

Shame on ye! What manner of man are ye? A bloody peepin' Tom?

Evidently, because when he discovered that the time she spent with the boy right after supper was a ritual, he watched every night. She would play with the boy first—rock and sing or talk to him—before she'd put him to bed.

To his continuing self-loathing, he now also knew exactly when she was in the habit of washing up at night. Many times he had seen her bring the big kettle into the room and pour steaming water into the bowl on the side table. Then she'd pull the shade, and turn the lantern to low. And his temperature turned to high.

God help him, but he couldn't keep from fantasizing about what went on behind that shade! At night, he'd lay sleepless on the cot with his hands clasped behind his head. It became a kind of sweet torment. He had only to close his eyes to conjure a vivid mental image—her undressing, standing nude in the center of the room, slowly rubbing a bar of scented soap over a washrag until she had built up a lather . . .

But, he had wondered, why turn out the lights? Was she in the habit of washing in the dark? Did she, even when married, undress in the dark? Certainly not!

There would sure as hell be no hiding in the dark if he were her husband! He could imagine nothing more delightful than watching her undress, helping her undress, then coaxing her to undress him. Lying on the narrow cot in the tack room, he fantasized about it. Facing each other across the wide expanse of the bed as she unbuttoned her dress and as he unbuttoned his shirt. They would both step out of their clothes. Smiling, he would reach across for her,

pull her over the bed and into his arms . . . Sean
stepped into her room.

It was like taking a bucket of bilge water in the
face! Painted robin's-egg blue with little yellow stick
figures stenciled high around the ceiling for decora-
tion, it was as pristine as a schoolgirl's room.

Ye blasted pervert! he cursed inwardly.

A small rag doll in a well-worn, dimity dress was
propped awry against the iron headboard. A heavily
embroidered navy counterpane covered the single
bed. The tiny crib with a rumpled blue pair of paja-
mas and a lonely-looking bootie was pulled up close
to hers. White, lacy curtains, swagged back with
yellow-checked ties, bracketed the window. The roll
shade, at half-mast, allowed only fragmented light.

A three-drawer oak dresser against one wall was
uncluttered except for a small circle of items arranged
on a tatted runner. Sean sniffed an empty cut glass
atomizer of Enchantment cologne. A small hand-
painted dish contained some shell hair pins and a few
colored buttons of assorted sizes. He lifted a heavy
jar of Ponds cold cream. He removed a few silver
blond strands of hair from a black-bristled hairbrush
and wrapped them round his finger. Finally he picked
up a sepia-toned tintype. The happy couple was typi-
cally posed. The boy sat stiffly with one hand inside
his jacket, the other holding a bowler-style hat above
his lap. His thin, straight blond hair, only slightly
darker in shade than Mae's, was parted in the center
and slicked down with pomade. Mae stood with a
small bouquet of flowers in one hand, the other
gloved hand rested on the groom's shoulder.

They both looked owl-eyed and scared spitless.

He was careful to put the tintype back in the same
spot. He ran his finger down her image. He had
known Peter had been young, but until he'd actually

seen the picture of him, he hadn't realized how young was young. He was a mere boy. Little more than a kid.

The thought cheered him no end. For a boy that age does not know how to please a woman. Certainly, not like the McGloin.

The scene outside the window cheered him even more. She was still playing with the baby. The child's cheeks were rosy and so were his lovely mother's. Sean heard the child's shriek as he flailed his arms and bounced around like a marionette. The laundry basket was, for the time being anyway, forgotten nearby.

"Good!" He muttered gruffly. He stood and took a last, reluctant look around. He crossed the room and closed the door silently behind him and made for the kitchen.

The large room had a thick battered oak table as its centerpiece. A faded oval rag rug covered the plank floor, extending out for a few feet around the table like a picture's matting. Pots and pans hung neatly above the cast-iron stove and familiar breakfast dishes drained on the sideboard next to the sink. Centered over the longest wall was an ornately framed watercolor of a castle nestled in some alpine mountains. On long, curved legs under it stood a well-made, cherrywood cabinet with brass handles. The wood-burning stove, the main source of heat for the house, was against the opposite wall on a raised red brick base.

Sean laid down his hammer and rapped his knuckles along the ceiling, listening for the slight difference in sound that would indicate the presence of a ceiling joist. In no time he was pretty sure he had one located. Pretty sure was nae good enough, however.

He tested the strength of the old stairs leading up

to the attic. "These are a bloody hazard!" he muttered as he ascended. Creaking and straining noises came from beneath his feet. A person could keep busy for months, for years maybe, fixing this old place up. He was surprised that the prospect of himself being the one to do the fixin' pleased him a great deal. He climbed cautiously, testing each riserless stair with every step. When he pushed the square door up and over, rusty hinges creaked and a puff of dust rose.

Sean worked his wide shoulders through the small opening, then looked around with interest. The attic had a higher-than-normal ceiling height. At sometime someone must have had plans to finish it off, adding on one or more large rooms as their family grew. Sean carefully counted the joists and checked the support beams. A person would need to construct some new, wider stairs with a handrail but with a couple of dormer windows, plastered walls and a polished, plank floor, the attic area could be made into a large, private room. Say, a large and very private bedroom. For example.

For the hell of it he took some preliminary measurements. In his mind, he had already calculated to the nail what would be needed to renovate the space.

Six

Sean had added four new supports to shore up the ridge beam on the barn roof. Now, riding the beam like a bronc buster, he was attempting to correct its sag. Mae was hanging laundry in the yard below. He cursed emphatically and forced himself to look down at the nail head.

That was the second time he had rapped the tar out of his thumb because he was attempting to hammer and ogle simultaneously. He shifted position and dug in his pocket for another spike and pounded it home without looking up once. But within seconds his eyes had strayed again.

It was barely perceptible, but it seemed to him that she walked as if she were especially tired today. As a consequence his disposition grew more surly by the minute.

For whatever reason, he was as attuned to the woman as if he were an appendage. When she smiled, he was happy. When she laughed, he felt like laughing too.

But when he saw her struggling with a load of laundry, or her mother, or when he noticed the fine lines of fatigue around her mouth, he felt it. Worse than a gut wound.

Mae went from the clothesline to the porch and Sean groaned. Not that all his thoughts were chaste and selfless. When she walked, she had a way of throwing back her shoulders. He closed his eyes and envisioned a lovely mental picture. God but he wanted her!

Well, of course I do. 'Twas never in doubt. 'Twas what I had in mind from the first.

He was no nearer his goal than the day he'd arrived. Damn! He shifted on the narrow board.

Yer liable to fool around and fall off the blasted roof!

Within seconds he was watching her again. Why— when his taste in women leaned toward trashy—was he so entranced with this girl? The answer continued to elude him.

T' say nothin' o' the gel.

Right. To say nothing of the girl. Matter of fact, she barely noticed him. Had he lost his . . . touch, for want of a better word?

He chewed the inside of his cheek. Was it possible?

Nah. That women were attracted to him was like saying he had a bent index finger. It was simply a fact of life. Puzzling, but there you had it.

He didn't think it was necessarily his looks or manly physique, although some women had come right out and asked him if he was as big all over as he was tall. He supposed in those instances it was the same as how some men had to fight him—some women had to have him. Like Augusta Ahearne. Sean paused, remembering the first day he'd attracted the attention of Squire Ahearne's wife. God, that was at least a hundred years ago.

Actually it was twenty-one years ago. He was twelve years old and had been doing a man's work since his mother's death two years earlier.

Stripped to the waist and working one of the horses in the paddock, he had felt someone's eyes on his sweaty back like the point of a sword. He'd turned and the squire's young wife had crooked a finger at him from just inside the cool interior of the stables. He went, perplexed. She pushed him against the side of a stall and had his pants unbuttoned before he knew what hit him.

For months afterward, under the rapacious tutelage of Mrs. Ahearne, he'd spent hundreds of hours "perfecting his technique" as she was wont to say.

Then one hot afternoon her husband caught them rolling around in the hay and had Sean tossed in jail on a trumped up charge of pilfering. Had it not been for a well-placed bribe by an old friend of his father's, he would have been hung. After narrowly making it out of Castletown with his life, he lost himself in the slums of Dublin.

After Castletown there were two things that always came easy to him: women and trouble. He was as randy as a cat with two dicks and possessed a boulder-sized chip on his shoulder. There followed a period when he had thought the proof of his manhood was most easily verified in a bar fight or between some willing woman's legs. He'd commenced proving his manhood just as often as humanly possible.

Sean set another nail and hammered it home. Some things a man outgrows and some he doesn't. He'd outgrown fighting for the sheer fun of it when fighting became a business, a deadly business. About that same time he outgrew having to have every woman he laid eyes on. Now, he did not turn any down. He was no idiot! But aside from the fulfillment of a healthy, purely physical manly need, he had become vaguely disinterested in women. This ambiguity seemed to have the exact opposite effect on the opposite sex.

Except for one woman. The only woman he had ever wanted. Could fate be so unfair?

The sad answer was apparently yes. Could and was.

Sean brushed his sweat dampened brow against his sleeve. Then, reminding himself that he needed to get the beam replaced before the snow flew, he concentrated on nailing the long spike into the wood without crucifying himself upon the barn roof.

He could always go to town for a woman, but the thought of a woman, just any woman, was about as appealing as being keel hau . . . He glanced down to where Mae had been standing only seconds before. She lay, arms and legs spread, flat on the ground.

The hammer skimmed the roof and fell to the ground with a thud. He crab-walked the steeply-pitched roof and pedaled down half of the ladder, then skipped the last several rungs to drop to the ground and run across the yard. Scooping her into his arms—he swallowed a shocked exclamation when he realized how little she weighed—he carried her swiftly into the house. Her head fell back over his arm, exposing her neck. Long, pale and translucent looking. "Sweet Jesu!" he muttered and laid her gently on her bed. The boy was asleep in the crib with his diapered rear heavenward and looking like a morel mushroom. He didn't stir.

Sean dampened a rag in the kitchen and folded it with shaking hands as he went back into the bedroom. He pressed the cloth to her forehead and temples, debated a quick second, then loosed three buttons of her woolen work dress. A pulse beat in a tiny blue vein below her fragile collarbone.

"Ma'am?" He brushed silken hair back from her brow. Her lips were slightly parted and her chest moved slightly with each shallow breath. "Mae?" he whispered and leaned closer. Her dress was saturated. Where the hell had all the water come from? "Bloody hell!" he muttered and tried to blot it up.

Mae opened her eyes just a little, enjoying the cool, gentle presses on her face and neck and chest. Chest? Her eyes flew open and filled with the Irishman's face.

Something had sure upset him. His mouth was pinched white and a bump of determination stood out on his jaw feverishly going up, down, up, down. Thick brows beetled over his downcast eyes. My, but his lashes are incredible, she thought. Suddenly, he looked up and skewered her with his sizzling eyes!

Goodness sakes! The man was livid! With her!

"Be it yer plan t' work yerself into the groun'?" Tossing the rag down on the dresser with a loud splat, he straightened, arms akimbo.

"What?" His brogue was so thick his words were unintelligible!

"If'n tha' be yer plan, ye're abou' t' get yer wish!" Grasping her shoulders, he lifted her slightly and shook her. "An' then, what'll happen to yer bairn?"

What was this ranting maniac doing in her bedroom? And what had she done to infuriate him so?

"Ye dinna ha' the weight of a nit!" Looming closer, he stuck out his jaw aggressively. "Jesu! Me very life passed afore me! An' 'tis nae somethin' I care to relive, thank ye very much!"

Mae pressed into the bed. "Mr. McGloin! Please stop hollering at me!" She drew the two edges of her dress together. "Did I, uh, faint?"

"I though' ye was dead! Scared the pee right outa me!"

Her mouth dropped open. "Mr. McGloin!" Insanely, she had an overwhelming impulse to laugh! She pressed her hand to her mouth and bit her lips to keep from doing so.

He shook a big fist in her face. "Ye'll be killin' yerself with work! An' meself too! Me heart willna take it!"

Looking at his flushed, angry face, Mae felt a twinge of something. Fear? No. Anger? No, not anger. Excitement?

Yes, excitement! Why, she could light a match from the sparks coming out of his eyes. She had never seen such contained strength or felt the might of such power before. It was wonderfully exhilarating! Like going down the rapids on the river in the little home-made canoe. Like flying down cemetery hill in the sled. And she'd thought that there were no feelings behind that tough, contained exterior!

She smiled—only a small, tentative smile—and he slowly lowered his hands. She heard his long exhalation of breath. Her smile waned when their eyes locked. Something in his expression rendered her incapable of movement. She was a little afraid but could not look away. The air became close and heavy, like before a summer rain.

"Mae!" The guttural word was like a primitive battle cry. He pulled her up to her knees and crushed her to him.

"Oh," she said.

"Yes. Oh." His eyes ran over her hair and her face and then centered on her lips. Her lids closed of their own will when she felt his lips seal hers. Holding her head easily in a large hand, he pulled back—only far enough for a feather to pass between their parted mouths—and whispered "Mine!" or "Mae!" She stared into his steamy eyes for several heartbeats. "Sweet Jesu, woman!" Again their lips met and his tongue trespassed, entering into the chaste sanctuary of her mouth. He began a slow, thorough exploration. Totally comprised of greedy lips and hands, it seemed as if he wanted to absorb her. She fought an insidious desire to let him. Increasing apace with the rough thrusts of his tongue was a throbbing ache between her legs. Something made her think of . . . It was almost like when . . . when Peter had . . . when he had . . . Suddenly afraid, she struck his arm. Abruptly, he released her and turned away.

Without his support, she collapsed on the bed like a wet dishrag. Belatedly, she croaked "Mr. McGloin!" Truthfully, her astonishment was more at herself than at him. She felt feverish, close to swooning. Her senses whirled. She had never experienced such feelings.

He walked out and a second later she heard the screen door close. She touched her bruised lips with trembling fingers.

Crimany! What on earth? That was indescribable. Like being in the middle of a . . . a tornado! She felt so weak, she didn't think she could stand without assistance. Her breasts felt tight and full. Deep in her core, she felt a cramping and dewy moistness.

She stiffened. Could she be getting her monthly? She covered her face with her hands and thought.

No, she'd just had it.

"There's those whores! Mae Elllla? There they go!"

Mae put her hands over her ears. Blushing, she turned her face into her pillow and curled into a fetal position. Not now, Mama!

With long, angry strides, Sean covered two miles in about as many minutes. Finally he stopped. He leaned against a molting cedar and looked down at the farm. He remained thus for several moments. After cupping a match to his cheroot, he walked on, slower now. The small cemetery seemed to beckon.

Many times he'd seen her walk this way, often with that old hound following close behind. Sometimes she would even bundle up the bairn and the three of them would sit on the hill. Profiled against the sky they made a picture that was as sad as anything he'd ever seen.

He had never come up to the graveyard before, thinking she might look upon the place as private to the family. Hands on hips, he stared sightlessly at her da's grave. The earth was still raw and denuded of grass. A few dried mums—yellow, orange and white—had been stuck in a wide-mouthed Mason jar and buried lip deep at the foot of the grave.

He could just hear the old man . . . "What the devil do you think you're doing?"

It was a reasonable question. One he'd asked himself as a matter of fact. Many times. "Damn it!" He kicked a clod of dirt.

At first he'd told himself his actions were predicated purely on simple curiosity. He had to find out why she looked familiar to him. Later, when he'd remembered Bolivia and the puzzle was solved, he'd told himself it was pity. Her smile had touched a soft spot in him an' . . .

An' 'tis time to stop foolin' yerself. Curiosity an' pity dinna fill ou' the front o' a man's denims.

Lust then. Was it lust? Lewd, carnal desire? Corrupt and impure hunger? Was that what he felt?

No. He'd experienced lust many times before. Lust did not evoke the depth of emotion he felt.

Somehow, somewhere along the line, the emotions governing his actions had changed. Instead of simply having her in his bed, now he must keep her in his life.

He saw her as she had looked a few moments ago—smiling tentatively up at him—and he realized that everything he had ever wanted was before him. After knocking around hither and yon, here he had found one thing that mattered most to him in the world. A fine, lovely girl with a soul as pure as molten gold and a backbone of steel.

Ah, wha' a woman! Memory of her sent a ripple of longing through him and he was hard as iron again.

He rubbed his hand over his jaw. 'Twould no' do. This was not a woman to roll in the hay with. This was a woman to love. When he looked at her before, he had seen only her body. After today, after looking into her eyes, he had seen her soul. The gel was as innocent as a babe. Pure. Untainted. Chaste.

Exasperated, he kicked a half-buried log and his leg vibrated like a tuning fork. It was a bigger log than it had appeared. He spat a word, then slumped down onto it. "God help me, but do I love her?" *Since first I saw her? Is that possible?*

Crazy as the notion was, it had to be true! His obsession with her well-being, his powerful need to protect her, his desire to please her . . .

Shit! He loved her.

An' the gel dinna return the feelin'!

He spat an extremely coarse word.

'Tis a terrible blow to a man's ego!

So have ye tossed in the towel, then?

The McGloin? He rolled his shoulders. He would win her, he vowed. Although obviously not by a frontal attack. She was unawakened, an innocent for all her womanly appearance. He'd map out a plan, just like any successful campaign. First strategy, then planning, then patient carry-through. He would not allow himself to be distracted. He would be focused.

He would be invincible. As usual. He was, after all, the McGloin. He rolled his shoulders again.

Now, he thought, the first thin' to do is . . .

. . . figure out how to stop every drop of blood in his body from racing to his groin when he was in her presence.

"Bloody hell!" He pulled out a tuft of dried grass and shredded it.

The wind sighed in the trees and the air carried the smell of pine cones and wood smoke. He looked at the river bluffs and then down at the farm below. A single thought hit him. A man could be buried in a lot worse places.

He looked at the grave and ran a hand through his hair and cleared his throat. If the man was alive, he'd ask his permission to court the gel. Of course, if her father had been alive, Sean would not have been on the farm to begin with.

Not a man normally given to prayers, he felt a powerful need to say one now. He went to one knee and bowed his head. "I dinna wan' to leave her. I wan' to stay an' help her, the babe. I will work yer land, keep it fine. I would gladly cut off me arm 'fore I'd hurt her."

'Twas a strange prayer, but one he felt better for saying. Was it heard? Would the old man approve? Sean imagined his own reaction to someone such as himself courting his daughter—especially if he knew what had just transpired—and blanched.

The gel deserves better than ye. Yer too old, too used, too . . . he glanced down at the farmhouse then abruptly stood. He threw the grass down. Mae was running around the yard like a chicken with its head cut off! Something she cried out floated up toward him like a warm breeze. Was it . . . Mama?

He tossed aside his smoke and charged down the hill.

"Mama?" Mae ran through the barn peeking left and right into every stall. She stopped dead at the ladder to the loft then tucked her skirts up. She climbed it quickly. "Mama?" Craning her neck, she turned her body first one way then the other, peering into all the dark corners of the loft.

Nothing!

She ran to the tack room. After she had already thrown open the door, she considered the impropriety of not knocking first. What if the Irishman had been inside? She pressed her hand to her warm cheeks but stepped inside.

The room was neat, the bedspread smoothed. New hooks were affixed to the wall for clothes. The collapsed duffel bag and the jacket he had worn the first day he arrived hung on two of them. A red-and-black-plaid blanket was folded lengthwise across the bottom of the bed. The little coal heater was placed safely a few feet out from one of the walls. Dropping to her knees, she looked under the small, sagging bed, thinking the Irishman couldn't possibly find it comfortable!

No sooner did she think of him than, as if by magic, he filled the doorway. "What is it?"

"I'm sorry to be in your room uninvited . . ."

Waving her words away, he repeated. "What is it?"

"I can't find Mama." She blushed. "I heard her cry out, but . . ." She couldn't bring herself to say that she had been clutching herself for a long time after he had left her bedroom, reliving his kiss. "I didn't go to her right away." She looked up at him. "Only five minutes, even less. Then when I went into her room, she was gone!"

Sean snatched a bridle off the barn wall and went into the horse's stall.

Uncle Ed appeared in the barn doorway. "What's all the hollerin' about? What's goin' on?" He squinted.

"Mama's missing, Uncle Ed." She hurried by him.

"You know, I can't be sure, but I thought I saw a flash of white go right by me about five minutes ago . . ."

"Where?" Sean and Mae asked together.

"Headed toward the river bluffs."

"Please!" Mae held onto the bridle as Sean was about to kick the horse into motion. "Take me!"

Reaching down, he grabbed her and effortlessly slung her up behind him. They were about a half mile from the bluff's sheer drop to the river when Mae saw her mother. "Mama!" Mae held her hand out, hopelessly, in a staying motion. Wearing only her nightdress, her mother ran swiftly toward the edge, then without pause, sailed out over the water and dropped out of sight. "Mama!"

"Bloody hell!" Sean muttered, kicking the poor horse even faster. Pulling it up to an abrupt halt at the edge, he jumped down, flinging "Stay there!" over his shoulder as he ran down the narrow path to the bluff. He paused on the rim of the bluff for a second, then disappeared over the edge in a neat dive.

Mae stood stunned for a second then ran to the drop-off and looked down the sheer face of the cliff to the swiftly running water below, a distance of many feet.

The Irishman's slick head appeared above the water for a second, then disappeared again. Mae ran down the circuitous path to the water's edge, unmindful of the branches that scratched her arms and face. Reaching bottom finally, she waited ankle-deep in the water.

Her heartbeat stepped up in tempo each time his head broke the surface alone. "Oh, God! Please! No!"

At last, he appeared. Her mother's head was in the crook of his arm. He swam toward shore.

"Hurry!" She paced, never taking her eyes away from his bobbing head as he cleaved the water with a strong arm. "Oh, hurry, please!"

When they were within a few feet of shore, Mae splashed into the turbulent water thigh-high. With a lunge, she got a handhold and started tugging on her mother's nightgown. Sean carefully laid his burden down.

"Mae!" He encircled her waist and pulled her a few feet away. She struggled to twist away.

"Mae, her neck was broken in the fall. Mae!" He clasped her to him, holding her easily while she pushed at him, crying. "Mama!" Her hands pressed with less and less strength against his wet shirt. Finally she collapsed against him, sobbing. "Oh, God! Not Mama too!"

Seven

Mae must've felt obligated because of his efforts to retrieve her mother's body. That was the only reason he could figure why she'd insisted he attend the small gathering for friends and family in the parlor.

Several people had seemed perplexed by his presence. He could imagine what they were thinking. A hired hand might attend a family member's funeral but a hired hand would not stay for the reception.

Sean had said little and kept to himself, holding his empty teacup and saucer like they contained the host and shifting from one big foot to the other. He was very glad when it was over. Now he and Ed stood in the yard looking up toward the cemetery where Mae sat. The last mourner had left an hour earlier.

"She still up there?" Ed ran a finger around his collar, obviously uncomfortable in the starched shirt and the brown serge suit that was several years out of style.

"Yes, damn it!"

"I'd best go back up then. She's liable to grieve herself sick."

"Let me go. All right? She . . . she may need help coming down. Could you keep an eye on Jack?"

"Yeah. He was sleeping, but I'd best go inside so I can hear him."

Ed headed toward the house and Sean toward the cemetery.

He stood at the fence, reluctant to intrude. Mae sat in front of the new grave. He could tell by the set of her shoulders that she had heard him approach, but she didn't turn. She was staring straight ahead with one arm across her midriff as if she was holding something inside. The other arm was around that damned dog.

"Please come down now, ma'am. The ground's too cold to be sitting on." He waited in vain for a response. "You'll catch yer death."

Silence.

All right, he thought. We'll sit up here till hell freezes over if that's what you want. He propped the sole of his boot against a tree and studied her. Leaves were mounded against her back and trapped in the folds of her skirt like ornaments. He had never seen her with her hair done so formally. It was poufed out on the sides in what ladies called a pompadour. On her the mass looked way too heavy for her fragile neck.

She's pale as paste, he thought and clenched his jaw. She turned her head slightly, offering him her classic profile.

There's something, he thought not for the first time, almost ethereal about her. She reminded him of a religious card his mam used to mark her place in her bible. On one side was an uplifting prayer. On the other was a painted picture—Saint Teresa or Saint Rita, he couldn't remember who—of a very young, very beautiful, but very tragic woman. A virgin martyr, he remembered, who had died a horrible death because she refused to sleep with some powerful man.

The blasphemous thought made him more uncomfortable than the drizzle seeping into his collar. He turned it up and looked around. The woods were quiet and most of the trees bare. It was a poetic day for a funeral—cold, damp and dreary. The kind of day when a man's breath will form a gray vapor whether he was smoking or not. Mae's voice startled him.

"Peter isn't buried here, you know."

"No," he replied. "I knew that."

"They . . . his family . . . insisted that he be buried over on their place. His father told Papa he wasn't about to let his son be buried in a nest of bead rattlers. Wasn't that an awful thing to say?" She sighed. "At the time I just didn't have the heart to argue." She shook her head. "If they only knew."

Sean frowned, puzzled. A long silence ensued, then she said, "Granny and I used to come here all the time. Coming back from gathering black berries or looking for wildflowers or on our way to the river to fish, Granny'd say, 'Let's stop and say hello to Helmut.' And we would. We'd sit right there," she pointed, "under the oak tree, and Granny would tell about her early life with Helmut." She looked at him. "Helmut was my grandfather."

"Yes."

"Granny said that when they moved to Minnesota from Weisbaden they were so poor they couldn't even afford to buy a chicken! You wouldn't believe some of the awful things that happened! Granny'd say, 'Der vas dis time ven de river flood . . . Der vas dis time ven de Indians kom . . .' She'd tell about some devastation then say, 'Vel, Helmut und me kom from goot stock, you know, liebchen? Not so easy to knock us down. Maybe can knock down but not keep down, you know, liebchen?' "

She sat still as stone for several minutes then

turned to him. "Were you ever . . . fanciful, Mr. McGloin?" Her look was expectant, hopeful. He pretended to think but the answer was easy. *Never.* In so many ways she was still a child. And as for himself? Hell, he'd never been young.

"Of course I was, but it was . . . long ago," he said gruffly. He watched her pet the dog.

The dog's tail acknowledged her attention to his ears. "Sometimes I talk to myself. Just inside my head, you know, I don't . . . ah, move my lips."

"Is that what you consider fanciful?" She nodded. "Well, hell, I do that all the time."

"You do?" She looked at him, hopeful again.

"Sure, all the time." He would say he was Kaiser Wilhelm if it would bring color back to her cheeks.

"Sometimes I imagine I hear my granny talking to me."

"Me, too."

She looked up, incredulous. "You hear my granny?"

"No, I mean I imagine I hear a . . . a voice," he said, feeling like a fool.

"Who?"

He smiled a little. "Me conscience, I think."

"Oh." There was a pause. "That's good to know. I was beginning to think I was getting a little, you know . . ." She twirled her forefinger around her temple. ". . . dotty."

"You're right as rain, as you Americans say. Although I've never understood that phrase." He struck a lucifer with his thumbnail and prayed that they were done with fanciful.

"I was sitting up with Mama one night . . . She often didn't sleep very well so I would leave my mending basket in her room. I would sit with her and sew until she went back to sleep."

She was rambling. Was she in shock? The thought

dried his mouth and had the opposite effect on his armpits.

"Doc Neimark had been to see her that day. He said things were going to go downhill fast now. I was close to rude to him. I said, 'Can't you give me any encouragement. Must you be so pessimistic?' It didn't phase him in the least." She deepened her voice. " 'You want sugar-coated words, Mae Ella? Or the truth?' Why, I was certain Mama could hear him. We were standing right outside her room and he's got such a big voice.

"That very night when I was sewing a button on Uncle Ed's work pants, I remember thinking how mortified Mama would be if she knew how she really was . . . if she . . ."

Mae covered her face with her hands. Sean pushed off the tree and knelt beside her. He laid a gentle hand on her rounded shoulder and felt her tremble. "Here! You're cold." He shrugged out of his jacket and wrapped it around her shoulders.

She shook her head but pulled the lapels together under her chin. "I was never that close to Mama. She was always so . . . serious. Maybe if I hadn't had Granny I would think that's how people of different generations were supposed to be. But I did have Granny. She wasn't at all like Mama. She was so much fun! When I was little, it was always Mama and Johnny and Papa, then Granny and I. That's the way we sat at the table, that's the way we rode to town in the sleigh. I loved Mama." She glanced at him quickly and he nodded. "Very much. But I've always wanted to be like Granny. Practical, but a lot of fun, you know?" He nodded again. Wind blew hair across her face and a few strands caught between her lips and he had to clench his fist on his thigh. "That night, after Doc said that, I thought . . . I remember thinking . . ." She swallowed visibly, staring into the distance. ". . . that Mama would prefer to die. I know her. I know what she would want and then I thought maybe I should . . ." She covered her face again and started to sob, great choking sobs. "God help me!"

He extended a hand to her, hesitated, then sat back on his bootheels. Long moments passed. He lit another cheroot with unsteady fingers and exhaled. Her crying tore his guts, but he wasn't sure what she was talking about and didn't want to say the wrong thing. Why was she was beating herself up? Unless . . .

"I read once that it's common for people who are caring for the dying to wish them dead, if only to give their loved one peace and freedom from pain. It's also common for families to feel guilty when the sick person finally dies."

Her bleak expression lightened a little. "Really?" she asked, her amethyst eyes awash with tears.

"Sure. A proven fact. It's very common."

"Sometimes I believe I'm . . . that I'm bad luck. A jinx or something."

"Where do you get such thoughts, anyway?"

She looked about her as if he'd asked where are your gloves? "You know, I don't honestly know."

He held out a balled up handkerchief. "Here." She looked askance at it. "Go on. It's clean, just not ironed." She took the handkerchief and wiped her eyes.

"Tell me something. Did your mother ever have lucid moments?"

"Yes, every so often. It was somehow even worse when she did." She blew her nose. Sean hid a smile. Dottiness might not run in the family, but honking did.

"She would look around at her room, at herself in a diaper, in bed in the middle of the day. And then she'd look at me as if asking, why am I here? Once she said something like—why are you doing this to me, Mae Ella?"

"Maybe she made a decision in one of those lucid moments, right before she headed for the river." His voice trailed off.

"No. If Mama was in her right mind, she would never have . . . done that."

"But that's just it. She wasn't in her right mind. And therefore she was not accountable for her actions. You must remember that some decisions are made by a higher, wiser power and we must simply believe that that higher power's judgment is better than ours. Now, dry your eyes."

Mae did as ordered. The handkerchief smelled like him, like the woods, earthy and clean. She had seen him washing out his clothes in the bucket in the barn. She could easily do his laundry for him, especially now that she didn't have Mama to care for. And she would too. Gladly. Would he stay, if she did? God! Please, please!

She had an unexpected thought. Would something awful happen to him if he did? She didn't want him to die! She looked at him, suddenly fearful. "Maybe . . . maybe you'd be smart to move on, Mr. McGloin. Everybody around me seems to die."

He snorted derisively. "That's a crock and you know it. I'll not leave. Not until you run me off." Standing, he held out his hand. "Let's go down now. Give me yer hand, Mrs. Herrmann."

"You'll stay then? For a while longer?"

He nodded slowly. "Absolutely."

Promise. Promise. Promise! She fought further tears. She looked at his hand then up into his eyes and put her hand in his.

Eight

"How about if you and me do a little turkey huntin'?"

Sean almost swallowed the nail he was holding between his teeth. The thought of being anywhere near Ed while he wielded a loaded gun . . . He took the nail out. "Have ye lost the little sense ye were born with?"

"Oh, not me! You! I'll do the callin', you do the shootin'."

"Calling?" Setting down the hammer, Sean turned to face him. "What the hell are you talking about, man?"

Pulling the skin away from his neck with thumb and finger, Ed rolled his eyes skyward. He resembled, Sean thought, a man trying to have his daily constitutional.

"Gobble, gobble, gobble."

"Is that how wild turkeys sound? Man, they deserve to get shot!" Sean tilted a cigar can over on the bench, spilling out an assortment of different sized nails and brads.

"Yes, that's exactly how they sound!" Ed was clearly offended. "If I was a female turkey, I'd be practically faint with excitement." The man leaned over and spat. After a minute, he asked. "Any good with a rifle?"

"Fair." Sean hammered a wire brad into the pine cabinet.

"Well, we might get lucky then and get us one. Say, what the Sam Hill are you doin' anyway?"

"Making a nice cabinet. With doors." With his head bent, Sean missed Ed's gap-toothed grin.

"A cabinet! Huh! For out here in the barn?"

"No. Does it look like it will be for a barn?"

"No. Looks like it might be for Mae Ella's kitchen. Right?"

"Yeah." He looked up just after Ed had composed his face. "Do you think she'd prefer to have it varnished or painted?"

"Well, I guess I don't know. Guess you'll have to ask her."

Sean fitted the brass hinge to the cabinet carefully. He knew exactly why he didn't ask her. He didn't want to remind her that he was still on the premises!

She seemed almost in a daze in the days since her mother's death. If she had not forgotten what had happened in her bedroom that day, maybe she had forgiven.

She must have. Otherwise she'd have thrown yer arse off the place.

That thought brought the memory. He clenched his jaw. After the funeral, he had promised himself that what happened that day in her bedroom would never be repeated.

But he was like a boy hoarding a cookie and, at the end of the day when he was alone in the tack room, he would allow himself his treat. With his hands behind his head, his legs exceeding the cot's length by a yard, he would close his eyes and unwrap the memory. Ah, but it was like polishing fine silver, for each time he did it, it became cleaner and brighter. Except, lately, the image intruded when he wasn't willing it to. He had become like some mates who'd got hooked on opium. Poor buggers. No matter how they tried, they couldn't leave the stuff alone.

Ed pushed up his battered hat to scratch his crown then pulled it back on. "If we get a couple of turkeys, we could smoke one. Ol' Bill, Mae Ella's father, and I always used to go this time of year and try to get at least one for Thanksgiving." Then, "You know what Thanksgiving is?"

"The Pilgrims and Indians, right?"

"Right! You got Thanksgiving in Ireland?"

"No."

"How come?"

"No Pilgrims."

"Huh. Well, anyway, I was thinking that we might be able to get a deer. It'd sure help the larder this winter. I'm mighty partial to deer and pork sausage." After a pause, he added the clincher. "It'd be cheap food, too."

Sean studied the old man in the dusky light. "How much of a problem is there with money?"

"Ha!" Snorting, he leaned over and spat again. "When does anybody have enough?"

Sean sat next to him, wiping his hands on a rag. "Does she have enough to get by?"

"Well, that's hard to say. Last night, she was addin' up some figures from the bank. She said she must have added them thirty times, and got a different figure each time."

Sean stared at the yellow light coming from the kitchen window and imagined her inside, sitting at the table. He knew there were money problems but he hadn't known the extent of them until the incident at the grocer's the day before.

Everyone had made the trip into town. Mae had made out a list before they left the farm, asked Ed to make sure it was filled properly and then she handed the list to Sean.

Sean stood in front of Watson's and watched as Mae and little Jack went into the Farmers Bank building. After a minute, he followed Ed inside the store.

The old-fashioned store was jam-packed with merchandise, everything from feed and fertilizer to food and fixtures sectioned off by signs hanging on cross beams overhead.

Beneath the sign for mens & boy's apparel in the back Sean found a fleece-lined winter jacket large enough for himself. As he strolled back to the front of the store he was presented with a cacophony of pungent smells. From the grocery section, onions, garlic and licorice. From households, soap and vinegar. And from hardwares, turpentine and paint.

John Watson periodically consulted Mae's list, then added items to the cardboard boxes containing their order. When he paused and looked up, Sean laid down some cash on the counter. "For the jacket." Sean glanced at Ed, standing near the door. Bent almost double, he was peering into the glass enclosed case containing the chewing tobacco. Quietly Sean asked, "What's the status of the Botts' account?"

John Watson's eyes dropped down to the other bills Sean held in his hands then fled to the list. "Uh, well, it's owing," the proprietor answered in an equally discreet tone.

Watson and his wife had attended Mae's mother's funeral. Unlike some of the townsfolk who had seemed nonplused by his presence, Watson had shaken Sean's hand and introduced him to his wife.

"I'm not pressing Mae for the money at all. I know she's had more than her share of trouble this year." He glanced up at Sean then back at the neatly printed list in his hand. "I'll be glad to wait."

"How much?" Sean reached into his back pocket and took out a number of bills.

"Oh, no. That's all . . ."

"Listen, Bill lent me some money a few years back. Matter of fact, that's how come I'm here. Came to pay him back but I arrived a week too late. I still owe the money of course but Mae feels funny accepting it. Can't understand why . . ."

"Oh, I can. Mae's like that . . ."

"But you and I both know the family can use the money. Right?"

Sean could see conflict on the shopkeeper's moon shaped face. "I'd consider it a real favor," Sean added.

Common sense finally won out over propriety and Watson sorted through several cards in a little wooden box next to the scale then pulled one out. After adding the supplies still on the counter and the items packed in the boxes, he named a total figure.

Sean doled out the money, then, hands wide-spread, leaned on the counter. "It can be our secret. You can say there was an existing credit or something. How about it?"

"I could. You bet!" He added. "This is sure kind of you, Mr. McGloin."

"Sean. Call me Sean." They shook hands.

When they left and Sean assisted Mae into the wagon, she glanced in the back of the wagon at the supplies and then at Uncle Ed. Sean heard her softly question Ed as he rounded the wagon. "Was there any problem with filling our order, Uncle Ed?"

"Nope. Filled it lickety split!"

"So, whadda ya think? About the hunting, I mean?" Ed had to say it twice before Sean heard him.

"All right with me."

There was blessed silence for a while.

Ed, in the habit of joining Sean in the barn for a chew before dinner, had also gotten in the habit of pumping Sean for information about himself. The old man had the tenacity of a badger.

Sean had tired of side-stepping questions like "How come you know so much about farming, Irish?" and "Where'd you say you learned to do that?" So almost in self-defense, Sean had told him about his life in Ireland. Over time, in bits and pieces, he'd described where he and three previous generations of McGloins had been born. About the drizzily days and cold nights and a thatched-roof cottage poorly warmed by an ever-present peat fire. About his two younger brothers and a sister and about their deaths from smallpox.

In the jargon every farmer understands, he complained about the backbreaking toil required to feed a family on poor, rocky soil that was incapable of yielding a good harvest even in the best of years. About the bugs and the blight, and finally, about the beauty of the land and how much he had loved it.

Now, at last, their conversations were general. The old man was content to sit companionably chewing while Sean worked on one project or another. They had discussed the latest war and the next. Women's right to vote and men's right to imbibe. Everything from adultery to Zulus and then adultery among the Zulus. Sean found he enjoyed the old man's company, especially his dry wit and easygoing temperament.

Having decided to go hunting on the morrow, they spent the evening discussing scat and spoor and gauges and blinds and tracking. With great relish and outrageous exaggeration, they each recounted previous hunts.

If asked, both men would agree that their conversation that night was so splendid it was almost spiritual.

Sean stood abruptly, went to the window and placed one gloved hand on its frame. All was quiet except for the animals moving in their stalls and the bark of a dog in the distance. The moon endowed the frost-covered yard with a silver sheen. Even in the barn their breaths hung visibly in the air. Sean stared at the house and thought he saw a shadow pass the window.

'Tis a clever man who recognizes an opportunity when he sees it.

"Can you get your hands on those figures she's been worrying over?"

Ed leaned over and spat. "I guess I could. They were spread all over the kitchen table last night and the night before. Might be tonight, too."

"I've got a real head for figures." The porch door slammed and Sean watched Mae come toward them. She wore her father's ratty old coat.

Damn, but he had wanted to buy her a new coat when he was in Watson's! A nice, fitted one to match the color of her eyes. Most of her clothes were worn and too large, but one dress was worn and far too tight! When she came out of the house wearing that particular work dress, Sean, fearing for his sanity—or his limbs if he happened to be wielding an axe— would head for the fields. She wasn't aware of it, modest as she was, but the bodice on that dress was so tight practically nothing was left to the imagination. She hadn't ever worn it when they were headed to town, which was fortunate. He would be forced to spill something on it or stand on the hem. 'Twas a double-edged sword. He wanted her to look nice, but not too nice.

Someday, he vowed, he would buy everything new for her. From the skin out. Lovely sheer things. Then he would sit in her rocking chair and have her model the stuff for him. Silk chemises. Satin nightgowns. Camisoles. Pantaloons . . .

"Hello." Mae said, stopping a few feet from them. She shot a quick look at Sean. "Mr. McGloin."

"Ma'am."

She folded her arms against the cold. "Well, Uncle Ed? Dinner's in about five minutes. Are you hungry?"

"Starvin' to death! I'll come in right now and wash up." He stood and brushed off his seat.

She glanced at Sean and blushed and hated herself for it. Her eyes skittered away. "Please take your meals in the house with us from now on, Mr. McGloin. At least until you . . . as long as you are . . ."

"Thank you." He replied quietly. "I appreciate that, ma'am."

Mae pretended absorption in the characterless, gray sunset. She was thinking about that day in her bedroom. How his tongue had tasted, how he had made that hungry growling noise like he wanted to eat her. She shivered.

She was apparently obsessed. Or was it possessed? Instead of outgrowing her flights of fancy she was getting even more fanciful. Just take, for example, what happened to her today.

She'd been feeding Johnny, like always. First thing she knew, she heard the baby's piercing screech and realized she had been holding the spoon in front of his open, baby-bird mouth, probably for several minutes. But she'd been thinking about Sean. Again.

She'd given herself a good talking-to right on the spot, but an hour later only her full bladder alerted her to the fact that, instead of strolling in a rose garden, she was leaning against the smelly outhouse door, staring dreamily into space. Guess what she was thinking about then, hmm?

Then the last straw was burning the wild rice soup so badly there was an inch of crud on the bottom of her best pan. She could soak it until she was a hundred, probably. What on earth does a person do about a problem like this? She shifted from one foot to the other. When a person loses all control over their thoughts, who do they see? Doc Neimark?

Sean watched Mae fidget like a water bug on a trout stream. Were her senses electrified? Was being close to him a bittersweet torment? Did she ache with desire?

It was something he devoutly desired her to feel because, for himself, it was all that and more. If only he could make her feel as he did.

An' so ye can. Ye only hav' t' liv' with yerself after.

His years in the Orient had included a stint in a samurai dojo. While becoming skilled in the martial arts—karate and jujitsu—he'd also learned the ancient art of saiminjutsu. Suggestive thought. In others. It had been a long, long time. Still . . .

Silence descended and time seemed to be held in abeyance.

Suddenly Mae's head snapped up. She licked her lips and looked around. She shook her head slightly and stuck her finger in her ear and opened her mouth.

Sean hid a smile.

"Well, I'm going on in." Her voice was unnaturally high. "If you'd like to wash up in the house, Mr. McGloin?" Turning, she walked swiftly away.

"Thank you, ma'am," he called.

Ed snickered, showing what teeth he had like a shark. Sean cuffed him on the shoulder. "What's so funny, you little squint?"

"You know, Irish, sometimes a man who can't see

can see better'n someone who can't see for shit!" He straightened his hat, resettled his coat, snapped his suspenders and grinned slyly up at Sean. "Know what I mean?" Not bothering to wait for a reply, he strolled after Mae.

Sean watched him spit out his wad just before he got to the back stairs. The little tur'! His step was downright buoyant, almost a damn jig.

Nine

"More sweet potatoes, Mr. McGloin?"

"Yes, ma'am. Thank you."

Mae plunked a ladleful on his plate.

"These sweet potatoes are especially good, ma'am."

"Thank you. It's the . . . ah . . . brown sugar. I found some brown sugar in one of the grocery boxes. I didn't order any but . . . there it was. I'll have to ask Tom Watson if he charged us for it because if not . . ." Her voice trailed off. Both men were addressing themselves to their food.

Under the veil of her lashes she watched the Irishman cut a piece of baked ham, then add some potatoes to his fork. He had excellent table manners, but he made everything—kitchen, table, silver—look too small. Coarse, black hairs grew in little tufts between his knuckles and in increasing density on the backs of his hands and forearms. His shirtsleeves, rolled up almost to the elbow, looked tight around the well-muscled thickness of his arm.

He did not wear a union suit. The thought made her slightly dizzy. She looked at her plate of virtually untouched food.

At her uncle's suggestion he'd cleaned up in the kitchen. He had opened his shirt a couple of buttons and turned his collar inside and then washed his face, neck and hands. A patch of hairy chest—and nothing else—showed in the opening. She'd been trying to set the table, but the fluttering in her stomach somehow transmitted itself to her fingers and she'd dropped all the silverware on the floor.

She knew some men had hair on their bodies. It was just that she'd inadvertently walked in on Peter once when he was getting dressed and discovered that his chest was as hairless as her own.

Her sick, sick, mind replaced Peter's image with another and the piece of smoked ham she forked into her mouth might as well have been smoked cow pie. She was becoming obsessed.

Her uncle's voice intruded. "I saw Einar in town. He had a good Ole and Sven joke." Welcoming any distraction from the obvious onset of insanity, Mae urged him to tell it.

"Well, Ole goes over to Sven's farm and sees Lena in the kitchen. Where's Sven, Lena? he asks. Oh, he's out in the chicken cuuuup, Lena says." Ed was enjoying himself, laying on the Norwegian accent. "So, Ole goes out to the chicken cuuuup and there's Sven smearing chicken puuuup on his lips. Sven, Ole says, what are yuuuu doin'? Well, Sven says, I got this terrible problem with chapped lips, so I'm smearin' this chicken puuuup on them. Ole says, does that help cure chapped lips? Sven says, I don't know but it suuure keeps me from lickin' 'em."

Mae tried to join in the men's laughter but her mind had one track.

How was she ever going to get used to him eating in the house? To his throwing his head back and displaying his corded neck and big U-shaped jaw? Now he was looking straight at her, following her hand as she smoothed her hair back and tucked a loose tendril into her braid. She looked at her plate.

"Einar had another one of 'em killer muskie stories too." Ed said and started relating it.

As if hearing voices wasn't bad enough, now she was seeing things too. Out by the barn earlier she'd had the strangest . . . vision.

She'd seen herself reclining on a hundred colored cushions without a stitch of clothes on and, apparently, without any modesty as well because she was making absolutely no effort to cover herself. If anything she seemed to be . . . preening. The same soft breeze that swirled silky curtains played the chimes that decorated the windows. (By then she'd figured that it wasn't Minnesota.) She was wondering: where on earth am I, when the Irishman stepped between herself and her view. He was buck naked. She was beckoning to him when the picture turned grainy and then faded away completely.

"Mae Ella?"

"Huh? Oh, sorry."

"I said Sean and me's thinkin' about goin' huntin' tomorrow. Unless you got somethin' else lined up."

"That's a good idea." She smiled at Sean. "It would be real nice to have a turkey for Thanksgiving."

Mae looked from one man to the other but they were both applying themselves to their food. Did he mean to stay to Thanksgiving? She hadn't meant to insinuate that she expected him to. Granny'd said men are contrary by nature. If they know a thing is expected of them, nine men out of ten will do just the opposite.

Oh, but she hoped he would stay. But he couldn't stay in the barn much longer, she countered. It would soon be too cold, even with the coal heater cranked to high. And he sure couldn't stay in the house. People in town would talk.

The thought zipped across her mind: *How will they know?*

This was not, she was sorry to say, a new thought. She had first had it while cleaning Mama and Papa's room. She'd stored away a few mementos and then, while she was airing out the mattress, she'd thought about the Irishman sleeping in the barn. And then she'd looked around the room. The empty room. Just . . . empty.

Realistically she knew that she and her uncle could not run the farm on their own. Not for a cash crop. Last season, even with her father's labor, there'd been barely enough money to subsist on. And if there was no cash, there was no money to pay the taxes, much less the bank.

The bank. There was a sobering thought. She had to do something. She—and the farm—were in very serious trouble.

Last week Mr. Jameson had informed her there was no money left in her father's account. "No money? But that can't be, Mr. Jameson." As a matter of fact, Mr. Jameson went on to say, two tax payments were due and her father had a small crop loan unpaid. He had apologized for bringing it up when he saw her stricken face but, nonetheless, he had handed her a copy of the bank records.

Last night she'd added all the figures up once again. Her father's personal records were in a rectangular blue ledger and went back the last six years. There were hundreds of tiny numbers printed in it. The amounts he had borrowed each spring and the amounts, plus interest, that he'd paid back. Years before, there had always been some money left over— not a great deal, but a decent sum. Last fall and this fall as well, he hadn't paid back a red dime. Mae speculated that the combination of her mother's doctor bills and the poor growing season caused by the unusual amount of rain was the reason. She would study the figures again tonight but her head ached just thinking about it. Arithmetic had never been her strong subject in school. She'd been much better at history and spelling, spelling in particular. Either she or Marta Hoff had always been the last pupils to sit down when there was a spelling bee.

Marta Hoff, my goodness, I haven't thought of Marta in ages. Wonder where she is now? She married one of the Steinforths, Mae recalled, and moved . . . where? Eau Claire, I think.

Mae pictured Mrs. Dinwiddie with her large dictionary opened on her desk. She would fold her hands on the book and look over her glasses at the two girls. "Well, ladies? Now your next word issss . . ." She would drag it out, building the suspense. Standing by their desks Mae and Marta would cast furtive glances at each other. All the kids in the room twisted around in their seats, staring and there'd be the usual ploys designed to rattle them. Marta's brother with his one eye crossed. Arne Hecktner with his tongue protruding like a hung man. Ernst Osten-sacker with his pencil—or worse—stuck up his nose.

Mae would try to concentrate on Mrs. Dinwiddie but she couldn't help sliding looks at Marta. Although Marta was three years older, she'd only come close to besting Mae once. Mae could always tell when she was unsure of her answer. She'd purse her lips and narrow her eyes and her whole face would fold inward like a morning glory at sundown.

First prize was always a blue ribbon with a little yellow bee embroidered on it. Mae looked at the doorframe leading to the hallway where several blue ribbons used to hang, fading until they were more purple than royal blue. That same door was where

Papa had measured their growth. One side was notched for her and one side—the marks reached much higher—was notched for her brother.

John. How she wished he were here now! Happy-go-lucky and hardworking. And so handsome! All the girls were crazy about John. Not that he got much chance to do anything about it. Not with his kid sister following him like a bad odor.

Sighing inwardly, she sprinkled some nutmeg on her applesauce and told herself to quit wishing for what could never be. She could not call on a big brother's help nor could she call on a husband's help. Not a husband's family either.

For a while she pretended interest in her uncle's monologue about hunting but not for long.

At one time she had wished for a better relationship with Peter's family. Not that she would ask for their help financially but perhaps if she had to get a job, one of Peter's sisters could have taken care of Johnny while she worked. She would have been willing to pay, of course. She soon realized that would never happen.

Only five miles separated their farms—but they would not even travel that distance to see Peter's son. One time, a few days before Papa died, she'd run into two of Peter's sisters in town. They had barely glanced at their nephew. I just can't understand people like that, she thought.

They were strange, strange people. Peter had started telling people when he was six years old that he and Mae were going to get married. His family had been about the only people in the world who were shocked when they set a date. Adamantly opposed for religious reasons, they raised all sorts of objections and even threatened to disown Peter, all of which made his life miserable. Not that they were wealthy, but the hateful words had wounded him. After they were married, Mae discovered just how rigid and formal Peter's family truly was, even toward Peter, their own son! Little things when they were growing up should have tipped her off. All the rules and regulations which kept Peter from doing the things other children could do. The way they isolated themselves from other people. Small as the community was, she had seen Peter's mother and father only twice during her entire childhood. And those meetings had been accidental.

Lost in her thoughts, she was surprised to hear the scrape of dishes behind her. Sean stood at the sideboard, dwarfing it. She hopped up. "Oh, no. You don't have to do that!" The arm she pressed was warm, hairy and harder than brick.

"Believe me, I'm capable of stacking a dish, ma'am. Say, Ed," he said over his shoulder, "how about handing me those plates?"

Oh, God! There wouldn't be a dish left in the place. "No, no, really! That's not necessary."

"I insist."

She tried to hold onto her plate but there was a little tug-of-war which, like always, the bigger, stronger contestant won. She watched him carefully take each stack from her uncle's hands. By the time she'd taken an apple pie out of the wooden pie safe, set out fresh plates and refilled everyone's coffee cup, he had, without mishap, scraped the scraps into the slop pail and stacked the dishes in the dishpan. A lot of men, she mused, would consider helping with the dishes woman's work. It was interesting that the most manly man she knew did not.

Mae dished up the pie and her mind returned to the columns of figures in her father's book again. Soon as they were finished, she'd . . .

Suddenly a whispered voice startled her, "Look around you, Liebchen!" Sean and her uncle were bantering back and forth, oblivious to any voice but then it came, clear as a bell. "Look, Liebchen!"

Granny. She always used to say people couldn't count their blessings if they didn't take the time to see them. She looked at her sleeping baby, swaying gently in his swing and at her uncle and the Irishman, and then around the lantern-lit kitchen aromatic with the scent of wood smoke. Contentment stole over her. *You're right, Granny. There is much for which I should be grateful,* she thought.

Before she sat back down, she put the ham bone in Sandy's dish and rubbed his ear.

"He appears glad to be inside," Sean commented.

"Yes." Mae watched the dog worry his treat. "Sure signs of winter for me are fat pumpkins in the patch and the geese migrating and Sandy's bath. Late every fall, Papa would bring him in, heat the two big kettles and wash him in the biggest laundry tub we had. The bath was a concession to Mama who didn't much care for animals in the house. After his bath, he was allowed to sleep inside at night until spring. Every winter that I can remember, he's been sprawled on that rag rug by the wood stove." Mae swallowed. "Course, Papa would be sitting right beside him . . . working on his books."

Sadly, her little period of contentment fled.

Ed opened the barn door. Sean was leaning over the cabinet. The barn cat crouched pantherlike on one of the rafters, patrolling her domain.

"Here's them papers and the ledger. Mae's givin' the boy his bath so she'll be busy for a while." He laid the papers on a bale of hay and joined Sean. He fitted a new plug in his lower lip and bent until his nose practically touched the wood. "By golly, you're just about finished, aren't you? That's gonna be right handy."

"I hope so. I noticed that Mae keeps a lot of her pots either in the storage room or in the cellar. Once this cabinet's hung, she can put them in here. It'll save her having to run up and down those stairs so many times."

"Leona was always after William to make another cabinet for the kitchen but he wasn't much for working with wood."

"I like it." Sean finished attaching the last hinge and lit a cheroot. "Well, I'll take a look at those figures." Unhooking the lantern above his workbench, he carried it over to the pile of papers and rehung it on a spike on the overhead beam.

Ed observed him for a minute, then asked, "Are ya addin' those numbers up in your head?"

"Yes," Sean replied without looking up.

Ed turned his head slowly. "You're a man of many talents, Irish."

For a few minutes, the only sound was the animals moving around in their stalls and the rifffff of pages turning in the ledger. Scanning from the beginning of the ledger, within no time at all Sean had found five minor errors. A few moments longer and he closed the ledger with a loud clap that made Ed, leaning back against the post and dozing a little, jump.

"The bank has made a seventeen-dollar error in your favor but there're still over two hundred dollars owed on the bank note and back taxes." Sean rested his forearms on his knees, flipping the ledger back and forth slowly as if fanning his face.

"Two hundred bucks!" Ed whistled long and low. "Shit-house mouse. Bill had said he was gettin' a bit behind but I didn't know it was that much. I've got right around twenty-five bucks saved up for a rainy day. Figured I would hold onto it until it was really needed. Guess this is it!"

"Save your money." Ed waited. The silence spun out. Finally, Sean stood and handed him the ledger. "I've got a . . . ah . . . a plan that . . . ah . . . might work."

"Oh, yeah?"

"Yeah. Kind of a proposition, like."

"What kind of proposition would that be, Irish?"

"Ye know, yer a pretty obnoxious little squint."

"You have feelin's for Mae Ella, don't you?"

"Yes, I do." Sean cocked his heel on the mud scrape and looked at his boot as if he'd never seen it before. *Bloody Hell! I don't believe I just said that!* The words slid out of his mouth so easy he felt a bit queasy! "Don't say anything."

"I ain't gonna say nothin'." Ed watched the other man pace.

"I need to find the right moment. It's all in the timin', you know? Like knowing the exact second to fire a gun when you're hunting."

"I was wonderin' what you were waitin' on."

"What do you mean?"

Ed chuckled and stood, resettling his battered hat. "You've been smitten since the day you got here."

"Is tha' a fact?"

"Smitten. S-M-I-T-O-N! With a capital S." He strolled off.

The little tur'! "Hey, what time tomorrow?"

Sean's question stopped Ed halfway across the yard. He turned. "I'll come for you. It'll be in the pearly early, as they say. That means early, Irish. Real early."

Poor guy, Sean thought, watching him walk toward

the privy. Yesterday, with the wagon loaded with fire-wood, he and Ed had taken a shortcut back from the bluffs. It was a road Sean hadn't traveled before. The wagon rattled across a shallow, sandy-bottomed stream. Then, after passing a large copse of white pines, they had come upon a clearing. It wouldn't be a clearing for long. The woods were fast encroaching with bracken fern, wild sassafras, hazel and dogwood. Vines entwined a red brick chimney rising out of the charred remains of the homestead. Rotted wood and roof timbers were all that remained of a good-sized barn and two outbuildings. Sean pulled up on the horses and pointed with his chin. "What happened over there?"

"Fire." Ed replied succinctly.

"Anyone hurt?"

"Three people. My wife Frannie and my two girls died in it." He turned his face away. "And in a manner of speakin' myself as well."

Sean searched for adequate words but found none. He had wrapped an arm around the older man's shoulders and squeezed and then, with a lump in his throat the size of an orange, he had urged the horse past the desolate site.

A few minutes later, the door to the privy smacked shut and Ed shuffled toward the house. About midway there, the old man must have sensed Sean's presence because he turned and waved. Sean caught himself, like an idiot, waving back.

Sean remained in the doorway long after Ed disappeared inside. With a shoulder against the barn door, motionless except for occasionally bringing his smoke to his lips, he studied the sky with a sailor's eye, noting its color and clarity, the position of certain key galaxies.

Suddenly, he speared his cheroot butt to the ground.

An extremely alien emotion was snaking through him. One he'd only encountered a few times before but one he was having no trouble recognizing. It was fear. Mouth-dryin', armpit-wettin', bowel-loosenin' . . . fear.

"Bloody hell!" He shot indignant glances at the farmhouse. "Who said I have to be responsible for these people? Where is it written that I have to live on this godforsaken, rundown . . ." He pushed off the barn door and paced the rectangle of light spilling from the barn like a sentry on patrol. "A person'd have to be a blithering idiot."

Or sick.

"Yeah, that's it." he muttered. "I was probably bitten by something last time I was in Asia. I've got that disease that leaves the body hard but turns the mind to oatmeal."

Aye, but those people never recognize that they're sick.

Maybe I only have a slight case, he countered. Yeah, that's it. Thank God I recognized the symptoms before I did something foolish.

Greatly relieved, he was silently celebrating his good fortune when he glanced across the yard at the old farmhouse. The lighted windows on either side of the porch were shining like yellow eyes. Beyond the canopy of bronze leaves the land lay in stark and eerie silence.

It *does* have its own kind of unearthly beauty.

There ye go again! 'Tis a mess! The whole place's a mess. Take the barn, for instance. Just look at the north side. Practically rotted through. It'll be a miracle if it lasts the winter. And the roof. Sure it's shored up now, but a good snowfall could cave it in like a house of cards. And the house? Hell, the whole place is . . . is . . .

Perfect, his inner self supplied.

Perfect? He turned up his collar and ran his fingers through his hair. It is! God, I better see a doctor, he thought. Nobody who knew him—really knew him—would ever believe this.

An' who migh' tha' be? Those that really know ye?

Why, me ol' fightin' mates, o' course. Me ol' buddies. At the thought of them he was immediately nostalgic as hell. Wonder where they are right now? Ol' Snake was probably upstairs at the Blue Parrot in Calcutta with a blonde sitting on one side and a redhead on the other. God, we had some fine times together! An' Digger . . . Good ol' Digger was probably anchored somewhere off the Marianas in that dilapidated sloop of his.

Hell, if somebody told Digger or Snake what he was considering, he knew exactly what their response would be. First they'd spew their drinks all over. Then they'd say. "Go on with ye! Sean McGloin? A farmer? In where didya say? Minnesota? Har har har! Not the McGloin. Not in a million years! Ya've got the McGloin mixed up with some other bloke!"

I really miss 'em, Sean thought.

Nae ye don't. Ye don't give a rat's arse abou' 'em.

No, he realized with a start, I don't. Digger got his name from digging a dead man's gold tooth out with his penknife. And the rumor was Snake was not a nickname but the name his own mother gave him—she'd known he was a snake the minute she'd laid eyes on him. And she hadn't been wrong.

All right, he thought, making a last ditch counterpoint to that annoying inner voice, so we were not exactly friends but we were sure as hell comrades. For brief intervals, we participated very intensely in one another's lives.

Aye, strange and powerful bonds can be forged

when men stand against those who would shoot yer balls off.

Yeah. Powerful bonds. Any chance meeting had always been cause for a major celebration. First there'd be a lot of back-pounding, then God help the owner of the nearest tavern.

The next morning, however, each man was quite content to go his own way. No regrets. Not even a backward glance.

It had always seemed a fine way to live.

'Twas a damn lonely existence.

Well, maybe. But you've got to admit it was . . . exciting.

"Yeah!" Sean muttered, damned exciting and . . . and . . . Hell, exciting was plenty good enough. At least it wasn't like this place, where everybody, himself included, started yawning the instant the sun dropped below the horizon.

Besides, why should I care what happens to these people? Who'd willingly take on that wagonload of responsibility? With the wagon broke to boot? I only came 'cause of a lovely face and eye-popping figure. Once I'd bedded the woman . . .

There was the crux of the matter. If he'd been able to have the woman, he certainly wouldn't be considering such a rash move as marrying. No' the McGloin, no' in a million years. So the woman hadn't responded? So what? There are hundreds of women. He kicked a pebble which thudded against the barn and startled an evening grosbeak into flight. He watched its shadow cross the moon.

Hundreds, did he say? Hah! He flung his arms out. Bloody thousands! Tens of thousands!

Civilization! Ah, he could hardly wait! He rubbed his hands together. Women would drop in his lap like tree ticks in the Amazon! He paused. When should he leave? Tomorrow? He shrugged. Why not? No ball and chain on him.

He paused again. Should I pack now?

Nah. He resumed pacing. Plenty of time for that. He would pack up in the morning, head into town and catch the first thing smokin'. Yeah! And he was gone. S-M-I-T-O-N? Hell, he was G-O-N-E. A day or two between some sweet thing's thighs and this place—most particularly *this* woman—would be but a dim memory.

A feeling stopped him cold. He rubbed his stomach. Bloody hell! His gut felt like the time he'd been knifed in Marseilles! Must be a hitch. Placing his hands on his hips, he rotated his upper body and then bowed his back.

Ah! There. Much better.

He was lighting a match when suddenly he jerked his eyes up. What the hell was that? The match burned unheeded while his arm hairs stood at attention. He was nae alone! In a matter of seconds, Irish lore and deep-seated superstition, vanquished thirty-two years of harsh pragmatism. He sensed the proximity of something or someone! Without conscious thought he checked his weapons, running a reassuring hand over the revolver in his coat pocket, touched the stiletto under his shirt. He cocked his head. The snowy owl hoo'ed and he heard a rustle in the corn crib, then the night was still again. He looked skyward, at the pale moon, at the myriad, low-slung stars and waited for the sensation to subside.

It did. The moment passed and reality returned. He took a ragged breath.

Shit, for a moment there it was as if someone were telling him this was his destiny. This farm, these people, that girl. *Hah! Next ye'll be tellin' yerself there's a master plan for yer life!*

He stuffed his fists in his pant pockets, and decided to take a walk. A very long walk. Maybe, he thought as he set out, he'd try whistling.

The next day Sean walked back to the farm to get the wagon. He carried a hen turkey in each hand. They'd gotten a deer too. It lay where it had been shot, close to the tree line. Ed and Sandy had gone up to stand guard against any foraging scavengers.

He reached the crest of the hill above the farm just in time to see a flatbed wagon pull out. Two ladies in large-brimmed hats sat stiffly on the wagon seat.

Better tell Mae about the turkeys, he thought. By the time he got back to the ridge, dressed out the deer and returned, it would be at least a couple of hours.

He stopped at the house, laid the turkeys in a tub on the porch then knocked at the interior door. There was no answer. He opened the door a crack and called inside. There was a slight pause before he heard, "Come in, Mr. McGloin."

After wiping his feet and removing his hat, he stepped into the kitchen. "We've had good luck. Got two turkeys and a buck. The turkeys are on the porch. I've come back to get the wagon . . ." He looked closely at her averted face. "Is anything wrong?"

The wood stove hissed, an unnaturally loud sound. She tucked in her chin. "No."

He twirled his hat by the brim. "Something's wrong. Please, what is it?"

"It's nothing." She walked to the stove and lifted the cover on a pot, stirred something, then replaced the lid. "Just some bad news about someone you don't know. It's nothing."

She had just lied to him! Why? Sean looked around

the room. Before her company had interrupted, she had been canning. Three big pots sat on the stove. Rows of Mason jars with neatly lettered labels were crowded on the kitchen and side tables. "Ap. Sauce." "Blkby. Jam." "Stewed T's." The jars had been pushed aside to make room for her company. An empty pie glass sat next to three coffee cups. Someone had polished off last night's apple pie. He had a twinge of disappointment. He'd been thinking of doing just that himself in the woods earlier.

He eyed the curve of her cheek, which was the color of a maraschino cherry. The gel would never make a liar.

In the blink of an eye he was all done equivocating. He now knew that a divine force had bound him to her. Had ever since that day at the cemetery. Didn't she sense it? Didn't she realize that she belonged to him? "I'll no' be leavin' until you tell me what's wrong," he said softly.

She glared at him through red-rimmed eyes.

Sean waited, frustrated. What he wouldn't give to take her into his arms.

"God but you're nosy!" She put her hands on her hips. "This is not your business, Mr. McGloin. This is a family matter." And you are not family, she added silently.

"And I'm not family," he said startling her. "This is true."

But nae for long, gel. "An outsider can sometimes see a solution right off the bat. A fresh approach and all. Besides it's a known fact that men and women don't look at things from the same angle."

"Are you saying a man has better problem solving abilities, Mr. McGloin?"

"No' atall. Just different." Arrogantly, he leaned

one hand on the wall, crossing one booted leg over the other.

She stacked the pie dishes and coffee cups in the sink none too gently, then flounced to the table and sat.

She rested a forearm on the table and drummed her fingers.

He curled his fingers into a loose fist and studied his fingernails. "Like I said, I've got all the time in the world. Unlike your elderly uncle. He's probably getting plenty cold up there on that ridge."

"Oh, all right! Those were my in-laws. My mother-in-law and Peter's oldest sister."

"Ah!" He lit a cheroot. "Come to see the bairn, then?"

"No. I wish that were the case." The sand went out of her. She propped her elbows on the table and rested her chin in her hands and sighed. "They never go out of their way to see Johnny. They didn't approve of Peter and me getting married."

"You mentioned that."

"I did?"

"Yes, that day at the cemetery, remember?"

"Oh, yes."

Sean was more than a bit put out. Didn't she remember their intimate conversation that day?

"It still amazes me." He turned a chair around and straddled it. "That boy is one of the nicest babies I've ever known."

"Have you known many babies, Mr. McGloin."

"Sean. Not many."

"How many?"

"None. But a person can tell."

She seemed not to have heard. "They're very strictly religious. Their religion is the only religion." She sighed again. "After all this time, they've finally decided to take an interest in Johnny. They don't think I can keep up the farm, which is probably true. They want me to sell it to them." She looked up at him. "They say they'll take Johnny now too because I can't provide for him." Angrily, she clenched her fists. "I'd never give Johnny to them. Never."

Sean's eyes scanned her face. His lips crinkled. "Ah!" he commented enigmatically. *Timin', Sean me boyo! The key to every successful campaign. Timin'!*

She eyed him, dying to remove that complacent look from his face. "Also, there was a very pointed comment about you, Mr. McGloin."

"You don't say!"

"Yes. About your living here. I told them you did not live in the house, that you were leaving soon, and that it was none of their business anyway!" She huffed and a curl lifted on her forehead. "I am surrounded, it seems, by people who cannot mind their own business!"

"Ah!" he repeated. After a minute, he stood. "Well, I'll be going up the ridge to get your uncle and that deer now."

Sean had a rough wagon ride back to where Ed waited. When he got close, he could see the old man was kneeling next to the deer.

"What's the matter," he asked and jumped down.

"This here deer must've died of a busted heart. There's not a mark on him."

"Check the left ear." Sean was clucking to Jocko, backing the wagon up.

Ed leaned close and then softly exclaimed, "I'll be damned!"

* * *

Meanwhile, Mae was inquiring of the empty chair, "Is that all you have to say? *Ah?* Fat lot of good it did, telling you my troubles!"

She planted her elbows on the table and pressed the heels of her palms into her eyes. Well, that settles it. She must somehow keep the farm and make it pay. After all, it was Johnny's heritage and about the only thing she had to give him. She would have to get a job someplace. But what would she do with Johnny while she worked? And what about Uncle Ed? He could watch Johnny, but then who'd see to the animals? If she lived on the farm and worked in town, she would have to get to town and back every day—almost sixteen miles one way. She could take in laundry or sewing but they were the last farm out, too isolated for business from the townspeople. If they lived in town, could she rent a place? Then who would care for the livestock? Could she rent the farm out? Probably not. Not with land as cheap as it was now. So that left selling out, except if she did sell, rented a house in town and could not make enough to support herself, Uncle Ed and Johnny, the money from the sale of the farm would be gone eventually and then what?

Maybe she should first sell some or all of the livestock? The spinet? Granny's earrings?

If only they could get in one or two good harvests. Too bad they didn't have the money or the proper lodging so they could keep the Irishman on. The man worked harder than Papa. He was clean and . . .

She rubbed her brow. Well, a person could go on and on about him. Actually, about the only thing wrong with the man was his proprietorial attitude toward her. It was almost like having another uncle! Only bossier. And much more distracting.

Unfortunately the people around Otter Tail have long

memories—not always accurate, but long. Among the older generation, the trip from the fatherland was weeks ago and their recollection of its hardships fresh and crisp as spring cabbage. It was the same for imprudent indiscretions by their neighbors. No, she'd assured her in-laws, he would not be staying. Soon as the snows come, the Irishman goes.

Tears welled. The only assistance her in-laws had offered was to take her farm and her son off her hands. Well, there wasn't a chance of them getting either. Not as long as she had a breath left in her body! She blew her nose.

"You really have no choice but to accept our offer," her mother-in-law had said, "unless, of course, you plan to get married again."

The one thing she could not do again, even if she wanted to. Which she most definitely did not. She shuddered. I'd sooner take in laundry for free.

When she had first gotten her monthly it had been Granny, not Mama, who had a talk with her about what it meant to become a woman. Having grown up on a farm, Granny could and did dispense with the mechanics. Instead, she talked to Mae about passion. And about romantic love. That summer day when they had strolled along the river bluffs was one of her most precious memories. Her beloved Granny had died the following winter.

"Ven you lov someone, Liebchen, you vil vant to touch. You vil velcome passion und it vil be de most vonderful thing in your life. At first, you vel vant your luf's touch every minute." Granny laughed. "I know. Myself, I couldn't think of much else. Den, later ven you are together, you vil share un look or un laugh und suddenly you vil be like de first moment you met. Dat's how is passion if is goot. My Helmut, ah Liebchen, my Helmut could make my juices flow until de day he died." Leaning close, Granny whispered, "De older de bull, de tougher de horn!"

They'd walked further while Mae mulled that unusual bit of information over.

"How will I know who to love, Granny?"

"You vil yust know. First you must haf trust und den koms luv. You vil look at your lofer und you vil say, 'Dis person vil never villingly hurt me' Und ven you luv, vil be vid all you heart. Dis is how ve are, our family.

"Ah Liebchen, I envy you! Vil be so vonderful."

Well, it was a far cry from wonderful! On her wedding night, Peter had gotten into bed, nervously snatched up her nightgown and stabbed painfully into her. After a few seconds he fell heavily on her. It was quick, uncomfortable, unpleasant, and later, whenever she met Peter's eye, embarrassing. Immediately afterward, Peter had thrown on some clothes and left their Minneapolis hotel room while Mae, bruised physically and emotionally, had been incapable of movement. When Peter returned that night, acting as if nothing had happened, she noticed that his hair was damp. He had bathed! At that time of night. The implication, intended or not, was that there was something unclean about either what he had done or about her!

Her wedding night was the high point of her honeymoon. She didn't know what to expect from marriage but surely it wasn't what transpired over the next two weeks—a nightmare of fumbled gropings, painful attempts at intrusion and then hateful words of blame. Was that how marriage was supposed to be? Surely not!

Love as Granny described it and how it actually

was with Peter was as different as night and day. The harder she tried to please, the more unhappy he was with her and, she came to realize, with himself.

Except for a chaste kiss or two and the occasions when they had held hands, they hadn't touched before they were married because people weren't supposed to touch before they were married. Or so she'd been taught. Then, when they were married and could touch all they wanted to, apparently Peter didn't want to! As a matter of fact, Peter had never touched her at all after their honeymoon unless they were under the covers in a completely dark room.

One night, lying rigid in the bed, Mae nervously waited for him to poke her with his stiff dry fingers then curse her when her body did not do whatever it was he wanted it to. Tension had been building all day. She was so anxious, she actually felt feverish. She had to say something. As Peter, garbed in his night shirt, leaned over her, she had pressed a hand on his chest. "Peter, we have to talk." He froze with his hand on the hem of her nightgown. "Peter . . . ah . . ." She tried to speak quickly but the words were so difficult! She wished she could see him, wished she could search his eyes and see a tiny bit of concern, maybe—was it asking too much?—a hint of love. "Peter, something is wrong," she whispered, "because it hurts me terribly when you . . ."

He jumped out of bed, pulled on his pants and was out the bedroom door in a flash. She sat up. "Peter?" The apartment door slammed a second later. Apparently "that" wasn't something one talked about!

Having cried herself to sleep, she never heard him return that night. In the morning she found him on the battered divan they'd bought from a second-hand store for three dollars.

Her whispered, "Good morning," went unacknowledged. When she was packing sandwiches in his metal lunch pail, he startled her, coming up behind her and hissing, "If something's wrong, it's because of you, Mae Ella! Otherwise it would work." He glared at her, picked up the lunch box and stalked out. "Even dumb animals can procreate."

She cried again, all morning, wondering what was wrong with her?

She must have conceived that first night and felt doubly blessed because as soon as she told Peter she was pregnant, he stopped his weekly attentions.

Fine with me, she had thought. She remembered looking in the mirror and hugging herself. A mother, she thought. Me! Mae Ella Botts!

She wrote letters home that were full of joy about the baby—but that was all—and she went about happily preparing the apartment and herself for her child. She bought material for baby clothes. Started knitting caps and booties. Made an afghan.

She loved babies. Always had. Far as she was concerned, it was too bad doing "that" was the only way to get them!

There wasn't one happy word from Peter about the baby. Matter of fact, there was hardly a word, period. Except for conversations more aptly held between polite strangers, Peter and she ceased talking.

How different it had become, Mae thought. Best friends since they were six, she and Peter could always talk about anything. She'd even told him about the time at school when Otto Steinforth grabbed her breast behind the outhouse. But after they were married, his quiet assault on her body in the dark of the night, then his reticence, effectively dried all but the most necessary words on her tongue. She catered to his moods and cooked his favorite dishes in an attempt to patch things up. All in vain. As her pregnancy progressed, their relationship deteriorated. She rekindled her friendship with Moira and started meeting her on the sly. She'd simply had to have someone to talk to.

Mae stewed about her problems all that day and the next, even though she knew stewing to be a pointless and ineffective pastime. She saw the Irishman, of course, at meals and here and there about the farm. It still rankled her that he hadn't been more solicitous about the dire depths of her predicament. She didn't expect him to have a solution; only to be more sympathetic. Easy for him to be cavalier, she thought, with his confident, brash attitude and wings on his feet. A comeuppance wouldn't hurt him a bit, she decided.

It came the day after.

A hard rain the previous night had left the worn path to the barn a muddy quagmire. The wind had picked up to gale force proportions and it smelled like more rain soon. After Mae'd had to clean her boots on the broken scythe that served as a mud scrape—for what must've been the hundredth time— she decided to spread some straw between the barn and the coop and the barn and the house.

She opened the barn door with difficulty and the blustery wind propelled her inside. A metal bit hanging on the wall dropped onto a oil drum with a loud *blam*. The sound was not unlike a gunshot.

The Irishman came out of one of the stalls and arced across the barn like a shooting star. He tumbled twice, head over heels, and landed flat on his back in the mud—and worse. Teeth bared and panting, he looked like a swamp alligator with only its eyes showing above the water.

Except where he had landed was not water.

She walked closer. "Did I startle you, Mr. McGloin?"

He closed his mouth and swallowed before he answered. "No' atall."

Mae caught her lower lip in her teeth and smoothed her skirt. She looked at a sore spot on her finger then back at him. "You're . . . ah . . . laying in some ah . . . horse puckey, Mr. McGloin."

"Is tha' a fac'?"

She folded one arm at her waist to support her elbow and laid a finger across her lips. She had frightened him! The brash, confident Irishman! "Yes, it is. Horse pucky."

"I'm checkin' for shamrocks."

She stuffed her hands in her pockets. "Shamrocks? Are there shamrocks in the pucky in Ireland."

"Aye. 'Tis the first place to look."

"I see. Well, good luck!"

"Thanks."

This last was like a growl. "Bye for now," she said.

Outside the barn, she flicked the air like a bug and whispered "Gotcha!"

Actually, exactly the opposite had occurred. Of course, she didn't know that at the time. That came much later.

Ten

Einar greeted Sean like a rich relation who had no kin and a wasting disease.

"Sean! By golly, I'm glad ta see yew! Why, I vas yust talkin' ta Mr. Yameson here aboot yew."

Einar's current customer in the barbershop was an elderly man with an impressive moustache à la Grover Cleveland. Since the barber was holding a razor to his gullet, Jameson only rolled his eyes in Sean's direction.

"Do yew know Mr. Yameson, Sean? Da President of da Farmers' Bank?"

Sean sat in the other empty seat. "No, I have not had the pleasure." He leaned to take the limp, white hand that emerged from the smock.

"Mr. McGloin," the man mumbled as Einar wiped off the residual shaving cream.

"You know, Jameson, I was going to stop and see you today."

"Mmm?" The banker elonged his upper lip while Einar trimmed his moustache.

"Suppose it'd be all right if I stop by after Einar's finished with me?"

"Mmm!"

Talcum powder flew as Einar vigorously dusted the banker's face. Leaning back in his chair as far as possible, Sean resisted the impulse to wave his hand in front of his face. He met Einar's twinkling eyes over the banker's head as he slapped on about a gallon of bay rum cologne. Bloody hell, Sean thought, and lit a cheroot in defense.

After the banker left, Einar held the door open and waved the used smock around. "May gootness!" He waved a few more times. "I better prop dis door open for a minute." He took a good look at Sean's hair. "Yust looook at dat hair. Yewr vay overdue for a cut!"

"Yeah!" Sean looked at himself in the mirror and crooked his eyebrow. *A foin figure of a man even if I do say so meself.* "Matter of fact, give me the works. Shave, hair cut, trim my 'stache—careful now—and so I don't have to haul all that bloody water, I'd like a hot bath also."

"Well, by golly, let's yust get to it." Only to be sociable—he did not consider himself to be a nosy man by nature—Einar inquired, "Vat's da big too do?"

Sean left the bank a couple of hundred dollars lighter but with the sweet smelling banker's undying gratitude and directions to St. Olaf's Catholic Church. He headed toward the steeple in the distance, moving slow . . . very slow . . . getting slower all the time. *Ye'll have moss on yer north side soon.*

Having decided to ask Mae to marry him—and not doubting for a minute his ability to get her consent because he had a plan, God help him, for a kind of extortion—he wanted to save time by anticipating the next step. He had no idea what the process involved, but was giving even odds that the first thing the priest was going to ask was how long since his last confession.

Sean approached the walk leading to the red sandstone church at a pace only slightly faster than a slug's. He paused to read the little granite marker—*St.*

Olaf's Roman Catholic Church—Founded in 1866— and he tried to imagine the town back at the time of the Civil War. Then he admired the lawn around the building, brown now, but obviously well-tended in season, and then he appreciated the leafless branches of a poplar tree and then the starkness of the steeple against the gray sky. It was starting to drizzle. Sean looked down and a bit of water dripped off his hat brim. Bloody hell! 'Twas worse'n the waitin' afore battle.

He paced. His plan was to get the priest to waive the reading of the banns—a six week process, if he recalled right.

Hell, 'twill take that long to hear yer confession!

He had a smoke and counted his pocket change.

Almost as bad as confronting the priest would be confronting his own conscience! Man, there are some things a man would sooner leave forgotten! He combed his hair carefully then cleaned his fingernails with his penknife. He looked at the heavy double doors to the church. He looked at the toe of his boot then back at the door.

He'd sooner fight a room full of drunk Legionnaires. Sell ladies' hats! Eat okra!

Closing his eyes, he conjured up the image of Mae Ella Botts Herrmann. By holding that lovely picture in his mind's eye, he was finally able to force his anchor-laden feet to ascend the stairs.

The door to St. Olaf's rectory opened to his knock, revealing a stout gray-haired lady with a ruffled mobcap. She had a feather duster tucked rakishly under her arm like a riding crop.

"Why, I barely heard you knock, sir. If I hadn't been dusting this table right here . . ." She pointed behind her. ". . . I'd've never heard you." She leaned closer. "What did you say?"

"I SAID I'VE COME TO SEE THE PRIEST."

"No need to holler."

She directed him into a small anteroom that was rife with the scent of beeswax, lye soap and vinegar water. "Please wait here, in Father's office. As she exited, she added. "I make no excuses for this room. Father won't let me move a thing."

The center of the room was dominated by a cluttered claw-foot desk. Bookcases lined three walls. The jumble of books, magazines and artifacts looked as if they'd been thrown on the shelves, like mud on a wall. Sean was drawn to one shelf where a ghoulish ceremonial mask from some aboriginal tribe was propped up by *The Life of St. Thomas Aquinas*. He was puzzled. The priest who officiated at Mae's mother's funeral didn't look to be the sort to collect such things.

Standing on an intricately designed but threadbare Turkish carpet, Sean glanced up at a giant wooden crucifix hanging in front of a ceiling-to-floor stained-glass window. He rimmed a finger in his shirt collar. The room was as quiet as a friggin' tomb. He twirled his hat and muttered "Christ!"

"Here!"

Sean whirled. A diminutive man with wire spectacles, scant tufts of reddish hair and dirty, knobby knees had sneaked up behind him.

"Christ is here, o' course! He's everywhere! All around us, but He might be unable to respond right at this moment. A busy man, Our Lord! I know I'm a poor substitute, but will I do?" He stuck out his hand. "Lawrence Fitzgerald."

Knees? "Lawrence Fitzgerald?" Sean repeated and tried not to look down. 'Twas true! Dirty, knobby knees! "Wha . . . What happened to . . . Father Perry?" Yeah, that's his name. "I met him a few weeks back at a funeral."

"Ah, Father Perry! A saintly man! He was kind enough to fill in for me while I was at a retreat in Chicago. An' you are?"

Reluctantly, Sean gave the man his name and then his hand. "You're Irish!"

"Astute of ye t' notice."

Sean withdrew his hand and looked at his palm. The priest's hand felt like sea weed.

"Sorry! I didn't take time to dry me hands." The priest wiped his hands on the rear of his grubby short pants. "I was working in me rose garden when Mrs. Deetz said I had a visitor."

Rose garden, Sean thought. In this weather? The priest rounded the desk and sat in the high-backed, leather chair. Sean doubted his feet reached the rug. Where's his dog collar anyway? What in the hell was he doing wearing short pants? Was the man addlepated?

The priest said, "Yer thinkin' I'm addlepated to be wearing these cut-off pants . . ." Sean's jaw dropped. ". . . it being so chilly out and all, but ever since I had my missionary time in Guyana, I have had terrible jungle rot on me lower legs." He lifted one knee above the edge of the desk. Red angry blotches covered his calf.

Sean wiped his right hand on his trousers.

Jungle rot! Great! Just friggin' great!

"Long pants makes me knees itch like crazy so, when I'm working in me little indoor greenhouse, out of the view of me parishioners, I wear these shorts." The priest grinned, revealing the most poorly arranged teeth Sean had ever seen.

What a weird little guy, Sean thought but found he

couldn't help but grin back. Who'd have believed? A fellow mick! He relaxed a little.

Maybe 'tis a good omen?

Yes, he decided, it is. It must be. "Where are ye from?"

"Dublin," the priest said and lifted his brows. "And ye?"

"Castletown."

"The devil ye say!"

They grinned at each other.

Ah, Sean me boyo, 'twill be a piece of cake.

From the desk drawer Father Fitzgerald removed a pouch of tobacco and a cardboard folder of papers and offered them to Sean.

"No. Go ahead."

"I hope ye'll not mind if I . . . ?"

Sean lit one of his own cheroots then watched the priest ritualistically prepare his cigarette.

"I keep these in the desk drawer here so I have to come all the way into this room, either from me own quarters or from the sacristy or from me flowers, and pass directly under the crucifix of our Lord . . ." The priest looked balefully back at the crucifix. ". . . who knows I have sworn to quit—in order to get my smokes." The priest inhaled with an orgasmic expression. He jumped when the housekeeper opened the door. She carried a tray with teacups and a teapot covered with a knitted cozy.

"Father! I'm ashamed of you!" The priest shriveled like a swatted spider. She set the tray down and placed her fists on rather robust hips. "Didn't I hear you vowing to quit again? Just this morning?"

"I'm only having one with Mr. McGloin, Mrs. Deetz," he whined and held his hands in supplication. "Only to be sociable, so to speak."

She shook her finger. "But you know where one

leads, Father. You haven't the will power of a gnat."
She tsk'ed as she exited.

"A good bu' very strong willed woman," the priest
said. "German, you know."

A pleasant half an hour ensued in which they discussed who had the best rugby team in Ireland that
year (the Dublin Old Boys), what was the best beer
in Minnesota (Lancer's, made in Wisconsin), and how
to send money to the IRA (Flaherty's Pub in the lower
Bronx). Then Father Fitzgerald, fixing his fourth or
fifth smoke, asked. "An', so, then. These important
things aside, what be yer need of yer priest today?"

Sean picked up his hat and tested its crease between his knuckles. He opened his mouth, closed it,
tried again. He tossed the hat on the desk like a gauntlet. "I want to make arrangements to get married."

"Married?" Father Fitzgerald grinned. "An' who
might the gel be?"

"Mae Botts. Mae Herrmann, I mean."

"Ah. Wha' a lovely gel she is." Father Fitzgerald
rose, walking over to stand at the window with his
hands behind his back. It had started to rain in earnest, falling with soft sluicing noises on the roof.
"Yesss, a lovely, lovely gel." Posed next to the crucifix and with the water-blurred stained glass as a
backdrop, the priest looked pious, even saintly. Unless
one looked down at his thin, stork-like legs and dirt-
stained, bumpy knees. And, Sean allowed, not many
saints have been depicted with a cigarette bobbing
between their teeth.

"I married Mae Botts and Peter Herrmann, you
know." He held the cigarette between thumb and forefinger and looked over his shoulder at Sean. "I heard
about Peter's death. Tragic. Truly tragic. She's been a
widow how long now?"

"I don't know exactly how long. Is there some official waiting time?" The hell with that! "I'm in no mood to wait."

"I've not seen much of her or her family since her mother became ill."

I might as well be speaking to meself, Sean thought. Father Fitzgerald sat down, rested his elbows on the desk and steepled his hands. "Did you know that the day before they got married somebody broke this window behind me?" He waved at the stained glass. "I suspected one of the Herrmann brothers at the time because the family was so opposed to the match but I didn't say anything to anyone." He shook his head. "There's something odd there."

"I've no' had the pleasure o' meetin' any o' the Herrmanns." Sean pulled himself together and leaned forward. "Look, I'd like to marry as soon as possible."

The priest held up his hand. "Now, just hold yer horses, man."

Sean rolled his eyes.

"I normally speak to both the parties. Is the humor upon the lovely bride as well?"

"I've not . . ." Sean resettled his butt. ". . . asked her just yet."

"Ye've nae asked the gel?"

"I'm planning on asking tonight, tomorrow at the latest." He gave the priest a fierce glare. "I don't expect to be turned down."

"I see." Is this to be a courtship or a siege? the priest wondered.

"Well, will ye do it or should I be takin' meself to the Protestants?"

"Now there's no need to get yerself in a big dither. I'd be honored, o' course, but there are certain proprieties to be observed."

Sean slumped. The little squint! Now's when he

will try to throw his weight around. Like all small men in power. The priest took a paper out of the desk. "Now. Have ye never been married before?"

Sean shook his head.

"An' have ye been a good Catholic? Attendin' mass and goin' regular to confession?"

Sean swallowed hard. "Well . . ."

"How long has it been?"

"Ah . . . it's been . . . a while."

The priest waved his hand. "Well, that's easy to rectify. A good confession and we'll have ye back on the straight and narrow in a wink. . . ."

As a prelude to nap time, Mae nibbled Johnny's toes, then his knees then blew air on his stomach. He giggled. She had her feet on Granny's chest, the baby in her lap. They played for a while, then the baby yawned for the third time in as many minutes and she lifted him into the crib. "Here you go, Johnny cakes. Beddie-bye." She laid him on his stomach and rubbed his back. He stuck a fist in his mouth and closed his eyes immediately.

With her cheek on the crib rail, she daydreamed, rubbing and patting. She sighed and focused. She was looking right at Granny's old humpbacked chest. Granny had called it "Liebchen's hope chest" but Mae and everybody else had always called it Granny's chest. The steamer had come from Germany with newly wedded Ilse and Helmut.

She gave Johnny a last pat—he was already breathing deeply through his mouth—and opened the chest. A blue and white wedding-ring quilt Granny and Mama had made together lay on top. The intricate quilt had taken them most of a long winter, working practically every night. She laid it on the foot of the bed then added four embroidered pillow covers. Wrapped in an eiderdown comforter was a figurine of a shepherdess and her dog. About a half-foot tall, it was, Granny'd said, very very old and very valuable. She laid it on the quilt. There were handpainted plates and silver candlesticks, cut-glass bowls and fine flatwear, but mostly there were linens and fine women's things. Her trousseau.

Soon the chest was emptied and the bed was covered. She sat back on her heels. Her eyes touched lovingly on all her things.

Her things!

She hadn't taken the chest to Chicago because their apartment in Chicago was only temporary. A year maybe two. She'd planned to have the trunk shipped once they found their permanent home, the farm in southern Minnesota that she and Peter were supposed to be saving for.

With the insight that only time can bring she suddenly realized the primary reason she had married Peter. It was in order to have a home of her own, a home that was hers and only hers. And now she had one. This farm was hers. Not Granny's. Not Mama's. This was where her things should be displayed and used.

Mae spent a happy afternoon incorporating the things from the trunk into the house. By dinner she was finished and very pleased with the results.

Unlike her father or her brother, who could probably walk into a house where every stick of furniture had been removed and only ask, "What's for supper?" Sean noticed the additions right away.

"Where did these come from?" he asked, leaning closer to the small charcoal drawings of wildlife that Mae had artfully grouped above the breakfront.

"My grandmother drew them for me. A long time ago. Aren't they good?"

"They are indeed." He looked carefully at each. A vixen and her pups playing in tall marsh hay. Two deer feeding beneath quaking aspen. A plump brown rabbit in its winter burrow. "Really good. You've an artist's eye yourself. They were just what was needed here."

"I remember those," Uncle Ed said. "Where'd you dig them up from?"

"They were in my . . . in Granny's chest."

"That big humpback thing in your bedroom?" Sean asked. Mae blushed. Of course, knowing about the chest meant that he'd been in her bedroom, but Uncle Ed didn't seem to put it together.

"Could I take a closer look at that chest, Mae?"

"Just an old chest. Made about a hundred years ago, I expect." Ed quipped.

"Well, yes, but why, Sean?" She followed him into the bedroom.

"It's a beautiful piece of work. All that carving and the scrollwork here on the edges. Bet it cost a pretty penny once."

"Granny said it took a lickin' on the crossing."

"I imagine it did." He was running his palm over it. "It wouldn't take long to fix it up a bit. I could reline the inside with fresh cedar slats, polish the brass fittings. I couldn't do much about those deep dents there but it would look much better. You could store winter things in it in the summer." He glanced up at her. "Do you have moths here?"

She nodded.

"Would you like me to give it a go over?"

"You know," Ed said from the doorway. "I thought Germans were supposed to be industrious and Irish were supposed to be lazy, ne'er-do-wells. I get tired just watching you."

"Who said the Irish were lazy ne'er-do-wells?" Sean asked, looking from Ed to Mae.

Mae noted his narrowed eyes and wondered if he was offended. But Sean had noted a tiny mole just below her left ear and was thinking about kissing it.

So, the chest exited the house and entered the barn where it was set on two wood crates covered with a tarp. After dinner it was scrutinized by Sean from all angles. Ed sat nearby.

"This is a fine piece of work. Not a thing cheap about it."

"No, I would guess not," Ed replied. "Ilse came from money. Had a governess and the whole shebang. Chucked it all for Helmut!"

"Is that so?" Sean already had the leather straps off and was in the process of removing the lid.

"Ilse was a real looker. Believe me, I could see real good back in those days and she was the best-looking woman I'd ever laid eyes on." He cut off a wedge of Red Dog then closed his jackknife. "Besides being pretty, she had a pleasing aspect to her, a way about her that drew a person. Mae Ella favors her."

"Then Ilse must've been a beauty."

"And, you know, Irish, since you've been here I think Mae Ella's become more like Ilse in her personality as well. More . . . uplifted."

The old man's heading somewhere, Sean thought. "I'm a happy man if that's the case," he said, in the process of removing the old lining in the bottom of the chest.

Ed cleared his throat. "You know, Irish, there's

something else I've been wanting to know about you."

"Another bleedin' question? 'Tis the only thin' ye've been doin' since the day I arrived. What more can ye want to know?"

"Well, you never said how come you came to be here to begin with. Seemed sort of odd to me right off, you know? A man such as yourself, walking up one day . . ."

So Sean told him about seeing Mae at the train depot, about the days after and about how Mae had absorbed his thoughts. And then he told him about John and Cuba.

"Oh, Lord." Ed shook his head. "Don't ever tell Mae Ella that. It'd hurt her something awful to know that her brother died that hard."

They were silent for a time, then Ed chuckled. "She used to wrap herself around his leg like a garter snake and he'd walk around with her like that, pretending he didn't notice she was there. When he got older, she about drove him nuts. She was like shit on his shoe. But, you know, I never saw him do anything hateful to her. Ol' John would've been . . ." Ed's voice cracked. Sean kept his back turned while Ed composed himself. "He would've been a fine man, you know?"

A time passed without talk. Sean worked. Ed chewed. Sean could practically hear the cogs and wheels turning.

"But how come you came to be traveling through here in the first place? If you didn't put John together with Mae until that day we was cuttin' wood?"

Sean laid down his tools, debated, then he sat. "Hand me those smokes behind you."

Ed did as asked.

"It started about six months ago. I'd ended up a

two-year stint as a first mate on a tanker in New York City. I'd been there before but I'd never been further than the coastal towns of the States and got to thinking that I'd like to see a bit more of the country. I had the time and the money but trouble was, I didn't know where to start. So I was lollygagging around, killing time. A guy I'd met in Caracas told me about a friend of his owned his bar down near the waterfront. Flaherty's, it was called. A dive and a front for the IRA, but it's a place where people such as meself are welcome.

"I made Flaherty's my headquarters. Until I could decide what I was going to do next. I ended up there most nights, not because I'm a man that fond of John Barleycorn or seditious talk but it was . . . someplace to go. There was usually a poker game in the back room. And I'm very lucky with cards.

"Somebody must've said that I might be available for a job." He snorted. "My specialty, you know, quick jobs for fast money on a short-term basis." Sean looked quickly at Ed who moved his hand like used-to-be-my-specialty too.

"One night I was sitting having a beer and this guy swings a leg over the barstool next to me. 'Wanna make a lot of extra money? Fast?' he asked. Having been asked that same question dozens of times in as many countries, I didn't bother to answer. 'Money's good.' the guy continued. 'Light work for someone of your talents.'

"I didn't ask how he knew what my talents were. I did ask him if he was a copper. He hemmed and hawed. Three more 'chance encounters' and he admitted that he was. In a manner of speaking, he said. I can spot a copper a mile off, you know?" Sean glanced at Ed and Ed gave a me-too snort.

"Somehow the guy had heard about me. About

how I can remember things." Sean ran a hand through his hair. "Anyway this guy—O'Brien he said his name was—had a deal I could hardly pass up. I was to get a job with these guys, get some information the feds needed to prosecute and they'd pay me a bunch of money."

"What guys?" Ed asked.

"The head man's name is Spinelli. He must have a hundred guys on the payroll and twice that on the dole. Highly organized. Nobody does business on the waterfront without Spinelli knowing about it and getting his cut. They've got the New York waterfront covered better than the smell of fish.

"Most of their profits are from smuggling. Opium, booze, illegal arms, kids, whatever. They aren't selective. If there's a buck to be made, and it's illegal, Spinelli's got his thumb in it. I'd heard of them even before I arrived. Somebody told me that a guy I knew was doing some of their 'collection' work for them."

"No foolin'?"

"Well, not any more. He got bumped off in a war with a rival group from Queens a few months before I hit town."

"Garrrgh . . ." Ed was either gargling or strangling but Sean was too caught up in his tale.

"Well, I had done my share of espionage. And I liked O'Brien once we got to know each other." Sean chuckled. "Nervous little twitch." He looked at Ed. "You know the kind of guy never stops moving?"

Having recovered, Ed, with his smirk and rolling eyes said, Known-hundreds.

Sean smoked a bit. "Yeah, we hit it off all right and the money became a factor. Funny thing. I never cared how much money I had. No place to spend it except on booze or women, and the kind I liked were

both damned reasonable, if you know what I mean?"
Sean glanced at Ed.

To a T, Ed's slowly nodding head implied.

"But then I'd started thinking I'd like to settle
someplace. Get some land and . . ." He shrugged. "I
don't know. All of a sudden the money was too good
to turn down. So I agreed. And I got the information.
But somebody tipped Spinelli off. They were waiting
for me one night. Two of 'em jumped me as I was
leaving Spinelli's office. I killed one. The other one
probably. I was just going to make sure when a third
guy came in. I took off." Sean paused to light another
smoke and Ed fidgeted until he did.

"The heat was on all over town. I figured I was a
dead man. I couldn't go back to the place where I
was staying. I laid low a couple of days, until I could
hook up with O'Brien. He outfitted me in all new
stuff, paid me most of the money I had coming and
had someone drive me to Allentown, Pennsylvania. I
hopped the first thing headed West."

"So, did you give O'Brien the information you had
and you're done with it?"

"The information is in me head. Even if I wrote
it all down, they'll need me to testify in order to put
Spinelli behind bars. But first they want to find out
who the traitor is in their own organization before
they start arresting people. Spinelli's lawyers are the
best money can buy, O'Brien said. It'll take an air-
tight case to nail 'em. And they don't need somebody
feeding Spinelli their strategy."

"What happens now?"

"Well, supposedly I hide out until they let me know
they're ready for me. I go back and testify."

"Do they know where you are?"

"Only O'Brien."

"What will you do?"

"I don't know. I could send them all the information. Maybe sign something in front of witnesses."

"If you don't need the money . . ."

"No. I've enough. More than enough." There was a period of silence. "You know those last two guys? It was either them or me but I swore then that that would be the last time . . . the last man . . ." He dug his heel into the dirt. "I'd like to be done with the killin', you know?"

Don't I, Ed's wave said. Then he shook his head. "Mighty thrillin' life you've been living, Irish."

"But not one I want any more." Sean paused. "Not if Mae will marry me."

"Do you think this here farm'll be excitin' enough for you?"

"More than. 'Tis all I want." Sean threaded a leather strap through his fingers. One of the cows lowed. "I don't want . . ." His voice sounded tight.

Ed had time to spit twice before Sean went on.

"I don't wan' t' die with me back to some wall, fightin' like an animal, an' no' a soul t' mourn me."

"Hell! Seems reasonable to me." Ed replied.

Using the pretext of looking out the darkening window, Mae eyed Sean with sidling glances. Why was he all spruced up tonight, wearing a shirt she had never seen before and smelling faintly of a manly cologne? She watched a piece of venison steak disappear between his lips and looked at her uncle. Why, even Uncle Ed looked spruced up. His hair was slicked back and his shirt buttoned clear to the top. The very air was anticipatory. What was happening?

Sean'd never been so antsy in his life. Well, except maybe for that time when he was in jail in Marrakesh and got body lice.

No. This was worse than Marrakesh. Much worse.

His original strategy had been to get her someplace casual-like, and ask her when she was unawares. Having come to the realization that he was willing to do whatever was necessary in order to have her, now God help him, he planned to get her between a rock and hard place and squeeze. Manly appeal wasn't enough? Fine. He'd stress security for her son and herself, a home for her uncle in his declining years—whatever it took.

He never got a chance. She was always scurrying in the opposite direction. Once when he had managed to put himself in her path, Ed was with her. Or he got a glimpse of her—the bottom of her dress and her boots beneath a flapping sheet, but by the time he worked up his nerve, the flutter of her apron strings was disappearing around the corner.

'Twas damned frustrating. The only thing he could liken it to was having someone yell "Charge" and then say "oh, never mind."

The feelings of futility, building and building, resulted in some very strange urges. To . . . display himself! Assume a John L. Sullivan pose and flex his muscles. Tear apart his shirt and beat his chest like a gorilla. Thrash around in the woods and butt horns with something while bellowing like a bull moose.

Peculiar. Very very peculiar.

"I saw Einar today," Ed said. "Got a new joke."

"Tell it, Uncle Ed."

"Well, it seems this dumb Swede named Ernst went to Duluth on business. Goes into a saloon up there to have a drink and a big Indian guy comes over to him and challenges him. 'Tell you what,' the big Indian sez, 'you answer this riddle right and I'll buy you a drink. Answer it wrong and you buy me a drink. Waddayasay?'

" 'Well, okay,' Ernst sez, 'shoot!'

" 'My mother and my father had one kid. It wasn't my brother, it wasn't my sister. Who was it?'

" 'Ooooh yeepers!' sez Ernst. 'That's a toughie!' He thinks a bit and then he gives up.

" 'It was me!' the big Indian crows. 'Har! Har! You owe me a drink, big dumb Swede.'

"Well, Ernst goes back to his home town and sees his old buddy Sigfrid in the bar. 'Sigfrid,' he sez, 'got a riddle for you.' And he goes through the whole deal about who buys who a drink then asks the riddle.

" 'My mother and my father had one kid. It wasn't my brother and it wasn't my sister. Who was it?'

" 'Ooooh yeepers!' says Sigfrid. 'That's a toughie!' He thinks a bit and then gives up.

" 'Dumb Swede,' Ernst sez, 'It was a big Indian fella up in Duluth.' "

"That's awful, Uncle Ed."

"It really is," Sean said.

Silence fell like a guillotine.

Well, Sean thought, 'tis now or never. He ran a finger around his collar.

"I'd like to have a word with Mrs. Herrmann, if I may, Ed. I wonder if I could ask you . . ."

Mae paused with her back to the table, frozen in the act of putting the last dish away. She wiped her hands on the dishtowel.

"Yep. I'm just going out for my chew."

Before Mae turned around to look at Sean with surprise, Uncle Ed had put on his jacket and was shuffling out the door.

Her heart sank. The Irishman's leaving! What will I do now?

She sat and folded her hands on the table. He turned his penetrating, silver-eyed gaze on her.

Eleven

"Marry you?" Stunned, Mae steepled her fingers on her sternum as if adding—Me?

"Why I've never contemplated such a possibility." Considering her situation, this statement was entirely true.

"You haven't?"

Someone looking in the kitchen window—as Ed was doing at that moment—would see two people sitting at the table, relaxing after their meal. Except, Mae Ella's face was the color of Otter Tail's new fire engine.

"Why ever would you want to marry me?" She waved her hand. "Surely you could do better than this."

"But can I do better than you?"

Her eyes, skidding to a stop, met his. A moment passed. "Oh . . ."

He smiled quizzically. "Surely you knew I had feelings for you?"

She met his eyes and the memory of their kiss roared into mind. Her blush deepened. "Yes. I guess I . . ." She stood and was weak-kneed as a newborn colt. Think, Mae Ella! Stalling for time, she checked the level of coffee in the enameled pot. When she found it almost empty, she got down the long-handled, wooden grinder to make another pot.

If she said no, simply no, would he pick up and leave? She measured out the coffee precisely. She didn't want that! She turned up the fire.

She stared at the pot on the stove, wiping her hands on her apron. Squaring her shoulders, she returned to her seat, where the full force of his steady regard made her even more nervous.

For a long moment the only noise in the room was the tick of the wind-up clock on the wall, the rumble of the blue speckled coffeepot and, Mae was quite sure, the thump of her heart.

Sean cursed his miserly habit with words. Now was the time to reveal the depth of his feelings, to wax poetic. He was about as eloquent as a friggin' rock.

Mae looked at him with entreaty. Wasn't he ever going to speak? "I don't know what to say."

"Can ye truthfully say ye dinna see me as a man?" *An' a foin figure of one, even if I do say so meself.*

"Of course I see you as a man."

Reaching into his shirt pocket, he removed a small blue book and a many-times folded piece of paper and laid them on the table. Mae looked at them curiously.

"Ask yourself why not? You would keep your farm, you would have all the money you or the lad will ever need and you have no further problems from your relations or the townfolks. You married for love before. Why not marry for security?" He played with the little blue book, turning it over. "Before you say yea or nay, there are a few things I'd like to add in my behalf."

Stop him, Mae Ella! Tell him now before he opens his heart. But she'd been struck mute.

"I am thirty-two. Quite a bit older than you, I realize. But my da was fifteen years older than me mam and it didn't seem to affect their marriage. They rarely passed each other without touching, exchanging some teasing banter or a wink and a certain look." He chuckled until he noticed Mae's burning face. He cleared his throat, assuming a more serious tone of voice.

"I've done a man's labor since I was ten. I'm healthy as a horse and not afraid of work. I've no strange . . ." How does one say something like this? His eyes circled the room then settled on his dessert plate. ". . . tastes."

That's good, thought Mae. The only Irish dish she knew how to make was that stew Moira gave her the recipe for.

". . . come from good people, common hardworking people who were . . ." He smiled a little. ". . . for the most part, Godfearing." He lit a cheroot, cupping the match out of habit.

"My family had had the same small farm for generations. My da died when I was seven. Stepped on a spike and didn't tend to it." Mae watched him unconsciously rub his jaw. "I . . . I remember him well. A big man, kind, gruff-voiced." He paused, his voice and features softer, and Mae was saddened. "So. After he died, my mam had a struggle. I did as much as I could, of course, but we got behind on the taxes. Before his death my da was pretty vocal in expressing his politics, so the powers that be weren't inclined to give us much leeway."

"Don't," she whispered, "please don't say any more . . ."

"Have the courtesy of allowin' me to finish me speech." He gave her a half grin. "I've been workin' on it night an' day."

"But . . ."

"Now. Where was I? Oh, yeah.

"Well, we lost the farm and my mam had to get

a job at the local tavern waiting tables. Room and board was included so we lived right there, on the top floor. I worked odd jobs around the place and went to school when the thought appealed to me." He winked. "Or when I figured me mam would find out if I didn't. She raised me best she could. She died suddenly when I was eleven and that, aside from meself was the last McGloin in Ireland. At least the last McGloin that was a relation of mine. So I left not long after . . ."

Eleven! Mae thought.

". . . had to make my way with my wits or brawn, I know I'm a bi' unpolished." *There's a wee bi' o' understatement there!*

He turned his cup. There was a prominent pause. "I've not had much family life but I've had enough to know I'd like one. I am not a man for the drink or gambling or . . . the other, although I've done my share of all." He cleared his throat. "I've walked on the wild side and sowed my oats there." *There's another wee bi' o' understatement!*

"Like an outlaw?"

"A man can hardly be an outlaw where there is no law."

"Oh," she said and chewed on that a bit.

"But even before I came here I'd had enough. I was beginning to think that I'd like to settle somewhere. Find a place and put down some roots. America always appealed to me more than Australia or New Zealand. I was in New York about ten years ago. I was between jobs and sort of at loose ends for a time. I decided to learn everything there was about this country. I ended up spending hours in the library." He laughed. "I must've looked like a nun in a brothel." He glanced up.

Are ye proposin' or auditionin' for vaudeville?

"Anyway, I read up on all different parts of the country. Iowa. Missouri. Idaho. I decided to head for the midwest. But then another war started down in Cuba and I never got there." He searched her eyes intently. "I'll not lie to you and say that I don't care about this farm at all. I would be proud to work this land. 'Tis foin land. But I can buy any land I want. It's you I want. Even little Jack."

He leaned forward. "If you will marry me, the lad'll never want for something to eat or have to work before his time. I would treat him as if he was my own. As I would always hold you and yours dear."

Nae bad, he thought, for a first go at it.

He pushed the book and paper under his wide hand toward her. "I paid the note at the bank and I paid your taxes last year, this and next."

She just stared at him, speechless then because he expected it, she unfolded the official-looking paper. A big black slash with the word "PAID" was written diagonally across it. "Oh, Mr. McGloin! Sean!" She opened the small book. "Oh, you should not have done this. I cannot possibly accept this." The first page had her name printed on it. The second showed a dollar figure that stunned her.

"I've no designs on owning your farm. If you like, I will sign a legal paper so stating."

"No. You don't understand. I cannot marry you because . . ." Sean looked at her down bent head, the soft flush on her cheek. ". . . I am already married."

Someone had lowered the boom and he was under it. "Wha'?"

"Because I am still married."

"Your husband died."

She shook her head. "No. He did not die."

Sean lifted her chin. Her eyes were brimming, her chin wobbling. "Tell me," he insisted.

"I cannot."

"But I carried the man's casket meself!"

"No. It was some hobo's casket. Not Peter's."

"Not Peter's?"

She shook her head. "Please don't ask me more."

"Don't ask more? Where is the man now, now that you and your boy need him?"

She shook her head again.

"Please."

"I couldn't possibly . . ."

He pointed at the table cloth. "Look here, not at me." He started speaking, soothing, nonsensical words in a hypnotic voice while his thumb drew circles on the back of her hand. Time passed. Fear fled. Modesty followed. Briefly, before something dreamlike settled over her, she wondered how does he do that!

"You were in Chicago?" he asked softly.

Mae herded some bread crumbs into a small pile. "Yes."

"With Johnny and Peter?"

"Yes."

"You weren't happy?"

"No."

"You and Peter argued?"

"No. We hardly ever argued. We hardly ever talked." Her voice was less than a whisper.

Sean leaned closer and so did she. Her lips were close to his ear. The impression of confessor/penitent came fleetingly to her mind.

"Why? What was wrong?"

"Peter didn't like me as . . . as a man does a woman."

"But there's the boy?"

"Yes but that was only that one time. The other times, he didn't . . . he couldn't . . ."

"Go on," he said and kept up the spellbinding motion of his thumb. "But start at the beginning. Go back, way back to when you first met."

She sighed. "I was six and Peter was seven and we met in the schoolyard not ten miles from here." Still looking at the tablecloth, Mae smiled with the memory of a fall day so long ago. "Papa drove me to school that day. I cried all the way. I remember I had on a new dress that Granny made. It was a really pretty madras plaid with white cotton collar and cuffs but I hated it because I hated having to go to school. My older brother, John, had been poking fun of me for days, calling me a uh, a tittie baby. Out of Papa's hearing of course." She circled the crumbs with her finger. "By the time we got to the school, all the other children were lined up outside the door, I thought according to height—little ones in the front and big kids in the back—but it was according to age. I noticed Peter right away because he was a head taller than all the other kids around him. And I liked him right off because he was bawling, too!"

She smiled. There was something so encouraging about the way the Irishman listened, as though what she had to say was the most important thing he'd ever heard. For the first time in months, thinking about Peter was not painful. And as the words flowed, the hurt she'd held inside for months started to ease.

"At recess, I walked over and sat next to him. Neither one of us said anything but just sat together quietly. After that, it seemed natural to be together. I . . . I was always drawn to Peter for some reason. I guess maybe because we were both so shy. Peter's sister, Hilde, was the oldest of the five Herrmann children in school that year and she came right over to Peter. 'Peter, come over here with us and sit.' She looked at me as if I was a horse apple. Even though his face was red and he looked like he was ready to cry again, he told her no. I was so proud of him. Hilde was always so bossy."

"You stayed friends as you grew older?"

"Yes. We were inseparable. People would say wherever Peter is, Mae is nearby and vice versa. For as long as I had memory, I knew I would marry Peter."

"When did you decide to get married?"

"Peter decided when we were both eighteen. Actually, it was on my birthday." Mae remembered she had met Peter at a spot on the bluffs not far from the area where Mama had run over the edge.

She felt compelled to tell him everything. Words welled and spilled. "Peter never really asked me *if* I wanted to get married, he just expected me to marry him. I guess I expected to marry him also but I was sort of disappointed that he didn't ask me." She shrugged. "I don't know. I suppose I never thought about marrying anyone else. I mean, who else *was* there? My friends were all paired up with boys. Girls get married young around here. Nobody was surprised. Except for Peter's family."

"Why was that?"

"I guess they thought that when it really came down to it, Peter wouldn't go against his family and marry me, but they were wrong."

Sean squeezed her hand, his palm warm and rough.

"What could they have again' ye, as fine a person as ye are."

"Thank you," Mae tucked her chin onto her chest. "But when they found out that our children would have to be 'signed over to the Church' then that's when they told Peter they disowned him. That's why they don't come to see Johnny. And why I wouldn't think of going to them for help."

"But Peter changed. Did that start when you were in Chicago?"

Drifting in her dreamy reverie, she felt no embarrassment. "I'll say he changed! He acted like he disliked the very sight of me. I got bigger and bigger with Johnny and I know I looked awful but oh what I would have given for a hug. I was so very lonely. I didn't know a soul except for my friend Moira. Peter had insisted I stop seeing her but when he was never home for, it seemed, days at a time, we started meeting again."

"Did ye nae talk to him about what was wrong between ye?"

"Only once. I asked him if he was sick. If maybe a doctor could help. He got furious. Said there was nothing wrong with him. It was me."

"Ah. So he is alive, living in Chicago and you are here. Why?"

"That's where the hobo came in."

"Yes?"

"I think Peter got the idea about two months before I had Johnny. From a friend of his friend Spiro."

"Spiro?"

"There was a deli on Fullerton Parkway called Thiro's where Moira and I used to go. We would buy feta cheese and big black olives the size of guinea eggs. I used to get terrible cravings for those olives!

"Sometimes we ate right there at a little iron table. We had a dish . . . I forget what it was called but it was meat and rice wrapped in leaves. It was wonderful! A Greek lady usually waited on us but occasionally it was a young man. He was uncommonly handsome. Moira said she wished she had his curly black hair and long lashes and one time, when he brought our check, she asked him if he was Thiro. He said he wasn't. Thiro, he said, was his father who was deceased. His name, he told us, was Spiro. We exchanged a look. Later, walking home, we laughed, thinking Spiro and Thiro—how funny. Then we thought of Moira Mary Maureen O'Toole and Mae Ella Botts Herrmann and we really laughed.

"Anyway, one day I was taking my walk alone. Moira had given me an article about how it's supposed to be good for expecting mothers to walk so I tried to walk at least ten blocks every day. I was strolling down the block where Thiro's is, looked in the window and there, of all people, was Peter. I remember for a brief second thinking Moira must've told him about how I loved those olives. I waited outside. I watched some children playing stickball for a while. Still Peter didn't come out. I thought—I'll finish my walk to the corner. By the time I came back, there was a CLOSED placard on the door and the shade was drawn. But still no Peter. That's odd, I thought. Then I noticed the lights on upstairs, above the store. The sound of music came out the window. Strange music from an instrument I'd never heard before. There was a side entrance to the apartment so I walked up the stairs and knocked on the door. 'Peter?' I called. I heard a thump and the music stopped. Peter opened the door. He was draped in a sheet. His face was flush, his eyes wet. I looked into the room. He appeared to be alone although some striped curtains were settling behind him. I looked at Peter. 'What ever are you doing, Peter?'

" 'Spiro is a ah . . . a sculptor. He's paying me to pose for him after work.'

" 'Oh,' I said, but I looked again at what I could see of the cluttered room. I couldn't see any clay or any statues.

" 'He was making some preliminary drawings,' Peter said."

Mae looked at Sean who, except for his jaw muscle, could've been a statue himself. "I'd known Peter all his life and so far as I know, we'd never lied to each other yet I knew he was lying. Something was up."

" 'Will you be home for dinner, Peter?' I asked. I couldn't think of anything else to say. 'Yes, yes,' he said and practically shut the door on my face.

"But he didn't come home until very much later. Not that night and not many others either. I had the baby a few weeks later.

"After that he even stopped making excuses for being gone so much. I had to beg for money for rent and for food. He gave it very grudgingly. Many times I smelled licorice on his clothes or on him. I thought, what on earth, until I discovered it was a kind of Greek liquor.

"What was wrong with him? What had happened to the boy I thought I knew so well? Where had this cruel, cold-eyed stranger come from?" She shook her head. "A few weeks after Johnny was born was the first time he suggested that I return to Otter Tail and he remain in Chicago. 'Why?' I asked. 'I want to be with my friend Spiro,' he replied. 'So be with Spiro,' I said, 'and be with us too.' But no. He told me that would not work. I refused to leave. To punish me one time he went ten days without ever uttering a word. I know. I counted. 'Peter? Will you have coffee?' He'd whistle and continue whatever he was doing. He'd become a man obsessed with his friend and 'having fun.'

"One morning I woke up to find the crib empty. Johnny was gone! I ran around and around the bedroom like a chicken then out the door. There was Peter, arms folded, in the center of the living room. He calmly opened the closet door and there lay

Johnny on the floor among the boots and cleaning things. 'It would be easy, Mae Ella.' Peter said and walked out. I was shaking so much—from fury, from fear, I don't know—my teeth were clacking. After I put Johnny in his crib and made sure he was all right, I pulled the valise out from under the bed." She missed seeing Sean light a smoke with trembling fingers.

"What about the casket? The hobo?"

"Spiro had a friend who was a medical student at Cook County Hospital. Between the three of them they cooked up a scheme so that Peter could stay in Chicago with a whole new identity. This friend would wait until some John Doe was delivered to the morgue. I would take that body home and say it was Peter. And no one need ever know Peter wasn't dead."

"Except you."

"Except me. And Moira. I didn't tell her about the hobo. Just that Peter and I were separating."

"Ed doesn't know?"

"No. No one else but me and you, and you must swear never to tell."

"I swear. His secret's as safe with me as it is with you."

"Thank you.

"I trusted him," she said softly, "I trusted him to always be . . . Peter." Several minutes lapsed.

"You should have seen him that last day, Sean. Crying like a baby . . ." Sean made an angry sound. ". . . he said he couldn't help himself and please forgive him. He pleaded with me to never ever expose his whereabouts and to never, ever tell his father. I had to do it for him. He is . . . he was my best friend."

Silence stretched.

"God! What a mess!" he said and touched her hand in such a way that ended her curious reverie.

"Yes."

Sean stood and looked at her. "Divorce was never a consideration?"

"No," she said shaking her head. He nodded once then started to leave.

"What about this money, Sean? I want to make some arrangement to pay you back."

"Later. We'll worry about that later."

Mae kept her eyes downcast until she heard him leave then she closed them and put her head on the table. She was exhausted and drained of all feeling. How could she have actually said such things? Color suffused her face anew. She remained thus for a long time.

At last, she forced herself to sit up. Her chores waited. She pressed her palms to throbbing temples then scooping up the bank book and paper off the table, she circled the room, looking first at the Bible, then at the tall rose-colored vase on the cabinet that was just for show. Finally, although she didn't want to imply permanence by her choice of a hiding place, she pried up one of the bricks under the wood stove with a knife and dropped the bank book and paper inside. The scooped-out hole already contained a small leather tobacco pouch with seven dollars and Granny's sapphire earrings.

After putting Johnny down for the night, she returned to finish cleaning the kitchen. Pulling the chairs away from the table, she swept the floor and rug. She folded the tablecloth corners to the center, walked to the back door and shook the cloth out. All her functions were by rote, as if performing her chores as usual would lend normalcy to this night. It wasn't working. There was nothing usual about this night. She paused there a moment, looking at the closed barn door with amber light leaking from its edges. An owl hooted. She looked and imagined she saw a bit of white on one of the fence posts. She had heard that the Indians think the owl is a bad omen, that one hears the owl call his name right before death.

She closed the door and stood there thinking of Peter, poor Peter.

Twelve

The day was as bleak as Sean's spirits. The temperature had been stepping down as the weather made the transition from fall to winter. Ed, claiming an inexplicable knowledge of cloudy origin, had emphatically predicted a "serious" snowstorm by Thanksgiving. He might be right. Each day was noticeably shorter and the nights frost-laden.

Sean drove slowly down the rutted road with two wide-planked, wooden crates rattling around in the back of the wagon. Seemingly oblivious to his clattering passage, two ringnecked pheasants, with long, sweeping tails and brilliant feathers, pecked in a strip of marshy grasses beside the road.

By following Ed's directions, Sean had just taken two hogs to a farm about ten miles distant. The farmer, coincidentally the one who had given Sean a ride from town that first day, offered his neighbors a slaughtering service. In return for one shoat in the spring and two bucks a hog up front, the farmer would render everything edible that ensued as a consequence of his service by either curing, smoking, stuffing or pickling the yield.

Earlier in the week—before Mae had cut him off at the knees—Sean and Ed had stood in front of the pigpen, looking at the subject of their discussion eyeball to eyeball. They had briefly discussed the merits of doing the job themselves. Very briefly.

"We could do the job ourselves." Ed had said.

Sean had almost choked on his cheroot. "The devil ye say! Are ye daft?" He knew exactly what "ourselves" meant. Sean would "do" and Ed would "instruct and observe."

Sean shivered, in truth, more from the thought of drawing a razor-sharp knife across a hog's throat than from the frosty air. He'd paid the farmer the four bucks. Gladly.

He pulled up on the reins and rested his forearms on his knees. Unlike some, he had never found pleasure in tormenting a stray cat or throwing rocks at a mongrel dog. Matter of fact, there was an occasion back in Ireland when it gave him a great deal of pleasure to beat the bejesus out of a boy who was preparing to torch a kerosene-soaked kitten for the benefit of his drunken friends loitering nearby. Still young enough to want to avoid being teased, Sean had tucked the bedraggled cat inside his jacket and walked the long way home. It had taken, he recalled, hours to wash all the gas out of the cat's fur.

Had he come so far in his life, he wondered, that he could contemplate an act far more dastardly? When had he come to believe that murder was his only choice?

Accustomed to approaching problems with a head-on, clear-cut perspective, his habit was to define the difficulty, decide upon the best solution then execute same. Simple. He had been thinking about this "obstacle" incessantly and still he had found no other solution. Which was why he'd been committing cold-blooded murder in his heart.

Divorce or annulment was out of the question. The former because it was contrary to all her beliefs and the latter because to request an annulment would reveal the whereabouts of that . . . Sean used a particularly vulgar phrase to describe Peter. Loyal as Mae was to her "best friend," she would never break her promise.

Best friend me arse! Sean did not fault Peter for his sexual preferences—to each his own—but he would gladly snap his miserable scrawny neck for sending his wife and child away to fend for themselves.

"Wha' manner o' man is he?" Sean muttered. A person could argue that he could not know her mother was ill, that her father would soon die, but neither argument tipped the scales in Peter's favor.

So Sean was, as described by the proverbial saying, on the horns of a dilemma. He could stay—make a crude hand-signal to convention and the proprieties—and they would end up living in sin because if he stayed, he would seduce her. Even if he swore he wouldn't. So, if he knew that was a foregone conclusion to his remaining on the farm, then he also knew that staying would mean he would destroy her. Her neighbors would castigate her, other children would taunt her son. And should their efforts fail to prevent conception—it's been known to happen—what of that child? What then?

That thought brought him back to the surest, simplest method to remove the obstacle—murder. Cold-blooded assassination.

The question was not if he could do it. A man does not live by the sword all his life then toss it aside when facing his biggest battle. Through the ages men less combative than himself had done much worse for much less. The question was could he look at the man's son for the rest of his life?

Clucking and slapping the reins lightly, he started

the old horse moving again. Maybe he should leave town for a time, give Mae's in-laws the impression he was out of the picture. Standing back, maybe he could get a better perspective. He would regroup, reconnoiter then come up with a plan. He could return to Minneapolis and while there he'd check in with . . . what was the guy's name? Hanson? Once in Minneapolis, if Hanson couldn't give him an update, he could send O'Brien another wire.

Sean had sent O'Brien a wire the same day Sean had arrived in Otter Tail. *Let me know when you're ready. Send a letter to Otter Tail, MN General Delivery.* And then he'd waited, stopping to check for a response whenever he was in town. But on the rare occasions when he'd seen a Minneapolis newspaper there'd been no mention of a waterfront scandal in New York. Of course, that didn't mean much. New York news wasn't Minnesota news.

Originally, when and if O'Brien had contacted him, he had planned to take a circuitous route to New York, probably via Toronto. Slip in, testify, slip out again. But if Mae had said yes, then he would have had to reconsider—a trial could mean a lengthy separation. He didn't need the money. He figured returning what money he'd received canceled his debt. By a big margin, Mae and the boy's well-being was far more important than the conviction of a bunch of criminals. He recalled having the fleeting thought before the disastrous talk with Mae that he would not want to take a chance on leaving her widowed again. Ha!

But now?

Now he was inclined to go to New York. Might as well. Although it wasn't written in blood somewhere that he had to testify, if he couldn't have Mae then it didn't much matter one way or the other.

At the crest of the hill he stopped the horse again

and stared down for a long while at the small farm.
Cottony puffs of smoke were spiraling out of the
chimney.

His life had had meaning since the day he arrived.
It was crazy, but the place had become a port, finally,
in his stormy life. And he wanted it—the woman, the
bairn, all of it—more than he'd ever wanted anything
in his life. The responsibility and the commitment and
the obligation? None of it worried him one whit. Well,
he shifted on the hard wagon-seat, maybe a tad. But
everything was incidental compared to Mae. She
needed him, not only as a provider but as a man.
With infinite patience and with all the love he had
in him, he had hoped to show her exactly how much.

He smiled sadly. Sassy little nit! She tried to act
so . . . he searched for the right word . . . Prussian.
My granny this and my granny that, as if she were
descended from some Amazon warrior.

The fact of the matter was, the gel was about as
thick-skinned as a grape and fierce as a kitten. An
inveterate daydreamer. How many times had he come
upon her, lost in thought, with that beatific half smile
on her face? And her not even aware of his presence.
No, the gel hadn't a mean bone in her body.

"Foin," he muttered, smacking the reins on the
horse's rump, "for I am mean enough for the lot of
'em."

Sean tossed hay into the stalls. Ed, sucking on his
tooth, stood behind him. "Turned you down flat?"

"Yes."

"Didn't say, I'll think it over or nothin' like that?"

"No."

"I don't know what in the blazes is wrong with
that gal." He moved out of Sean's path—or end up

with footprints on his back—and raised his voice to be heard in the tack room. "Do you want me to talk to her?"

"No," Sean said as he returned with the bridle and harness. "I want you to say not one bleeding word."

"Shit-house mouse. I feel like I've got a sock stuffed in my mouth."

"Not a bad idea. I'd never thought of it." Sean led the horse out. "All I want you to do is ride with me into town so I can catch the Minneapolis train then bring the wagon back."

"Well, I can do that."

"Then you better get a heavier coat on because I'm leaving now."

"How long are you gonna be gone?"

"I don't know."

"How come you don't know how long you'll be gone?"

"I've got things to attend to."

"On that New York problem?"

"Listen," Sean faced him and put his finger close enough so Ed didn't have to squint to see it. "You agreed to keep quiet about that. I'm holding you to your word. I shouldn't have even told you."

"I ain't sayin' nothin' to nobody nohow. What did Mae say when you told her you were goin'?"

"Not much." Having finished hitching up the horse, Sean went back into the tack room and returned with his new coat. He hadn't seen Mae since he told her. "But I can't stay here indefinitely. Not unless I can figure some way . . ."

"Mr. McGloin?" Mae stood just inside the barn door. "I've packed some sandwiches for you for on the train, and a jar of cider." She held out a burlap bag. "I wrapped the jar in a towel but I don't know how warm the cider will stay." She eyed the toe of her shoe, then looked up at him. "Have a . . . nice trip."

"Thank you."

"Ah, I was wondering if, when you return, you'd be willing to accept some land, say the southernmost fifty acres to pay back that money and then later . . ."

"We'll talk when I return."

"Oh. Well, then, how soon . . . ? Do you think you'll be back by the weekend?"

"I doubt it. Probably early next week."

"Oh? Early next week?"

He looked at her long and hard. Her fair cheeks, normally the color of ripe apricots, were apple red from the wind. He wanted to crush her to him. He wanted to sweep her up and run with her into the house.

He got into the wagon. "Comin', Ed?"

Her positive attitude lasted as long as the wagon was in view. The sense of well-being she'd glimpsed and sometimes sustained during the last weeks reverted to bleak despair. A sense of foreboding grew.

During the long days of Sean's absence, all her problems—Peter, the farm, the bills, the in-laws—came crushing down on her.

Oh, Sean had bought them some breathing room when he paid off the bank note and the taxes. But all she could think of now was how on earth would she ever pay it back? How were they to get a crop in next spring, she and Uncle Ed alone? One year without a paying crop, one year of having to buy feed for the stock instead of producing it themselves and they were right back in the same predicament. She started to feel—as she had earlier in the fall, before the Irishman—desperate, besieged, a house of cards in a tornado. She couldn't shake the sensation. And she castigated herself mercilessly for her inability to do so.

What a terrible failure you are, Mae Ella Botts. Hopeless. Useless.

She wished she'd thought of deeding over that fifty acres earlier. She could have done a lot better job of selling the Irishman on the idea. Maybe she could have convinced him to build on that acreage and work his land and theirs as well and they could share the profits. Or something. Fifty acres wasn't very much land. Not enough to feed a family should the Irishman decide to have one.

With that thought, a huge knot formed in her throat and her house of cards collapsed with an explosion of dust.

She got Moira's letter the day before Sean returned. They must not have spelling bees in Ireland.

Deerest Mae: I tak pin in hand to tel yu about yur husband Peter. He was kilt!! I wood haf never noed about it xcept that Tim's onkle Fogarty (he is the won who is a poleec man, rember?) kaim to our apartment invesi [this word was drawn through] loking into where Peter used to live to see if innyone knew innyting to help them find out who dun it!

Mae held the letter to her chest and closed her eyes. Peter dead! Oh God! After a long moment, she read on.

A bun found Peter in an aly in the seedyst part of town. He had all his clo [this was drawn through] things. So he was not kilt for his mony. I tried inkwiring but Tim an Fogarty loked at me and dropped tha subjickt reel quik. Tim later sez it waz entirely too riskay for me. So I don no wot reely hapened I jest no he wuz kilt. I no yu wood want to no rite away.

I will keep trying to get the hole storrie. I supose to get the mony he was carrying yu wood hav to say who yu were to him. If it is inny consol [this word drawn through too] help, it waz only ate dolars.

It has ben raining all the time lately an Tim got a raze but that's not the big noos. I think I'm prag [drawn through] pegn [drawn through] going to hav a babe!! I lov yu, yur frind, Moira.

P.S. Plez escuse my slopey hand writin.

"What's the matter, Mae Ella?"

She realized she hadn't responded to something her uncle had said. "It's a letter from my friend Moira in Chicago. She's going to have a baby."

"Oh? Her first?"

"Yes." She folded the letter and slipped it into her apron pocket. "Uncle Ed, I don't feel so good. I think I'm going to lay down for a few minutes." She lifted Johnny from the swing.

"Want me to keep an eye on Johnny?"

"No. I think I'll take him along."

"Sure. Take a nice long nap. You've been looking a mess lately."

"Thanks, Uncle Ed," she replied dryly.

"You know, Mae Ella? I wanted to say . . . er . . . well, about the Irishman?"

Mae looked at him. "Yes?"

He shuffled his feet, snapped his suspenders and sucked his tooth.

"What, Uncle Ed?" With only a tenuous hold on her emotions, she wanted to get to the privacy of her bedroom.

Shuffle. Snap. Suck, Suck.

He slapped on his hat and rocked it about ten times. "Oh, shit-house mouse! Never mind."

Mae crawled into bed with Johnny and pulled the quilt over both of them. She held Peter's son and pressed her lips to his head. "Oh, Peter! So alone and so far from everyone who loved you." Though profound, her grief was blunted. In her heart she had lost Peter months ago in Chicago.

Still, she cried herself to sleep.

Something woke her as abruptly as ice water on a sleeping sunbather. She sat bolt upright and pressed a hand to her mouth, trying to bring her breathing back to normal. She listened but the house was quiet.

Oh, God! she whispered. She rested her head on her knees. What a heinous thought! It's not possible.

Heinous, yes. But impossible?

No. It was possible but was it true? Was her dream an instinctual sort of premonition? A revelation of what she intuitively knew without the conscious use of reason?

Neither, she insisted. Just a bad case of nerves. The Irishman wasn't capable of such a deed.

But a splinter of doubt had been lodged in her mind. She stared out at the night with unseeing eyes.

The Irishman was a man who, by his own admission, had walked on the wild side. A man who took what he wanted and who wanted her. Fiercely. But did he want her bad enough to commit murder?

She simply couldn't believe it of him.

Why not? she asked herself. Because she really believed him to be incapable of such an act? Or was it because she didn't want to believe she could be falling in love with a murderer?

There was the crux of her problem. Who was he really? The only thing certain about him was Sean McGloin was a man of contradiction! Ruthless yet compassionate. Cocksure but strangely troubled.

She had no trouble picturing him as a scarred and cruel warrior wearing breastplate and chain mail. And yet, conversely, he was a man whose gentle hands had fashioned a swing because a small child saw too little of his mother.

Unable to sleep, she was stoking up the stove long before dawn. Nothing was resolved other than that she now knew she not only mistrusted the Irishman, she mistrusted her own judgment.

He had been gone eight days. Eight virtually sleepless days for Mae. Counting travel time, getting back and forth to the train station, which accounted for two days, Mae figured he actually had six days to tend to his business. "A little matter" surely could be taken care of in one day, two at the most. So, what was he doing all those other days? Going to fancy restaurants? Taking in a musical review or two? She knew there was lots to do in Minneapolis. (Not that she had done much when she and Peter were there.)

Finally she heard a familiar step on the porch. "Ma'am?"

"Come in, Mr. McGloin." He looked tired, travel weary and cold. He pulled off his hat and smiled. "You're a sight for sore eyes, as they say."

"So are you." She wondered why he hadn't hung his coat on one of the hooks beside the porch door. Then he reached one hand in each deep pocket for fat jars encased in wide-woven burlap. He set them on the table.

"What's this?" she asked and skinned one side down to reveal the label. DELPHI FOODS.

"Black olives!"

"Do you like them all the time? I mean, when you're not . . . ah . . . you know?"

"Like them? The only difference between now and the months before Johnny was born is now I won't eat both jars at one sitting. Thank you!" She set the jars on the shelf. "Did you get them in Minneapolis?"

"Yes. At a Greek grocer's that was smack in the middle of a big Polish neighborhood in northeast Minneapolis. Say where's Ed?"

"In town. The pump handle broke and he's getting it refitted at the blacksmith's." She set coffee and two sugar cookies in front of him and tried to look into his soul. "I'm surprised you didn't run into him."

"I wish I had," he said between bites, "I had to rent a horse in town and . . ." He glanced up. "Aren't you going to join me?"

"Yes." She got coffee. When he looked up at her questioningly, she sat.

"Did you have a good trip?"

"Yes. No. I worried about things here." He searched her face. "You look tired."

"I'm fine."

"How've things been here?"

"Fine."

He took a sip of coffee. "I've decided to look into buying some land nearby. Maybe you know of a neighbor who might . . ."

"Peter's dead," she said and watched his reaction.

"What?" His eyes widened and he sat forward. "What did you say?"

"Peter's dead."

"What happened?"

"They don't know yet. He was killed by a person or persons unknown."

"Sweet Jesu! that this should happen now." Talking more to himself than her, he was unaware of her scrutiny. He shook his head. "It's hard to believe."

"Yes, my thoughts exactly."

He looked at her. "What does that mean?

"Sean, were you truly in Minneapolis."

"Yes, of course. I said that's where I was going."

"I know what you said." She watched him carefully. "Why were you gone so long? What were you doing?"

"Why do you ask? I had some business I had to . . ."

"What business?" she asked then waved her hand. "No, never mind. It's not my business to ask what business." She leaned closer. "But you weren't in Chicago?"

"No."

She searched his eyes.

He set down the cookie. "Why do you keep asking?"

"It all seems too pat."

"So you think that I went to Chicago and . . .

"I don't know what to think."

He spread his hands on the table and shook his head. "That you would think that of me!"

"You weren't there, you swear?"

"Of course, I swear. How can you even think . . ."

"I'm sorry." She rubbed her eyes. "I'm so sorry. I don't know what's the matter with me. Please forgive me."

There was a barely perceptible pause. "All right."

"It's only because I had just told you about Peter and not a week later he's been killed. It's so coincidental."

"I understand. However, it's still unfair to you to believe that I would stoop so low. You must not have a very high opinion of my character."

"Oh that's not so! I think you are a wonderful man." *But I'm still going to mail the letter to Moira asking her to find out the exact date of Peter's death.*

"A man who would do murder?"

"No. No. I know you wouldn't." She rubbed her forehead. "You are one of the kindest, most compassionate men I've ever met and . . ."

"Worthy of marriage?"

She looked at him. "I . . . I"

He covered her hand with his. "Don't you understand, gel? Some higher power has taken a hand in our lives. We were meant to be together. 'Tis fate."

"Do you really believe that?"

"Sure! Don't you? Especially now?"

"I don't know what to think."

"I honestly can't say I'm sorry to hear of Peter's death. The man had done a dastardly deed. Leaving you and his son to fend for yourselves to say nothing of the fact that he'd consigned you to live the rest of your life alone."

"That was not a hardship to me. Other than having more children, I was not unhappy to know I would never be getting married again. I didn't like being married one bit."

"Great!" he muttered. "just bloody great!" He ran his hand through his hair. "So you will not marry me under any condition?"

"I didn't say that. But we've only known each other a few weeks."

"That's not important."

"It is to me."

"Well, either we marry or I go. Which is it to be?"

She looked at him then at her clasped hands. "I *have* been thinking about it."

He stood. "Do you think you could speed it up?"

"Yes, but why?"

"Because I'm freezing my arse . . . rear end off in that tack room!"

"Tomorrow." She smiled in spite of herself. "Give me until tomorrow."

That night, while Ed was in the barn with Sean, and Johnny was asleep in his crib, Mae got out some paper and pencil and sat at the kitchen table. "Remember the three P's" Granny'd always said. Precise. Punctual. Practical. Very, very important, but of the three, the most important is practical.

She wrote For and Against at the top of the page then scratched it out. Pro and Con. She drew a line through those words too. Ditto for Good and Bad. Finally she settled on Advantages & Disadvantages to Marrying. She stared at the words but added nothing to the paper. She got up and looked in on Johnny then wandered dejectedly back into the kitchen. She repositioned the doily in the center of the table then she sat down again. Stop dillydallying around, Mae Ella.

Number one, she wrote and then started writing short sentences down the page. When she was finished the Advantages column extended to a second piece of paper. The minus side had one three-letter word.

She sat there, looked at the word and felt like bawling. She rested her chin on her hand. Maybe she would bawl. She covered the word on the Disadvantages side with her hand. "Yuccht!" she said and shuddered.

* * *

"Mr. McGloin?" She stood just inside the barn door.

"Ma'am?" After replacing the pitchfork on its hook, he walked toward her. It was impossible to read her expression. Though wearing her coat she had pulled out a small bit of her apron and was looking at the hem.

"I accept your offer of marriage on one condition."

He levered one hip on the work bench and swung his booted foot, waiting.

"Peter has only just died and . . ."

"To the rest of this town he's been dead for months."

"This is true but not to me, Mr. McGloin. For that reason and the fact that I need time to come to think of you as my husband, I ask that you give me time before we . . . before we . . ." Her face flamed.

"Before we consummate our marriage?"

"Yes."

"Yes?"

"I want to wait until we know each other much better."

"No problem. I'm in no hurry. I'll be glad to wait until you're ready."

"Oh?" Mae tried not to show mild surprise. She would have thought that that word written on her sheet of paper would be very important to a robust man like Sean McGloin.

"It's not like it's something a person can't control, you know," he said.

Boy, that's good to know, she thought. The idea of the Irishman out of control was downright scary. She breathed an audible sigh of relief. "Well, then, if we're agreed?"

He stood so quickly the work counter rattled. Mae jumped. "We'll take time to get to know each other better. 'Twill be sort of a courtship." He offered her his hand on it. " 'Twill be a pleasure to court you, ma'am."

She placed her hand in his then he captured her other hand and held them to his chest.

"My granny said there was something very important a person should know before she loves."

"What."

"Can I trust you, Mr. McGloin, to never knowingly hurt me?"

"Sean."

"Sean, then. Can I?"

"Yes, implicitly."

"Will you promise never to leave us? Johnny and I?"

"That goes without saying," Sean said and mentally kissed his gang-busting career good-bye.

"Do you also swear that you will never lie to me?"

"Yes, I promise."

"I should probably ask you to change your cocksure, arrogant attitude while I'm at it . . ." He made a sound of mock shock. ". . . but I'm beginning to find something endearing about it."

"I should certainly hope . . ."

Mae, listening with half an ear, fixed him with a baleful eye. A shaft of sunshine pierced the barn's dimness, encircling his head like a halo. Halo, indeed! She looked at his mischievous eyes, his mobile mouth and thick shiny hair and sighed. Her guardian angel? Or a snake in the grass? Maybe she'd never be completely certain which. She knew only one thing—she was powerfully attracted. And she'd always been fascinated by snakes.

With two big tents and wild animals galore, there had never been a bigger circus in Otter Tail. Coincidentally it was also Oktoberfest. The townspeople normally gathered in a field north of the depot where the ladies would display quilts, fine needlework and jams and jellies while the men talked farming and sampled homemade brews. That year, the year before John left, the locals pitched their tents and set up their rough-hewn tables adjacent to the circus grounds.

"The World's Most Venomous Snakes & Man Eating Reptiles," said the sign. Mae was petrified. Yet, at the same time, she was captivated. While keeping an eye peeled on the ground around her feet, she wondered—Were the snakes in glass cases? Had their fangs been removed? Was one of them wrapped around a naked lady's body like the painting outside?

Boy, she'd give just anything to see them.

She'd hung around the tent for a long time trying to screw up her courage. She left twice—"Santana the Sword Swallower" and the "Death Defying Daring of the Dantini Brothers" were intriguing also. But she came back time and again to the snake exhibit.

Maybe John would take her, she thought. Resolved, she decided she would ask him. She no sooner had the idea then she saw the tent flap close behind John and three of his friends.

"Shoot!," she'd said. Then she snapped her fingers. Why, I'll just go find Papa, she thought. He said he'd be at the livestock pens.

She no sooner got *that* idea than she heard, "Time to go home, Mae Ella," Papa called, "Your mama'll be waiting supper on us."

She had waited too long! Oh, she was disappointed!

In the years after that two other circuses had come through Otter Tail. One of them even had a snake exhibit but they didn't have "The World's Most Venomous Snakes & Man Eating Reptiles."

* * *

No sense giving him more of an advantage than he already enjoyed. "One more thing, Mr. . . . Sean?"

"Yes?"

"Whatever you do to me to get me to do what you want? I want you to stop doing it!"

"What are you talking about?"

"That business with your thumb."

"What?"

"You know what."

His brow was furrowed in a who-me-I'm-innocent frown. God, she could just imagine him as a child. Oh, he would've been a tough one to scold. She removed her hand and brushed off her skirts. "So, when should we . . ."

"Tomorrow."

Her turn to frown. "Tomorrow?"

"Well, I'll talk to the priest tomorrow about setting a date. The sooner the better as far as the neighbors and all." They walked together toward the door. "I can woo you just as well married as not."

She paused. Better make the terms perfectly clear. "But we would wait on . . . consummating until we know each other much, much better? You're sure you don't mind?"

"No' atall."

Feeling like a boulder had been removed from her back, she smiled at him over her shoulder. God she was clever! She'd bought herself a two- maybe three-month reprieve from B—E—D.

Good go, mate! Once ye get yer foot in the door, yer lookin' a' one, two days, max.

"Dinner will be in about ten minutes." She twirled

to face him and continued walking backward. "You know, I've never been courted."

Sean grinned.

She waved.

He waved.

Then he turned into the barn and grinned wider. 'Twill be like taking candy from a babe. Like falling off a log. He rolled his shoulders and swaggered into the tack room for a fresh shirt. A day.

Nae, yer a migh' rusty.

Two days then. He started whistling softly. ". . . the humor is on me now, lads, the humor is on me now. For I will and I must get married, the humor is on me now . . ."

Despite the chill, Mae paused on the porch stairs. *First you must haf trust und den koms luv.* Oh, Granny, have I put my horse before my cart?

Thirteen

Having read the banns, exactly according to canon law and in strict compliance with the Church's ancient decrees, Father Fitz married Sean and Mae.

Present were the members of their family—little Johnny and Ed, and a small group of friends—Mrs. Deetz, their nearest neighbor, the widow Weltes and Einar Torkelson. Mrs. Deetz held Johnny during the ceremony and, while the baby didn't cry once, Mrs. Deetz and Mrs. Weltes sobbed through the entire proceeding. Mae thought she had never attended a Nuptial Mass, or any Mass for that matter, that was over so soon.

Mae had intended to wear the dress she wore when she was married before but Sean wouldn't hear of it. " 'Twould be bad luck," he insisted.

A pattern was chosen, then fabric, and no expense spared so that Mae could wear the most wonderful creation imaginable. She felt like a princess. The ivory, watered silk had a soft primrose pink overskirt with rose-colored piping down the bodice, sleeves and waist. "I've never seen anyone so lovely," Mrs. Weltes said "You look like that Gibson girl from the magazines."

At Father Fitz's insistence, refreshments were offered in the anteroom of the rectory. There Mrs. Deetz had arranged a small white tier cake and fluted glasses for serving the chilled, amber-colored German wine. When everyone held a glass, Father Fitzgerald made the toast. "May yer days be long and full of happiness. May yer children be many and full of health and may they live in peace and freedom."

Mae regarded Sean over the rim of her glass. He looked very handsome in a snow white starched shirt with a high collar, black and silver necktie and black broadcloth suit. Her husband. Oh, my! Her stomach fluttered.

"I think you're supposed to feed me some of that." He pointed to her plate containing a wedge of wedding cake. "Tradition, you know." Mae held a small piece up to him. Bending at the waist, he leaned to within a few inches of the fork and opened his mouth. She inserted the minuscule piece of cake and her stomach reacted as if she'd swallowed a live animal. As she did when she was feeding Johnny, she closed her mouth and pressed her lips together when she tilted the fork handle up and out. He licked his lips. She licked hers as well. The smallest bit of white frosting remained on the end of his black moustache. He chewed and swallowed.

He smiled.

She smiled.

He clinked her glass lightly in silent salute and they drank. The noise around them faded. The others receded. It was as if they were behind a wall of glass. The crystal of sugar twinkled like a star in a midnight sky.

Then he wiped his mouth with a napkin.

"Your turn now." He made a fussy production of getting just the right-sized piece of cake. Obligingly, she opened her lips. He held a cloth napkin under the fork and inserted the cake. She looked up at him but his gaze, dark and glittering, was fixed on her mouth. The cake became as chewable as a peach pit.

He cleared his throat and looked around. Mae's odd little trance was abruptly broken. She was shocked to find she'd tied her lace hanky in a knot. She picked up her glass with trembling fingers and felt his hand at her elbow. "Well, Mrs. McGloin, shall we join the others?" He motioned to Mrs. Weltes and Einar.

Mrs. McGloin!

"Oh, here's Sean and Mae." Einar moved aside to include them. "Ve noticed yew two sparkin' over in da corner, didn't ve, Mrs. Veltes?"

Mae thought Einar looked splendid. Smelling of expensive bay rum, dressed to the nines, he wore a pearl gray suit only a tad tight across the middle and carried a matching, brushed homberg. Mrs. Weltes, however, was looking at him as if he were an open sore.

Mae greeted Mrs. Weltes again. When they touched cheeks she smelled the vanilla and lemon verbena she had always associated with their nearest neighbor. A widow for many years, Mrs. Weltes had been like another mother to Mae and her brother, dispensing homemade hard candies and affection with equal generosity. She was no stranger to tragedy. Mrs. Weltes' two boys had died in bizarre accidents with a year of each other. A wagon rolled with one and a tree fell on the other.

"Yewr yust in time, Mae," Einar said. "I vas tellin' Mrs. Weltes here aboout dat time last summer.

"So, as I vas sayin', dere I vas. Vas early in da mornin', vay before sun up. Still an' quiet, dere vasn't a lick of wind. A mist hung over da vater like a ground fog."

Father Fitzgerald, Mrs. Deetz and Ed had joined them. Sean still held Mae's arm in a proprietorial manner. Johnny sat on the rug in the center of the circle of people, chewing on a rubber ball.

"All of a sudden, my line yerked—vhy I could barely keep a holt of it! Den dere come a afful turmoil in da vater, vas like being on the ocean in a hurricane. I thought—Yumpin' yimminy! I'm gonna swamp! I shoulda knowed."

Einar paused dramatically, playing the audience like a vaudeville trouper. Mae noted that Mrs. Weltes' eyes were glazed.

"Vas Ol' Yewelry Mouth, yewsee."

"Vel, by golly, den dere come a fight." Mrs. Weltes groaned softly. "I held onto my rod vid vun hand an' my hat vid da other an' Ol' Yewelry Mouth pulled da boat all over da lake. Up vun side. Down da udder. May gootness, I got a afful vindburn . . ."

As always, the story seemed interminable and as always, ended with another of Einar's favorite lures decorating the mouth of the monster muskie.

Finally. Sean leaned close to whisper in Mae's ear. "Maybe we should leave for home soon?" Her tiny neck hairs did a dance. "It's getting dark and Ed says it might snow tonight."

"Yes." Mae picked up Johnny. She saw Sean slip Father Fitzgerald an envelope and then clasp hands with him. Father Fitzgerald punched Sean playfully in the shoulder. They seemed to have established a very close relationship, more like longtime friends than priest and parishioner. Mae joined them. "Father, now that Mama has passed away, we should be able to get to town more often for Mass. Weather permitting, that is." On an impulse, she asked. "Ah, do you have plans for Thanksgiving, Father?"

"No, actually, I don't. Mrs. Deetz will be going to her sister's in Minneapolis for the long weekend. So far anyway, I'm to be on my own."

"Then please come to our home for the day." Mae said.

"Why, thank you! I'd be delighted."

"Mrs. Weltes will be coming and bringing some of her wonderful candies." Mae said, turning her upper body slowly back and forth. The sleepy-eyed baby had rested his head on her shoulder. "What about you, Einar? Would you like to come to our house for . . ."

Sean heard Einar decline, saying he was going to his brother Lars' house.

Our house! Sean thought and practically choked up. He cleared his throat. "Here, let me take Jack." Sean lifted Jack into his arms where the baby resettled promptly. He rubbed the boy's back and rested his chin on his little bald head. Our home, he thought and felt another rush of emotion. If hearing those words could have such an effect, what would happen if she were to say—I love you? He snorted to himself. Ye'll probably start bawlin'!

Father Fitz held Mae's hand in both of his, smiling, patting it. The woman was so lovely! He couldn't take his eyes off her. If she ever said those words, they'd be more healing to his sick soul then a hundred stints to the confessional.

Which reminded him! Scowling, he looked at Ed and the priest, who were shaking hands. He'd been babbling Our Fathers and Hail Marys for days! Thanksgiving dinner, indeed! He'd be lucky if he'd have time to eat, seein' as how it'd mean taking time away from his bloody penance. He'd promised Father Fitz that if he married them now, he'd do all his penance by December 1st but Jesu! it would be damned close!

The priest agreed to arrive as early as possible on Thanksgiving in order to spend the day with them.

Then they bundled up and went out into the cold night.

On the ride home Mae was acutely sensitive to everything, as if somebody were poking her in the ribs and saying, "Pay attention, Mae Ella! This is important!"

She closed her eyes and listened to the carriage wheels crunching on the ice, the clip of the horse's hooves, a dog barking in the distance. Tilting her head back, she admired the tiny sliver of the silvery moon, the inky black sky—overcast and devoid of stars. She felt the bite of chilly air on her face.

But most of all what she noticed was what a tight squeeze it was on the seat. A very tight squeeze. Holding Johnny, wedged between Uncle Ed and Sean like a piece of meat in a sandwich, Sean's thigh felt as unyielding as the wood seat under her rear.

As soon as they left town and turned off onto the less-used road toward the bluffs, the ruts in the dirt road bounced them around like marbles in a tin can. Except the Irishman, who was solid as a boulder. Mae found herself leaning into him. Only for stability, mind.

Now that the four of them were alone, it seemed no one had anything to say. The silence stretched like too-washed underwear. Mae poked her uncle and he started to chatter.

"Well that was a real nice ceremony. I like the way the good Father said the Mass in the little chapel area where Johnny was baptized, you know, instead of usin' the whole big church. We'd have felt lost in there."

And then. "I've always thought there's something

real soothin' about them Latin words. Like he's speakin' magic over you. I've always liked that."

He was silent another moment. "Another thing I liked is how my nephew behaved himself. I laid him on the pew there and he kicked off his blanket and played with his feet. Right obliging little boy. Mrs. Deetz didn't have to hold him but I think she wanted to."

"Good boy, Johnny!" Mae kissed her sleeping baby, or rather she kissed the blanket covering his head. A few more minutes of silence.

Fumbling inside his heavy coat for his tobacco, Uncle Ed managed to get most of it inside his lip, then brushed his coat front off. "I thought it was real nice of that Mrs. Deetz to make that little cake. Didn't you?"

"Yes," Mae said. Her uncle gave up. She slanted a look up at Sean. With his hat pulled low, only the hollow of his cheek and length of a beard-darkened jaw was visible in the moon glow. When she closed her eyes, she imagined she still saw a tiny piece of white frosting glistening among black shiny hairs.

"Ah, Mr. McGloin . . ."

"Now, just a minute. Doesn't it seem pretty silly for you to say Mr. McGloin all the time? What should I call you, Mrs. McGloin?"

"I forgot . . ."

Uncle Ed had gone to bed. Johnny too. The newlyweds had agreed to share the coffee which Mae had heated up. They looked at each other across the width of the kitchen table.

Married, Mae thought. They were married! Oh what have I done? "Did you say anything to Uncle Ed?"

"About our sleeping arrangements?"

They'd agreed to separate rooms during their "get acquainted" period. He took a sip of coffee.

"No, did you?"

"Oh, no!" She blushed.

"Should I have a little chat with him about it?" Sean asked innocently.

"Oh, no!" She blushed deeper. "I'll say something . . ."

He lit a cheroot, precariously tilting the chair on two legs. "I'm not sure you have to. He's an uncanny little tur- . . . squint." He grinned. "Not that you need to go telling him so, but I've grown quite fond of him."

"Yes, he's quite a character." She stood, pressing the fingertips of one hand on the table. "Well . . ."

Sean continued to smoke, squinting up at her. He raised that one eyebrow. "Yes?"

"I thought I'd show you to your room, uh, if you like. Show you where things are."

"In a bit." Sean waved toward her chair. "Please."

She sat down like the chair was covered with spit.

"You know, for us to get acquainted, it's going to be necessary for you and me to talk, to have little chats. I thought we might start tonight by telling each other something about ourselves. Then, we could alternate. You know, take turns asking questions of each other."

"Oh? Well, that's a thought." Nervously, Mae drew circles with a spoon. She was dying to know more about him. "So . . ."

After a long pause, Sean leaned up, placing his forearms on the table. "One of us needs to go first."

"You go."

"No, you."

"We'll draw straws. Fair enough?"

Mae grinned at him. "Fair enough."

Sean tilted his chair back for two kitchen matches from a metal holder on the side of the oven. Breaking one off, he picked up an empty coffee cup and dropped it and the other match inside. He covered the cup completely with his palm, held it high above them and flipped it slowly back and forth.

"So, whoever gets the short match has to answer—honestly now—any question the other one asks. All right?"

Mae nodded.

"Then the other one has to answer next time. Same terms. Fair enough?"

She nodded again.

"You pick." Sean held the coffee cup high in the air. Under it, their eyes met and held. Lifting her rear up off the chair seat a good foot, she reached into the cup.

"No cheatin'!"

Twisting her mouth, she laid a short match on the table. "Darn!"

"Well!" Sean set the cup down with a loud thump. She jumped. "Let's see now. Any question I want answered . . ."

She looked into his mischievous eyes and blushed. "Well, within reason . . ."

"Just a minute now! Will ye be makin' changes in the rules after the game has started?"

"No." Grudgingly, Mae drew more circles on the table cloth with the spoon handle. "I guess not."

"All right, then. I'd like to know about your brother John."

"John?" She was delighted. "Oh, well, where to start about John? I was quite young when he died. Did you know my brother died in the war?"

"Yes, Ed told me. I'm sorry."

"Yes. I loved him very, very much."

"You remember him well?"

"Oh, very well."

"What was he like?"

She smiled. "Kind. My brother John was kind to things smaller than himself. Which was me. And very adventuresome. I don't know what he would have ended up being but whatever it was, I think it would have involved traveling. He wanted to go everywhere, see everything." She drank some coffee. "I remember one summer." She shook her head and chuckled.

"What happened?"

"He and Willy Steinforth decided to build a raft and sail down the St. Croix to the Mississippi and then clear to New Orleans. I know John was the driving force behind this venture. Among his friends he was always the one with the ideas.

"Anyway there's a little secluded cove to the north here. It's pretty but we never go that far north to fish because it's too shallow until you get way out from shore. Actually I think it might be on Mrs. Weltes' property anyway.

"Well, John had rolled some old rusted barrels down there. Then he got some wormy barnwood some place or another and hauled that down there too. As was my habit, I had followed him and so was on to him from the start. I watched them from my secret hiding place. He and Willy Steinforth were going to build a raft! Hammering, sawing, lashing everything together. Just working like beavers. It looked like they had enough rope to stretch clear to Minneapolis.

"They discovered me, of course, and tried to run me off. But I kept creeping back, circling them like a hungry cur around a garbage dump. I started inching my way closer every day. Pretty soon I was standing right out in the open, watching them. Willy said

I gave him the willies, standing there, staring. He offered to run me off for real.

" 'Go on home, Mae Ella!' John said. 'This is the last time I'm gonna tell you. Next time, you're gonna catch it.'

"I knew he was bluffing.

" 'Can't you get rid of her," Willy whined.

" 'Oh, leave her. She ain't hurtin' you any.' John said.

"So they gave up and swore me to secrecy instead. But they didn't want me any closer than necessary to the 'construction area' because they were talking 'man talk' and didn't want to have to watch their language.

"They got practically the whole thing built and decided it was too small. Boy, it looked huge to me. But they took it apart and added two more barrels and several more planks.

"Naturally I had started begging to go along.

" 'First night out you'll be cryin' for Mama,' John said.

" 'Nuh-uh, nuh-uh,' I said.

" 'There's river pirates,' John said, 'all up and down the river. They'll cutcha throat and feed you to the fishes.'

" 'I don't care,' I said, 'you won't let them get me.'

" 'Wouldn't be any help for it. We'll probably have to fight them off and I'll be too busy trying to save my own neck to look out for yours.'

"Well, nothing I said swayed them in the least. Two fourteen-year-old boys about to embark on the greatest adventure of their life didn't want a little kid sister along.

"Finally the big day arrived. They attached the flagpole. One of John's good shirts had been nailed onto it by the arms and the words "New Orleans or

Bust" written on it in indigo ink. They distributed their load very evenly. All the canned food they'd purloined from the house on one side and the whole hams and smoked turkeys and all the other meat from the smokehouse on the other. It was riding pretty low but was proclaimed seaworthy. My job was to take the wheelbarrow full of tools back to the house, wait until dinner and then tell Papa and Mama that John had gone to New Orleans with Willy Steinforth, not to worry and that he would write upon safe arrival." She grinned at Sean. "I had repeated the message many times and had it down pat.

"So, with the long birch poles they'd cut down and several 'Yippees' and 'Whoo Haas,' they propelled themselves out toward the middle of the river. It was so exciting! I was crying my eyes out but my heart soared.

"They sank like a dart."

Sean chuckled.

"I couldn't believe my eyes. I blinked. One second they were there, the next second they were gone. Along with about every bit of food on the farm.

"Well, you should have seen my papa! Boy he was madder than I have ever seen him. John got a whipping. The first and only time I've ever known Papa to give one and he was confined to the farm for the summer. As further punishment, he was to replace the larder. Poor John. He was hunting for weeks. Grouse, pheasant, turkey, goose, duck. He not only had to shoot them, he had to clean them and pluck them and smoke them. The works. He had feathers sticking on him for weeks. One time I snuck back behind the barn and tried to help him pluck.

" 'Mae Ella!' I practically jumped out of my socks. Papa stood there at the edge of the barn giving me

The Stare. He just pointed toward the house and I slunk off."

"How long was John in the doghouse?"

"Well, that summer for sure and some of the fall. John finally shot a deer and Papa said enough—his punishment was over.

"I felt so sorry for John at the time but a farmer who has to take off to hunt isn't farming and it was harvest."

"He sounds like he was quite a rascal."

"Oh, he was but very good-hearted and kind. I hope my Johnny grows up to be like his namesake."

"Sean is Irish for John."

"Really? I didn't know that."

"Yes."

"Well. That's kind of nice, isn't it?"

"I think so."

They sat silently for a few minutes, listening to the clock tick. At some point in her story Sean had covered her hand with his.

Mae looked at the clock. "My, it's getting late. Would you . . . like more coffee?"

"No, thank you. Maybe you'd better show me where I should sleep."

"All right." At the door to her parents' room, Mae glanced over her shoulder and waited for him to pick up his cheroots, matches and the ashtray. She'd cleaned the room again, top to bottom, and even whitewashed the walls. It looked nice. She inhaled. It smelled wonderful. She watched Sean look around.

She'd put a glass jar on the dresser and filled it with crushed sage, pine nettles and a few marbles for color. She'd switched washbowls, giving him Granny's hand-painted one from her room. It had red tea roses on it, which wasn't terribly masculine, but at least it didn't have a big chip like the one in her room now. Although the quilt was a little ivoried with age, its colorful maroon and navy blue checkerboard pattern went with the ivory lace curtains. She'd sewn some navy tie-backs out of a tablecloth just last night.

" 'Tis very nice." Conveniently placed alongside the bed—where warm feet would otherwise meet the cold floor—was an oval rug he recognized from her bedroom. Her thoughtfulness touched him.

"Everybody leaves their doors open a bit in the winter for extra heat." Mae whispered.

"I may be able to do something about that. I sent for some how-to books and one of them is on heating." Setting his smokes and ashtray down on the dresser, he turned, leaned his rear against it and crossed his ankles.

"Really? Well . . ." The lantern behind him projected a huge bogey man shadow on the wall. She backed up.

"Oh, one more thing . . ." He pushed off and came toward her, stopping so close she had to tilt her head up. "My family was real big on one thing. My mam, da, everybody." He drew a line down her jawbone with the tip of a long finger.

"What?"

"Kissin'! Hello. Good-bye. And especially goodnight!" Leaning down, he paused, searched her wide eyes, then he dropped a quick, soft kiss on her lips. "There now," he said, "good night!"

She left quickly. In spite of her suggestion to leave the door ajar, she closed it. Leaning her forehead against it, hand resting on the knob, she breathed, "Oh, my!"

As she struggled with one of the cast-iron stove lids in the predawn light—the darned thing was stick-

YOU'RE GOING TO LOVE GETTING
4 FREE BOOKS

These books worth almost $20, are yours without cost or obligation when you fill out and mail this certificate.
(If the certificate is missing below, write to: Zebra Home Subscription Service, Inc., 120 Brighton Road, P.O. Box 5214, Clifton, New Jersey 07015-5214

Complete and mail this card to receive 4 Free books!

Yes! Please send me 4 Zebra Historical Romances without cost or obligation. I understand that each month thereafter I will be able to preview 4 new Zebra Historical Romances FREE for 10 days. Then, if I should decide to keep them, I will pay the money-saving preferred publisher's price of just $4.00 each...a total of $16. That's almost $4 less than the publisher's price, and there is no additional charge for shipping and handling. I may return any shipment within 10 days and owe nothing, and I may cancel this subscription at any time. The 4 FREE books will be mine to keep in any case.

Name _____

Address _____ Apt. _____

City _____ State ____ Zip _____

Telephone ( ) _____

Signature _____ LF0495
(If under 18, parent or guardian must sign.)

Terms, offer and prices subject to change without notice. Subscription subject to acceptance by Zebra Books. Zebra Books reserves the right to reject any order or cancel any subscription.

*A $19.96
value.
FREE!*

*No obligation
to buy
anything, ever.*

ing lately for some reason—Mae heard the door to the porch close.

Wondering who on earth was up before her, she walked into the hallway. Sean was shrugging out of his heavy coat and wiping his feet on the rug. "Good morning!" he boomed as he hung his coat on one of the pegs. He kissed her slightly open lips then proceeded into the kitchen, rubbing his hands together.

"What's for breakfast?" He laid a palm on the coffeepot, then reached for a mug hanging from a hook on the underside of the shelf. "Great! It's done. That's good timing. Yes, good timing. Timing is important. Strategy an' o' course, patience. Yes. A grea' deal o' patience."

What on earth has gotten into him? Mae walked back to the stove and looked at the familiar blue speckled pot as if it were a poisonous reptile. She'd been so intent on removing the lid, she hadn't noticed that he had stoked up the stove and started the coffee already.

"I left the milk pails on the porch. I thought to keep them cool but I'll tell you, they just may freeze over." Sean added a log to the heating stove from the adjacent wood box. "It's that cold out!"

"Good morning!" Uncle Ed came in, yawning, poking one arm through his suspenders.

"Hey, Ed, how'd you sleep last night . . . I slept . . ."

She knew she was as animated as a dead carp, but she was just so shocked. The Irishman had milked both cows and made the coffee already!

"Mae?" Sean asked. "Anything wrong?"

She shook her head. He wore a smile and freshly laundered denims. Stiff-armed, he had both long-fingered hands on top of one of the ladder-back chairs. One booted foot was casually crossed over the other. He was freshly shaved, his hair still damp and curling over a bulky, cowl-necked sweater.

So handsome, she thought, handsome enough to eat for breakfast!

The thought popped into her mind. Her jaw dropped. She turned away. Whatever's gotten into me? I *have* gone dotty.

She took up the knife and tried once more to lever the lid off the burner.

"Here! You'll cut yourself." He was beside her, gently took the knife and in seconds, removed the lid. "Hmm. I think the latch is broken."

When he leaned close to examine the lid, Mae smelled soap, tobacco and the early winter morning air on his clothes. Her head swam. She braced herself with one hand on the sink.

"It'll have to be repaired but I think I can fix it. If I can't, I'll take it with me when I go to town . . ." Laying the heavy cover near the door, he sat back down at the table. ". . . which I thought I'd do today, Ed, unless Mae has something else for me to do . . ." He looked at her.

Shaking her head, Mae cracked an egg into a bowl. Things are going to be very, very different around here!

"Do you want to go along, Ed?"

"Hell, no! It's too danged cold. I'll get my outside chores done, then I'm gonna be right inside here. What do you need to go to town for anyway? We was just there yesterday."

"Well, I could hardly haul lumber on my wedding day."

"Lumber?" Ed asked. Mae listened carefully as she added some chopped onion to the butter sizzling in the black iron skillet.

"I want to fix those stairs going to the attic and

there's some other things that need fixing. I thought this winter . . . Well, you know, keeping busy helps prevent cabin fever."

Chuckling, Ed sawed off a piece of bread Mae had placed on the table and buttered it. "What do you know about cabin fever? A newly married man shouldn't have to worry about that, leastwise, not the first winter."

Running the wooden spoon around the mixing bowl to get all the eggs out, Mae felt the back of her neck redden. Darn you, Uncle Ed.

He continued. "Boy! You're sure full of piss and vinegar this morning!"

"It's the snap in the air. Gets me blood moving!"

"Hmm? Is that so? Snap in the air, you say? Funny it ain't affected my blood that way."

Mae heard the grin in Uncle Ed's voice. With a wooden spoon she started beating the hell out of the pancake batter. It was that or beat her uncle about the head and neck.

"Bye! I'll be in the barn. I've got a bit of sawing."

"Bye!" Mae automatically lifted her face and pursed her lips.

Sean looked her over. Wrist-deep in strudel dough, flour garnishing one cheek, she stood at the kitchen table with eyes closed and lips puckered. He grinned. *Ah! Sean, me boyo, yer a bloody saint!*

He kissed her briefly. But not quite as briefly as he had the day before when he had kissed her just a bit longer than the day before that. Ach! Sean stepped into his heavy leather boots and wound a plaid scarf around his neck. At this rate, ye'll be old an' gray before ye get yer own wife in the hay!

Fa' lo' of good ye'll be doin' the gel with rigor mortis o' the privates!

When the screen door slammed, Mae opened her eyes and licked lips that felt like they'd fallen asleep.

Pounding the dough with renewed enthusiasm, she congratulated herself on her astute decision to marry the Irishman. The man was pleasant to be around, interesting to talk to, neat as a pin, had all his teeth and hair and was a working fool! Never had she seen such energy, such natural talent, such able hands.

What a smart cookie you are, Mae Ella! No flies around your head. No sirree bob. Sharp as a tack and twice as shiny.

She smiled to herself as she took the narrow glass strudel-pan out of her new cabinet above the stove. She stepped back to admire it again. So nice! She especially liked the way Sean had put small grooves in the top to display some of Granny's fine old, hand-painted dishes. He had painted the cabinet a nice medium blue and painted the store-bought knobs white. Then, he had painted the kitchen white. After that he added a rough-sawn wooden border around the ceiling and, like wainscoting, a matching border five feet off the floor. Why, it was amazing what he had accomplished in less than a week! She would hardly recognize the room. Now he was working on installing new stairs going down into the root cellar. "They have to be replaced. I'll not have ye goin' up and down those stairs a minute longer than necessary."

And, my goodness goodness! Could he kiss! Left and right! It seemed that he didn't even consider going to the privy without a kiss! And touch! All the time! Why, the difference between Peter and Sean was like fire and water. Like dark and light. Like German and Irish?

She sat, the half-greased pan forgotten in her hand.

No, she decided and resumed her work, Papa was German. And Granny's beloved Helmut—ol'-one-look-and-flowing-juices-Helmut—was German.

Still, even Papa and Mama had not been that big on kissing and touching. She'd sensed as a child that there were certain times set aside for that kind of thing. A kiss good-night, a kiss or a hug on parting. But not so with the Irishman.

Picking up the pan, she finished running the greased cloth in it. The Irishman was always patting her shoulder, squeezing her hand or clasping her to him when they stood side by side. She was certain it was totally instinctive because he'd go on about his business and there she'd stand, staring after him with stupefaction.

She arranged the dough just so in the pan and brushed it with melted butter. She shook her head. Poor Peter! Maybe if they had kissed more, if they touched more, it would have been different between them. Maybe she could have even made Peter happy.

Then again, maybe not. If she assessed her entire relationship with Peter, she had to conclude that he had never, ever made her feel like the Irishman did. And he probably never could have no matter what he did. There was just something about Sean. Something magical.

She paused once again then frowned. With sudden insight, she thought she knew why she had been drawn to Peter. Was it for the same reason she'd been drawn to the smallest of the barn cat's kittens, or to the runt of the pig litter? Was it because Peter had needed her?

After washing her hands, she drew a damp cheese-cloth over the strudel, making certain the cloth didn't touch the dough. Then she poured some coffee. She sat with her chin propped on her hand, looking outside. It was a blustery day. A strong wind was blowing the last leaves off the trees, leaving the branches starkly unadorned. The ground was covered with swirling leaves, tempestuous as her thoughts.

She picked up a narrow black case and smiled. Her uncle's new specs. Sean must have asked Watson to order them from Minneapolis weeks ago because he brought them home the same day he hauled all that lumber.

Although they were just magnifiers, they allowed Ed to see well enough to play dominoes, to mend a harness, to help Sean some with his projects in the barn.

She thought Uncle Ed was going to cry the night he got them.

Mae heard a gruff "Here, ye little squint. I picked these up so you'd stop droppin' things on me foot," and turned.

"Well, what the hell . . ." The black case opened like a clam. "Glasses?" Uncle Ed removed them.

"Wha' do ye think? 'Course they're glasses."

Her uncle unfolded the fragile stems then looped them over his ears. There had been tears in his enlarged eyes when he turned toward Mae. She was watery-eyed herself. They stared at each other and smiled then she rushed to him and gave him a huge kiss on his whiskered cheek.

Later, after dinner, Ed asked. "How about I beat you in a game of dominoes, Irish? You made a big mistake gettin' me my new specs! Now I can see you cheatin'!"

"You're on, mate!" Sean replied. "I'll be delighted to give you another lesson in dominoes. Soon as I finish me coffee." He covered Mae's hand where it rested on the table.

He and Ed discussed their last match and made outrageous bets. No one paid the least attention to Mae's captive hand. Except Mae. Sean's large hand was curled around hers and he started rubbing his thumb slowly back and forth. With every slow stroking, slightly abrasive caress, the back of her hand heated like a hot coal. Sometimes he pressed, almost like a tiny massage, other times, he brushed by with a touch as soft as eiderdown.

She could feel it clear to her toes. While her mouth dried, other places dewed and swelled and tingled. "Stop that," she hissed.

"What?" he asked so innocently she knew he wasn't doing anything unnatural to her hand. Could he make her have that kind of unusual reaction without trying to now?

"Well, let's go in the parlor and have at it." Uncle Ed said as he stood and stretched.

"What will you do, love?" Sean turned to her.

That was another thing! Right in front of Uncle Ed and, she suspected, anybody else if they happened to be around, the Irishman was calling her "love." She wasn't sure how she felt about his doing that. Surprised. Peculiar maybe. The first time he did it, sort of like that hot, summer day when she wrapped her mouth around the spigot on the water barrel and a wasp flew in her mouth.

Sean and Uncle Ed were waiting for her reply. "I'm going to crush some cranberries for Granny's cranberry salad." The cranberries had to sit in sugar for a day before she added the other ingredients; then they had to sit another day before they were ready for eating. The salad was a lot of trouble to make but if anyone was going to keep up the family traditions now, it was her.

"Well then, if you don't need me for anything . . ." She shook her head and almost groaned aloud with relief when he finally released her hand. He leaned over and tucked a tendril of hair behind her ear. His fingers brushed her neck. She swallowed hard. He cupped her head with his hand, leaned down and kissed her. A long and vastly different kiss. With his hand on the back of her head, he turned her head so their lips met more completely. His mouth was as hot as her wash-day iron. Her stomach tightened. Her nipples puckered beneath her bodice.

"Are you gonna spoon, Irishman, or play dominoes?" Her uncle's voice came from far away, farther than the parlor.

"Well . . . ?" He looked down at her rosy face and moist, pouty lips and raised his eyebrows.

She stood so fast she almost swooned.

The next day was Thanksgiving. While she worked, Mae couldn't help thinking about the vast difference the past year had made in her life. Thanksgiving last year she'd been in Chicago, virtually alone, pregnant and very miserable. Peter had been alive. Papa too. Mama had been, so far as Mae knew, hale and hearty and happy.

She reached into the cupboard for a small wooden box, flipped back the lid and sorted through the folded pieces of paper within until she found the cranberry recipe. She closed the box and carefully unfolded the spattered paper. Since Granny had never learned to write in English, all the recipes were written in her mother's spidery scrawl. Granny and Mama had sat one winter's night, Mae recalled, and written down all their favorite recipes. Mae'd been seven, maybe eight. She smoothed her hands over the paper, touching it as others had before her.

Suddenly on an emotional edge, she went into her room and picked up Johnny. Sitting in the rocking chair, she tucked his small head into her neck and rocked. She loved the fresh, clean smell of him and holding his warm sleepy body. She loved the view out her window. Her home.

She was counting her blessings when the Irishman came out of the barn. He latched the door and, turning his collar up, ambled toward the house. He appeared to be whistling.

Interestingly enough, the big Irishman loomed very close to the top of her list.

Mae wrestled with the huge Tom turkey. She had gotten up quietly, an hour earlier than usual, in order to get the bird in the oven. Stuffed, it probably weighed twenty-five pounds. The job was made all the more difficult because it was covered with butter. "Darn!" she muttered as the turkey slid one way and the greased black roaster another.

"Can I help?" Sean asked, startling Mae.

"Did I wake you?" She whispered apologetically. "I'm sorry!"

"You didn't. I was . . ." Sean looked her over from head to toe and his smile waned like a new moon. ". . . already awake." Her dress sleeves were rolled up revealing slender, white forearms. Her hands and a good portion of her forearms glistened with butter. She ran her hands over the turkey and her tongue over her lips and Sean gritted his teeth. God! Patience. Planning . . .

Ah, bloody hell!

Some days were decidedly worse than others. Today, if its beginning was any indication, promised to be difficult.

T' say the leas'.

Just how long, he wondered, is this get-acquainted period going to last? When would the world-renowned McGloin charm kick in, rendering her helpless and unable to resist him?

He pulled his eyes up from her hands. "Wha's goin' on?"

"I'm trying to get this turkey into this big sack. The sack is greased, the bird is greased and I'm greased." Mae chuckled.

Sean tried to join in, croaking like a stepped-on frog. He washed his hands. "Let me help." In no time the turkey was in the sack, sack in the pan and pan in the oven.

"Whew! Now, I'll get the giblets going on low . . ." At that moment Johnny whimpered in her bedroom. "Darn . . . Johnny's awake already."

"I'll see to him!" Sean was out of the room before she could protest.

Shaking her head, Mae poured water over the giblets, added salt and adjusted the heat on the burner. Again, she couldn't help making a comparison between her two husbands. Peter had not felt comfortable with his son at all. Of course, Johnny had been terribly little. Why, initially, she'd been a bit afraid of how tiny he was herself.

"Hey!" The Irishman's voice boomed from her bedroom. "Ye little tur'!"

Banging down the giblet pan, Mae ran toward the bedroom. She rounded the door and took in the scene. Holding his shirt out from his body with two fingers, Sean glared down at Johnny on the bed. A fresh diaper, ready to pin, was folded beneath the baby. She covered a giggle. She knew exactly what had happened.

He looked up at her then scowled at the baby and pointed a long accusatory finger. "The little tur' pee'ed all over me shirt!"

Gurgling happily, Johnny kicked both feet in the air, his little peter wiggling like a tomato worm. Mae covered her face with both hands and peeked through her fingers. Laughter threatened.

" 'Tis no' funny! Me clean shirt's got baby pee all o'er it!" His sparkling eyes belied his fierce growl. "The bairn's a regular fountain!"

Mae wiped her eyes. "Oh, my! The expression on your face was so funny!" Sean laughed with her, then chuckled then finally, they were smiling at each other.

The silence intruded. They both became aware of it and their smiles faded faster than new denims.

"I . . . I didn't know you liked babies."

"I like your babies! I love your babies!" He restated huskily.

Shy blue eyes locked with sultry silver ones. "Mae!" he said and there was a moment in which all sounds were magnified. The baby's little spitting noises, the tick of the clock on the endtable. Outside, somewhere, Sandy barked.

She looked away and stood abruptly. She walked stiff-kneed to Johnny. She deftly pinned the baby's diaper, picked him up and set him in his crib. She looked at Sean. "Let me have your shirt." He had already unbuttoned his shirt and was yanking it from his belt. He wiped his chest with a clean diaper and Mae's eyes followed its path as if they were attached by a string. Ropy muscles rippled under skin the color and texture of smooth butterscotch. The black, wiry hair on his chest looked like a open umbrella with a narrow handle that went down somewhere below his belt line.

With her breath captive somewhere between her lungs and her lips, Mae folded one arm across her waist and pressed a hand to her lips. She knew she was staring like he was devil's food cake but she couldn't help herself. God, look at him!

Finally her gaze rose and met his eyes. He threw the diaper down. A long stride and he pulled her roughly to him, capping her shoulders. He shook her a little. "Mae! Please!"

The air crackled, sizzled then ignited. She sagged against him. He kneaded her body, malleable as bread dough, as he brushed kisses over her brow and neck.

His coaxing lips were close to her ear. "Ah, sweet gel, I'm dyin' for ye . . ."

Then at the corner of her lips, promising "I'll make it so foin' for ye, love . . ." And seducing . . . "Come with me. Where we can be alone."

She allowed her neck to roll to one side, silently offering it to his mouth. His nimble fingers were already through half the buttons of her dress. In a yet untouched place deep within her, a heated response waited. It sighed out with one word, "Yes!" Threading her fingers into his hair, she parted her lips. "Yes!"

Lowering her lids, she felt his warm breath on her lips. "Ah! Sweet . . . At last!" He pressed his arousal into the apex of her thighs. She stood on her tiptoes to feel it more fully then her feet left the floor. They both sighed.

"What's going on?" Uncle Ed's bedroom door across the hallway opened then shut with a bang. "The noise out here is enough to wake the dead."

Mae hit the floor running.

"Bloody Hell!" Behind her it sounded like a palm met the wall with quite a bit of force.

* * *

"Wonder what time Father Fitz will arrive." Uncle Ed asked.

With breakfast out of the way, Sean and Mae sat drinking coffee like any two normal people, as though neither one of them had any recollection of what had transpired a scant hour earlier. Every time he looked at her, Mae suffered a hitch in her breathing. And he looked at her constantly.

"I think early. When I saw him in town he said he planned to spend the day." Tilting his chair back, Sean reached for the coffeepot and refilled their cups. "You know, he's just a little guy, Mae, and you've been cooking for days. Who's going to eat all this food?"

"You two men are going to eat like lions!" Mae shook a finger at Uncle Ed and Sean. "You'd better bring your appetites to my table today. That reminds me," she took a folded piece of paper from between the salt and pepper shakers. "I'd better check my schedule." She scanned the paper. "Oh, see! I'm supposed to be putting the cream into Granny's salad right now. It says three hours before . . ."

"Where is it?" Sean stood. "I'll get it."

"On the porch in the blue porcelain bowl." Mae looked over her menu. Desserts—done. The apple strudel and pumpkin pies—on the porch. Cream for the pie and strudel topping—whipped. Granny's salad would soon be in its final phase. Turkey with dressing—in the oven. By the time Sean came back with the large shallow salad bowl, Mae was down to mashed potatoes and vegetables.

Sitting back down, Sean lit a smoke, and indicated her list. "What are you doing?"

"Well, I made a written schedule for myself of when to put things on. I want to make sure everything

will be ready at the exact same minute. This is my
first Thanksgiving with just me doing the cooking."
She consulted the list again. "I don't see how I can
possibly mess up. All the recipes in this little box are
either Granny's or Mama's. They were both wonderful
cooks. Still . . ."

"You're a wonderful cook." Covering her hand on
the table, Sean started that caress that was so disturb-
ing. "You're a good mother, a fine woman . . ."

Flushing, Mae pulled her hand out from under his.
"Please don't," she whispered for his ears only. She
simply couldn't take any more of his attention and
continue to function.

"He's right, Mae Ella. You can hold your own with
anyone in the cooking department. Matter of fact, I
think I've gained weight since you've been in charge
of the kitchen." Uncle Ed scooted his chair under the
table then patted Mae's back. "I'm going to check
the livestock. Have my chew." He left.

The tension in the room escalated along with Mae's
pulse. She searched her mind for something to say.
Something normal. Anything so it wasn't so quiet!
"Well, while I peel these potatoes, I think it's my turn
for our chat."

"I'll help." Taking a bumpy Idaho out of the burlap
bag propped against the table leg, Sean pulled over
a piece of newspaper Mae had spread on the table
earlier. He started wielding a knife. "Ask away, me
darlin'." Potato peelings gathered with amazing ra-
pidity on the paper.

"Why did you come here to Otter Tail?"

"Because of you." Dropping the peeled potato in
the waiting pan of water, he picked up another one.
"Next question."

Believing he was teasing, she cried angrily, "That's
not fair. You expected more detailed answers of me."

She picked up the potato he had just peeled, quartered it then dropped it back in the pan.

" 'Tis a true answer." Sean picked up another potato. "I saw you on the train."

"I don't remember seeing you." Her lips stretched petulantly.

"My ego is crushed," He covered his heart with his hand. He actually was a bit hurt. "But you were terribly distracted that day. Anyway, what matters is that I saw you. Ever since then, I couldn't get you out of my mind. You'd been crying. That bothered the hell out of me! I found myself thinking of you, wondering what was wrong. I became obsessed with seeing you again." He looked into her shocked face. He leaned closer, whispering. "Don't you know I love you?" Smiling, marveling at how easy the words were to say, he repeated them. "I love you."

"You love me?"

"Yes, I do."

She searched his face. The truth was there, naked and plain as day. "Really?"

"Really." Lifting her hand to his lips, he pressed a warm kiss onto her palm. His moustache tickled. "But I promise not to make a fool of myself. At least not any more than I already have."

She closed her hand, put it in her lap and covered it. The Irishman loved her!

He sighed. "I guess, long as I'm being so honest, I have to tell you the truth about something else as well." He frowned at the potato as if it had blight. "The word *lied* seems a bit harsh but that's what I might as well have done. And that isn't the way I want to start this marriage."

He stood and walked to the window and so missed Mae's stunned deer-in-the-lights stare. "Li- . . . Lied,

Sean?" she choked out before covering her mouth with her hand. She whimpered. *No! Oh, No!*

"Well, I definitely misled you."

She stood and put a hand on the table for support.

He turned and met her eyes. "I misled you by letting you think I wasn't anxious about bedding you."

Her mouth fell open. "Bedding me?" she cried, incredulous, "Is that what this is all about?" She thought he was going to tell her that he had gone to Chicago and murdered Peter in cold blood.

"Yes. I was afraid to overwhelm you with me ardor so when you asked me if I didn't mind waiting, I said 'oh, no problem,' as if I'm neither here nor there about it." He brought her hands to the center of his chest. "That's not so. I've a powerful craving for ye, gel."

If she doubted what he was saying she had only to look into his eyes. They burned with desire. Blushing, she asked, "Why did you say that then?"

"So you would consent to marry me." he said, adding softly. "I had to make sure ye would be mine someday." He cleared his throat. "But . . ." He patted her hands then sat and picked up the potato again. "A deal's a deal. Ours stands. Now, where was I? Oh, yeah."

Mae was admonishing herself. How insidious distrust is! With only a few words she had been prepared to believe him guilty of treachery. Was her confidence in his integrity so fragile?

"Why I left New York at the exact moment I did? Well, that's a whole other story completely. I left because I had gotten a job offer I couldn't refuse. A way to make a lot of money acting as a sort of informer for the police. Well, more for the government I guess."

"A spy, Sean?"

In for a penny, in for a pound, he thought and succumbed to a desire to tell her everything.

Everything?!

Well, not everything. Not after listening to Father Fitz's strangled noises in the darkened confessional. "Faith n' begorra! Faith n' begorra!" the priest had said over and over like a Gregorian chant.

"Sort of a spy," he allowed.

He briefly summarized his meetings with O'Brien, the terms of their agreement, and finally the events that led to his getting out of New York. "The government paid me to get some specific information. It was a trap and I had to shoot my way out. Two guys . . . died." Dropping another peeled potato into the pan full of water on the table, he raised his eyes to hers. "It was them or me."

Mae had stopped her movements. As outrageous as his revelations were, his tone of voice remained so matter-of-fact. "My God, Sean!"

"Well, it was them or me," he repeated. For a moment, there was silence then he said, "I vowed that those men—miserable crooks that they were—would be the last to meet their maker at my hand. An' I mean to keep my word."

Without realizing it he had just put her last misgivings about Peter's death—and any involvement he might have had in it—to rest.

Uncle Ed's shuffling entrance precluded further conversation. Mae touched the back of his hand with her fingers. Turning his hand over, he enclosed her much smaller one in his. They sat for a moment thus. Emotion gathered, triggering an almost irresistible urge to be held by him. "Sean . . ."

"Well, Father Fitz should be here just about any time now." Uncle Ed sat.

"Oh, no!" Shakily, Mae jumped up. "What time is it?" Her legs felt like the stems of a delphinium in bloom. "I want to bathe first!"

Fourteen

Mae was putting on Granny's sapphire earrings when she heard the wagon pull into the yard. Oh, my, Sean, she thought, back from picking up Mrs. Weltes already.

She hurried to the front door and caught a glimpse of herself in the oval mirror in the hall. She turned her head. The earrings tinkled and glittered. She smoothed her hair. It had been still slightly damp when she worked it into a figure-eight chignon. She'd anchored it with every bone pin she had, but hair was already starting to escape and curl around her face.

Oh, well, she thought and grimaced at her reflection. She smoothed her bodice. Her dress, a plum-colored taffeta gored with light blue insets in the bodice, skirt and hem, was her second best now, after her wedding dress. The insets, goring, and hem had been added two years earlier when Mae's bosom strained the seams and she started showing an inch of ankle. Dear Mama, Mae thought and was saddened. Only Mama, who was the best seamstress in the county, could have made it look like it was supposed to be that way.

A burst of cold air accompanied Sean and Mrs. Weltes inside.

"Hello, my dear Mae Ella. My, it's bitter out. The snow's stopped but I don't know for how long." Mrs.

Weltes removed her snow dusted hat. "I hope the girls will be warm enough until I get home."

Mrs. Weltes' girls were two fat house cats.

She switched a large tin from hand to hand while Sean helped her remove her coat then she lifted the lid like it was a treasure chest. "Look, Mae Ella, all your favorites."

Mae dutifully peered inside the tin, which was triple-layered with homemade hard candies. "Oh, Mrs. Weltes, every color of the rainbow. You've outdone yourself!"

"Here comes Father," Sean said and opened the door.

"God Bless all in this house!" The priest said, stamping his feet then stepping over the threshold.

"I'll see to your horse, Father."

"Thank you, Ed."

Sean took the priest's black three-quarter length jacket into one of the bedrooms.

"I hope you don't mind that I'm out of uniform, Mae Ella?"

"Oh, heavens, no . . ." Mae got that much out and then was at a loss for words.

"I decided I'd dress like you normal folks today."

Normal folks? Leaving his dog collar at home was the least of it. Wearing a woolen sweater with a diamond pattern like Uncle Ed's argyle socks, pants with big navy and white checks and a tartan plaid scarf, Mae thought the priest looked like the clown that ran out and entertained the crowd between acts during a traveling show!

"It smells great in here!" Out of a burlap bag, Father Fitz drew a bottle of John Jameson Irish whiskey and a bottle of German Riesling, both of which he handed to Sean. To Mae he made a courtly bow and extended a box of Becknell's Finest Chocolates. "An' may I say you look like a breath of Irish springtime, Mrs. McGloin!"

Mrs. Weltes looked pointedly at the chocolates and frowned.

Mae thanked him for the compliment and the chocolates, and set them on the hall table. "Dinner's in about an hour."

As he had been directed to do, Sean steered the priest and Mrs. Weltes into the parlor. "We can have a glass of wine in the parlor." Like a kid, he looked back at Mae for her approval.

Mae nodded and followed. She was proud of the nicely furnished room. She smiled inwardly. Father and Mrs. Weltes should have seen the place yesterday. In order to clean thoroughly, she'd asked Sean and her uncle to carry everything into the hallway. Amid mutterings like ". . . you'd think it was the second comin' . . ." and ". . . heard fumes from that cleaning stuff is poisonous . . ." they complied. Early this morning she replaced the hand-washed, tatted doilies and antimacassars on the arms and backs of the matching brown couch and settee—after pressing the fabrics flat between two Sears Roebuck catalogs. She lit the two glass lamps with tasseled shades on the end tables, and uncovered the spinet. It sparkled and Mae glowed with pride.

Mae perched nervously on the edge of Granny's great aunt's ornately carved spool rocker. She watched Father Fitz take a circle of smoked sausage and slice of cheese off the plate strategically positioned on the side table.

"So, Sean," Father Fitz chewed on the appetizer, "how's that renovation project going? The one you were telling me about last week?"

Concerned with whether or not the sausage might be too spicy, Mae had intended to observe Father

Fitz's expression after swallowing. Instead, she looked curiously at Sean. "What renovation project?"

"Well, I was going to surprise Mae . . ."

"Oh, me an' me big mouth! I'm sorry, man!" Father Fitz looked chagrined.

"No, it's all right." Absolving him with a wave of his hand, Sean looked at her. "Mae, I was playing around with some plans for the unfinished attic area, thinking maybe I could make it into a nice big room up there, add a fireplace. Even put a fireplace in this room if you like—right about over there." Sean pointed right behind Mae to the common wall between the parlor and the kitchen.

"Oh, wouldn't that be nice, Mae?" Mrs. Weltes exclaimed.

Mae twisted in her seat and looked at the blank wall. A fireplace! She looked at Sean. The man shocked her—left and right! Fireplaces, falling in love on sight . . .

"I was thinking of one that would be open on one side into the kitchen and on the other side in here."

"That's an intriguing concept." Father Fitz said with interest. "I have always enjoyed doing that sort of thing myself! I love to putter around and build things. Do you have a sketch done?"

"Why, yes. As a matter of fact, I have drawn up some preliminary blueprints."

"Blueprints?" Mae asked. "What are blueprints?"

Father Fitz stood. "I, for one, would love to see them. That is, if you don't mind, Sean?"

"Well, of course, I'm still in the development stage, you understand . . ."

The three men left the room, trailed by Mrs. Weltes. Mae heard Uncle Ed comment. "I've seen those plans. Boy, they are pret-tee darned fancy, I can tell you. I'll just get my glasses out of my bedroom."

Alone, clutching her small glass of wine, Mae looked at the virtually untouched appetizer tray. Her plan was for everyone to sit in here until dinnertime, chatting! From the kitchen, she heard the underlying excitement in Sean's voice and the sound of chairs being moved around.

"Now, Father Fitz, set the salt and pepper shaker on that edge and the sugar bowl on the other so I can unfurl . . ."

Unfurl? Mae jumped up like she'd been goosed.

"Mrs. Weltes, will you hold that edge? Ed . . . ?"

"Got it."

Mae stood in the door.

All four of her guests were bent over a large piece of cream-colored paper that covered a good fourth of the kitchen table. With difficulty, she elbowed her way between Father Fitz and Uncle Ed. She looked at the drawings. Blue ink lines went every whichway. "So, that's why they're called blueprints," she murmured to herself.

Tiny numbers in precise writing ran up and down the edges. Arrows pointed from several small sections to big boxes where those sections had been redrawn on a larger scale. Sean pointed at the paper then towards various parts of the house. Mae tried to follow what he was saying.

". . . right about there. Now, Father, if you please . . ." Father Fitz held up the salt and pepper shakers and Sean removed the top layer of paper, revealing another intricate and just as elaborate drawing beneath. Father Fitz rolled up the first paper, stuck it under his arm and leaned over again. "Here's the second level." Sean anchored the second drawing, smoothing a large hand down it almost lovingly. "The fireplace is here. I figured I'd cut the hole in the ceiling there." Sean pointed with a short stubby pencil to the ceiling above the wood burning stove and all heads rotated like at a lawn-tennis match to look in that direction. "That'll take care of additional heat up there. I can cover it with a cast-iron grate so it'll look nice. I was thinking of a custom-built armoire against this entire wall." Everyone including Mae tilted toward the far side of the paper where there was a furious concentration of tiny lines. "And, over here . . ." Looking up, Sean met Mae's wide eyes and pointed with a sweeping flourish. ". . . is the bathroom!"

"Ah!" Mae released the breath she had been holding.

Father Fitz whistled through crooked teeth, and shook his head in amazement. "Can ye do all that yerself, man? 'Tis quite an undertaking!"

"Yes, I can!" Sean folded his arms confidently.

Mae believed him implicitly! There wasn't anything the Irishman couldn't do. "Oh, Sean! A bathroom? Right inside the house?"

"Yes! I've sent for all the books I need to figure out the piping. I'll need steel pipes for the water supply lines and cast-iron pipes for the sewer lines. Unfortunately, I have to wait until spring to actually bring the water lines in." Sean smiled at Mae then looked at Ed. "What's your opinion, Ed, about diggin' an extra well this spring? How far down are we talkin'?"

Her uncle's face took on a thoughtful look. Mae could tell he was pleased and she could have kissed Sean for bringing him into the thick of things.

"You know, I think that you'd be mighty smart to do that, Sean. Wouldn't take much either. I remember Mae Ella's father said his folks only had to go down about twenty-five feet. And, if you ran an extra line, it'd be a good backup in a dry spell. We could try just north of the garden."

Father Fitz and Uncle Ed walked back toward the

parlor, talking. Apologetically, Sean looked at the drawings then at her. "Mae, I was going to draw up these plans then ask if you wanted me to make the changes. After all, this is your home. I don't want to overstep myself."

"And now this is your home too, Sean." Mae laid her hand on his arm. "I'm just so surprised! Very surprised." She smiled at him. "And very, very pleased."

"Really?"

She returned his smile and let her eyes run over him. She rested her hand on his chest and spread her fingers. She felt his heartbeat, the heat of him. She leaned closer.

Father Fitz came back into the kitchen, rubbing his hands in anticipation. "Ed said, if there's time before dinner, maybe I could get a look at the construction site."

Sean and Mae, lips an inch from joining, sprang apart.

Sean swallowed a word unfitting for a priest's ear. "Sean?"

"All right. If you don't mind climbing into the attic. At least I can assure you that you won't be meeting your maker. I just finished replacing the stairs."

Father Fitz looked up the new, wider, as yet unpainted staircase. "That was a job in itself, wasn't it?"

He looked at Sean who smiled and replied, "Not really," then at Mae.

"It was a big job but Sean made it seem easy." Mae smiled at Sean.

"Well," mentally Father Fitz did a Lady Macbeth with his hands. So tha's how 'tis, he thought. "Let's have a look see!"

"I think I'll stay down here and help Mae," said Mrs. Weltes.

The three men's legs disappeared up the attic stairs. Mae'd seen that old dusty attic. She had no intention of getting her dress all dirty. She planted her elbows on the elaborate drawing, studying it. Mrs. Weltes joined her. "Isn't this amazing, Mrs. Weltes?"

"I'll say!" She angled her chin sideways. "Wonder if that little rectangle over there is the front door?"

"No, I think it's the bathroom window!"

"Or maybe the hearth . . ." Mrs. Weltes leaned closer.

"I'll ask Sean when he comes down, Mae said and was embarrassed to learn it was a rather artistic ink-blot.

"Dinner couldn't have been better, my dear!" Father Fitz smiled at Mae.

"I'll second that. Superb, love, simply superb!" Sean held his wineglass up to her in a salute.

"Yes, indeed, Mae Ella," Mrs. Weltes said.

"I think I'm gonna need either a nap or a long walk." Indeed, Ed's eyes were heavy lidded.

Bowing her head, Mae said, "Thank you," and repeated the same in her heart to Granny and Mama.

Everyone carried something into the kitchen until there were so many platters and dishes, there was no room left on the kitchen table. Mae practically had to restrain Sean and Father from helping with the cleanup. "I'd really rather have a few minutes to get things organized myself. Really!" She knew it was hopeless to try and keep Mrs. Weltes out of the kitchen.

Dessert choices were discussed and voted upon but it was unanimously agreed that the actual serving should be delayed until later. Father and Uncle Ed took a brief walk then returned to the dining room. Mae heard snatches of their conversation as she and Mrs. Weltes washed the dishes and straightened the kitchen.

". . . a fella by the name of Jim Thorpe at the Carlisle Indian School in Pennsylvania . . ." Mae carried the covered bowl with the remaining pork sausage and sage stuffing out to the porch.

". . . that crazy Kaiser . . . keeps fartin' around . . . war . . ." She pulled a chair over, stood on it and replaced Granny's nice serving dishes to their display area above the cabinet. Passing the open door to the parlor, Mae peeked in.

". . . liked the way Roosevelt handled that miners' strike . . ."

She shook her head. The cigarette smoke was so thick the room looked like it was on fire.

". . . we need less government, not more. I bet the first thing that new Commerce and Labor Department tries to do is tell people how to mind their own business . . ."

She placed a small bowl of pickled beets in the wooden icebox on the back porch and in spite of the cold, stood there a minute. She wrapped her arms around her chest. There was about an inch of snow on the ground but it smelled like more. Opening the back door, she leaned out and turned her face up to the dusky sky. Their weather normally came from the northwest but the part of the sky that looked ominous was toward the south. Very ominous. Mrs. Weltes joined her. "You probably want to save this carcass for turkey soup . . . Oh, my," she said, looking out at the sky, "I hate to drag Sean away but I think I better get home."

"Oh, he won't mind in the least. I'll go call him."

* * *

Mrs. Weltes untied the apron she'd used to protect her twill dress. Sean, with his coat on already, held hers open for her. "Mae. Sean. I hope it isn't in poor taste to bring this up now . . ."

Her tone of voice caused both of them to look at her. Sean thought her face, long and sallow as that of a Goya king, had become longer still. ". . . but I wanted to let you know that I'm going to put my place up for sale after the first of the year."

"Oh, Mrs. Weltes. The Weltes have lived over there longer than the Botts!"

"Yes, I know. Believe me, I know. But what can I do? I can no longer handle it, financially or physically." She sighed. "I hate to but it's just too much for me, riding herd on the hired help and being totally alone all winter. And . . . ," she folded the apron and patted it, ". . . I need the money. Even after the sale of most of my things, I'll still have to get some sort of work in town."

"Oh, Mrs. Weltes." Mae went to her.

"Will you talk to us first, ma'am? Before you sell?" Sean asked.

"Us, Sean?" Mae asked.

"Yes. We, Mae and I, might be interested in buying."

"But Sean, if you plan to work all of Uncle Ed's fields and all of ours too, don't you think that will be plenty to handle?"

"Maybe. But I can always hire on help." He helped Mrs. Weltes into her coat. "A person can never have too much land, to my way of thinking. I want enough so any child we have, boy or girl, can stay right here if they choose to and there'd be enough land for them to make a decent living."

Mae's heart swelled.

"Good-bye, dear. Thank you for a wonderful day."

"Bye, Mrs. Weltes." Their cheeks met.

"I'll be right back, Mae." Sean kissed her briefly.

"All right." She walked to the door with them. Enough land for everyone. What a wonderful thought.

"This is a fine old instrument. Bavarian, isn't it?" Father pointed to the spinet.

Mae trailed her fingers lovingly over the inlaid wood border. "Yes, it is. It came from the old country when Granddad and Granny moved here. It was about the only thing they had of any value. I guess it was a bone of contention between my grandparents. Granny told me she wanted to sell it many times when they were financially strapped but Granddad always refused. They used to have big arguments about it. "Ve'll starf to death first!" Granny said Granddad would try to be very bossy with her, if she let him."

"Do you play, love?" Sean asked.

"You know, it's the craziest thing. I had about a hundred lessons from both Mama and Granny but I never got the hang of it. For some reason, I just don't have the ability to take the notes from the page and make them sound like they should when I play." She smiled up at Sean as his arm encircled her shoulder.

"Well, I can play! Not very well but I can play!" Sitting down, Father Fitz heavy-handedly banged out a tune Mae had never heard before and exclaimed, "Ye'll be rememberin' this one, Sean me boyo!" Surprising Mae with his exuberance, he burst into song, ". . . Jack Duggan was his name . . . he was born and bred in Ireland in a town called . . ."

Setting down his glass of Irish whiskey, Sean folded his arms, leaned his hip against the spinet and sang.

Mae's mouth dropped open. She looked at Father Fitz and Uncle Ed and saw similarly surprised faces. Sean's voice was . . . was like nothing she'd ever heard before!

Smiling and swaying, Father Fitz harmonized with Sean. Uncle Ed, sitting on the settee, swung his crossed leg and his shot glass of sippin' whiskey in time. At the end of the tune, everyone looked at Sean, who had the decency to turn a little red under his tan.

Father Fitz commented first. "Ye've a foin Irish tenor here, Mae. Foin as any I've ever had the pleasure of hearin'."

Mae just stared with awe at her husband. She finally found her tongue. "Why, I've never heard such a beautiful voice in all my life!"

Uncle Ed piped in. "You should consider vaudeville!"

Sean scoffed and jerked his chin. He clasped Mae to him again, fitting her shoulder neatly under his. " 'Tis only what the Irish are known for—making love and singing!"

Trying gamely to join in with the mirth making, Mae's laugh sounded more like a bleat to her. Boy, if he made love anything like he sang . . .

"Aye, 'tis true, aye, God knows, 'tis true." Father Fitz shook his head. "Tha' an' the drink, God bless 'em!" Father Fitz pulled one ankle over his knee and prepared a cigarette. "Seriously, have ye ever thought of singing professionally, Sean?"

"Nah! But it got me a few good meals in New York."

Uncle Ed asked, "How so?" Halfway to the kitchen to get the coffeepot, Mae abruptly detoured. Sitting down, she folded her hands primly and looked with interest at her husband. For another bit of personal information about the Irishman, the coffee could wait.

"Well, one time I was at a place near where I worked . . ." Sean glanced over at Father Fitz. "Uh, maybe you've heard of the place, Father. Flaherty's?"

"Ah, yes, Flaherty's. Indeed, I've heard of it. Just recently, too." Father Fitz's head was wreathed by a ring of blue smoke.

Flaherty's? Mae wondered if Flaherty's was anything like that famous place Delmonico's. She'd read about all the rich people who frequented Delmonico's, about its gold fountains and plush carpets. She made a mental note to ask Sean later.

"On St. Pat's last year, I don't know if I had a bit too much or what but some of the guys started singing a tune I'm fond of. For whatever reason, I joined in. I was never one to sing in public but everybody could sing in my family. You should've heard me Mam! Singing certain seditious tunes—you know the ones, Father—she could make a grown man cry like a baby." Striking a match off his boot, he lit his smoke and inhaled deeply before continuing. "It was not long after that that, two little old ladies come knocking on me flat door early one morning. Seems some mick died, all the way out in the Sheepshead Bay section of Brooklyn. The ladies had come to see if I'd sing at his wake! Well, at first, after I got over the shock that those two ladies had traveled all that way just to see me, I said, "Go on with ye!" They were serious! And stubborn as mules. They wouldn't take no for an answer. I couldn't ask them into me flat and I couldn't very well close the door smack in their faces. They said 'twas their only brother had died. Finally, I said I would do it. You know, I figured I'd just get rid of them. But then me conscience started to bother me and I thought, what the hell? I knew I'd get a free meal out of the deal." Shrugging, Sean looked over at Father Fitz for confirmation.

"You know how good the eats are at an Irish wake, Father."

"To say nothin' of the free booze." Father Fitz's eyes sparkled.

"Anyway, after that, seemed like three or four times a month some ladies would come tapping at me flat door. Always traveling in pairs like nuns, they would be from St. Jerome's Rosary Society or St. Peter's Ladies Auxiliary, asking if I would come to their church on such and such day. Sometimes one of them would be the relative—the sister or the wife—of some mick." He laughed. "They were like maggots in an open wound."

Mae blanched, then steadfastly refixed her smile.

As he was looking intently at the toe of his boot, a faint slash of color brushed the Irishman's high cheekbones. "Guess I'm a sucker for a sad story. I pretty much did it, time permitting." He looked at the three people watching him. "Well, dinna look at me like that. 'Twas sad to me, you know, that some bloke should die with nae a person to sing for him."

"I think that's wonderful!" Mae whispered, interrupting the silence that followed Sean's story. "Just wonderful!" Walking over to him, she pulled on his shirt until he lowered his head and kissed him softly, lingeringly. "What a good person you are, Irishman."

Pulling her to him, Sean deepened their embrace, kissing her back thoroughly. "Ah, woman, ye'll be the death o' me!" he whispered hoarsely.

He forgot where they were.

She forgot where they were . . . until reason returned. Pushing away, she smoothed a hand over her hair and inquired somewhat breathlessly. "More coffee, Father? Uncle Ed?"

"No, thank you." Father Fitz waved an arm to her.

"Come on over here, Mae. I'll bet you know this one!"

Feeling blazing eyes on her, Mae joined the priest at the spinet. Her skin felt so warm, she was tempted to open a window. Drawn like a sailor to the Lorelei, Sean moved to stand beside her.

Father played the familiar introduction of the most popular tune that year, then launched into "In the Good Old Summer Time!"

Smiling and humming, Mae rested her hand on the spinet first, then sang softly along with the priest until she was certain she recalled all the words. Then, with a burst of enthusiasm, she sang.

Father Fitz's fingers faltered. He almost stopped playing. He looked up at Sean with a deeply furrowed brow.

Swinging his head toward the awful noise, Sean looked down. Mae, not a dying animal, swayed within the curve of his arm.

Standing with her eyes closed, hands clasped prayerfully, a rapturous expression on her upturned face, she was singing her heart out. There was the click of toenails against wood as the dog left his spot by the fire.

Sean's words stumbled. He glared at Father Fitz. Hanging his head between skinny shoulders, the priest was doing a pee-poor job of disguising his laughter. The sight almost caused Sean to lose his control. He bit the inside of his cheek. Painfully, displaying what he considered extreme control and a fortitudinous character (to keep from laughing, he thought of the time he had had that bad case of body lice), he managed to continue singing until the end of the tune.

"Oh, Father! That was so much fun!" Mae's lovely face was flushed, radiant with happiness. "Let's sing another one! Do you know 'Sweet Adeline'?"

Sean moved fast. He was already at the kitchen door. "You two go ahead. I . . . I want to get some more coffee."

Leaping up, Father Fitz practically flew from the room. "I'll be back in one second to play it for you, Mae."

Mae strolled over to the settee and straightened the antimacassar behind her uncle's head. Leaning down, she whispered conspiratorially, "Did you see how fast Father Fitz was moving just then? He must have waited too long to go to the privy." She cupped her mouth and chuckled. "Even his voice sounded strained."

"Hmm? Yes, well . . ." Uncle Ed pried himself off the couch. "I think I'll just . . ."

While waiting for everyone to return, Mae reflected on what a lovely day it had been! She sat on the polished bench and trailed her fingers across the worn spinet keys without exerting pressure. Maybe I should start trying to play again, she thought. I was pretty young when Granny and Mama suggested I might not want to continue my lessons. I just love to sing! Mae pictured long, wintry evenings during which she and Sean, backlit by a roaring fire in the new fireplace, could harmonize together. He could teach her those lively Irish tunes. Oh, how nice! She sighed contentedly.

"You'll have to stay now, Father. You can't travel in this mess." Sean shrugged into his fleece-lined jacket, preparing to see to the livestock.

Everyone stood on the back porch staring into the swirling whiteout. "See," Uncle Ed said proudly. "I told you guys we'd have a serious snowstorm by Thanksgiving. Well, here it is!"

Snow was falling so rapidly and with such magnitude that a good six inches had accumulated already. Natives Ed and Mae knew it was the kind that fell and stayed.

"You won't see the ground again until April," Ed said.

"I thought it smelled like snow earlier. I meant to come back out but I got so caught up in the singing." Mae wrapped her arms around herself. "You know, I think the temperature has dropped quite a bit in the last hour. No, there's no question of your traveling tonight. We wouldn't find you until spring!" To herself, Mae added, in spite of your outfit! Smiling, she walked to the door, rubbing her arms. "There's no problem, Father. I'll just get a room ready for you."

Uncle Ed slipped into his high-top galoshes and leaned down to snap the few remaining buckles. "I'll latch these porch shutters down then take care of the milking."

As she entered her parents' old bedroom to prepare it for Father Fitz, Mae saw one of Sean's shirts lying across the bed. The air left her lungs like the day she fell out of the red oak and her stomach met with a pumpkin.

"I can bunk in with Ed or sleep in the barn," Sean said.

"Oh no! Don't do that," Mae whispered, blushing. "I don't want Father to know that . . . well, you know . . ." Pacing a few feet away, she chewed on her lower lip. "And it's too cold in the barn now."

"Oh? Well, if you think so."

The twinkle in his eyes annoyed her. Mae thought through the alternatives once again and concluded, again, that there were none. Earlier, she'd changed the linens on the bed Sean had been occupying and, while Father Fitz was elsewhere, had tiptoed across the hall into her bedroom with armloads of his belongings. Her parents' old bedroom, the nicest, largest and closest to the heat was the only one she would consider offering to the priest. There was no alternative! They would have to sleep together. "We'll have to sleep together, just for tonight!"

"Oh, no!" He made a tsking sound with his tongue but had turned away. "Well, I suppose if you insist." He pulled his shirt out of his pants.

Something was suspect about the Irishman's voice. "Are you laughing?" Mae hated to be the butt of someone's humor. "Boy, you just better not be laughing. This is not a bit funny! We had a deal to . . . you know . . . to chat and . . . you know . . . chat some more." Of course, he wasn't upset by these untoward events. He had made no bones about what he wanted.

He smiled innocently, sat on the bed and pulled off one boot. She kept her eyes glued to his face, purposely not looking at his bare chest.

"I can converse in a horizontal position."

"As well as a lot of other things," he added under his breath.

"You know what I mean! I don't intend to be rushed!" She turned around, arms folded and paced the length of the room. After everyone was asleep, she could slip out to the couch in the parlor. Oh, if Father Fitz caught her sleeping on the couch in the parlor, she would just die of embarrassment! Still, she was going to die of embarrassment anyway, crawling into bed with a person she barely knew from Adam!

Wrenching open the door, she tiptoed down the hallway, pulled on her father's old coat and started wrapping a plaid scarf of unknown ownership around her neck.

"Where're you going?"

She jumped at the sound of his booming voice behind her. Shirt hanging open, flaunting his manly chest, he stood in the doorway in his socks.

In his socks!

She waved frantically. "Go back!" Quickly glancing at the door into which Father Fitz had just disappeared, she scurried toward him. "Father might come out and see you any minute!"

He stretched to rest his forearm on the doorjamb. Mae's eyes crossed. His furry armpit was at eye level and an inch away. She stepped back, refocused and wrenched her gaze upward. "Go back inside!"

"What's wrong with Father Fitz seeing me?"

"Practically naked?"

"I don't think I'd shock him." Sean scratched his taut stomach indolently then smiled at her. "You didn't say where you were going, love."

God, if that's a whisper! "Shhh!" Mae ran in place. "Well?"

She spoke through clenched teeth, too upset to be ladylike. "To the blamed outhouse!"

"I'd better come along . . ."

Her jaw dropped. "Come along? Absolutely not! Why ever would you come along? I've been going to the . . . privy on my own since I was three."

"Why don't you use the . . . ?" He waved behind him.

Use the chipped china chamber pot under her bed? She looked at him as if he'd just asked her to eat worms. "Absolutely not!" Even if he waited outside and she hummed he would know, she would know . . . "No," she said.

She'd only opened the door an inch when the storm's ferocity hit her full force. The wind grabbed the door out of her hand and slammed it against the house. It almost whipped off her scarf before she snatched it back. Sinking down into the soft snow over her boot tops, her face, the only part of her exposed, prickled and was immediately glazed with frost.

Every year word would come of some farmer who had frozen to death within inches of shelter. Holding her coat closed with one hand, she reached for the thick lifeline rope coiled to the right of the door, found the end of it and started trudging blindly toward the outhouse.

Mae always thought there was something awe-inspiring about the first snowstorm of winter. When she was a kid, she imagined that God looked down on the little farm and said, "Hey! You guys down there! Watch this!" Forgetting to inhale shallowly, she took a deep breath. Frigid dry air seared the moisture in her lungs and caused stabbing discomfort in her chest.

Finally, she slowed, sensing she was close. With both arms straight out, she connected with the privy door. She patted blindly up and down until she felt the metal latch. Holding onto it with one mittened hand, she wrapped the end of the rope around and around the hook on the outhouse wall before attempting to open the door. A big bank of drifting snow blocked it. She kicked at the snow with her boot and simultaneously tugged on the door. "Bugger!" One day a few weeks back, Mae had been on the other side of the barn door when she heard the Irishman say, "Bugger, Ed! Ye drapped tha' rock righ' on me foot."

"Well, your damned foot's a yard long."

"Nae any more!"

Obviously *bugger* was an Irish swear word! Mae decided on the spot that she liked it a lot better than *darn!* Last week, when Johnny threw up his lunch on her unprotected shoulder, she'd laid him down. "I'll be right back, sweetie." Elbows out and pumping, she had scurried down the hall and into the storage room. She closed the door. "Bugger! Bugger!" Well, no wonder men like to curse, she'd thought as she experienced a wonderful release.

"Double bugger!" she shouted, challenging the wind tumultuously, and losing.

At last, she wedged the door open and swung it back and forth several times leaving a fan-shaped swath in the snow. "My own fault. I should have brought the shovel," she muttered. Soon as she stepped over the wooden ledge and the door slammed behind her, she sighed with relief.

In the dead silence and pitch darkness, standing in the outhouse was like being inside a block of black ice. With chattering teeth, she removed one mitten and held it in her mouth, afraid to lay it down for fear she would never find it again. She pulled up her skirts with one hand and pulled her underpants down with the other. She felt behind her, scraping her knuckles twice on the rough wood wall before her frozen fingers found the stack of damp paper.

Her exposed derrière came into contact with the frost-caked wood around the seat's open circle. "Arrgh!" Arctic air blew up through cracks in the old structure, seizing her goosebump-covered privates like a fist and instantly halting any release. "Oooh!" She concentrated. Nothing. She told herself she was warm as toast. Nothing. She did what had worked when she was a child. She closed her eyes and transported herself back in time.

Ah, there she was! Sitting on the riverbank, wearing her lucky straw bonnet and fishing for sand pike. Boy, was it hot! She had just been swimming. Her petticoat was pulled up under her arms, her legs bare to the sun. She counted the May flies that dipped and soared over the lily pads.

Nothing! It wasn't working!

Maybe it was because her mental picture was a little girl one.

She closed her eyes again. "Ah!" A wonderfully warm image was forming. She was standing in a sun-filled, saffron yellow room. In its center, on a raised platform strewn with pink rose petals, was a claw-foot bathtub. Slipper-shaped, the zinc tub shone like a new penny. Little snaky lines of heat rose from the azure water within. Scented soaps and a quart bottle of Enchantment cologne lay cushioned in fluffy, bedspread-sized towels. An oval-shaped, gilt-edged mirror hung on one wall. It was covered with steam. A row of green plants with wide, variegated leaves sat in the deep sill of a bright, mullioned window. The window was open and white eyelet curtains fluttered in a light summer breeze.

She could see it, plain as day. "Oh! How lovely!" A bathroom, right in the house! She sighed, rubbing her arms in sensual delight. Suddenly, a bare-chested, sock-clad Irishman floated into her mind's eye and stood grinning at her from the doorway. Her eyes flew open! "Oh! Bugger!"

When Mae returned to the dimly lit bedroom, the Irishman was already in *her* bed, propped up against *her* headboard with *her* pillow folded double behind his back. Irrational as she knew it to be, every bit of her pique returned. And then some. Obviously he wasn't planning to wear a nightshirt. The thought made Mae's heart thump and her skin prickle with warmth.

With warmth? How could that be? She stood in the open doorway with big globs of snow clumped on her hair. She glared openly at him. Big, hairy (did he have hair everywhere?) forearms lay across his middle and a glowing cheroot stuck rakishly out of his clenched teeth. Folded neatly back over the counterpane were white sheets that bisected his chest right under his nipples and contrasted like night and day with the darkness of his skin.

She knew it was irrational, especially in view of their rapport earlier, but the mere sight of him just bedeviled the hell out of her. Somehow the storm, the cold, the sleeping arrangements—the fact that she'd gotten a C-minus in geography when she was eleven—*all* could be directly attributable to the cocky Irishman.

She wanted to stomp over there and smack him!

Besides, he was taking up so much room in the bed there wasn't any more than an inch of space on either side of him. Where was she supposed to sleep? On the rug?

And where was she supposed to get undressed? In the kitchen? She also didn't care one bit for his cat-and-the-canary grin.

She curled her lip and tiptoed to the side of the bed. He smiled. She fumed.

In a hoarse whisper, she inquired, "Mr. McGloin! I hope it isn't going to be necessary to remind you of our agreement?"

"Sean. And no. I most certainly remember our agreement. Yes, indeed, I do." He had removed the cheroot to facilitate his reply then stuck it back in his mouth.

Leaning closer, she pointed behind her. "Father Fitz is just across the hall and he can hear everything, especially if he's left his door ajar for heat." A large glob of snow melted, slid down the nape of her neck and into her dress. She rolled her shoulders. "I don't want to have to . . . to argue with you . . ."

"Argue? I have no intention of arguing. I've barely said a word. You're the chatterbox."

She stuck a finger in her wet collar and held it away from her neck. "I'm just not ready for this yet."

"Ready for what, love?"

"You know what! *That!* I can see by . . . I told you before we were married that I can't crawl into bed with someone I hardly know!" She whipped a towel off the washstand and started toweling her hair.

"Why not? People do it all the time."

Lifting the towel, Mae peeked wide eyed at him. "They do?"

"Well, yes actually." How, he wondered, could the gel look like a drowned rat and the most beautiful thing he'd ever seen—simultaneously.

"They do?" She repeated.

"That can be one of your questions when we have another of our get-acquainted chats." Stubbing out his smoke, he flipped the covers back. "Here you go!"

Gasping, Mae dropped the towel over her face again.

"Hop in 'fore you catch your death!"

"Just a minute!" She snuck a quick look in his direction from under the towel. "You have to turn off the light so I can get into my nightgown."

"All right."

She waited a few seconds then chose an unfortunate moment to peep.

He was sitting up and stretching across the bed for the lamp. The covers dropped below his waist. The light went out.

Frozen, she stood with the image of a navel imprinted on the inside of her tightly closed eyelids.

God, didn't he have anything on? Not even his underwear? It was obvious from his bare chest that he wasn't wearing a nightshirt but, certainly, at the very least, he would have the decency to leave his knickers on! Oh, God. Wouldn't his knickers cover his navel? She found her navel and stuck her finger in it. Decidedly, definitely below her waistline.

Under the cover of the towel, Mae chewed her cuticle. She'd seen the men in her household at one time or another over the years. Her father wore a nightshirt. Uncle Ed wore a nightshirt. Sometimes, if it was really cold, Uncle Ed wore his union suit too. Peter had always worn a nightshirt. She'd just assumed that all men did, but obviously some men didn't.

It was pitch black. She shuffled to the dresser, remembering to be wary of rubber balls or wooden toys and opened the second drawer. She fumbled until she found her most decorous nightrail. All noises seemed magnified in the total dark. The scrape of the drawer opening. Sean's polite cough. The rustle of the covers. Another polite cough. The creak of the bed when he moved. Unbuttoning her dress she could hear the snick of bone button against fabric. God! She could even hear Uncle Ed snore. Under normal conditions, she never heard Uncle Ed snore. There was another cough.

Had consumption set in?

She stepped out of her dress and laid it over the nearby rocking chair. It would be wrinkled in the morning but she would rather press it again than have to delay this any longer. She struggled into her nightrail, buttoning every button carefully. Shuffling slowly toward the bed, when she met the mattress with her knee, she tentatively put out a hand. And connected with smooth warm skin. *"Arghh!"*

"Well, what do ye think? 'Tis me arm." His voice smiled. *"Shhh!"*

"Did ye forget I was here, or what?"

"Shhh! I told you these old walls are so thin, you can hear everything!" First sitting on the bed, after a long, courage mustering minute Mae's feet left the floor and she slid under the covers. Lying back, she encountered a long, rock-hard arm behind her. She sat bolt upright immediately. "Oh!"

"Sorry." His voice sounded sincere. "Here, let me move further over."

"All right. Well, yes, if you could . . ." She lay down and the back of her head met his shoulder. She popped back up again. "Do you mind?"

"Sorry. Here, I'll just turn on me side."

Gingerly, Mae lay down. He made a big flip onto his side, the bed folded up and they came together like the clap of two hands. "Ah!" Mae stuck her butt out and pushed him away. Her palms rested on a warm, thumping chest. She snatched them back and slowly slid into him. She sat up.

"This really is a small bed, isn't it?"

She heard and felt his accommodating movements. Cautiously, she reclined again and encountered only her own pillow. "This will never work!"

"Why not?" he asked innocently.

She felt his breath on the side of her face. A hard thigh pressed her leg. Chest hairs brushed against that part of her arm that was exposed below the elbow. And she was perched against the very rim of the bed. "It just will never work." A long, wide foot came in contact with her small, cold one. She slid both feet over until they stuck out from under the covers.

"Sorry."

He realigned his legs. Slowly, ever alert, she

brought her freezing feet back under the covers. Having become accustomed to the poor light, she was able to see him. Lying with one arm curved back under his head, apparently he was studying her profile. Out of the corner of her eyes, careful not to move her head, she watched him. If she kept her eyes riveted sideways for long, she'd have a terrible headache. As a matter of fact, she thought she felt a headache coming on already.

She would never ever be able to sleep a wink! She was lying next to a brick wall. A hot, hairy brick wall.

"Well, since neither one of us is going right to sleep, whose turn is it?"

"Turn?"

"Whose turn is it to ask a question?"

"Yours, I think. Yes. Yours."

"Good! Give me a minute." Rolling over onto his back, he reached for his smokes and the old feather mattress folded up again on the edges, flipping Mae into his side.

"Sorry."

"That's all right."

"Are you warm enough?"

"Yes!" Mae was burning up! Heat radiated from him. Only her toes were a teeny bit cold. She moved them closer to the center of the bed.

"Well, let's see."

She relaxed a bit. Their question-and-answer time had become a familiar ritual. A match flared and his face was illuminated in its glow before he shook it out. She relaxed further.

It was the Irishman. Not a total stranger. Actually, she reminded herself impatiently, her husband.

There was a particularly loud snort from Ed's room

and Sean said, "How on earth did his wife ever sleep with him?"

"You know, it's funny but I've never heard him before tonight. Isn't that odd?"

"It sure is. Suppose he's especially loud tonight because of all the food he packed away?"

"He loves to eat but, in spite of what he said, he's never put on a bit of weight. His wife, Frannie, was a good cook."

"Did you know her well?"

"Not very. I only remember little things about her. Her chocolate pie. Her big amber-colored eyes. And the fact that she used to crack her knuckles."

Mae felt the rumble in Sean's chest. "You're joking," he said.

"No, I'm not. Uncle Ed has always snapped his suspenders and sucked his tooth and Auntie Fran used to crack her knuckles. Granny said they got married so they could make wonderful music together.

They both laughed quietly. After a minute, Sean said, "Well, okay, here's my question . . ."

"Just a minute," Mae whispered. "You've already asked your question. Several actually."

"I did not!"

"Did too."

"Which questions?"

"How on earth did Aunt Frannie sleep with Uncle Ed and did I know her well and . . ."

"No fair."

"Uh-huh."

"You little cheat." He stubbed out his smoke. "I can't let you get off scot free. A quickie then."

Mae heard a yawn and turned her head toward him. There was little natural light. His face was an inscrutable shadow. She waited, nervous as the fattest hen on Sunday morning. Johnny was making a snuffling noise. The snow tapped the window like feeble fingers.

"You like me, don't you Mae? Answer honest now."

She fingered the sheet's wide hem. It pressed restrictively across the fullness of her breasts. "Yes . . . very much." She whispered and curled her toes into the mattress.

"Good. And you trust me, don't you?"

Nodding, then remembering the dark, she croaked, "Yes . . . well, pretty much." Not always, she added to herself, and especially not right now.

"Trust me now." He leaned over her on one elbow, his shoulders filling the world. Surely, she thought, if they were to mate, he would crush her. Her head further indented the pillow.

"Let me kiss you good-night."

The blurred outline of his head came closer. Their lips were a whisper apart. He paused. She nodded then sucked in her breath and clasped the sheet in a death grip. Kissing in the prone position was lots different than being on your own two feet. With a finger under her rigid jaw, he tilted her chin up. Lowering his head, he brushed his lips lightly across hers with a kiss so soft and so gentle, he was done before she knew he had begun!

"That was all right, wasn't it, love?" he whispered.

Wide-eyed, she strained to distinguish his features. She tried to nod again but his finger still supported her chin.

"Let us have one more then."

He sealed their mouths, fitting his lips to hers like the last piece of a jigsaw puzzle. A pleasant innocuous kiss ensued, one that, in Mae's opinion, ended all too soon.

"Mmm?" she protested when she was able.

"Once more then," he rasped. "Let me taste ye!"

When his mouth returned to fasten on hers, dazedly she parted her lips and heard a throaty groan. His? Hers? His tongue plowed into her mouth and she was beyond caring.

Long moments passed during which the air was filled with only soft moans and long sighs.

"My, Sean, that was . . . especially nice."

"Yes, it was, wasn't it."

Twisting, turning their heads to merge their open mouths more completely, the next kiss heated up . . . got hotter . . . became incendiary. Instinctively, her tongue met then mimicked his.

"Sweet gel!"

Persuasive. Potent. Seductive. His words incited. Mae was compelled to get nearer. She rubbed her palm across his chest. Heated skin strained and flexed under her palm. She followed the curve of his powerful shoulder while he kissed her senseless. The tumult of their passion mingled with the sounds of the night. The wind whimpered. So did Mae. "Oh, Sean . . ."

A loose windowpane shook as bad as Sean's voice. "Ah, sweet, let me kiss ye here . . ."

The old house groaned and shifted. Inside, the occupants of the small bedroom did likewise.

Lips glued to hers, Sean rolled onto his back and brought Mae with him. Her legs dropped between his widespread ones, fitting the length of his arousal into her cleft. He tilted his pelvis and pressed into her. "Sweet, sweet Jesu . . ."

His hands were everywhere, on her back, her buttocks, brushing down the sides of her breasts. She should stop him, she thought, and did nothing.

"Turn a little, love!" Sean implored, frustrated at being unable to reach the distended nipple that drilled into his chest.

The sound of someone's—was it Father Fitz?—

cough inserted itself on Mae's consciousness. She tensed then rose on her forearms. Sean's hands were on her breasts in an instant.

"No, sweet, don't pull away from me!" Relentless, he directed her head down toward his questing mouth. Mae melted on him like butter on griddlecakes. They both groaned. Another cough in the other bedroom and she broke the suction of their lips again.

"Bloody hell!" Carefully, he turned her onto her back. Then slowly, he lay back on the pillow. He raked a hand through his hair. Through the mattress Mae felt the shuddering rise and fall of his chest. In a minute, he stacked his hands behind his head.

"A man canno' make love under these conditions!" he muttered emphatically.

Really? Mae wondered. Why not? If they were only going to do what Peter had done, they most certainly could make love. A moment passed. Raising her hand to bruised lips, she realized she missed the feeling of his mouth on hers, the rough stubble of his beard on her cheek and the weight of their bodies pressing together. There was something else, something elusive and just beyond her comprehension that she wanted. She was sort of . . . irked!

"Well . . ." His voice was close to her ear. ". . . Good night, then."

Licking swollen lips, Mae just managed to squeeze out, "Good night."

Fifteen

Waking slowly, Mae first thought that if it was this hot so early in the morning, it would be a good day to go down to the river and have a swim. Her second thought was to wonder who was breathing in her ear. Her body stiffened like a corpse. Her eyes flew open.

Dawn's early light barely breached the windows, glazed with snow and ice. Moving only her eyes, she looked across the room into the bureau mirror. It wasn't only herself she saw reflected therein. Covering her like a second skin, the Irishman's body so entwined with hers she could hardly tell where he started and she left off.

They both lay on their right sides, spoon fashion. His arms were wrapped tightly around her. His head was buried in her neck, his hair peaked and tufted like a well-beaten meringue. His lips and moustache pressed into a sensitive place below her left ear. Her nightgown was pushed up waist-high. Wedged between her legs was a thick, hair-rough thigh. The entire length of an enormous arousal pressed against her buttocks.

A very long, extremely hard arousal.

O Lordy, Mae swallowed a gasp. His hand cupped her breast, leaving her straining nipple untouched and the nubby material of her nightgown tightly drawn over it. Ever so slightly, his thumb moved, making the circlet of his fingers smaller. She held her breath. Her nipple tingled and beaded painfully. An overwhelming yearning beset her: to feel his touch on her nipple.

What has gotten into you?

She flung off the covers, disentangled herself and leapt up. Swirling into her robe, she scooped up Johnny and fled the room.

Through slitted, bleary eyes Sean watched her go and gratefully acknowledged the end of the longest night of his life! He brought his legs up and moaned.

Before he would go through something like that again, he would rather walk on coals in the Sandwich Islands. He'd rather have his head shrunk in New Guinea. He'd rather be permanently shipwrecked on Devil's Island where, for fun, he would stick pointed things up his nose.

Rolling onto his back, he pressed his hand hard on his groin. Speaking of things needin' to be shrunk . . .

"Bloody hell!" Soon as he could stand and provided he was still able to walk, he would seek out Father Fitz and ask him to send a letter to the Vatican. Surely, after such a night, he would qualify for canonization.

Sean looked out the window. Snow. Sweet Jesu, would you look at the snow!

Maybe ye should pole vault, buck naked, into the biggest drift ye can find.

Groaning, he rolled up and sat on the edge of the bed.

Patience, Sean me boyo! Remember how you were going to have patience? "Bloody Hell!" he muttered, "I canno' stand up!" Sean heard snuffling in the bedroom next door and buried his head in his hands.

The damn walls might just as well be made of cheesecloth! Father Fitz had a chronic smoker's cough and Ed snored with more toots and whistles than the New York City Hibernian Band. A branch scraped stridently against one of the parlor windows all night. The logs in the wood-burning stove clunked loudly against the cast iron each time they settled. Worst of all was some tiny critter racing back and forth and back and forth between the bedroom ceiling and the attic floor. The pitterin', patterin' feet had driven him crazy! Sean looked up at the ceiling with narrow, speculative eyes and muttered, "I wonder . . . drill a hole on the outside of the house . . . measure carefully . . . just the right height . . . hole large enough to get both barrels . . ."

"Ach!" Standing, Sean walked to the basin and threw frigid water on his face. The upstairs room was his only hope. He would renovate it, get a bed in it and get his wife into said bed. A married couple needs privacy.

As he stretched for his pants, he paused. In their respective bedrooms, Ed passed wind and Father Fitz started whistling Galway Bay.

Sean spat a short, very graphic word then sank back onto the bed and held his head.

Standing on the porch, Mae thought the farm looked like a Currier & Ives print. Ice crystallized the trees and sheathed the outbuildings with silver. All windows were decorated with snow like cotton batting.

Sean had to put on snowshoes to get to the barn— nobody had thought to bring the shovels to the house—then all the men went to work, digging paths from the barn to the house, the house to the coop then to the privy beyond. Watching from the window, Mae thought they looked like mice in a maze. Bet they'll work up an appetite, she thought as she put on a clean apron.

Mae had rolled the dough out on the table and was cutting biscuits. She paused, pressing the rim of the battered metal cup into the small mound of flour next to the dough. She left her arm outstretched a full minute, her mind far from making biscuits.

She could still feel its imprint as if it were burned on her buttocks. It had been huge! The Irishman's youknowwhat must be at least . . .

"Fourteen inches!" Uncle Ed walked in holding a yard stick like a symphony conductor.

Mae collapsed into the kitchen chair. The cup rolled off the table and plinked onto the floor.

"That's how much snow we got." Ed threw the wooden marker on the work counter and turned to greet Father Fitz.

"Good God! the priest said, incredulous. "It seems impossible to get that big a one that fast! Twelve inches, didy' say?"

"Fourteen inches!"

Good God, Mae thought, I wish he'd stop saying that!

". . . I told you that was going to be a serious snow. Under normal circumstances we could chain a log behind the sleigh and drag it up and down the road. Clear a path to town in no time. But not with that much snow. No way you're going to be able to get home today, Father. Might as well plan on an extended stay."

She bent over to retrieve the cup, hoping the action covered her strangling noise.

* * *

Three days later, only seconds after waving good bye to Father Fitz, Mae heard Sean start to move his belongings back into her parents' bedroom.

So, she thought, smoothing a pair of Sean's underwear then folding the legs for a minimum of creasing, they would not be sharing a bedroom tonight. Now, contrarily, she wasn't at all sure separate bedrooms was what she wanted.

The Irishman had allayed her fears about sharing a bed with him after that first night. "Any time we spend in bed, until the upstairs is finished, is for talking. That's it! Talking!" He was quite emphatic.

Once over the tremendous shock of waking up in his arms every morning, Mae found she didn't want to wake any other way. Not that it didn't take a bit of getting used to. It did. By sheer size, he hogged the bed, the covers, the pillows and her! But once enclosed in the strong ring of his arms, she had never felt more secure or more safe. And warm! In spite of telling herself she would never be able to get to sleep, in actuality, she had never slept better.

And true to his word, talking was almost all that transpired before they went to sleep. Almost. Lying face to face, their bodies inches apart, they had had wonderfully long, by necessity, whispered talks. Most of the time, the Irishman talked and she listened. Gladly. Although their conversations lasted way past her usual bedtime, the tales the Irishman told were so colorful and captivating, she hadn't minded the lost sleep in the least. Matter of fact, listening to the Irishman talk was about the most interesting thing she'd ever experienced. Except for kissing the Irishman. But that was another thing completely!

He told her about Ireland. His liltingly, descriptive words painted such a vivid picture she'd felt she was there . . .

. . . standing atop a winding rock wall, sur-
rounded by rolling fields of purple heather, a mist-
filled breeze stirred her hair.

. . . On a soft summer eve she strolled through the
eerie, moss-covered ruins of a centuries-old castle.

. . . In the spring she waded knee-deep in fast
running, icy streams and fished for trout and salmon.

One night he told her about his tropical ports of
call. Oh, what romantic, exotic names! Raratonga.
Bora Bora. Samoa.

. . . She felt warm sand between her toes and the
touch of a sultry breeze through swaying palms.
Flamboyant birds of paradise and tiny monkeys with
impish expressions flitted between vine-festooned
trees. She heard macaws and garishly colored parrots
call out from deep within the steamy jungle.

. . . Mahogany-skinned, laughing natives pro-
pelled long canoes out to meet her many-masted sail-
ing ship. They threw flowers at her feet and dove
gracefully into the aquamarine lagoon after coins.

Lying in her bed in the little farmhouse on the Minnesota border, Mae went places!

Oh, but it was magical. Lots better than a stereo-
scopic travelogue like the one she and Moira had attended in Chicago.

"Well, I suppose we'd better get some sleep now,"
he would say, his breath warm on her face. "Besides,
I've been waitin' all day to kiss ye good night, love."
And he would touch her parted lips with his.

Then she really went places!

One of his earth-shattering good-night kisses and
it sure wasn't Mae Botts Herrmann . . . McGloin . . .
in that bed any more! Last night that other person
had thrown herself into his arms and explored his
back clear to his waist!

She loved the texture of his skin, smooth and tight

over lumpy muscles, the hard indentation of his spine. Brushing his lips over her eyes, her cheekbone, the valley between her collarbones, he had whispered her name like a pagan chant while his hands pressed her up and into him. When he had trailed his fingers inside the opening of her nightgown then followed them with his lips, she had wanted to lift her shoulders, wanted to part her nightrail for him. She wanted to offer him . . . everything!

And were there juices flowing? Yes, indeed-dee doo! By golly, Granny had been right!

Again last night, when he lay back and whispered a strained, hoarse good-night, she hadn't felt relief but terrible . . . disappointment.

Mae folded a diaper and laid it on the stack. She set aside the folded towels and quickly, before she could change her mind, she walked down the hall. She pushed open the door to her parents' room. Sean was leaning over the bureau drawer, placing a few items in neatly arranged stacks within. "Sean?"

He turned and smiled. "Hello, love. Done with the laundry?" He added the last two items he held to the drawer then closed it with his knee.

"Ah, no. Not quite." She stepped inside and closed the door. Sean looked so tired! A lot of work had been accomplished in the past week. Father Fitz was surprisingly handy with tools and truly enjoyed helping Sean so the two men, trapped inside by the storm, had worked almost nonstop on the attic room. Her uncle had helped too, taking care of all the farm chores then assisting with whatever he could. But the real workhorse was Sean. She wondered, seeing how exhausted he looked, if he hadn't bitten off more than he could chew.

"Sean . . ." She walked closer, wiping her damp palms on her apron.

He turned. "What is it, sweet?"

"Well . . ."

"Yes?" He cupped her shoulders and bent his head in order to hear her soft spoken words.

"I . . . I'll miss having you with me at . . . in my room." She buried her blazing face in his chest.

He smiled and kissed her head. "And I will miss being there."

Like hell, he thought. Last night was the worst torture imaginable. He'd finally fallen asleep around dawn then something woke him. Groggy and disoriented, he had looked around the room with red, bleary eyes then down. Mae lay with her head on the middle of his chest. Through parted lips she blew warm, soft air across his nipple. Beneath the tented sheet, her relaxed hand was curled around his balls! Around his blasted, friggin', bloody balls!

'Twas too much! The final straw! He knew at that moment that he wouldn't last another night. He had been within seconds of losing the small modicum of restraint he had heretofore—marginally and with great difficulty—been able to maintain. It was more than an ordinary man—even an extraordinary man, could take. And contrary to certain rumors, he was only human!

He would carry the little midget priest home on his friggin' back if he had to!

He'd made a horrible mistake. Yes, he'd willingly admit it. He'd done way too good a job on the kissin' phase of his seduction. Not only was she now an expert kisser but she wanted to do it for hours. So did he—nobody liked to kiss more than himself. But he sorely desired a progression to stage two. In a manner of speakin', a part of him was stretched to the limit with the desire to thrust itself into the next phase of things. In a manner of speakin'!

He tilted her chin up with his thumbs and caressed her cheek. "I think it'll be easier for everyone if I sleep in here until I get the new room finished."

"Oh," she said, her averted face crestfallen.

He kissed her lightly. When she leaned into him and kissed him exactly as he'd taught her, he whispered, "Jesus!" then jolted them both with a searing, open-mouthed, tongue-mating kiss. By the time he set her away from him, they were both hotter than a firecracker on the Fourth of July.

He ran his hands through his hair. "We must have some privacy, you and I, and then . . ." He sat on the bed and started pulling on his boots. He had to work off this frustration as soon as possible. ". . . I don't want to rush you or anything, but do you think, when the room is finished, you might be ready to try out that other side of the marriage—just once. Just to see if . . . ah . . . you like it?"

Dismally, she looked down at the rug. Just once? Would he try it once and find her so lacking, he'd not want to do it ever again? Peter hadn't wanted her either, not after that first time.

He continued. "Ah, I'm ready to give it a go if you are." He stomped down on one bootheel. "I mean, no hurry but if you think you would be ready." He looked at her a long moment then turned away. *Damn, I canno' face her until I'm sure I won't embarrass meself.*

It seemed so matter-of-fact to Mae to discuss it thus. She wished they could just *do* it instead of *talking* about it. "Well, yes. I think so." She wished she could see his face but his back was to her. He seemed to be adjusting something. "Maybe you'll change your mind by then." Oh, what an awful thought. But then Peter had certainly changed his mind, hadn't he?

Sean picked pocket items off the dresser. "I rather

doubt that. Course, one never knows but I rather doubt it."

He turned toward her. She searched his face. Well, I never! Now he's sounding lackadaisical!

I'll never understand men, she thought. Sometimes Sean seemed to be full of ardor. Then other times, like right now, he seemed downright stand-offish. He said, "Bye," and the door closed behind him. Why, it seemed he couldn't get away from her fast enough!

Mae wandered back into the kitchen. How could she have been so unlucky as to have married *two* men who had such unusual attitudes about *that*. Peter had been . . . finicky and now the Irishman, apparently, ran hot and cold.

She put her hand into one of her uncle's socks and spread her fingers. There was a small hole in the toe. She tied it and its mate together and put them in her mending basket then sat, her hands idle in her lap.

After the last few days—well, actually, the last few nights, she'd started to think it would be better if the Irishman just . . . took the bull by the horns, so to speak. At least it would be over and done with then, once and for all, and she could quit stewing about it.

She stood, walked to the cherrywood cabinet and picked up the small framed daguerreotype of Ilse and Helmut. She studied her grandfather's image. Somber-looking and barrel-chested, his big handlebar moustache looked sort of like those Texas steers.

She blushed. She never looked at his picture without remembering what Granny said about Granddad's ever-ready, ever "stiff horn."

She would have been better off if she'd married somebody like Granddad. At least he hadn't been wishy-washy.

"Boy," she informed the picture, "they just don't make good men like they used to."

* * *

They had their first argument that morning. It all started, in Sean's considered opinion, because that busybody Ed couldn't keep his mouth shut.

Sean had been working like a man possessed. Which, of course, he was. He thought of little else but getting the renovation project finished. That morning was no exception. While listening to Mae and Ed's conversation with half an ear, he ran through his master plan in his mind.

'Twas a simple plan. Finish renovating the new room by mid-December. Finish constructing a big, custom-made bed by Christmas Eve. Get his wife in the room and posthaste, into the bed, by Christmas. Do not allow her to leave it until New Year's.

New Year's? St. Pat's! Yeah, St. Pat's!

It was a sound plan and entirely realistic, thanks to Father Fitz. An able woodworker and possessing a fine eye for detail, Father Fitz offered to come out once a week, weather permitting, to help. Sean had gratefully taken him up on it. Not that he couldn't do it on his own, but speed is of the essence here. Quality, yes, but speed above all else.

In the last two weeks, with the priest's help, he'd constructed a support pillar in the root cellar for the fireplaces. On the first floor the fireplace would open into both the kitchen and the parlor. On the kitchen side, Sean planned to build a rustic stone wall and hearth using some of the rocks from the pile in the west pasture. On the parlor side, Mae said she thought she'd like something more formal, perhaps red brick. He was still thinking about what wood would be appropriate for the mantels for each room. The clay tile flues, unfortunately, had to be ordered all the way from Chicago. He checked on them at the little train depot receiving office whenever he went into town but they were still in transit. When they arrived, his first problem would be getting them from the train station to the farm. Every farmer was responsible for clearing his own roads of snow but some did a better job than others. Sean had cleared the Weltes' roads as well as their own, but the Fagers' roads, on the other side of the Weltes' place, were less meticulous. Also, there'd been two more mild snowfalls since the Thanksgiving Day storm.

His main focus, understandably, was the attic bedroom. The subfloor was finished with the newspaper insulation laid between the joists. Thankfully, Father Fitz had never thrown away a newspaper in his life so the priest had supplied a lot of the needed insulation.

Sean slathered another buttermilk biscuit with blackberry jam, took a bite and masticated energetically.

That was his whole problem. Too much bloody energy. Sometimes he felt like he was about to explode. Of course, he knew exactly how to relieve it. He glanced at Mae, sitting next to him and bouncing Jack on her lap.

"Mommy's gonna eatcha." She growled and buried her face in Johnny's neck. The child squealed with delight.

"Suppose Johnny's ever going to grow some hair, Uncle Ed?"

Ed looked thoughtful. "Maybe likely. Ilse had an uncle, I recall, who was bald as a croquet ball his whole life."

"Oh, no." She licked her fingers and tried to make a spit curl out of four hairs.

Bloody hell! Sean shifted and swung his head toward the wall. *Where was I?*

Only one small section of tongue-and-groove maple flooring was yet to be done. He could have that in by noon. The matching wood ceiling was unfinished, waiting for the delivery of the rest of the wood. Maybe the shipment would be on this afternoon's train. The plumbing pipes were in. They were exposed in the root cellar and where they went through the storage room but Sean planned to conceal them within the walls in the new room. He would have to figure some way of mixing the mortar—the cement, sand and water—to lay between the bricks for the hearth and get it installed before it froze. If he mixed it and quickly carried it in small batches . . . He was just considering that stage of the operation when Ed spoke.

"So, you workin' in the barn again today? Then runnin' back and forth?"

Mae lowered her coffee cup and looked inquiringly at Sean.

Sean swung his head toward Ed, silently glaring stilettos at him.

"Why are you doing that, Sean?" Mae set down her cup. "Don't you do most of your work upstairs? Right on site, so to speak."

Now that she considered it, she had seen Sean hauling wood upstairs—then ten minutes later she'd watched him haul what looked like the same wood down again. "Why do you do that, Sean? You must be up and down those stairs a hundred times a day."

"It'd be too messy . . ." Drizzling some honey on the last piece of his biscuit, Sean popped it in his mouth before wiping his hands. "Sawing upstairs."

He made, Mae thought, a Ziegfeld production out of folding his blue and white checked napkin beside his place. His idea to cut down on laundry was that the three of them would keep careful track of their napkins and reuse them at dinner.

"Just a minute." Mae placed a hand on his forearm. "What do you mean, messy?"

"I don't want to saw upstairs. Sawdust would filter down the stairs. Be bad for you and the baby." He waved his hand. "Dust everywhere."

"Is that what you're doing?" Mae held his arm as he prepared to stand, effectively preventing him from doing so unless he would rudely snatch his arm away. "Running out to the barn to saw your boards and running back into the house and up those stairs?"

"That's exactly what he's doin'!" Ed stuck in.

"Boy! That's a lot of running, Sean."

Sean looked at Ed and spat. "Keep out of this, you little squint! I'm not in the mood to take any shi- . . . to take anything from anyone."

"Sean, this is not like you. This . . . crankiness." Mae put the baby in his swing.

"Cranky? You bet I'm cranky."

Ed snorted and Sean glared at him. Ed wisely pretended a great deal of interest in the remains of his oatmeal.

"I'm warnin' ye to stay ou' of this. 'Tis no' yer business, ye . . ."

Mae tugged on Sean's sleeve. He looked at her.

"I can't allow you to do that any more, Sean." She smiled then started scraping the remains of her breakfast off her dish and onto another. She stacked the dishes, not even glancing in his direction.

"Say what?" She'd spoken as if she was saying have a good day!

"I said, I can't allow you to do that anymore, Sean." She met his eyes, and thought suddenly of rain clouds.

"Can't allow? You . . . *you* can't allow?" Sean was

unable to remember ever being so mad so fast. His crown felt hot and wet, like when he'd eaten Caribe pepper pot. "I can't believe I actually heard you say you can't allow . . ."

"Why not?"

"Why no', says she?" Sean looked around the room.

"I'm gonna check the livestock." Ed's chair scraped back. "And catch a breath of cool air."

Neither Mae nor Sean paid any attention whatsoever to Ed's shuffled exit but Mae ended her nonchalant act and frowned at Sean.

"This is my kitchen, Sean and my house to clean. Lord knows I hate dust but . . ." Sean leaned across the table. If she was of a mind to, he was close enough for her to count every one of his silky black lashes.

"Now listen t' this! 'Tis the man who wears the pants in a McGloin house! Think o' i' as a family tradition."

His lips, curled like a vampire, didn't move one bit when he spoke. She couldn't recall ever seeing that done before.

"Me word is, an' always will be, final. I willna have it anither way!"

"Well, that's rather too bad. Because if we are going to be a family, you and I, then we're going to have our own set of traditions. Different ones." She broke their sizzling eye contact to brush crumbs off the tablecloth into her hand. She hoped he didn't notice how her fingers trembled. "I won't have you working up there and then running outside. You'll catch pneumonia! I can put up with a little dust. And that . . ." She dusted her hands over the basin, ". . . is that."

"Tha' is tha'? says she."

She walked stiffly to the stove. "There's no call to get upset, Sean."

"Nae call . . ."

Leaning down, she struck a match and adjusted the flame under a pot already filled with water. "You've gone and gotten yourself so riled a person can barely understand you."

Sean stood abruptly. His chair crashed to the floor and startled the baby in the jump swing. He gave a frightened little yelp.

Mae walked over to Johnny and ran a soothing palm over his head. She handed the baby a small piece of toast which he tried to put in his nose. "This is a silly argument, Sean."

"Silly! 'Tis nae a bi' silly. 'Tis an argument about a man's inalienable right to be a man. 'Tis about a woman knowin' her place and no' oversteppin' the man's authority."

Mae faced him and folded her arms.

He was distracted briefly by the mutinous set of her jaw. "Barely understand," she'd said.

He forgot about her jaw and concentrated on suppressing his brogue.

"The woman gives the man unquestioning obedience and acknowledges that the man has sole responsibility to make all important decisions. The man's word, after he's made that decision then, is final. That's the way it has always been. Always will be."

"Really?"

"Yes, it's a commonly known, scientific fact that a man has the inherited characteristics necessary to lead while the woman . . ."

"Bull drop."

"Bull . . . ?"

"Bull drop."

Sean closed his lips on a repertoire of vile curses

the likes of which are only accumulated by the most seasoned of sailors. A long minute passed.

"Now you listen!" Her voice was perfectly modulated. She held up one finger. "I'll say this only once more. This is my house. My dust to clean. My husband to have to nurse if he gets sick. I say you do your sawing in the house."

"God, I willna be dictated to . . . I . . . !" His jaw muscle worked but his mind would not. *Nobody—Nobody had ever talked to the McGloin in this manner.*

"Then . . ." Walking back to the table, she sat and adjusted the folds of her skirt then her apron just so. ". . . whatever there is between us is over."

"What?" Sean snapped his jaw shut, stunned and once again, speechless.

Mae slanted a look at him. She didn't know whether to think Uh-oh! or Wow! Legs spread, pelvis out thrust and fists planted on his hips, he was the epitome of manly aggression. "Exactly what do you mean by that?" he asked softly.

The black kettle started making the kind of humming noise that preceded a whistle. She should get up and take it off the fire but she was afraid to move. She licked her lips. It was like a Mexican standoff.

Finally, she sighed dramatically. "It's so sad that we had to argue like this because . . ." She fingered the doily. ". . . because today was the day I had decided to tell you I've fallen in love with you."

Her words had the same effect on his anger as a slammed stove door on an eight-egg soufflé.

"Eeek!" Mae squeaked when he grabbed her.

"Mae!" He searched her face. "Do ye mean it, woman? Can ye love me? *Me?*" She jerked her head. Her feet dangled a yard off the floor.

Sean enfolded her in his arms, holding her so tight

she could scarcely breathe, much less speak. "Oh God, sweet gel."

She flung her arms around his neck as their lips met. All she could think was . . . Yes, yes, yes!

Sean opened the barn door moments later. Ed huddled on a bale of hay, close to the coal heater.

"So, now you're probably gonna spend the rest of your married life in the barn, huh? Heh-heh-heh!" He spat, looking toward Sean with twinkling eyes.

"Listen, you old fart, I dinna need ye buttin' in an' stirrin' up stuff between us." His words were harsh but he was grinning. "God!" He leaned on the work bench across from Ed. He felt like he'd been pole-axed! "I canno' believe it!"

"Canno' believe what?" Ed mimicked him. "That a little slip of a girl like that could talk back to a big guy like you?"

Tha' she should love me.

He ran his hands through his hair then over his jaw.

". . . haven't had much experience with the German race," Ed was saying, "but let me tell you, there's nobody can be more stubborn than a German. And little Mae Ella's one hundred percent. Let her get the bit between her teeth and that's it. Might as well be written in stone as far as changing it. I've known Mae Ella all her life and I can bet you that she won't lay down many ultimatums but when she does, she means it. One hundred percent!"

"I just found that out." Sean grinned. "God, the gel's fabulous when she's mad!" He strolled to the lumber supply and started to stack long pieces of one-inch boards. "Ah," he paused dreamily, "we are goin' to have some wonderful fights!" When he finished selecting what wood he needed, he dumped a sack of nails in Ed's lap and handed him one of the saws. "Carry these into the house for me."

Ed stood. "Oh? Into the house, you say? Well, well. I'll be damned!"

Sean gritted his teeth and looked skyward. Ed sauntered along the shoveled path toward the door, the nails cradled in one arm, dragging the saw in the other.

God, fond as he was of the old fart, at times he would truly like to strangle him.

Word had arrived via a passing farmer that the clay flues waited at the train depot. Sean and Ed were going to town to get them. In the back of the sleigh was about every blanket on the farm, along with an entire bale of spread hay. Sean wasn't taking any chances on the rough, snow-packed road bouncing the flues around and possibly breaking or scoring one.

Shading her eyes against the sunshine, Mae waved good-bye from the back steps. Then she lowered her arm, sighed and went into the parlor. She planned to begin cleaning there first. She brushed her feather duster over the lamp shade, the table. The latest edition of the *Saturday Evening Post* lay on one of the chairs. She picked it up.

Their last days passed in a flurry of activity but their evenings were as leisurely as those of the Vanderbilts. A certain tradition had evolved—although Mae avoided using the word tradition around Sean, as she sensed he was still a bit prickly about capitulating to her so quickly.

As usual, they would all, even Johnny, have dinner together. Then while Sean and Ed saw to the animals, and Ed had his chew, Mae would put Johnny down for the night. Soon as he was settled in, she would grab some mending or needlework and hurry into the parlor. When she was ready, maybe with another cup of coffee by her side, Sean would read the latest installment of Jack London's *Call of the Wild,* which was presently being serialized in the *Post.* A wonderful story of adventure, it was made more fascinating by Sean's resonant voice and ability to mimic dialects. So he always read, except for the night when Mae had butter to churn. That night he brought the churn right into the parlor and chin on fist, elbow to knee, churned while Mae read. She had never known happier or more contented times.

" 'The crowd fell silent,' " Sean had read the previous evening. " 'Thornton knelt down and took Buck's head in his two hands and rested cheek to cheek.' "

Mae realized Sean was reading ever louder and looked up. Their eyes met, then went to Ed, who was sprawled on the divan. Knees locked and feet in a V position, he was snoring loud enough to ruffle the curtains. Mae covered her mouth and laughed.

"Jesu! I cann' hear meself think!" Sean said. "An' will ye look at the man's shoes?"

Dime-sized holes were worn in exactly the same spot on each shoe. "Aw, poor old guy." Mae tsked.

"Well, why dinna he say he needed new shoes?" Sean realigned the *Post* and recrossed his legs with mock annoyance. "I'll pick up some new shoes for him tomorrow.

"He has his pride, you know, Sean."

"Plain foolish for him to feel that way. We're all in this together, share and share alike."

"Maybe. It's hard for him to be beholden."

Sean muttered something about ridiculous and asked, "So, now where was I? I've lost me place."

"I think where the crowd fell silent."

"Fitting," he said and looked at Ed, still snoring to beat the band. " 'The crowd fell silent. Thornton knelt and took Buck's head in his two hands and rested cheek to cheek. As you love me, Buck. As you love me, he whispered. . . .'

". . . You are so beautiful."

It took a second for Mae to realize those weren't Thornton's words to his dog. She looked up and Sean smiled at her "Oh, Sean."

" 'Tis true. Like a lovely picture there in the lamplight."

She blushed and tried to concentrate on her mending but it was several heartbeats before he started reading again.

". . . as you love me . . ." He lowered the magazine again.

"You know, sweet, your uncle is just going to make us read this part over again. We might as well stop here and continue tomorrow night."

Mae put the *Post* upside down so it would uncurl, patted it and closed the drawer. Then she snapped her dust rag and got busy.

Sixteen

O'Brien didn't see the guy coming until too late. Juggling two boxes of groceries, he was watching his feet, trying to miss a puddle. He saw the guy's coat, black and almost ankle-length and he glanced up, but the guy was already on top of him. Collar up, head down so his face was shielded, the guy had his hand inside his coat. "Shit," O'Brien said and pushed both boxes at him.

"Keep walkin'," instructed a gravelly voice behind him. "Straight ahead." A gun jabbed into his back.

A third man stood beside an enclosed wagon, double-parked with the back doors open. "Manucci Meats. Manhattan's Finest," was painted on the side.

O'Brien shot a look down the deserted street. The two men had a hold of each arm and the gun bruised his ribs as they propelled him toward the van. The man standing at the doors seemed nervous. He tugged on his cap, looked both ways. "Come on," he said, "move it."

Stupid, very stupid, O'Brien thought, having both hands occupied like some green recruit. He stuck out his leg, tripping the guy on his right and tried to spin. Too late, he thought with odd resignation as he felt the sap strike the back of his head. Black oblivion descended.

An old woman watched, well back from the window. The man sagged between two men dressed in black. They pushed him inside the van and one got inside with him. The other two latched the door, climbed in the front and drove away.

The old woman's lips moved. "Pezzanovanti," she said and clucked her tongue, but she would not call the carabineri. Born in Palermo, she knew what happened to people who broke the law of silence. In Sicily, *omertá* was not a law, it was a religion. She pulled the drape aside, watched the meat wagon turn the corner then looked below her. A head of lettuce had rolled into the gutter. Eggs stained the sidewalk, mixing with a light drizzle and the contents of a small jar that had contained something orange. Otherwise all the groceries just lay on the sidewalk—flour, sugar—all getting wet.

Such a waste, the old woman thought, such a waste. She thought of the man in the van and crossed herself.

All morning Mae'd been looking with longing at the lovely day outside. It was so warm! When she attended to outdoor chores, she was able to do so wearing only her heavy sweater. As she was putting stew on for supper, she heard snow sloughing off the roof like a day in April. She walked to the window and looked out. A big blob of snow slapped the windowsill then slid slowly to the ground.

"That's it!" she muttered. She put the lid on the stew and turned the fire low. She took off her apron and draped it over a chair. "Let's go, Johnny."

He held up his arms. "Garght?" he asked.

"Yes. Go. We're going sledding. Won't that be fun?"

The elliptical sled hung on a hook in the barn. Balancing Johnny on her hip, Mae checked the tow rope. She wasn't surprised to find that it was frayed. After all, it had been a long time since it had been used. She set the baby on a bale of hay and, having found some new rope, used it to tie a U-shaped hand hold. Papa used to ride Jocko and pull her—and her brother too until he got "too old for that baby stuff"—all around the farm. One of her first memories was of John sitting behind her on the sled, holding her between his legs. She looked at Johnny. Would he remember his first time on a sled?

They set off, up to the cemetery, down the hill on the opposite side, as far almost, as the bluffs, then back. Amazing, but all that way and her feet didn't even get cold. Pulling was easy. The sunshine had compressed and slicked the snow. The apple-cheeked baby ate snow every time they paused then pumped his arms and fussed until she moved on. On the way home, she stopped at the top of cemetery hill and looked down. "This used to be Mommy's favorite place to slide, Johnny."

The hill looked like the side view of a rocking chair. The first and longest part angled straight down, leveled like a seat, dropped straight off again then swooped upward.

She looked at Johnny, debating. He had taken off one of his mittens and was trying to stuff it all into his mouth. She looked down the hill again. She chewed her lip. She walked over, replaced his mitten, then pulled out her handkerchief and wiped his nose. "Johnny?"

He furrowed his brow and looked at her as if saying, "What now?"

"Stay over here for a minute, sweet cakes." She took him off the sled and set him on a flat rock. In case he got adventuresome, he was almost level with the ground. "Stay right there, honey!" She patted the sun-warmed surface of the rock. He lay back and kicked his legs but the fresh air had had its effect. His eyes were heavy-lidded.

Hauling the sled behind her, she looked down the hill again, then at the baby. "Wait right there, Johnny. Mommy will be right back." Before she could change her mind, she lay down on her stomach and pushed herself off. She was heavier now; it took more effort to get going than it used to. The front of the sled tilted downward, perched precariously then slid over. It gained momentum. *"Whee!"* About midway down, she really picked up speed. Cold wind raced against her face. By Golly, it was exhilarating! She hit the flat part, didn't slow a lick and flew down the last part of the ride. At the bottom of the hill, the sled leveled out perfectly. Then something went awry. Shortly thereafter, so did Mae.

She flew off the sled and into a snowbank like a arrow. Shaded by a tree, the snow was soft. It was, nevertheless, a messy landing to an otherwise flawless ride.

Laughing, covered head to toe in white, Mae sat up and brushed snow out of her eyes and mouth. *"Thewey!"*

The first thing she saw when she cleared her vision was the Irishman. He glared imperiously down at her, booted legs planted in his intimidating, wide-legged stance. "Ye could've killed yerself."

"But I didn't, did 1?" She chirped, smiling widely. She scrambled up. Turning, she dusted off the back of her coat. She did feel a twinge in one of her shoulders and the pinky finger on her left hand throbbed terribly. She would never, even if tortured, tell the Irishman! She trudged over to retrieve the sled, which was buried nose first in an adjacent pile of snow.

"Here, where do you think you're going?" He followed a few paces behind as she started back up the hill.

"I'm going down again." She hadn't planned on another trip down the hill but now the Second Coming wouldn't stop her.

"You could spla' up again' tha' tree down there." He waved his arms around like a windmill.

"I don't intend to 'spla' up again' tha' tree.' Actually, I went exactly where I wanted to go. I was directing the sled expertly with my body the whole time."

"Is that a fact? Then I suppose you expertly directed yourself into that big snowdrift?"

"I hit something . . . a stump or something . . . under the snow. Just at the end. Caused me to lose a little control."

"A little . . ."

They had reached the top. She checked the baby. Sprawled in the sun, mouth working in pursing movements every few seconds, he was fast asleep.

"Well, here I go." She looked over her shoulder coquettishly. "Watch this, big boy!"

"Big boy?"

Just to be contrary, Mae screamed at the top of her lungs on the way down. She landed much better and hiding a grin, squinted up the hill. Sean stood looking down at her, shaking his head. His posture smacked of bossiness, his face, even at this distance, had a real you-are-such-a-kid smirk. He barely waited until she got within shouting distance before he started in.

"I suppose ye went exactly where ye wanted to go that time too, right into that blue spruce?"

She hadn't gone into the blue spruce. Close but she missed it by a foot at least. Her finger really throbbed now and she'd lost a button on her coat.

"If that's the best ye can steer, 'tis amazin' ye've lived to the age ye are!"

She retied her scarf, almost choking herself in the process. "You know, hot shot?" She dangled the rope between thumb and forefinger. "If you think you can do better, why don't you put your rear where your big mouth is?"

He waved at the sled as if it was a pesky fly, scoffing. "I could never fit on that thing."

"Tittie baby!"

He glared back at her. "Tittie baby?"

She flipped the rope end in front of her face. In a nearby birch two siskins fought over some seeds. A black-backed woodpecker pounded on a dead conifer.

He snatched the rope out of her hand. "Watch this." He pulled the sled back to more even ground and straddled it.

She giggled.

"What's so funny?"

"You! You're not supposed to sit on it like that. You're supposed to lie belly down on it.

"Allow me to ride as I see fit!"

"Well, pardon me!" She walked around the sled as he settled himself Indian style. "Say, Irishman? Your face looks kinda white to me. You aren't scared, are you?"

"Scared? I most certainly am not!" He scootched himself closer to the drop-off, moving his groin obscenely, digging his knuckles into the snow.

Mae snuck around behind him and gave his broad back a terrific shove.

"Hey!"

She continued to run behind him as he picked up speed, pushing as hard as she could. He went over the lip going at least a hundred miles an hour. His bellered "HEEEeeeeeeey!" was loud enough to shake the snow off of every tree within a five mile radius.

She jumped up and down, clapping her hands gleefully. Wow! she thought, he's really humming!

Halfway down, the sled hit the flat part and did a complete about face. The Irishman, bug-eyed, hanging on tenaciously, hollered again. "Shiiiiiiiiit!"

Crossing her legs so she wouldn't pee in her pants, Mae watched him continue down hill—backwards.

He never slowed a lick before he disappeared into a snowbank.

The sled scuttled away.

He didn't move.

When she stopped chuckling she cupped her hands around her mouth. "Yoo hoo! Irishman!"

Only his twisted legs were visible, sticking up out of the drift like bent matchsticks.

She snickered. "Hey, hot shot!"

Nothing moved, least of all the Irishman. Everything, even the woods were enclosed in an eerie silence.

"Hey, Sean!" she yelled louder. "Are you okay?"

She suddenly remembered a schoolmate of hers named Malcolm Manus. "Oh no!" she whispered. Malcolm had fallen off a toboggan and broken his neck. He died. "Oh God, no!

"Sean!" She started to half run, half slide down the hill. Slipping. Falling. Tumbling. Taking forever to get to him! Oh my God! Oh my God!

"Oh God!" She collapsed, breathless, at his side. "Oh, my God, Sean!" She grabbed a handful of his coat and tugged hard. Black dots swam in front of her eyes. She was afraid she would pass out from fear.

With an evil, deep-throated "Ah Ha!" he flipped her over and fell on top of her. "Now, ye sassy little nit!"

"Hey, quit it! You really scared me!" She struggled and punched his shoulder. Suckered! And by the oldest trick in the world.

"Get off, you big . . . possum!"

"Possum?"

"Oaf!"

"Oaf?" He captured her hands. "Tittie baby?" He held them above her head. "Hot shot hmm?" His purring voice was as smooth and sweet as warm honey. He looked at her mouth. "Ye've got a real smart mouth on ye!" His eyes flickered, narrowed.

Mae ceased squirming. She ceased breathing.

"Let's see wha' I can do abou' it." His lips were cold while his tongue was warm, sweet, springtime honey.

Mae's toes curled in her boots. For a second, she freed her lips "Sean!"

There followed a long moment of silence. A male goldfinch, his yellow and black markings standing out brightly against the denuded branches of a poplar was trying to complete his tune. Rudely distracted by the loud moaning coming from two figures lying in the snow below him, he flew to a higher branch to start his song again.

"Oh, Sean!"

"I'd like to show ye a tittie baby!"

There was another long silence. Snow fell off the windward bough of a jackpine and whooshed into the snow beneath it. Mae mewed like a kitten.

A black squirrel, stirred out of hibernation by the warmth of the sun and all the commotion, stuck his head out of a hole in the rotted stump of a white pine.

"Sean . . . we can't just lie . . . here in the snow . . . all day."

"Why not? I like it here. I may never leave! We're alone! 'Tis quiet!" He centered his attention on her lush mouth. "God, 'tis wonderful."

The goldfinch gave up—the neighborhood had become so noisy!—and soared sunward, searching for peace and quiet and, if really lucky, bright-red winterberries.

"Sean! . . . the baby's . . .

"alone . . .

"Up on the hill."

"Bloody hell!"

"Oh, Sean!" Mae viewed the progress of the room, turning slowly like a lazy Susan. Day by day, the changes amazed her. To protect the new floor, the pile of lumber for the ceiling was stacked on a long piece of broken-down cardboard. Assorted tools appeared to be scattered around the room. Actually they were very organized. "Yer Irishman is a master craftsman," Father Fitz had said, "but a real stickler for detail."

"Yes, but sticklerness sure shows in the finished product," she had replied.

The floor was completed, albeit at the moment it was covered with a fine layer of sawdust. The boards had been cut in random lengths, and Sean had painstakingly fitted them together tongue and groove. Even unstained, the highly textured oak had a clearly defined, multidimensional grain. Four dormer windows were roughly framed into the sloping roof, brightening and surprisingly, formalizing the room. Standing in one of the windows, Mae felt like she'd put on the hyacinthine sky like a picture hat. "Oh, Sean, this is spectacular!"

The late-afternoon sun tipped the lodgepole pine's long nettles with a reddish glow. Fat, ponderous snowflakes swirled seductively around her head then landed wetly on the panes. Inch-wide brackets of slushy ice had already formed around the mullions. "We can be in bed and look up at the stars." She blushed, then looked over at Sean to see if he'd heard her thoughtless comment. Apparently not, since he hadn't turned from his task.

It didn't take a whole lot to remind Sean of bed these days!

Speaking of which, after a last glance at the striking sunset, she strolled to where he wrestled, swearing under his breath, with the bed frame. She hunkered down. "Can I help, Sean?"

"Well, maybe so, actually." He positioned the footboard. "I'm trying to fit this end of the wood into this slot in the headboard and simultaneously get it into the footboard. If you could just hold that right there for a minute. Don't hurt your fingers now."

A second later he had tapped the metal male connection into the female one on the headboard. Sitting back on his heels, he wiped his sleeve across his brow. "Now let me get the other side in."

"Then let's take a break. I've brought coffee and cookies."

"Just like every helper," he teased, "ready for a break right off the bat."

Later, they sat companionably on a makeshift bench—a wide piece of lumber laid across two crates the windows had been shipped in. Mae unfolded a napkin and offered Sean the fresh-baked sugar cookies within.

He selected one, sipped his coffee and munched.

His eyes, as did hers, strayed to the bed. "Well, love, once that bed is together, it'll never be moved again."

"Why's that?" Mae bit into a cookie.

"Because I put the headboard together up here. In one piece, it will never fit through either the doors or the windows. Nae, unless 'tis taken completely apart, nail by nail and board by board, 'tis not going anywhere."

"It's lovely." The headboard fanned above the frame like a peacock's tail, its individual pieces fitting together like slices of a pie. The bed was Sean-sized.

"We haven't made a mattress for years and we've always saved all our goose and duck feathers. I'll bet if I gathered all the sacks in the barn and in the root cellar I'd have enough on hand to make one right here. You couldn't order one from Sears, Roebuck big enough to fit a bed that size anyway." Mae stood and walked around the bed's skeletal frame. "You know, I've got two small quilts. I wonder if together they might be big enough."

"Then we'd be set until spring. I can finish the plumbing then. I've ordered a bureau and a mirror. Two chairs for either side of the fireplace." Significantly, he looked at her over his coffee cup. "We can be up here before Christmas."

Mae smiled shyly. "I'd like that." She perched on the bed frame.

"So would I, gel." He moved his thick eyebrows and twirled his moustache.

She laughed. And loved him so much she ached. The words were so close to escaping, she had to press her lips together. Dare she tell him? Did people say such a thing when they were giggling uncontrollably? Surely, such words should be saved for more solemn moments?

Sean stretched then stood. "I'm not going to stain

the wood until spring. Even linseed oil smells too much and I don't want to freeze us out by opening the windows." He hauled her to her feet and dotted her face with soft busses. "Here!" He stopped and held her at arm's length. "What was that?" He hauled her closer. "Give me another taste!" He kissed her. "I think . . . yes . . . cookie. A deeelicious sugar cookie." He returned to her lips again and again then rested his chin on her forehead. "I canno' wait for ye much longer. I want to have ye alone and private. I'm nae sure ye understand how powerful . . . Do ye understand, love?"

She pulled his head down. "Yes, I understand," she whispered against his lips. "Now, I understand."

When it came to a choice, at least for Sean, of consummating their marriage on the sawdust-covered floor or parting, regretfully, they parted.

Mae heard a huge thump on the ceiling above her then a loud curse through the open heat grate. Quickly as she could, she turned down the fire under the venison stew and threw a damp towel over the bread dough. She put Johnny in the swing and handed him his rubber ball. Picking up her skirts, she ran up the stairs.

Sitting with his back against a wall, Sean had one denim-clad leg straight and his forearm resting on his raised knee. His eyes were closed. His shirt was open and spread wide; his shirttail hung out of his pants. His tanned chest glistened with a fine sheen of sweat.

Mae's eyes tracked the sleek line of black hair that halved his torso then arrowed down into his belt buckle and her eyes experienced a familiar tightening. "What happened?" she asked with a tinny-sounding voice.

He rolled his head in her direction. He smiled

tiredly. "Sorry for cursing like that!" He fished into his shirt pocket, took out a cheroot and lit it. "The flue slipped and I almost lost it. Scared the pee outa me! It would have taken months to get another one."

She came the rest of the way up the stairs, drying her hands on her apron.

"I've got to remember to watch me sailor's mouth," he mumbled to himself. Louder, he said, "But I finally got the blamed thing into position."

"You should have waited for Father Fitz to help you. He said he'd be out later today."

"I know. But he's so good with wood. I thought I could get this part done then I'd ask his help with framing the windows or building the furring strips around the flue." Sean leaned back again and his corrugated abdomen muscles flexed.

Mae knelt. Like the day before, it was unseasonably warm, especially upstairs. She removed a handkerchief from her pocket and patted his brow.

He caught her hand and brought it to his lips. "Mae!" His eyes gleamed at her. "How I love ye!"

She rested her hand flat on the wall behind him and leaning down, kissed him gently. Then again. "I feel like I'm the luckiest girl alive."

"Is something wrong?" He asked after moment.

"No, nothing." She shook her head.

"Sure?"

"Yes, well. I just . . . I . . ." She leaned against him. "Sometimes I worry that . . ." She searched his eyes. "That you'll leave. Promise you'll never leave me, Sean."

"Never. Haven't I already said I swear it?" He pulled her onto his lap. Their kiss deepened. He caressed her slender throat and pressed her backward.

His ardent mouth set her aflame. She rubbed the hair rough skin inside his shirt. Raking her fingernails across his flat nipple, she felt it spring up in instant response and was gratified. And empowered.

"Sweet woman, I wan' to lie with ye so very much."

She opened her lips to his tongue as nimble fingers unbuttoned her dress, parted it then eased it off her shoulders. She lifted herself to facilitate him. Their ravenous tongues mated, their lips twisted and slanted. Mae moaned and strained to get closer. Close enough to be inside, she thought.

He made her feel exceedingly feminine, looming over her with his big shoulders. She sucked in her stomach muscles. Through the thin fabric of her chemise, he was teasing her nipples, plucking and brushing his fingers over them. Her heart hammered in her chest. Her skin felt hot. So hot! Too hot! She wanted her clothes off. Now! Sean's fingers tugged at her chemise bow. She caressed his jaw and whispered, "Yes, Sean, yes!" When he released the drawstring of her chemise and bared her breasts, she watched him through slitted eyes. He held the cloth apart with wide-spread fingers. Possessive silvery eyes glinted down at her for a long moment. Mae's flushed chest rose and fell rapidly with intense expectation. She searched his face. His skin was drawn tight across his cheekbones, the marble-sized muscle jerked on his lower jaw, a long vein stood out on his temple. He lowered his head. His tongue dipped into the vale between her collarbones and his lips began a moist, fiery trail across her skin. Closing her eyes, arching her back, she directed his head down.

Mae heard Sean's "Yesss . . . !" about the same second she heard Father Fitz. "Hallooo? Anybody home?" and the galvanizing sound of his feet on the bottom stairs.

* * *

Later Mae sat in the rocking chair with the two quilts—one blue and white, one rose and ivory—spread on the parlor floor. She had marked the squares to be switched with straight pins and was ready to start the meticulous task of wedding the four colors harmoniously. After sewing on a lining, she would stuff goose down in between the lining and the finished quilt. It will be wonderfully warm.

Warm? In the Irishman's bed? She made an unladylike sound. She was wasting her time.

Closing her eyes, she leaned her head back and pressed the back of her hand to still tender lips. She pretended that the pressure was his mouth. Although the parlor was cool, the fantasy immediately escalated her body temperature.

See! Why, he didn't even have to touch her anymore! Just thinking about him was like standing next to the wood stove. She waved a quilt square in front of her face.

"What are you up to, Mae Ella?"

She jumped. Her uncle stood in the doorway. She blushed. "Oh . . . not much. How're you doing, Uncle Ed."

He sat on the settee and indicated the quilts. "Looks like you got your work cut out for you."

"Yes, I'm combining these quilts for our . . . for the new . . . ah bed." She pointed upstairs then bent over her work, stitching furiously. When she looked up, her uncle had put on his glasses. He picked up the corner of the quilt and fingered one of the squares.

"You know, I remember when Ilse was cutting material for this here blue one." He turned his head and looked wistful. "I wish you could have known her when she was young. Boy, she was a looker! And funny as a stitch!"

Mae smiled, the sewing forgotten on her lap. She loved to hear Granny stories.

"She was such a pleasure to be around. Ol' Helmut would get at her, teasing and she'd come right back at him, quicker'n spit. Well, it was obvious that they were just plain crazy about each other." He chuckled. "She thought he was fresh peaches growin' outside the front door and he thought the sun rose and set outa her . . ." He glanced at Mae and cleared his throat. ". . . smile. You know, 'course, how much you look like her . . ."

"Yes, and thank you, Uncle Ed. I can't think of a nicer compliment."

"Anyhow, guess what happened the other day?"

"What?"

"I got started thinkin' that the Irishman reminded me of Helmut!"

"Really?" Mae thought of the picture on the cabinet and the Irishman and thought day and night. "Really?" she repeated.

"Well, I know. Aside from both bein' big men, there's not much physically similar about 'em. Still, there was somethin' the Irishman was doing or somethin' about him that kept making me think of Helmut. I was thinkin' it was some mannerism then I got to wonderin' if it wasn't the way he acts about you."

"About me, Uncle Ed?" This was better than a Granny story.

"Yep. The both of you are startin' to act just like ol' Helmut and Ilse."

"Are we? Are we really?" She sighed and smiled. "Is it so obvious?"

"Obvious? Shit-house mouse! You think I'm blind or somethin'?"

They laughed then after a minute, she picked up her work again.

"Ah, say . . . you know, Mae Ella . . ."

Something in his tone got her attention. She laid the quilt down.

"I was wantin' to say . . ."

She waited, her eyes toward her lap and her mood, suddenly, toward uneasy. She could hear rasping as he rubbed his jaw.

"I know things ain't just right between you yet, sleeping apart and all and . . ."

She felt her face redden. The speed of her rocking increased.

". . . me just say this, Mae Ella. I know you love him and I sure as hell know he loves you. There's no mistakin' that. Now, I'm not pretendin' to know what the trouble is . . ."

She made some noise.

He patted the air. ". . . and I don't want to know what the trouble is but . . . well, I guess what I'm tryin' to say is . . . I know for a fact that that man thinks of you and your boy afore he thinks of anythin' else."

"I know that."

"I don't know what happened in your first marriage. But I get the idea it wasn't a bowl of cherries."

She said nothing.

"You got to put all that behind you and get a fresh start. He knows how to make you happy. What you got to do is trust him to do so." He stood up and came closer. He patted her shoulder. She covered his hand with hers. "Thank you, Uncle Ed."

"Yeah, ahem, well I better . . . Say, how come you're holdin' your pinky finger like that? Looks like you're puttin' on the dog."

Mae held up her left hand with a swollen finger.

"Well, promise you won't say anything to the Irishman?"

"Why? What's the matter?"

"Promise first, Uncle Ed!"

"All right. All right."

"I jammed it sledding the other day."

"Well, lemme have a feel of it." He took her hand in both of his and very gently felt her finger.

"Does that smart?"

"Yes, but not terribly."

"Well, it ain't broken. Probably just sprained real bad."

She leaned over and kissed his cheek. "I sure love you, Uncle Ed."

His eyes raced elsewhere. "Same here, Mae Ella," he replied gruffly. "Same here." He straightened, snapped his suspenders then sucked his tooth. "Well, I got things to do. Can't be jawin' all day."

After her uncle left, Mae stared out the window. Sean had hinted broadly that the room would be finished enough to occupy before very long. The knowledge made her stomach quiver with excitement. And dread. She wasn't sure which feeling was predominant.

Yes, she was. It was dread. She was worried sick. She smoothed out the square of material again but didn't begin to sew.

What if he were displeased with her, as Peter had been? What if, because of her inadequacies as a woman, he were to draw away from her in disappointment? Then would she spend the rest of her life with a silent, unhappy man? If she could not please Peter—inexperienced, unworldly Peter—how could she hope to please a mature, virile man like Sean? Maybe it would be better if Sean didn't know she hated it.

I wish I had the nerve to ask Uncle Ed if a man can tell whether a woman enjoys mating, she thought.

She stared sightlessly at the scene outside the window then caught her lower lip between her teeth and shook her head. No, she intuitively knew that trying to fool Sean wouldn't work. Not Sean.

She wished things could just stay the same, that's what she really wished because, if it wasn't for stewing over the impending wedding night, she had never been happier. No doubt about it, she loved the kissing and holding part. With a sultry, silver-eyed look or a husky word of endearment, Sean could make her "juices flow" faster than the rapids on the St. Croix. Every time they were together, standing in the middle of the attic or whitewashing the walls or looking through the Sears catalog . . . whatever, somehow she would end up in his arms. Instantly the room got as hot as a Swedish sauna. One time—honest to goodness she couldn't believe her eyes herself—but the windows in the parlor had steamed over!

A loud squeaking noise intruded and she realized she was rocking like a madwoman. Putting her toe to the floor, sighing, she resumed her former, much slower, pace.

Seventeen

Coney Island, New York

Grey clouds hung heavily in the sky and carried a suggestion of rain, even snow. The sharp blustery wind was raw but, to the boy, enjoying his first time out of doors in two days, the pure, clear salt air was welcome. A strong gust of wind pierced his coat and he put his chin on his chest. His coat was half open to accommodate a cast on his wrist. One empty sleeve flapped behind him.

"Nero," he yelled, "Neeeero!" The puppy was racing down the broadwalk flat out. "Dratted dog," he muttered, trailing the now-useless leash.

There's little activity at Coney Island in the winter. No souvenir stands or sideshow booths, no concessioneers selling things to eat. No people even. Just wind and salt-scoured buildings boarded up with protective pieces of fresh plywood that had already been decorated with obscenities and gang names. Any glass the stand owners had been foolish enough to leave exposed was now a testament to the rock-throwing abilities of the neighborhood rowdies.

The boy cupped one side of his mouth. "Neeero!"

Fatherless, regularly taunted by the street kids for being a momma's boy, the boy was a studious, solitary soul whose burning goal in life was to be an explorer.

So he could discover a heretofore unknown continent. So he could set himself up as a sort of benevolent dictator. He planned to call the new land Nobanoga— NO Bullys And NO GAngs allowed.

"Neeero!"

The dog bounced down the stairs and onto the sand, intent on flushing some sandpipers. After some spectacular but unsuccessful leaps for the scattering birds, the dog wheeled and headed back for the boardwalk. "You get sand fleas, Nero, and Mom'll skin us both."

The boy was pretty sure the sand fleas were gone now. Then he got to wondering where they went in the winter anyway? Deeper in the sand? Or maybe Florida, like a lot of the souvenir-stand owners?

The boy smiled, picturing a bunch of fleas headed for softer climes with pouches of belongings tied to sticks and slung over their shoulders.

Nero, out of view, was barking his head off. The boy walked to the railing, stood on the lowest rung and leaned over. If his mother could see him she'd have one of her vapor attacks. Climbing was what had gotten him a broken wrist in the first place.

On his back haunches, stomach low, Nero was barking non-stop—sharp, flinch-inducing barks. "Nero! Cut it out!" The boy went up another rung and leaned out as far as he dared with only one hand-hold.

A hand splayed out of the shadows. Dusted with reddish brown hair and sand, it was attached to an arm encased in a brown leather jacket.

"Come on, Nero." The boy said softly, thinking it odd that the bum didn't throw something at the puppy. Surely he wasn't sleeping through all that noise, not even if he was drunker'n a lord.

The hand didn't move and the dog wouldn't.

The boy walked down the stairs and trudged several feet straight toward the water. He paused a second or two before he turned and squinted into the dimness under the walkway. Later, talking to his mother—or rather talking to the cloth draped over his mother's face as she reclined on the settee with her worst vapor attack ever—he would say that he just knew, he just sensed something was funny.

The wind hit the boy's neck and flung his hair forward into his eyes but, unfortunately, he could see fine. He dropped to his knees.

The dead man lay face down in a swimmer's pose. Where his feet should've been were jagged white sticks.

As if responding to a muezzin's call to prayer, the boy bowed and then he urped his guts out.

Sean had turned down dessert again that night and it was his favorite—blackberry cobbler with cream. "I want to finish furring the mortar in the hearth tonight. I'll have some later."

Mae cleaned up the kitchen, folded clothes, bathed and played with Johnny. She set some bread dough to raise for tomorrow's breakfast. While she listened to the occasional footsteps overhead, she kept an eye on the time.

When it was almost ten o'clock, she looked in on the baby, who was sleeping soundly, then started heating water on the stove. She placed a deep, oval-shaped basin on the large tray, then filled it with the heated water. She added a bar of strong soap and laid a neatly folded towel on the side.

"Hello!" She called from the top of the stairs.

"Hello." He smiled back at her. "Only three more bricks to go."

She set her tray down on the workbench and joined him where he knelt in front of the hearth. Beside him sat a mixed bucket of gray claylike mortar and another bucket of clear rinse water. "Oh, Sean! It looks so nice."

The raised hearth was a half circle extending three feet from the center of the fireplace at its widest point. She watched him set the last bricks into the wet mortar. Using his thumb, he carefully made a perfect valley between each one.

"I started out using a trowel then a rag but guess what gives it just the right look?"

"What"

He held up a crud-encrusted thumb.

"Yuucht."

"Exactly."

With a wet rag which had been rinsed out in yet another bucket of murky looking water, he wiped the bricks several times, carefully removing all the excess mortar. "There!"

"That was good timing." She stuck a finger in the hot water. "Just right." She picked up the tray then returned to kneel beside him. "Give me your hand."

"Why?" He looked at the basin, towel and soap. "Oh, no, I'm a mess. I better clean up in the barn."

"No, you won't. There's no hot water in the barn. Give me your hand." Mae took one hand and pressed it into the warm water. "Soak for a minute." She picked up his cheroots, chose one and stuck it between his lips. It took three tries but then she struck a match and held it to his cheroot. Then, submerging both her hands in the basin, she rubbed up and down his forearm to loosen the cement. "You are indeed a mess!"

Sean squinted against the smoke. "It could take forever to get that gunk off."

"I have forever," she replied softly, smiling up at him. "For you, I'm going to have a lifetime."

He looked at her bowed head then down at her hands and didn't trust his voice. *Bloody hell!* Throat working, he contemplated the hearth.

She picked up the soap and worked up more lather. "Sean?"

"Hmm?" He replied, thinking, *God, that feels good!*

"Is it my turn?"

"Hmm? Turn for what?"

"For a question."

"I think so."

"Well, then my question is . . . have you ever . . ." She continued to run her hands up and down his arm. ". . . loved another woman?"

"Sure, me old gray-haired mam."

"No. I mean a young woman. You know."

"Oh," He was distracted. She was sliding her hand over each finger then between them, then she was turning his hand over and massaging the soap over his palm. She'd already repeated the procedure several times. Groaning, he turned his heels out and sank onto his haunches. "God, woman!"

She dried his hand carefully with the towel. "Now the other."

"I dinno think I can take it."

"Oh, posh!"

"Posh? You don't understand what you're doing to me!" He removed his cheroot with his dry hand and handed her the other. When she started soaping his arm, he groaned again. He closed his eyes and thought about body lice. It didn't work for shit anymore. Hadn't since the day he arrived.

"You haven't answered me, Sean. I know you must have had feelings for someone in all your years."

"In all my years? You make me feel like Methuselah."

She said nothing, waiting.

"There was a woman years ago. I didn't love her, certainly, as I love you. But we were together a long time and after she died . . ."

"Oh, she died. An Irish girl, Sean?"

"No, she was Italian. A Venetian. And you couldn't call her a girl."

"How did you meet her, Sean?"

"She hired me as a . . ." there was a barely perceptible hesitation, ". . . bodyguard."

"A bodyguard? How old were you, Sean?"

"Ah . . . nineteen, I think, when we first met," he answered, cursing himself for coming up with this stupid question-and-answer idea.

"Nineteen? You were a bodyguard and you were only nineteen, Sean?"

His cheeks had pinked under his tan. "I was full grown and appeared much older. And I'd been on me own since I was thirteen."

"How old was she?"

"Ah, a bit older."

"How much older?"

"Late thirties or so."

Mae looked up at him for a few seconds then down again. "How long were you . . . together."

"About four years, I think."

"Four years? That's a long time. Did you live in Italy then?"

"Yes. Venice. Lucia . . . that was her name . . . was the widow of a very powerful man—a doge."

"What's a doge, Sean?"

"Kind of like a duke or count."

"So she was a duchess?"

"Sort of."

"How exciting. A duchess!"

"Lucia would have disagreed because her husband came with the title. She was fifteen when she got married and the doge was sixty-five. She told me the first time she met her husband was three days before the wedding."

"How awful."

"Yes." He smoked a while. "Poor Lucia. Her husband was apparently a real bas . . . bad man. A descendant of the Borgias and worthy of them. Luckily he died not too many years after they were married. They had no children." He shrugged. "She never remarried!" He lifted her chin. "Don't make this into more than it was, Mae. I was not her first lover."

"Was she very beautiful, Sean?"

"Very striking would be a more apt description."

"What did she look like?"

He sighed again. "Like she could have stepped off one of the Renaissance paintings she was so fond of collecting. Tall and raven-haired with black, penetrating eyes."

They must have looked commanding together, Mae thought and asked, "Why did she need to have a bodyguard, Sean?"

"She liked to travel and she liked to collect things." Men included, he said silently. "Her palazzo was filled with rare and priceless objects and paintings by the masters. She thought her nephew coveted her things and would go to any length to get his hands on them. Turned out she was right."

"Why did she die?"

"She got a tumor here . . ." He touched the side of his chest, ". . . and it must've spread."

"How awful!"

"It was. I wouldn't wish such a slow and painful death on my worst enemy."

"You stayed with her."

"Yes. I used to carry her everywhere until it hurt

her too much to be moved. She weighed so little it was like lifting a five-year-old child."

"And you loved her?"

He took a minute to answer. "In a way, I found that I did. Toward the end she would ask me to tell her that I cared. When she finally died, I realized that I hadn't been completely lying."

"You stayed with her?" Mae said.

" 'Twas the least I could do. Her conniving nephew and his ferret-faced wife were practically carting her things off downstairs while she was upstairs, trying to die in peace."

"How awful. So then you left, Sean?"

"Aye. With a bullet almost giving me another part in me hair."

She looked up, frowning. "A bullet, Sean? Why?"

"Lucia's nephew claimed I had been stealing from her. Which was a crock. I only took a few things which she had given me. Some of the stuff he accused me of taking I had seen him remove from the palazzo myself. But the officials believed him, of course, so I had to get out of town quick. Barely had the clothes on my back."

"What things did she give you?"

"Some very valuable . . . er . . . objects that I can't tell you about because . . . well, just because . . ." She started to protest but he held up his palm. "There's no use trying to pry it out of me." She twisted her adorable lips. He leaned over and gave them a quick kiss.

"I want to surprise you." She smiled and he wanted to kiss her again. "A long time ago I sent them somewhere for safekeeping. Now it'll take some effort to get my hands on them again. But let's see. What other things?" He lit a smoke. "An emerald ring which unfortunately I had to use to buy my way out of a situation in North Africa. A stiletto purported to have been owned by Cesare Borgia himself. I still have that. And that's about it. Oh, she gave me more but I only took what I could carry on my person."

"I feel sorry for her. Lucia." They were silent for a time, each with their own thoughts.

When Mae finished, she set her cleaning things on the tray and held out her hand. "Give me a hand up and come downstairs now, Sean. I have your coffee and dessert ready."

"Dessert?" He tossed his cheroot in the nearest bucket. "I know what I want for dessert!" He pushed her gently backward. Stiff-armed, he poised above her. She smiled up at him, her hair poufed around her head like a cowl. "Do ye believe tha' I've never loved anyone as I love ye?"

She nodded shyly.

He lowered himself slowly. Framing her head with his hands, he brushed rough-feeling thumbs along her cheekbones then kissed her tenderly. "Yer so lovely, woman. Inside as well as out. 'Twas what I must have sensed that first day. Me black and sinful soul saw into yours and something told me that you were me one chance for happiness ever." She felt his lips on her forehead. "Thank God I saw ye! Think if I never had!" He buried his face in her neck, his voice tight with emotion. "I would no' want to live without ye!"

She kissed her way along his hard jaw. "We . . . will . . . never . . . be . . . apart!" She touched her lips to his. "Never!"

Later, standing across the hallway in the open door of their separate rooms, they gazed longingly at each other before closing their doors. Tomorrow, Sean mouthed and after a second's pause, she nodded.

* * *

Sean knelt before the flickering fire. He added a small piece of seasoned birch then a large wedge of oak. The birchbark caught with a flash of incandescent flames. Leaning back against the wall, he rested a forearm on his raised knee and looked sadly around the room.

The finished counterpane graced the mammoth bed invitingly. The aroma of fresh-cut lumber had won the war of scents over the strong soap used to clean the floor, the beeswax used to polish the furniture and the vinegar and water solution used to shine the windows. Multicolored rugs were artfully yet practically laid. His clothes were stacked neatly in the drawers on one side of the bureau. He had carefully arranged his hairbrush, comb and pocket items on a mirrored tray. A duplicate tray was unladen on the opposite side. The bridal suite he'd prepared was, unfortunately, missing one key ingredient.

Throughout the day, as they worked together cleaning and adding the finishing touches to the room, Sean had used every delicate nuance, every oblique suggestion he could think of to suggest that *tonight* was *the* night. He hadn't come right out and insisted. Hell, he'd tried to be . . . tactful.

Ye should've asserted yerself. Ye've been pussyfootin' around with the woman for weeks. An' it's done ye no' a bloody bi' o' goo . . .

A slight noise and he turned. Mae's head and shoulders showed in the stairwell.

"Hello," she whispered, peeping shyly at him between the balusters.

"Hello," Sean whispered back. For a long moment he waited, unsure. Should he go to her or wait for her to come to him?

She walked up another step, paused, then another. "The fire looks nice," she whispered again.

"Yes, it does." He looked to the fire then back at her.

"I love the way the light reflects on the window-panes. Can you see it from there?"

Nodding, Sean glanced up briefly at the reflection of blue, red and yellow lights flickering in the dark panes then back at her. "Why are we whispering?"

She shrugged then giggled. "I don't know. Especially since you just spent so much time trying to make the room soundproof."

Poised on the last step, she looked like she would jump and run if he said boo. Bloody hell, he cried silently. Fear was not what he had hoped to see in her eyes. He added another log to the fire, moving like she was a wild animal easily startled.

Her shining face was scrubbed, her hair brushed and rebraided. She was dressed for bed but like a vestal virgin, covered from head to toe in a pale blue flannel nightgown. But, just in case the nightgown's voluminous folds and heavy material should fail to conceal the body underneath, she had added a long cream-colored shawl over her shoulders. She played with the end of her braid which was tied neatly with a thin, black grosgrain ribbon.

Sean held out his hand, "Will you come and sit with me here by the fire?"

She straightened her shoulders, wrapped her shawl tighter and took a deep breath. Then she plunged headlong across the room and sank to her knees on the new oval rug. She smiled a little as if saying, "Made it."

Scared spitless, he thought. His heart, in direct parallel to another part of him, swelled and went out to her.

The silence spun out. The sound of the wind, moaning like an old lady with the miseries, should have enhanced the snug atmosphere of the room. Instead it amplified the lack of conversation. Chitchat, he thought sarcastically, something at which he'd always excelled.

"Too bad the wing-back chairs haven't arrived yet." *Wha' a stupid thing t' say. Ye sound like a blitherin' idget!*

"It'll be nice to sit here by the fire." She looked at him and he at her. "In a chair, I mean."

"Yeah, ha, ha."

Under the veil of her lashes, Mae shot a quick look from the fire to Sean then back to the fire. Since dinner, he had changed from his cotton shirt to a thick wool sweater. He'd shaved and washed his hair. Distinguishable from his black sweater only by its shine, it was still damp on the end and curled onto his collar. He's so handsome, she thought, handsome as the sunset. Inhaling, she smelled sharp, manly cologne mixed with soap, tobacco and wood smoke. She sighed, wishing he would take her hand but his fingers were splayed on his thighs, the tips of them indenting the fabric of his denims almost . . . almost as if he were nervous too!

"Ah, I'm no good at this!" He ran his fingers through his hair.

"Oh dern, dern, dern!" Mae sat flat on the rug, legs straight out like a kid. "I was hoping one of us was good at it!"

Sean looked at her. What the hell's that supposed to mean? Chewing her lower lip and blushing, she declined to meet his eyes. "What do you mean, you were hoping one of us was good at it?"

She tucked her chin onto her chest, picked up her braid and plucked at the end of it. "Well . . . good at . . . you know what I mean."

"No, what?" He waited, looking at her rosy cheeks

and at her fingers, nervously threading her shawl. She said nothing. He bit off a foul word. He stood. "I think 'tis time for another one of our little chats. But let's get comfortable first. Hop in bed."

Mae sprang up as if reprieved from some terrible punishment. Peeling back the counterpane, she slid into bed and turned her flushed face toward the window.

"Is it my turn?" he asked.

"Yes, I think so." She was about to ask Sean to turn out the light when she realized with dismay that the light was already out! The flickering fire was providing all the room's illumination.

Trying to ignore the rustling sounds of fabric against fabric, the clink of a belt buckle, and the thud of a boot, Mae concentrated on counting the stars outside the window. She only got to eight when she barely felt the bed dip—unlike the one downstairs that slammed them together like the screen door on a windy day. She shot him a quick look. He lay facing her with his head on his arm.

"All right, now," he demanded lightly. "I was talking about social graces. Did you mean you wish one of us was good at love-making?"

"Mmm, well, yes."

He snorted. "Why didn't you say so? Your worries are over."

"Really?" She raised her eyebrows.

"Yes, really. Because I am very, very good," he assured her softly, "an' I'll teach ye everythin' I know."

"Oh?" A small frown furrowed her brow. "Well . . ."

"There are a hundred ways to pleasure a woman. And I know every one of them."

"Really?"

"I could give lessons."

"Really?"

"I could write a book."

"Is that so?"

"Yes. You've only tried one way of love-making. That's obvious. Little Johnny's proof of that. But that particular way is not the only way a man and a woman can love one another." He paused and frowned slightly. "Not to say that it doesn't have fine aspects. It's one I myself am particularly partial to. But when I was in the Orient . . . well, suffice to say I did not spend all my time in the dojo studying saiminjutsu." He chuckled.

What on earth is he talking about? she wondered.

"If you don't take to making love one way, then we'll try another, then another and yet another. Until you find a way you like. What do you think? It's one of those things that's easier to demonstrate than to explain in words. Want to give it a go?" His lips touched her eyes, her brow and burrowing lower, his teeth found an earlobe and tugged on it. "Hmm?" He pulled her nightrail away from her neck with a long finger. "Mmm!" His open mouth on her neck felt piping hot. The achy feeling low in her stomach that always accompanied their kissing sessions started immediately and escalated rapidly.

He raised his head, and quirked his eyebrow in silent question. His shoulders gleamed, looking as rich in texture as the wood ceiling above them. She freed her hands and touched his hair. "I love you, Irishman!" Pulling his head down, she kissed him with all her newly acquired expertise then whispered against his lips. "Show me how good you are then, you braggart!" Then she closed her eyes.

And bit her lip.

And gritted her teeth.

And spread her legs.

"Ready," she said through clenched teeth.

He looked at her, rigid and white as a corpse, and he choked back a long and lurid curse. Great! The girl might as well be a virgin and he knew as much about virgins as he did about the cultivation of okra.

After taking a moment to gain control, he threw back the covers and gently hauled her out of bed. "If you are truly willing to learn, then we'll have to begin at the beginnin', and that's with our bodies."

"Oh . . ." Swallowing convulsively, she clutched the tip of her shawl, left behind and now tangled in the bed covers. "I don't think I . . ." She tried to inch her shawl closer, gathering it into folds.

"We can no' be peepin' and hidin' from one anither, love." With a finger under her chin, he bussed her lips lightly. "Come now. We've gotten to know each other's mind and heart, it behooves us to know our bodies as well."

Mae wanted to find some neutral safe spot on which to fix her gaze while he worked on the buttons of her nightrail. Instead her eyes darted back and forth to various spots on his mostly naked body. Except for knee-length cotton briefs, he was naked. She couldn't get her mind or her downcast eyes off of his groin area. The material of his underwear cupped his manhood like the palm of a soft hand, outlining its shape and delineating its length. Oh-my-God! Kissing her face and neck, he slowly worked open the buttons of her nightrail but his murmured sweet words of love were for naught.

"Uh, wait just a minute." Mae put a staying hand on his chest. "I think I'd rather learn another . . . ?"

" 'Twill be fine." He looked deep into her eyes. "I swear to ye."

She looked from the fireplace—she would love a bucket of water right now—back to the mounding of considerable magnitude in his briefs. Her throat clenched like a fist.

His busy fingers stilled at a tiny button between her breasts. He sighed and looked skyward. "Sweet gel, yer face looks like I just asked ye to hold me spider!"

"Spider?" She curled her upper lip. She looked at the bed, his groin, back at the bed. "Are we going to do something strange with a . . . spider?"

He threw back his head and laughed. "No. I only meant the way you looked when faced with the prospect of seeing my body.

"Basically I'm just like little Jack, only bigger. All in proportion, so to speak." Sometimes jumping in is less of a shock than a toe at a time, he thought. He hooked his thumbs into his briefs, pulled them down and stepped out of them. "Let's just dispense with all the damned mystery, hmm?" He straightened, tossed his knickers over his shoulder and crossed his arms.

Transfixed, eyes glued to his face, she took a deep breath. Her eyes dropped. And bugged. Then closed. Oh, God! No wonder it hurts! Bleakly, her eyes rose to his face.

He raised his hands as if saying, See? "Now, isn't that better?"

She shook her head balefully. "Not really."

Inwardly Sean sighed again. "Dinna be afraid. It will work fine. You'll see." Pulling her into his arms, he tucked her head under his chin and gently held her. Then he had a sudden thought. He hooked a finger around her chin and tugged. "Would ye like to touch me?"

"No." As an afterthought, she added politely, "Thanks anyway."

There was a prolonged silence during which Sean

eyed the gloomy expression on her face and considered the importance of the moment. It was like the few minutes just before a battle. The time when every man puts his life in perspective. This is it! Sean told himself. Everything. One mistake here and now, and that's all she wrote. It was a daunting thought.

"I think tonight we should just become acquainted with our bodies, and wait on the other . . . until another time."

"Oh, Sean!" Mae smiled up at him. "Could we? That would be so nice!"

Nice? Nice is it? He rolled his eyes skyward. "Sit on the bed there, love."

Sean walked to the dresser, naked as a scalded hog, and picked up a hairbrush. Mae averted her eyes but not until she saw broad shoulders, a small waist and tight, almost concave buttocks. He turned. Feigning nonchalance, she lifted her gown and inspected her bare toes. She snuck a look at the front of him—dark, hairy, big—and her toes pleated the rug.

"Come, sweet!" Sitting on the edge of the bed, he pulled her back to stand within the V of his legs.

Mae took a deep breath and, childlike, clasped her hands in front of her. She looked at their reflections in the bureau mirror. Thankfully, that particular part of his body was covered!

"This is a pretty ribbon, love!" Sean removed it from the end of her braid. "Let's put it here for safe-keeping." He fed it through one of her buttonholes and began to loosen her braid.

"I've wanted to do this for a long time." He shook out the three ropelike separations of hair. "Lean back, love. Relax."

She did and scrutinized him in the mirror, his wide cheekbones, the black slash of his brows, his long, almost straight nose, his lips—oh, his lips—wide, sensual, able to coerce such feelings from her. He was frowning slightly and concentrating intently on his task. A black wave of hair fell across his wide brow. Fine striations of gray winged at his temples. My husband! she thought, he's my husband.

He began at the cap of her head. Pulling the brush gently through the length of her hair, he followed the brushstroke with his hand. He held the first batch of hair in his work-rough palm for a long moment. Spreading his fingers, finally, he allowed the curling wisps release. " 'Tis like holdin' a moonbeam!" she heard him mutter.

He brushed and brushed. When he finished a section, he pushed it over her shoulder until a wide silver cascade rippled down the front of her nightrail. Long strands of hair crackled in the dry air, curling around his biceps, mingling with the crisp hairs on his chest.

"Now then," he said when she was leaning bonelessly against him. "To continue that frank discussion we were having. No, now don't stiffen up on me." He continued brushing. "You know how children are conceived but I'd bet that's the extent of your knowledge." Mae tried to listen carefully but seemed to be enjoying the feel of his hands in her hair too much to care. "What transpires between a man and a woman can be . . . indescribably beautiful. No. Beautiful's not strong enough. It can be the closest we mortals get to heaven. Unfortunately, because of the difference in a man and a woman's physical and mental make up, a man can get his pleasure from lovemaking easily while, for the woman, it is a bit more difficult. That's why a man needs to make a careful exploration of what pleases and what does not please the woman he loves. A very knowledgeable man can be a sort of a guide. He can cue the woman and help her to reach fulfillment. The key is the man's control.

That's critical. The man has to keep a tight rein on himself in order to delay his own release."

He brought her hand to his lips, kissed her palm, the fleshy pad of her thumb. He pressed his lips against the throbbing pulse in her wrist, her inner arm. He swept her hair aside, lowered his head and placed a hot kiss on her nape, then another, just below her ear then his eyes met hers in the mirror. "This control is something at which I excel. I swear I would put your pleasure before me own. Do you believe me?" The husky emotion in his voice touched her.

"Yes." Lolling on his shoulder, she was so relaxed now she was practically asleep!

With whispered sensual words, with nonsensical mutterings about the satin of her skin, the beauty of her face, the silkiness of her hair, he coaxed her to even further pliancy. Large hands kneaded her shoulders in a gentle but insistent massage that moved the fabric of her nightrail across her chest in concert. It felt like feathers brushing insistently across her nipples. She opened her eyes. Sean's head was bent, his lips buried in her neck. The material of her nightgown was ruched up in his hands and pulled tight across her chest. Her nipples spiked the fabric like the tips of fingers. Lifting his head, their gazes melded in the mirror for a long time. He tensed his fingers, drawing the material tighter still. "Sean!" she hissed.

She found herself flat on her back and her nightgown was gone and his hands were everywhere.

Eyes tightly closed, she licked slightly parted lips and felt his fingers between her breasts, over her waist and rounded hip, along the inner thigh of her legs. Her flushed chest rose and fell with shallow breaths. She raised trembling hands. "Nae sweet. Dinna cover yerself. Yer the most beautiful woman

I've ever seen." He threaded their hands and lay over her.

His soft, gentle kiss stretched on and on until it was one of twisting, searing intensity. Possessive hands lifted her breasts for his gleaming eyes then held them for his lips. He kissed their curving swell, and the valley between and the skin beneath them. Mae arched her back. His teeth grazed, then his mouth possessed. She pressed against his hair-rough thigh. "Oh, my!"

"Do you like this?"

"Yes."

"Yes?"

"Yes!" A hidden kernel he'd found throbbed.

"And this?"

His fingers worked magic. "Yes." Every nerve in her body had converged in that kernel!

"Yes?"

"Yes!" Her hips left the bed. "Yes! Yes!" Her voice warbled. "Ssssean!" Words deteriorated to mindless sounds.

"Christ!" he said through his teeth, "I'll have t' show you tha' other stuff later. I canno' wai' any longer t' begin!"

The little explosions between her legs were starting to subside and somewhere, far in the back of her mind, Mae thought . . . begin?

Breaths mingling, eyes locked, he eased slowly into her. Her eyes fluttered closed. It was exquisite, sublime, glorious. "Oh, Sean . . ."

"God you're so small. Any pain?" he gritted out.

"No." She opened her eyes slowly, dreamily then wide. The way he looked—teeth bared, eyes shut, sweat sheening his face—alarmed her. "You, Sean?"

"Me?" He gave a strange strangled laugh. "Nae. Yes! Terrible pain." Holding completely still he took

a deep shuddering breath then shook his head. "Giv'
me a minute, love."

Without conscious thought, in an inherently female
motion, Mae pushed her heels into the bed and tilted
her pelvis up in order to take him further.

"Aaah! Damn! Now ye've done i'!"

He lost all control. Utterly and completely. Mating
instincts took over and his mind went blank. He
thought he was going to croak. Then he did actually
die. He must've. Because he experienced heaven.

When he came back to life and when a bit of sanity
returned, he redeemed himself. Putting his extraordinary recall to work, he committed to memory forever
which movement elicited a gasp, which caress
brought a moan, which kiss placed thus roused a cry
of pleasure. Waiting for his love's slower passion to
grow, for her intensity to flower and to match his,
was a pleasure/pain unequalled in his life.

'Twas, he vowed, heaven on earth.

" 'Twas just a little cry. A tiny, tiny whimper."

The bed was a mess! One pillow was missing, who
knew where. The quilt was hanging half off and the
bottom sheet corner had pulled out. It was also wasted
space. Facing each other, legs and arms entwined like
vines, lips inches apart and touching where ever they
could, there was a huge expanse of mattress on either
side of them.

"Don't fib, Sean. I know I did. I . . . I heard myself." Mae blushed. The night was old but neither
wanted it to end.

Smiling, he kissed her forehead then the tip of her

nose. "What do you call those jackets the fox hunters wear?" He whispered.

She blinked, surprised and searched his eyes. "Why, I don't know. Whatever made you think of that?"

" 'Tis the exact color of your face, love."

"Sean!" She punched his shoulder. "This is not funny! What will Uncle Ed think? I'm sure he heard me scream. I think more than . . . more than once."

"Yes, ye did. To me everlastin' gratification." He hugged her to him. "In the morning, when I finally allow you to get out of this bed for a short minute, you can look and see my precautions against just such a thing. I covered the heat grate. The downstairs door is closed. The upstairs door is closed." She saw a flash of teeth.

"However, just to prove me point, I could endeavor right now to make you cry out again. Then, I'll run downstairs and ask Ed if he heard you."

When she freed her lips, she tried to push him back. "I knew it! I did holler, didn't I?"

"My sweet, you wailed like a . . . !" His words were muffled.

"Oh no! Sean!" She looked at the top of his head. His hair was finger messed something awful! "Like a what?" She tried to lift his head without success.

A moan escaped her lips despite the fact that she was biting her lip. His response was inaudible, his warm mouth wonderfully busy. The word she thought he said, before she ceased to think at all, sounded something like "banshee."

"Happy Christmas Eve!"

Mae, warm as a country kitchen in August, woke to the sunlit sight of her husband slipping out of his denims and picking up two steaming cups off the bureau. Oh my! She ran greedy eyes over him and tender muscles clenched in her nether region.

"I made you some coffee, slugabug. Changed and fed Jack and brought him up here." Sean pointed to the baby lying on a blanket in front of the recently refueled fire. "Are ye goin' to sleep yer life away?"

"Oh! My!" Mae sprung up, clutching the bed covers. A thick skein of tangled hair hung over one porcelain shoulder. Disheveled, disoriented, she rubbed her knuckles in her eyes. "What time is it?"

Leaning across, Sean set one cup on her bedtable and one on his own, then pressed her down.

"You've brushed your teeth." She said after he released her mouth. She scanned his face and added. "And you shaved!"

"Hmm! Have you no words of love for an old man? I thought ye would kill me!" He pulled down the covers exposing her love-swollen breast. "Hmm, this is nice . . ."

"Yes, well, you hardly let me sleep a wink! Mmm! Oh!" Mae's eyes drifted shut and her neck arched. She scissored her legs under the covers. "Oh, Sean!" she whispered. "Oh, my . . ."

By the time she sipped her coffee, it had grown well-water cold.

Sean leaned into the barn. "Ed! Hey, Ed, you little squint! Are ye in here?"

Ed walked out of one of the stalls.

"Milking the cows, are ye?"

Ed set a full pail of milk down next to two others. "Well, what else would I be milkin'? Chickens?"

"Don't be a wise ass! It's Christmas Eve, you know. Wise asses don't get naught but a lump of coal in their holey argyle socks."

"Is that a fact?" Ed pulled out his pouch of tobacco. "So . . . what's new with you, Irish?"

Sean shook his finger, grinning, Ed thought, like
a kid. "Dinna embarrass the gel with yer teasin'.
She's shy about . . . you know." Then he grabbed Ed
and pulled him into his arms, knocking his hat off in
his exuberance. He clapped him several times on the
back. Dust flew.

"Shit-house mouse!" When released, Ed picked up
his hat and slapped it back on his head. "I haven't
seen so much hoo-haa since the pigs ate my little
brother."

Sean stopped in midstride. "God, man! Pigs ate
your little brother?"

"It's just a sayin'."

"Oh." Sean shook his head. *What strange sayings
these natives have.* He took two of the pails and
headed toward the porch. Ed followed with the third.
"Mae and I want to go to get the Christmas tree this
morning. Could you stay with Jack?"

"I did that already. Most of the morning."

"I know. I'll make it up to you. We'd rather not
take him along."

"Oh, all right. I guess I can handle him for however
long it takes to get a tree . . ." He winked broadly when
Sean looked over his shoulder. ". . . what I'm worried
about is all the other stuff you've got in mind."

"Other stuff? Wha' other . . ."

The porch door closed silently behind them.

Sean harnessed the horse to the sleigh, singing
"The Wearin' o' the Green" at the top of his lungs.
Setting rags soaked with grease in front of each of
the runners, he walked the horse forward until each
runner was well slicked. It had warmed up for those

few days, then the temperature had plummeted. The snow should be frozen solid and packed hard, he thought and rubbed his hands like a miser.

He bad seen some old bells hanging someplace in the barn. "The question is, where?" he said, wandering around, looking in every nook and cranny. He located them, finally, hanging on the back of the tackroom door and affixed them onto the halter. He flipped them back and forth and grinned. "A foin touch, Sean me boyo. A foin touch indeed."

He gathered some rope to tie the tree on with, an axe and a shovel, and stored them all in the back of the sleigh. 'Twill be the best Christmas in me whole life! he thought, then realized it would be one of very few that he'd actually celebrated.

He mentally itemized the gifts hidden in the loft. For Ed he had a tin of imported Turkish tobacco, a fishing reel, fur-lined hightop boots, and a hand-carved Tennessee turkey caller ordered out of a hunting catalog.

For Jack, he'd insisted that Mae choose toys at Watson's and select some clothes from the Sears catalog. He planned to make a rocking horse for the boy's birthday. Next summer he'd build a teeter-totter outside. Then as soon as the boy was old enough, he'd buy him the sort of things every boy wants. A shotgun, a fishing boat, a football, maybe even one of those newfangled automobiles. The future spun out before him like a pasha's carpet. He and Jack would go fishing and hunting together. He'd teach him rugby. He could hardly wait.

Pausing, with the reins looped around his hand, he wondered if he and Mae would have other sons. God willing, he thought, and felt deep and strange emotions. A son. Maybe a whole team of ruggers! An' at least one daughter who looked like her mother. He paused. She'll have eyes the color of heather in the springtime. Heather. Now that was a pretty name for a gel.

Yer getting a bit ahead of yerself, aren't you? Ye've just bed the girl and already yer thinking of a bairn of yer own?

He walked the horse toward the door. When he reached for a cheroot, his hand encountered a draft of a wire he intended to send the next time he was in town. He pulled it out and unfolded it. It was brief.

> O'Brien: I'd notified you weeks ago that I wouldn't be testifying. Guess the message wasn't received.
>
> I'm married and have responsibilities that take precedence. I'm wiring you back the money you paid me, some interest plus an estimated amount for the clothes you bought. If I owe more, let me know. Sorry. Sean McGloin."

Sean replaced the draft. Had O'Brien really not received his earlier wire? Or had he chosen to ignore it? Sean had stopped checking at General Delivery weeks ago, so the clerk had asked Father Fitz to bring O'Brien's message out. It had said they were about ready to prosecute Spinelli and asked Sean to let Hanson in Minneapolis arrange his transportation back to New York.

Sean's decision, though final, didn't sit well. He was not a man to go back on a deal.

He pushed back both of the barn doors—and the niggling voice of his conscience—and turned his mind to the more comfortable task of his inventory of presents.

For his lovely bride he had a blue cashmere coat ordered all the way from Chicago and a bottle of Enchantment cologne. On an impulse he'd bought a new-fangled thing called a Kodak Brownie camera. It was really something—if it worked. Supposedly a person could take pictures one day, send the film away to be processed and in only a couple of weeks—pictures! Amazing! He'd been afraid the cold in the barn would hurt the mechanism, so Ed had it hid under his bed. The little squint was the first thing he was going to take a picture of. "That camera salesman must've seen you comin', Irish," he'd said more than once.

Let's see, he paused, what else? Oh, yeah, the ring. How could he forget the sapphire ring he'd bought to go with the earrings she prized. And a thin satin nightgown so sheer he could see the lines in his hand when he held it behind the material. A song book, *Old Favorites from the Gay '90s*. (If the gel wants to sing, he vowed, I'll sing. Even if it peels the paint off the parlor walls.) Sean heard the porch door close and he turned with a huge grin.

"Hello, Sean."

"Hello, love!"

Two blankets were thrown over her arm. The top of a jug showed between the folds of one. "I've got a container of cider here." Mae said.

"So I see." He kissed her quickly then lifted her, blankets, cider and all and walked into the barn. Behind the door, he held her captive against the barn wall.

While he pressed burning kisses on her neck, he lifted her knee and coaxed her leg around his waist. He settled himself and rotated his hips.

She felt his enthusiasm through the bulk of the blankets and all the layers of winter clothing. "Sean!" Behind them the horse tramped and snorted.

"I canno' help meself! 'Tis like I'm bewitched."

"Uncle Ed . . . We should go get the tree,

Sean! . . . Mmm!" Mae lost all ability to think. Next thing she knew, she was hearing bells!

Bells?

"Oh, Sean, let's go back upstairs. We can get the tree later."

"No. If I get back in bed with you we would never go. And it is Christmas Eve." He carried her to the sleigh.

"I can walk, you know."

"No need for that, love!" He covered the cold wooden seat with the blankets then he plunked her down and covered her legs with the lap rug.

After climbing in, he turned the horse in the direction of the river bluffs. He glanced at her, and smiled. She smiled back and adjusted her coat and the lap rug.

"Ah, before I forget. About that dress . . ."

"Dress?" She looked down but her dress was covered by her coat. She had to think a second to recall which one she had on. "What about it?"

" 'Tis a bit tight in the bodice, don't ye think?"

"Tight? No, I don't think so." It was too tight but she had already let the side seams out as far as she could.

He smiled at her again. "I don't mind your wearing it in my presence but I don't want other men . . . er . . . getting any ideas."

"Ideas? What other men, Sean?"

"Any man with eyes in his head who isn't dead."

"Oh, Sean. You can't be jealous."

"Possessive, aye. Jealous, aye. I don't want some man ogling what's mine and mine alone."

"Then I'll keep my coat on when I wear this dress." She pulled him down to kiss his cheek. He turned and kissed her fully. There was a prolonged period while the jingling horse plodded along totally directionless.

Within no time they were into the heavily forested area. Crisp clean air invigorated and chilled simultaneously. Winter solstice had just passed and the sun still hung in the south. The countryside's mantle of snow glittered in a radiant display almost painful to the naked eye. Trees, denuded now of their camouflage of leaves, revealed large, snow-capped nests high in the forks of their branches. Despite the slew of different-sized tracks crisscrossing their path, Sean and Mae experienced a sense of solitude as they passed through the still countryside.

Sean's sixth sense kicked in during Mae's bubbly recollection about snowfalls on previous Christmas Days.

". . . when I was twelve, I think it was the last Christmas before Granny passed away. Well, we had one of the worst blizzards in the history of the area. We were totally snowbound for mmm . . . must've been at least ten days. But we had so much fun! We pulled taffy . . ."

An ominous, eerie feeling stole over him, chilling him bone deep instantly. He pulled up on the reins. He looked behind them at the farm and outbuildings, small in the distance below, then toward the treeline ahead.

"What is it, Sean?" She smiled at him, her face aglow with happiness. "Oh, I was having such a good time I forgot all about the tree." Sitting up straighter, she looked around. "Do you see one already? I think you'll have to get closer to the bluffs. There aren't any good ones this close."

"No. It's something else . . ." He looked at her. A

short scarf, tied under her chin with a bulky knot, framed cheeks and lips that were a tempting cherry red against the white of her skin. His ominous feeling receded like a bad hairline. He shook his head and pulled her into the circle of his arm. "I don't see a good tree yet but I do see you, my sweet gel and I'm blinded to all else."

"Go on wit' ye!" She pushed at him laughing. "Yer full o' i', Irish!"

"Where did you pick up that awful accent?"

"Accen'? Wha' accen'?"

Shaking his head, Sean clucked to the horse. "Now then, you were talking about blizzards. I don't want horror stories about all the years before. I want to know about this Christmas. Will it snow or nae?"

"There's only one way to tell for sure. After you've lived here a hundred years, you'll be able to do it too. There's a certain smell." She raised her chin and sniffed like a rabbit. "Yep!"

Sean grinned at her. "A hundred years, hmm?" Her mittened hands were stuck up in her father's old coat's sleeves and he thought of the blue coat in the loft. He turned his rear impatiently on the seat. "Why can't we open our presents tonight?"

"Absolutely not! It's a family tradition to open our presents on Christmas Day, first thing in the morning. Saint Nicholas has to come on Christmas Eve! How can you get your presents before Saint Nicholas comes and brings them?" She shook a mittened fist at him. "That's the third time you've asked me. You're worse than a . . . Oh, look!" She pointed at a bushy-tailed red fox darting across the horse's path then into the woods.

After Sean lit his cheroot, Mae tucked her hand through his arm. They crossed a winterbourne stream lined with tall grasses, brown and bowed by heavy casings of ice.

Mae rubbed her cheek against Sean's shoulder, momentarily saddened that she didn't have much for him for Christmas. Sean was always pressing money on her to buy for herself or for Johnny or for the house. Still she did not feel comfortable spending his money, even on him. As a consequence, his presents were economical. And, for the most part, homemade. She'd carefully measured his hammer handle, screwdrivers and wrenches then sewn appropriate canvas holders of various sizes and lengths onto a leather belt she had asked the blacksmith to make. One of the construction workers had been wearing just such a handmade belt when she'd visited Peter at the building site one time. She'd noticed how everyone else was going back and forth to their tools and that man had just pulled whatever he needed out of his low-slung, gunfighter-style belt.

She'd also knitted a woolen scarf in a lovely pewter color which would match his eyes to a tee. Regretably, there hadn't been time to do a sweater. Next year, however . . .

Mae smiled to herself. Next year and the year after that and . . . Oh, she was so happy! She buried her nose in his jacket sleeve.

Sean's voice intruded on her thoughts.

"There's one!" He pointed to a tall Norwegian pine.

"Oh, my stars! That's got to be at least fifteen feet high." She curled her hand around her chin thoughtfully. "Well, now, wait just a minute . . . If we took out the floor in our room and made a sort of vaulted . . ."

"The first person to touch me new floor with more than a pat of beeswax is dead!"

"Now look, Sean, at all we have to choose from." They had reached the tree-studded bluffs. "There!"

Mae pointed to a long nettled balsam, top-shaped and about five feet tall, its windward boughs decorated with great clumps of snow. "It's perfect!"

"That's the one?" Sean asked, tossing aside his cheroot.

"That's the one. For sure!"

"Whoa, Jocko." Sean swung down and stepped into deep-drifted snow. After helping Mae alight, he removed the shovel and axe from the back of the sleigh.

"Let me have the shovel . . ." She snatched at the handle. ". . . so I can dig out around the base."

"No, I'll do this. Just wait right here."

"Absolutely not! I can help. Let me have the shovel."

"No!" Shovel tucked under his arm, Sean pulled on his gloves.

"Yes, I say!"

Mae latched onto the shovel just as Sean turned. Off balance, he started to fall and tossed the tools aside. He grabbed her coat lapel and pulled her with him. Yelping with mock surprise, Mae fell as heavily as she could on top of him. And knocked the wind out of herself.

Quickly Sean flipped her over and covered her body with his. The axe and shovel handles stuck out of the nearby drift like toothpicks in marshmallows.

"Get your nose out of there, Sean. It's freezing"

"Ah, yes, but me heart is warm." Angling his head, he kissed her neck once more. "An' anither part of me is hotter than a peat fire." Again and again, he was drawn to her lips.

They were spooning, Mae thought, as if they were in the middle of their warm bed instead of lying spread-eagled in a snowdrift. And she didn't care. Not a bit. The man had that kind of power over her.

He moved his hips against her. "I know it's cold,

but what are the chances . . . ?" He smiled down at her and started to dip his head again when, like a stag scenting danger, he rose stiff-armed above her.

"Well . . ." She looked dreamily up at him. Her eyes widened. There was something about the way he looked—jaw tense, eyes narrow and focused—that frightened her. She was suddenly chilled. "What is it, Sean?"

"I don't know." He stood and pulled her up with him. "Maybe we should head back."

She brushed the back of her coat off, perplexed. "Why are you acting so strange, Sean?"

"Didn't you ever feel like somebody walked on your grave?" He retrieved the shovel and axe and started toward the sleigh.

"No." She stuck out her lower lip. "I don't see why we can't get the tree as planned. We must have a tree, Sean. Sean! It's Johnny's first Christmas."

He looked at her face, the picture of disappointment. "All right. We'll get our tree." Wielding the shovel quickly, Sean removed the snow from around the bottom of the sturdy tree. Then he exchanged the shovel for the axe and smiled at Mae's worried face. "It's probably nothing."

Yet, it was. Sean tried unsuccessfully to force his uneasy feeling aside. It took less then five minutes to fell the tree.

Preoccupied with tying the tree securely to the back of the sleigh and wrapping the rope carefully so the boughs would not be damaged, he was totally unprepared.

Eighteen

A huge snowball splatted against the back of his head. Its wet residue held against his neck by his turned up collar. *"Hey!"*

"Gotcha, Sean!"

The second one caught him square in the face as he turned. He spat and tried to wipe his eyes and mouth clear with stiff leather gloves. "Yer about to meet up with yer worst nightmare."

"Oh, yeah? Sounds like all talk to me."

Obviously, the attack was planned with malice aforethought since the enemy had cleverly stockpiled ammo. As soon as he could see, he mounted a furious counteroffensive. Roaring like a bull moose, arms in front of his face to protect against the snowballs that were being pelted at him rapid fire now, Sean charged. Even with snow in his eyes it was a simple matter to track the attacker. He simply followed the squeals that sounded like those of a stuck pig.

It was over in seconds. He subdued his adversary and secured all positions. Then, he negotiated some very stiff concessions from the vanquished.

Ah, but the surrender terms were foin! Foin indeed!

They inched their way back toward the farm. By the time they reached the hill above the farm, Mae was paying the proverbial piper. And the piper, having secured the reins in order to free his hands, was pleasing her in ways she had never thought of.

Abruptly Mae broke the seal of their kiss and looked away.

"Is it too cold for such shenanigans, love?"

"Shh! Just a minute . . . Do you hear anything?" Mae cocked her head, listening.

Sean mumbled "Just the sound of me blood rushing down to me di- . . ." He turned his head toward the farmhouse below. They both looked down. It was a picture-perfect scene. The small farmhouse nestled in a snowy blanket . . .

Suddenly Sean picked Mae up by the waist and set her on the seat.

He whistled sharply and took the whip out of the holder. Jocko leapt forward.

"Is that Johnny crying? Oh, it is, Sean! I've never heard him scream like that!"

They raced into the yard. The barn doors that Sean had carefully latched an hour ago gaped open. High-pitched screams came from within.

"Oh my God, Sean! Johnny!" Mae jumped out of the sleigh before the horse came to a complete stop. Sean grabbed but just missed her coat. He caught up with her a few feet from the barn door.

Mae ignored his "Stay here!" and raced behind him. He turned too late to prevent her from seeing into the shadowy barn. Her screams joined her son's.

Her uncle's body slumped in his favorite spot, on the bale of hay closest to the coal heater. Head thrown back, leaning slightly askew against the barn beam behind him, he looked like he'd fallen asleep. Blood covered his blue plaid shirt like a bib. Twirling and frantically waving his arms, the red-faced baby hung by his ankles from a rope thrown over a rafter in the barn ceiling.

Wearing a bulky black overcoat and a wide-brimmed hat, both of which seemed to be several sizes too large, was an olive-skinned man with a gun.

"Come in, mick!" The man waved them into the barn with his gun. "O.K., Alf, you can cut the kid down now." A man brushed by them.

The second man pulled the stepladder over, unsheathed a long-bladed knife and slowly sawed through the rope holding the baby. He stepped off the ladder and held the screaming child a foot from the floor. He looked at Mae. He smiled then let the rope slip. Johnny jerked to a stop inches from the hard-packed earth. Galvanized by fear, Mae twisted in Sean's arms.

The gunman pointed at the baby. "Shut the kid up, lady. Now. Or I'll take care of it."

Sean released her.

As she passed her uncle, who appeared to stare at a point beyond her, her steps faltered. Uncle Ed's dead, she thought. Dead! Oh my God. Her child, still crying and dangling upside down, kept her moving.

She bent and cradled Johnny in her arms. Ignoring the man who looked over her shoulder, she plucked at the ropes on the baby's ankles and tried to soothe him.

"I told you to shut that kid up, lady!" The other man yelled.

Only two of them? Sean wondered to himself.

"Shhh, Johnny!" Mae swayed back and forth, her face close to the child's. Finally he quieted, his body jerking with great gasping sobs. Crooning, she laid him over her shoulder and rubbed his back. The baby hiccoughed and stuck a consoling fist in his mouth. He looked at Sean.

To Sean, the baby's young/old face was accusing.

"So. You've come for me."

"D'accordo, mick, and a long God-damned way

too." Without looking at Mae, he said, "Sit down, lady. Over there on the bench."

Stiffly, Mae complied.

The man used the gun barrel to push up his hat brim and uncovered greased hair, hanging jowls and BB-sized eyes.

The second, younger man shuffled into the light. He had the beginning of a black eye. Sean glanced at Ed and thought, *Good go, mate!*

Alf, standing so close to Mae his open coat seemed to enclose her, was holding the knife loosely but expertly. He touched himself, rubbing his hand down his groin.

Sean took two quick steps and was halted by a bullet that whistled by him and thunked into the barn wall.

"Where do ya think you're goin'? Dumb mick!" The gunman said.

Alf leaned over Mae again. His lips moved.

Sean spoke through clenched teeth. "Tell him to lay off."

The gunman looked at the younger man disinterestedly. "Save it, Alf."

Mae, shoulders rounded over the child, glanced behind her at the man, then at Sean, her fearful plea written plainly on her face. She unbuttoned her coat and tucked the whimpering baby inside.

"Hey, she's gonna give the baby some tit. Make her take off her coat, Angelo."

The man called Angelo looked with some interest at Mae. Sean moved a stride forward again.

Flat, soulless eyes returned to Sean. "I'm not gonna say it again."

"I've written everythin' down."

"Is that right?"

"Sure. An insurance policy in a manner of speaking. Something happens to me, the stuff'll automatically go to D.C." He nodded at Mae and the child, "Let them go."

Angelo smiled tiredly. "Don't try to feed me any crap. I'm not stupido." He walked a little closer.

Fifteen feet, Sean figured.

" 'Member O'Brien?" Angelo waited for Sean's head jerk. "It was your buddy O'Brien who told us where to find you."

Angelo paced when he talked. Ten feet now.

"He had to make it hard on himself. It was real . . . how you say . . . undignified, you know?"

"Ain't that right, Alf? Wasn't it undignified?"

Alf, standing behind Mae, was caressing himself and the blade of his knife. She was perched on the far end of the bench.

"Hey! Alf! Will you get your mind off your dick?"

Alf looked up. All limbs, he resembled a praying mantis. His eyes were the color of mold. He smiled and pale skin stretched across bones. "Yeah! Man, that guy was such a hard ass!"

Angelo walked over to the window and looked out, ignoring Ed's corpse less than a foot from where he stood.

"Screamed like a woman."

Alf was momentarily distracted by Mae once again. He watched her rock, her lips to the baby's forehead.

"I had to put my fingers in my ears he was so loud!" Alf chuckled softly.

"Like I said. Very undignified." Angelo folded his arms but kept the pistol, resting in the crook of his arm, trained. "Me and a couple of other guys was way in the back in the warehouse office, trying to have a meeting. We had to shut the damned door."

Sean's fists were knotted like his stomach.

Alf looked at Mae for a long minute then with a mournful look of regret, walked closer.

A little closer, arsehole.

Angelo spoke over his shoulder. "What was in the bucket."

He licked thick lips with a chalk-coated tongue. "Lye."

Angelo bowed to Mae. "Think about the little lady here. The kid. You don't want them to see something like that."

Mae's averted face was so white, Sean feared she would pass out. Throat working, she buried her face in Johnny's neck and started rocking again.

"All right." Sean took a long step forward. "I'll tell you what . . ."

Ed's body, hands still neatly crossed, tilted.

"Ebbene! You're in no position to bargain."

"You don't deal with me, neither of you will leave this barn alive."

Sean's bold statement brought a giggle from Alf and an incredulous look from Angelo.

"Pretty tough talk, mick. You must not've noticed what I got here." He held the gun out.

"If you believe anything, believe that yer gun will make no difference."

Behind Angelo, Ed's corpse tilted further, then toppled off the bale of hay.

Mae screamed.

The baby started crying again stridently.

Sean lunged for Alf. Alf fired. The bullet hit Sean in the shoulder. Another shot and pain seared Sean's thigh but he'd reached Alf. He grabbed his arm, broke his wrist and twisted the knife into him, entering just above the groin. Alf shrieked. His belt buckle stopped Sean's upward thrust. Like a fandango dancer, Sean twirled Alf between himself and Angelo. Angelo fired twice, the bullets jolting Alf's body.

Inches apart, their gazes met for a split second. The light in Alf's eyes dimmed. "So long, arsehole." The acrid smell of urine permeated the air. Alf slumped loverlike on Sean's shoulder. Sean used Alf's body like a battering ram. It jerked from the impact of another bullet.

Angelo and Sean grappled with the gun. An instant before they fell to the ground, Sean took a bullet in the knee.

Sean got the gun and tossed it aside. He gripped Angelo's neck and squeezed hard. Twisting and heaving, Angelo tried to throw him off.

It felt like someone was hammering a spike into Sean's knee. Sweat stung his eyes and blurred his vision. Consciousness ebbed. *Stay with it. Dinno' pass out now, man!* He could no longer see! He concentrated on sounds. Angelo's grunts and raspy breathing . . . Mae's cries . . . and on keeping his fingers . . . *Squeeze man, tighter* . . .

"Hold it, McGloin!" The command came from behind. "Don't move, DiAngelo!"

Stronger fingers than Sean's pried his hands off. Slowly, painfully, he was rolled over onto his back. Pain stabbed his shoulder, his knee. Everything dimmed. He looked into the smudged outline of a face. He was losing consciousness. The image blurred.

Sounds . . . then there were only sounds . . . Mae's screaming his name . . . Jack's cries . . . receding. Someone spoke O'Brien's name then there was a final shot . . .

Bloody hell, Sean thought. Groggily, he looked around him then closed gravel-encrusted lids. His head ached like he was coming off a three-day binge. Except it wasn't only his head that hurt. Slowly, he opened his eyes again and, turning his head saw Mae's pale, pinched face.

He smiled and said "Hello, love," but no sound came out.

Sobbing, "Oh, Sean! Thank God!" she covered her face with her hands.

"Here!" He croaked. He cleared his throat and tried again. "Here! Don't cry!" He started to sit up. Strong hands pressed on the only place that didn't hurt. He rolled his head clockwise fifteen minutes. It was Hanson! His escort in Minneapolis. It had been Hanson's face he saw before he passed out.

"Lay still." Hanson removed his hand from Sean's shoulder and sat back in a chair bedside. "You've lost a lot of blood."

Sean looked around his old room on the first floor. The last thing he remembered was O'Brien. And Ed. *Ah, no, God no.*

Sean woke feeling barely human. It must be a moonless night; it looked like the window pane had been painted over with pitch. Someone was moving quietly around the room. A chair scraped against the wood floor. A glass clinked. He turned toward the noise. Nothing seemed to have changed. Hanson was resuming his seat at the end of the bed. Mae still sat on the other side, her eyes red-rimmed. Reaching out weakly, Sean laid a hand against her cheek. Her skin felt smooth and cool. She turned her face into his hand and kissed his palm. "You look exhausted, love. And too pale."

Mae held his hand to her cheek. "I'm all right. Oh

God! Sean! I've been so worried about you." She smiled gamely at him, but a tear wet his finger.

"Here! None o' that now. Ye can see for yerself I'm all right."

Hanson picked up one of Sean's cheroots and at his nod, stuck it in his mouth then lit it. Sean inhaled raggedly. "Thanks."

"I deeply regret that this happened." Hanson said. "We were only hours behind them."

Rubbing a hand over his face, Sean closed his eyes. Bloody hell! For just a second he'd forgotten. The old man. Dead! O'Brien! Dead! Anger stained Sean's face. "Jesu! You regret? Fat lot of good that does, man!"

Hanson studied the crease in his pant leg. "You think you've taken every precaution to protect your investigator then they get to someone. To some men the prospect of ten times what they make in a year is just too tempting." He looked up at Sean. "O'Brien was one of the best. He . . ."

Sean jerked his chin toward Mae who was staring wide-eyed at Hanson.

The ladder-backed chair creaked as Hanson shifted toward the window.

"Mae, love. Will you please get me some . . . ah . . ." Turning his head on the pillow, Sean noticed two water glasses and a pitcher on the bedside end table. The coffeepot was on a tray on the dresser with three clean cups turned upside down on a folded napkin. ". . . tea."

"Tea?" Surprised, she asked, "Tea, Sean?"

"Yes, please, love."

"Yes, right away, Sean." She rose and hurried out of the room.

Wincing, Sean laid back. "Bloody hell!" His head

felt like it was going to explode. Cautiously and very slowly, he turned back to Hanson.

The government man apologized, holding his hands up like a gun was stuck in his ribs. "Sorry. I wasn't thinking . . ."

"I'd like to spare her any more of this . . . mess. She has seen an' heard enough to last a lifetime. Tell any others . . ."

Hanson nodded. "I'll tell them."

They both listened to Mae's movements in the kitchen. "I hate friggin' tea." Sean said tiredly, his pain as much mental and physical. "Now, tell me about O'Brien."

"It was his day off. They picked him as he was coming out of the grocer's. By the time his wife missed him and notified us . . ." Hanson lowered his voice to a gruff whisper. "Some poor kid found him. They'd dumped him under the boardwalk at Coney Island." Hanson's thin lips compressed. "He was a tough guy, O'Brien. Only seven years on the job but he was a damned good agent. He didn't make it easy for 'em, I can guarantee you that much . . ."

Staring out the window, Sean wasn't listening. He was remembering the last time he saw O'Brien.

Since O'Brien didn't think it was wise for Sean to go back to his place, O'Brien was to pick up some clothes, make arrangements to get Sean out of town and then they were to meet at a little Italian place on the Jersey side of the bridge. Gerardi's Trattoria.

The restaurant's only other patron—a wizened gumba wearing a shiny black suit with baggy trousers—lowered his newspaper and argued in staccato Italian with the waitress while she refilled his minuscule expresso cup.

Sean sat at a table near the window and wondered how long it would be before O'Brien showed. He was exhausted and famished. The waitress, built like a sumo wrestler, brought water, thick black coffee and some chewy breadsticks that Sean finished before she had waddled through the kitchen door. The door opened, then closed and Sean's nostrils filled with the titillating aroma of garlic, spicy sausages and fresh-baked bread. He looked around for more breadsticks.

Every table was identical. Embedded in a waxy pedestal was a red candle no higher than a spool of thread. A shot glass held toothpicks. The center-piece—a squat wine bottle with green, red and white paper flowers atop pipe-cleaner stems—was starting to appear edible when finally a shiny Ford touring automobile pulled up in front. O'Brien got out, slung a duffel bag over his shoulder, looked around briefly then sauntered toward the door.

The servings were monstrous and the food fabulous. Neither man had any problem putting away everything. Sean and O'Brien both sat back replete. With unspoken accord they had eaten their multi-course meal in virtual silence.

"You pack it away pretty good for a little guy!"

O'Brien waved his toothpick. "Hey, little? I'm growin' yet." He started methodically maneuvering the toothpick between his teeth. "Besides, I'm a nervous wreck. I always eat when I'm nervous." Glancing at Sean's face, noting the one raised eyebrow, O'Brien added. "Nah! Not about this deal, man. It's my old lady. She's p.g." He grinned wide enough to reveal two gold molars. "She's gonna have it any minute. It's our first."

"Congratulations." Sean said.

"Yeah, thanks." O'Brien's grin wavered then he frowned. "Except this kid may be our last, too. Megan, that's my wife . . . Meg says she's so miserable she's never even gonna do it again." He shook his head. "Can't say that I blame her. You should see her. She's normally so small. Really tiny." His laugh was forced. "Not now. She's as big as the Federal Building. And mean. Man, I heard women get a bit testy, especially towards the end, but Meg's like a damned pit viper!"

Sean laughed, and found himself wondering about O'Brien and his wife. Had they known each other long? Were they childhood sweethearts? Where did they live? Brooklyn? Queens? the Lower East Side? . . . and he felt a pang of something . . . envy?

Nah. Couldn't be.

"Last night," two deep creases had formed between O'Brien's russet eyebrows, "Megan's ankles were so swollen, I said, let's go. We're gonna go to the doctor." He ran his hand through thick, unruly hair. "Jesus, that woman's so stubborn. She worries all the time about money. Money money money. Hell . . ." There was a pensive pause while he turned the toothpick glass. "I don't care about money, you know?" Sean nodded.

Abruptly O'Brien sat up, looked out the window then checked a big stem-winder watch.

"Say, getting back to the business at hand . . ." He tilted his torso to one side, reached into his back pocket and handed Sean a folded note with a name on it. He laid a fat envelope on the table. "Here's . . ." Both men looked outside at the sound of an approaching automobile. "There's your driver. Looks like Palmer. He's good."

Sean stood. O'Brien pushed the envelope at him.

"Here's your payment, the name of a contact in Minnesota and a way to get in touch with me. If everything goes as planned, you won't hear from me until we're ready for you." O'Brien smiled and punched Sean's shoulder. "Hey! No need to look so grim. I just handed you more money than a lot of people see in a lifetime. Myself included."

Sean bent at the waist to see under the large sign that spanned the window, "Special Today—Spaghetti & Meatballs." The car was still running. He could see the shadow of a man's bulky form behind the windshield. He hefted the weight of the new duffel bag O'Brien had brought, then slung it over his shoulder; it wasn't light. "See ya."

O'Brien stayed him with a hand on his arm. "Listen, keep a low profile and a tight lip." He shook his head. "Hell, what am I doing? I don't have to tell you." He cleared his throat, coughed, looked away. "Hey, thanks, McGloin."

Sean dug his fingers into his eyes. "What about O'Brien's wife?"

"A widow's pension from the department, of course, and everyone kicked in for her and his daughter . . ."

"Bloody hell!" *A daughter. He had a daughter.* Sean lowered his hands. "I don't mean that. I mean what will Spinelli do about her."

"Won't touch her. It's sort of an unwritten law they've got. That guy, Alfonse, the one they called Al the Eel, he was an exception . . ."

Mae walked in at that moment. She smiled at Sean then frowned when she saw his flushed expression. She set the tray with the cozy-covered teapot and cups down on the dresser. Hurrying to the bed, she pressed a cool palm on his forehead. "Are you feeling all right, Sean? You look like you have a fever!" She scowled at Hanson. "Mr. Hanson, the doctor said Sean needs complete rest and quiet."

"I'm sorry, ma'am."

"And you," she turned to Sean, "you're not even supposed to be sitting up yet."

"I'm all right. I'm fine. And I've a bit more business with Mr. Hanson here." When she opened her mouth to protest, Sean held up his hand. "Give me a kiss, then I want you to leave us alone for a bit."

"But, Sean . . ."

"Mae, please just do as I ask! I dinno' have the energy to argue with ye."

Something in his tone or his expression, made her choke off a ready argument. She glanced questioningly at Hanson, who was pointedly scrutinizing his pant's crease again.

She leaned over and pressed her cool lips to Sean's. "Please don't make me leave, Sean!" she whispered and kissed his unresponsive lips again. "I just want to be near . . . I'll sit in the corner over there, quiet as a mouse and . . ."

"Go, sweet." Pulling her head down, he kissed her hard then turned away. "Go."

Sean waited until he heard the door latch then pushed himself up as far as possible against the headboard. "Give me another one of my smokes."

"You want tea? Or this?" He held out a flask.

"Both."

Hanson poured a good-sized shot of whiskey in the cup, added some tea and handed it to Sean.

Sean took a sip, waiting until the whiskey lit a fire within. "What now?"

"We still want to go ahead with the case against Spinelli. Now more than ever. And we want you with us. How about it?"

Sean ran his good hand through his hair. "I notified O'Brien that I wasn't going to testify."

"But not now, right?" Hanson stood by the bed, the knuckles of one hand indenting the mattress.

"O'Brien, your wife's uncle, you can't let that kind of injustice slide."

"Nae."

Hanson sat down heavily.

After a minute, Sean asked, "O'Brien was your man?"

Hanson nodded.

"This was your operation?"

Another nod.

"What in the hell were you doing in Minneapolis that day?" Sean held out his cup and Hanson refilled it, omitting the tea.

"Dedicating a new regional office." Hanson sat again. "I'm normally in D.C."

"Who else knows where I am."

"Myself and two of my men. The big boss. In Washington."

"Too many." Sean muttered under his breath. He lifted the covers with one hand and tried to move his legs. Through clamped jaws, he asked, "Who worked on me?"

"Local man. Neimark, I think. He'll keep quiet. He arranged to dispose of the . . . bodies also."

"Did you kill DiAngelo?"

Hanson shrugged. "I had to. He was goin' for his gun."

Sean stared at Hanson. Hanson stared back. Sean distinctly remembered wrestling DiAngelo's gun from him and tossing it several feet away.

Hanson shrugged. "Like you said, O'Brien was my man."

It took a second to equate. The gray-haired old man, sitting with his hands prissily folded atop crossed knees, an executioner.

I shouldn't be surprised, Sean thought, murderers come in all shapes, sizes and ages. There was a highly paid assassin who operated out of Lisbon, a hump-backed little grandmother who used an umbrella out-fitted with a curare-tipped rapier. "Dearie?" she'd ask her mark. "Can you give an old lady a helping hand across the street?"

She had no problem, he'd heard, getting her man.

Hanson was speaking, ". . . you're fit, we'll start the ball rolling." When Sean didn't respond, Hanson went on. "We need you, McGloin. We'll make it worth your while. There'll be a lot more money."

" 'Tis nae the money, man." A pounding pain in his shoulder arrested his angry movement.

Hanson leaned up and added more liquor to Sean's cup. "You've caused them to lose two of their peo-ple—four counting Calabrese and Lorenzo."

Sean looked puzzled. "Who the hell's Calabrese and Lorenzo?"

"The guys who surprised you in Spinelli's office."

"Oh, yeah."

Hanson continued. "You can put out the word that you've refused to testify. It won't even slow Spinelli down. He couldn't take the chance that you'd use what you know against them some time in the future." Hanson removed the cozy and poured straight tea into his cup. He drank it daintily, pinky stiff. A long mo-ment passed. "He'll just send someone else."

The irascible rooster crowed at the brightening ho-rizon. Sean looked out the frost-encrusted window. With dawn he could distinguish familiar shapes in the yard although the view was gray and bleak. The sleigh still sat in the yard with the tree still tied on the back. Patches of green showed through the fresh snow that covered its nettles. 'Twas to be Johnny's first real Christmas. Now it was to be the old man's last. He thought of the presents in the loft—the tobacco, the turkey caller—and rubbed his eyes. "Aw damn it! How many days past Christmas?"

"Eight."

"Eight days. Sweet Jesu! I had no idea I'd been out for so long!"

"So long? You're lucky you weren't out permanently, McGloin. The doc kept you sedated."

Sean snorted. "I was just thinking that meself. How damned lucky I am. Always have been." Some movement outside caught his eye. "What are the damages, anyway. My leg hurts like hell." Mae crossed the yard, wearing her father's old coat and carrying the milk pails.

"The bullet in your shoulder passed through. The bullet in your thigh had to be dug for but it's healing well. The third may be the most damaging permanently. The bullet missed the kneecap but just barely. It was the devil to remove, I guess, and Neimark isn't sure know how much damage there'll end up being to the muscles. An inch and he said he'd've had to take the leg."

"O'er my dead body."

"It might have been that. That's what I mean about lucky. Not many men can take three shots and end up with a stiff leg."

Mae set down the pails, wedged one of the barn doors with difficulty and slipped through small opening.

Sean spoke over his shoulder. "Have somebody move the sleigh into the barn, will you? And could you have someone drag that tree off someplace?"

"Yes. I'll see to it."

"Today. It's . . . depressing."

"All right. Right away if you like."

A minute later, Mae came out with the shovel and started removing enough snow so she could push back one of the barn doors. "What did you tell my . . ." Sean's voice failed, ". . . my wife?"

"As little as possible but what I did say was pretty much the truth." Shrugging, Hanson smiled a little. "She had plenty of questions. I told her the rest of her answers would have to come from you."

Leaning forward, Hanson rested his forearms on his knees. "Listen, McGloin. I'll be frank because we need you on this. You can't stay here anyway, man. Might as well come with us to New York and testify. You'd get those guys good for what they did. I can promise you that you'll have every protection. After the trial, you'd be free to go anywhere. We'll relocate you and your wife wherever you want. With the money, you can make a new start."

Hanson couldn't read McGloin's reaction. The man continued to look out the window.

Mae walked out of the barn carrying a bucket of chicken feed. She wore the same scarf she'd had on the day they cut down the tree. The same dress showed below her coat. When Sean spoke, his words were bitten. "I need some time to consider."

Hanson nodded. "I can understand that. Think it over. I believe you'll see it's your only option."

"In the meantime, I want you to take care of some things for me."

Hanson nodded again. He took out a small blue notebook and licked his pencil like a kid.

Sean closed his eyes tightly for a minute. Whatever medication he'd been on was wearing off. He looked back outside, then stiffened. His eyes scanned the yard, the path to the house.

Where's Mae?

He struggled to sit up. "Hey! Where're your men?" At that moment, she backed out of the chicken coop.

Sean slumped back. "I'm holding you personally responsible for the lives of me wife and child."

"The place is covered like snow. Even the train station. Same with all the roads. I've got a couple of men here who will not leave until it's totally over. Good men. Okay?"

"Okay." Sean rubbed his eyes. "Send someone into town for a Father Lawrence Fitzgerald. You'll find him at St. Olaf's Church. I want to see him as soon as possible."

"I'll send the car in for him if the road is passable."

"Bring me a gun. My own gun. Now. While my wife's outside." Sean explained in what drawer upstairs Hanson would find it.

In a moment Hanson had returned with the gun and a full box of shells. Sean checked the gun, spinning the cylinder then tucked it and the box of ammunition under the covers.

Hanson picked up his hat off the dresser. "Is that it?"

"For now."

He walked toward the door then turned, curling the brim of his gray fedora. "Will you think about it?"

Sean nodded. He heard the door open then close softly. Still, he stared out the window. Mae threw the feed at the clucking chickens. She turned the pail upside down, stuck it on a fence post then went back into the barn.

The yellow hound trotted across the yard, his tail like a comma. He circled the jackpine, anointed it then disappeared around the back of the barn. Mae stepped out of the barn and looked up at the sky, then with hands shoved deep in her pockets, walked toward the house.

The view shimmered.

In the sleepless, painful hours that followed, Sean caught himself listening. For the slam of the back door then the sound of work boots hitting the wooden box. For a phlegmy cough then that odd three-part gait—step—step—snap—as the old man made his way down the hall and snapped his suspenders against a bony chest. For nonstop monologue about something . . . anything.

"Good God, man!" Father Fitz perched on the end of the bed, chain-smoking as usual. " 'Tis a terrible development. Is there nae other way?"

Sean shook his head. "Not now. So, you see, I cannot stay. The only way I can protect Mae and the baby is by leaving." Father Fitz shared a match with Sean. "Soon as I can move, I'm gone."

"Canno' you take the gel an' the bairn an' head for parts unknown?"

"For a life on the run?" Sean shook his head again. "No. Those guys have a longer arm than the law. I'll not put Mae and Jack's lives in jeopardy." They smoked in silence a moment. "Once I'm gone, they'll be safe here. There's a weird code of ethics that includes not making war on a man's family.

"We can be thankful for that at least."

"Ironic, isn't it? She had to marry to save her farm and now the only way she could stay married would be to give up the farm."

"What can I do to help?"

"First off, I'll need a lawyer."

"Done! Soon as I get back to town I'll send Joe Barton out." Father Fitz lit another cigarette even though one already burned in the ashtray.

"Would you get in contact with our neighbor, Mrs. Weltes? You remember her?"

"Yes, indeed, from the wedding and Thanksgiving."

"Tell her I've agreed to . . ."

"Hold yer horses, man. 'Tis nae the time to be forgettin' somethin'." He searched his pockets for a piece of paper. "Ah, here we go." He pulled a fountain pen from between the buttons on his cassock. "Now, then, first off, the lawyer . . ."

Sean continued. "Yes, the sooner the better. I'm leaving in a few days."

"A few days, man!" The priest showed his shock. "Mae told me Neimark said complete bed rest for a month. An' then the prognosis is nae necessarily that good. He said ye'll be lucky to walk without crutches."

"Yeah, well, mark my words, I'm leaving." Sean pushed himself up, frowning with the effort. He wasn't bouncing back like he thought he should. He'd forced himself to use his leg. The pain was excruciating but he was determined. He would leave if he had to be carried on a stretcher. "Ah, I must be gettin' old, Father. In me prime it would've taken more than three small bullets to fell the McGloin."

His attention was elsewhere, so he missed seeing the priest's eyes roll skyward.

Sean looked back at the priest holding the pen poised over the paper. "Okay, listen up now, Father. About the Widow Weltes. Could you take care of that fairly soon? The Weltes farm is south of here."

"I know exactly where it is. I'll stop on me way home." The priest's small face was intent.

"Good. Tell her I'm accepting her price and that I'm buying her out, lock, stock and barrel. I think that's how they say it. Tell her I'm getting the lawyer to draw it up." Sean looked at Father Fitz's bowed, balding pate as he scribbled fiercely. It wouldn't be long until he'd have one of those monk's tonsures.

"She'll remember our discussion when I plowed for her last time. She can continue to live on her farm only I'd want her to come over here most days to help out with the housework and the boy." Sean told the priest an amount to tell Mrs. Weltes she'd be paid for her services.

The priest glanced up at Sean and lifted his eyebrows. "All right. Got it. Anythin' else?"

"Yeah, I'll need to hire some outside help here . . ."

There was a soft tap on the door and Mae stuck her head in. "Hello!" Obviously hesitant to enter, she put her hands behind her and leaned against the door frame. "Can I . . . get you two anything?"

"Not for me, love." Sean looked at the priest. "How about you, Father Fitz?"

"Ah, no, no, my dear. Not a thing!"

The priest observed the exchange of looks—Mae's pleading, Sean's flat and unreadable. Their eyes locked and the priest was at a loss to break the ensuing long (and at least for him) extremely awkward moment.

At last, Sean looked pointedly out the window. Father Fitz saw the girl's lip quiver. Barely audibly she said, "Well, if you do need anything, I'm just in the other room."

"Thank you, Mae." Terribly ill-at-ease, Father Fitz followed her into the hallway. "Ah, how's little Johnny getting along, dear?" He patted her shoulder, making a feeble try to be friendly.

"Fine. He's just fine. Thanks for asking, Father."

"He's a wonderful boy, Mae. As handsome as any boy . . ." Father Fitz spoke to the empty hallway, for the girl had covered her mouth with her hand and run upstairs.

Frowning and of half a mind to be angry, he returned to Sean's bedside. "Faith, Sean. Did ye see her face? What's wrong between you two?"

Sean rounded on him with so much fury, the priest stepped back a pace. "Of course, I saw her. Ye think me blind?" Sean jerked his jaw then looked outside again. After a long minute, he said, "Sorry, Father. I've had to distance meself from her. I canno' trust me resolve when I'm around her."

Father Fitz sighed and sank into a chair. "Ah. I see. 'Tis a hard thing ye do, Sean."

"Aye, 'tis." Sean whispered, folding his arms across his chest.

"Because ye love her very much."

No response was necessary.

"What will ye ever do?"

"The only thing I can. I can see that she wants for nothing and then . . . I can set her free."

"Free?"

Sean waved his hand. "First things first. I need your help with these financial matters."

"I'll do whatever I can, you know that." The priest picked up the paper and pen off the foot of the bed. He cleared his throat and both men affected a businesslike manner.

"I want you to help me hire two men to work this place. Familiar with farming. Jack-of-all-trades. They must, of course, be totally reliable. Good workers. No bums. I . . . I don't want them to live on the premises. They can live over at Weltes'. It's only four miles." Sean laughed and ran a hand through his hair. "I don't know what I'm I thinkin', man . . . I stopped meself just short of saying they have to be old an' ugly!"

Wordless again, Father Fitz simply squeezed his friend's arm.

"I'd consider it a true favor if you would get somebody to finish the remodeling job here. Maybe you could come out once a week and look in on the work, see how it's progressin'."

"I can an' I will. At least once a week. I'd even like to continue to help here and there."

"Take the prints with you if you like. Look them over." Raising his good leg, Sean rested a forearm on his knee.

"Sean, as yer priest, and as yer friend, I must ask ye. What about yer marriage?"

"That's what we need to work on. Long as I'm alive I'll keep in touch with you somehow. Say, once a month." He met the priest's gaze. "In the meantime, I want you to apply for an annulment."

"On what grounds, man?" The priest's brow furrowed.

"Whatever you have to use. Abandonment. I don't know anything about grounds for an annulment. That's your department."

"It dinno' work that way, Sean. Marriage is a holy sacrament. Ye canno' just toss it out the window like the slops. Unless . . ." Father Fitz cleared his throat. "Er, the marriage has been consummated, of course."

Sean hesitated, debated, then nodded. He grasped the sleeve of the priest's cassock. "I won't have her alone all her life. Would that be fair? When the gel is made for a man's love . . . when she's . . ." The silence strung out. Sean dropped his hand and looked away.

"I don't care what it takes. Money on the right palm . . ." The priest bristled. "Just do whatever it takes to free her. There must be some grounds for annulment. I'm leaving her and her boy flat."

"Well, it would be an unusual case . . . I dinno' know. I would have to check with Chicago. The cardinal might have to petition Rome."

"Wait until after the trial before you go to all that trouble." Sean executed a painful shift of position. "Chances are you won't have to bother."

"Now what exactly is that supposed to mean?" The priest stood, demanding that Sean look at him. "Suicide is a mortal sin. If yer plannin' to put yerself in the way of a bullet on purpose, 'tis the same as doin' the deed yerself. Where's yer head! Yer soul'll burn in eternal hell."

"Ah, don't get yourself all worked up." Sean lit a cheroot then tossed the match in the ashtray bedside. "I'm not going to make it easy but my chances of surviving after I testify in New York are as good as a bleeding sailor in shark-infested waters."

"I'm no' just speakin' as yer priest, Sean. I'm speakin' as yer friend. Yer throwin' in the towel before the bell's rung for round one, man!"

"I know." Sean's voice dropped, the angry tone faded and became resigned. "I guess I'm lookin' at me track record. Some men—old Ed and meself to name two—are just born unlucky." He swung his head toward the window. "I don't know what possessed me to think I could live a normal life."

"Surely ye willna give up without a fight!"

The priest waited for a response but none was forthcoming. He gave a resigned sigh. How often had he met with this kind of thinking before? Sean was just Irish enough to believe his life, as well as his bad luck, was predetermined. "I'll do what I can." The priest laid a hand on Sean's arm. "Ah, Sean . . . I wish there was something I could say . . . some words of comfort for ye."

Father Fitz stepped into the hallway and closed the door softly. He paused and with his hands clasped and head bent, he said a prayer Rome wouldn't sanction:

"May the road rise up to meet ye,
"May the wind be always at yer back,
"May the sun shine warm upon yer face
"And the rains fall soft upon yer fields
"And until we meet again,
"May God hold you in the palm of his hand."

"Sean, please don't go." Mae's whispered plea came from just inside the bedroom door. Sean threw his denims into the bag. Folding a gray knitted scarf carefully, he placed it in the bag as well.

"I must, love, but I'll be back before you know it." Pasting a smile on, he turned and waved her to the chair. She sat closer, on the bed next to the duffel bag.

"If you are going to be right back then why did you hire those men? We can get by until spring without help."

There was no response. "Sean, please," Mae turned him toward her with a hand on his shoulder. "You shouldn't even be out of bed. You aren't well enough to travel." He turned away. "What's the hurry anyway? They can't start the trial without you."

"I already explained that. Sooner I get there, sooner I'll get back." He'd returned with more clothes and tried to continue packing but she reached up and laid her hand against his cheek. Sean clenched both fists on the sweater he held.

"Why are you so . . . so distant to me, Sean?" She stood up and stepped closer. He held the sweater like a shield. "Is it something I've done?" She looked up at him with tear-filled eyes. "You seem so . . . strange." He had let his hair and beard grow, as if he were throwing off whatever trappings of civilization he'd acquired since coming to the farm. He looked wild and primitive and . . . scary. "If I didn't know better, I'd think you were avoiding me."

He tossed the sweater on the bed. "No. Of course not." He cupped her shoulders. "Nothin' like that," he said gruffly.

She leaned closer and tilted her chin up, silently requesting a kiss. It was perfunctory. "Don't you want to . . . don't you love me anymore, Sean?"

"Of course I do. You know I don't want to leave you with another bairn on the way and me not here to help . . . in the beginning."

She blushed. They'd had a terribly embarrassing conversation in which Sean had questioned her very specifically about her monthly cycle. "Now that we know I'm not . . . ah, with child, couldn't I go with you?"

"Please stop . . . pleading. We've been all through this before. There are times in life when a person is like so much flotsam. And there's not a thing that person can say or do to alter anything." He started stuffing things hurriedly, haphazardly into his bag. "This is one of those times for us. Besides you couldn't leave little Jack."

"Mrs. Weltes has offered to take care of him." Mae watched him insert a few more items. "Please, Sean. If it's such a quick . . . trip." He limped to the dresser and closed an open drawer. He looks like a fierce bird of prey, she thought, dragging a broken wing behind. "Sean?"

He turned on her and shouted. "God, no! Canno' ye understand English? Are ye so stupid? No!"

Mae backed slowly away, blue eyes swimming, chin jerking. "Oh! Sean!" Spinning around, she fled.

He sat on the bed and ground the heels of his hands into his eyes. "God Almighty, help me!" he muttered at last and then went to seek her.

She was upstairs, sprawled in the middle of the bed, crying her heart out o' course. He turned her over, gathered her in his arms and soothed her with meaningless words and tender hands.

"I don't want to whine, Sean, but I need to . . . I have to know when. When will you come back, Sean?"

He did not answer.

"Two weeks? One month? Two months?" She put a hand on his chest. "Sean? When, Sean?"

"I have nae lied to ye."

"No."

"Do ye think I'd've ever come here if I thought by doin' so I'd bring harm to ye or the bairn or that old man? Do ye think I would have done that?"

She shook her head.

"I feel so much guilt about that. Ye must at least allow me to do the right thing now." He leaned his head back and stared out the dormer window. " 'Tis the only way I can live with myself." His hand stroked her back. "Trust me to know when 'tis safe. Will ye do that?"

"Yes." She nodded, crying again.

"I don't know when exactly I'll be back but it will be as soon as I can." He brushed her cheeks with his thumbs. "Smile for me, my sweet, sweet gel," he said and she tried.

But after he left her to finish packing, all she could think of was another time when another person had asked her to smile then left forever.

Sean slipped into the darkened room and went to the crib. With a hand on each siderail, he leaned over. "So, yer awake, Jack?" The baby gave him a snaggle-toothed grin.

Bloody amazing, he thought, as he smiled down at the baby. With his knees locked, both legs straight in the air, the kid was able to hold one foot in each hand. "Can all babies do that or are ye goin' to be a contortionist when ye grow up?"

He scooped him up and pulled the rocking chair closer to the window. He sat and put the child on his knees. He stood immediately. "Yer soppin'!" Holding the child at arm's length, he carried him to the bed. "Well, at least ye won't pee on me."

Feeling like he had twenty fingers on each hand, he removed the soiled diaper and, as he'd seen Mae do, dusted the boy's bottom with the powdery concoction on the dresser then sat again. He held the child under the arms. The baby bounced on his thighs.

It was snowing lightly but the wind had been steadily increasing. Sean wondered if a storm were brewing. The weathervane on the top of the barn pointed directly north.

He missed Ed and his unsolicited weather predictions, his nonstop chatter, his wit. He missed the old man, period.

Out in the yard, Sandy halfheartedly chased the orange-striped barn cat back into the barn. Having accomplished this goal, he trotted around, tail high, then circled the jack pine with serious intent.

Sean laid the child on his shoulder and buried his nose in the baby's neck. He inhaled, then cleared a throat that felt barnacle-covered. "So, Jack." His voice sounded very loud in the quiet. He felt a bit foolish. The baby tried to get a grip on his moustache. He tilted his chin out of reach.

"Mama?"

"Nae, ye little squin', I'm nae yer mama. Can ye say da, Jack?"

"Mama!"

Sean laid the baby back in the crib. "See ya!" he whispered, but he stood looking at him for quite a time. The baby was chewing on a wooden carving as though it were a hunk of sirloin.

Before he opened the door, he pressed his thumb and forefinger into dampened eyes.

Little bugger had managed to give his 'stache a good tug after all.

Mae sat in the rocking chair, staring out the frost-covered window. Johnny slept with his head on her shoulder.

In the hour of dawn the windswept land gleamed with eerie incandescence. Between the barn and the house, the sleigh was hitched and ready. The roan gelding stamped and blew, his vaporized breath floating in front of him like an editorial balloon in the newspaper. Mottled and shaggy, the old horse's thick winter coat occasionally rippled with great shudders.

"I was just thinking about Uncle Ed," she said. "How he liked to tell about the river's first settlers, the French voyageurs and how they used to bring their dogs inside to sleep, one for every degree below freezing. 'It'll be a three-dogger tonight,' he'd say and then launch into his tale of the voyageurs. I've heard that story a thousand times. I'd give anything to hear it again now."

Bleak and bitter, with a biting north wind and below-zero temperatures, it would be a miserable day, a day to match her mood and a fitting day for her husband to leave her.

"You better go." She marveled that her voice sounded so normal! "I think it's going to get colder still." She hadn't done more than glance at Sean but she knew exactly what he was doing, even what he was wearing.

Elbows on his knees, he sat on the bed and fingered the crease on his black felt hat. It's the same hat he wore the day he arrived, she thought. His coat was still unbuttoned, but he was virtually ready to go, same as the horse. His seaman's bag, she supposed, sat in the hallway; she hadn't seen him carry it out to the sleigh yet.

"Mae, ye know I must go. I have to do it!"

Her quick shrug said . . . if you say so . . . and . . . makes no difference to me.

"Mae . . ."

She willed herself not to think about what was going to happen. She concentrated on the creaking of the rocking chair, Johnny's soft breath against her neck and the tick of her end table clock.

She heard Mrs. Weltes in the kitchen. Something about "bundling up." She fixed her eyes on the horse. If she looked at Sean she knew she would start to cry again.

He stood. "You know I'll be back as soon as I'm able."

"Don't bother."

"You don't mean that."

"I do."

"Look at me an' say that, gel."

She rocked steadily and kept her face averted until she heard the door close softly. After a second, he came into view, walking quickly toward the sleigh. The government man, Hanson, followed more slowly. Sean tossed his bag in the back of the sleigh and turned his collar up. Hanson walked around to the opposite side and levered himself up. Hanson's two men had left only moments earlier.

She started to cry, great racking sobs that hurt her chest.

He was pulling on his gloves.

He jumped into the sleigh.

He picked up the reins.

She stood. She laid Johnny in the crib. Turning so fast, she stumbled, she ran to the door, down the hall and through the porch. The sleigh, moving fast, was already on the road to town. The horse was practically running flat out. She cupped her mouth and screamed. "Sean!" Her voice was weaker than the wind and the ever expanding distance. She watched the sleigh until it sped over the crest of the hill then she slumped onto the icy step, remaining thus until she felt Mrs. Weltes' hand on her shoulder.

Nineteen

Mae marked time. She relived those last moments in the bedroom a thousand times. She started repeating Sean's words like a litany. *"Trust me to know when 'tis safe. Will ye do that?"* and outwardly she stayed composed. Inwardly she felt as if she were running a gauntlet, with emotions pummeling her from all sides.

She grieved hard for her uncle. Because she loved and missed him and because, right or wrong, she felt responsible for his death—if they hadn't asked him to watch the baby that day, if they hadn't stopped to spoon, if and another if . . .

The poor old man! Were some people, she wondered, destined to have hard luck all their life? Had he been one of them?

Was she?

Anger helped to carry her through the first several days after Sean left. Anger at life, at fate, and most especially at Sean. Remorse, despair and depression followed. She made crazy plans. She would go to New York. She would hire private investigators. She'd run advertisements in every major newspaper on the East Coast. On both coasts. When she found Sean she would make him come home. They would hire an army of bodyguards until the gangsters gave up. Then her mood would swing and the only thing she did was pine and pray. But none of her pining showed. She took pride in that fact.

"I swear, Mae Ella," Mrs. Weltes said, "I don't know how you do it."

"Strong stock, I guess, Mrs. Weltes. I guess I come from strong stock."

But Mrs. Weltes didn't know about when Mae found one of Sean's socks in the laundry basket. She'd had a long cry then, holding the sock to her lips as if it were a holy relic and thinking about the solitary sock he carried with him somewhere in New York.

Crying was the exception rather than the rule. She surprised herself. She could never figure, looking back in later years, how she did it. Maybe she was a lot tougher than she thought. Or maybe it was her son and her work.

Keeping busy, she would tell herself, there's the ticket. Like Granny'd always instructed, Mae put on a clean apron. She added more oats to the egg basket. She got the lead out and she got her face on straight. And surprisingly, she got by.

After supper she'd make a list of the things she wanted to accomplish, then the next day she'd try to see how many she could draw a line through. She was bone tired at night but too exhausted to dwell on anything. She took each day as it came but Sean was never out of her thoughts. When she read in the *Post* about Alice Roosevelt having the cheek to smoke in public or read the review on a vaudeville hit that starred an incredibly talented six-year-old named Buster Keaton, she never really thought about what she was reading. Only if Sean had read the same article.

During all those days and nights there was only one letter from Sean. Two lines long. Nineteen words. *I'm all right. Thinking of you.*

I love you. I'll be home as soon as I can. Trust me.

There was no return address, no word on the trial date, nothing.

All right, she told herself. I'm all right with that. To Mrs. Weltes and Father Fitz she said, "Well, good news! Sean will be home soon."

Johnny shot up like a weed soon as he started walking, which he did at ten months. In January her birthday came and went. Three weeks later so did Johnny's first birthday.

Except for the sock incident there were only two occasions when something cracked her facade. One occurred because of the dress Sean thought was too tight to wear in public.

She and Mrs. Weltes had decided to collaborate on a tree of life quilt. Mae was going through the rag bin in the barn, looking for scraps when she found her perfectly good brown dress at the bottom of the pile. Of course she'd missed it weeks ago and had looked all over for it. Very mysterious, she remembered thinking. But in those days right after her uncle's death and Sean's leaving, she hardly knew whether she was coming or going. Now she knew what had happened to her dress. She sat on a bale of hay in the barn and cried until she was physically ill.

A week after her birthday, she went into town to shop for groceries. She stopped first at the mercantile then automatically checked at the post office. There was a box for her, wrapped in brown paper, addressed in a large-lettered, childish print. There was no return address. Thank goodness, she was to think later that she waited to open the box until she got home.

"Becknell's Finest Chocolates." she read after removing the brown wrapper. Now, why would someone send her candy through the mail? Father Fitz had given her the same candy on Thanksgiving. Had he, in his kind way, sent her another box for her birthday?

She opened the box. There was no card inside either but paper wrapped candies framed an odd, small box. Wooden and shaped like a casket, it looked very old. A strange carving of a griffin decorated the cover. Inside on a bed of black velvet were several colored stones—red and green and icy white. She wouldn't even begin to try and guess what they were. Ruby and emerald and diamond came to mind but the thought astounded her. There was a single strand of fragile, perfectly matched pearls. A note was wrapped around them like a cigarette paper. It said "They will pale in beauty next to your skin."

The pearls lay forgotten on the table as, with trembling fingers, she touched the note to her lips. That was to be the last written contact she would have with Sean. It was well that she didn't know it at the time.

Mrs. Weltes said she recalled only one winter that was harsher than the winter of '95. Although Mae had been quite young, she remembered the winter of '81 as well. So much snow fell that year that the chicken coop was completely buried save for the little round galvanized pipe that came out of the roof. She remembered Papa had had to crawl up the snowbank on all fours in order to pour water and feed down the pipe.

So that February, when the path to the barn was banked with waist-high walls of snow, Mae put all the chickens in the barn and let them roost in the rafters. There were occasional unpleasant splats for those nonvigilant people working below, but better that, Mae reasoned, than thirty frozen chickens.

About two months after Sean left, word came that

Peter's family was pulling up stakes and moving to Texas. They were, so the rumor went, leaving to join a religious sect whose followers lived without modern trappings of any kind.

Mae wished them well but cared not one whit about seeing them before they left town. In her heart and mind, all ties had been cut long ago.

One of the two hired hands—a man named Brady with soft round brown eyes like Lottie the cow—said he'd heard that the Herrmanns wanted to sell their prize Angus bull. Without a moment's hesitation, Mae bought it and then worried for days about whether she had done the right thing. She would have liked to have asked Sean but there had been no further word from him.

"Why," she wondered to Father Fitz. "Why doesn't he write, at least?"

"I'm quite sure that Sean's spending every minute he can pressuring the government to get Spinelli's trial date set."

Bull drop, she wanted to say although Sean would want to get it over with. Lord knows, patience was not one of his strong suits.

A few weeks after she bought the bull, she went into town, as usual. Once a week, weather permitting, she shopped for supplies, picked up the Minneapolis newspapers at Watson's and, if Father Fitz hadn't been out to the farm recently, checked with him to see if he had any word about Sean. She believed the priest when he denied knowledge of Sean's whereabouts. After all, a priest wouldn't lie. But she felt sure he knew how to get messages to Sean and vice versa, because he hedged in response to her question about that.

The day she heard Sean was dead she had stopped in the mercantile to pick up a few items. She was searching her reticule for the list she and Mrs. Weltes had made out when John Watson came in from the back room. He gave her the strangest look then he came around the counter and took her hand. "Oh, Mae Ella, I just can't tell you how sorry we were to hear about Sean!"

"What?" She pulled her hand out of his grasp. "What about Sean?"

"Why, the shooting in New York." He looked at her face. "You hadn't heard! My God!" He turned. On the counter behind him lay a twice-folded Minneapolis newspaper. He picked it up but Mae snatched it rudely out of his hand. Her eyes skimmed down the article, grabbing random words.

Man Shot. Police Kill Assassin.

A government witness was shot on the Federal Bldg. steps only moments after testifying against the crime ring headed by . . .

Police opened fire on the assassin. . . . Cavanaugh . . . resulting bloodbath. The mayor's office spokesman.

The victim, identified as Sean McGloin was taken to Kings County Hospital and was pronounced dead on arrival . . .

Mae fainted, John Watson said later, and hit her head on the table displaying women's fabrics.

She came to in Doc Neimark's little examining room. John Watson and Werner Steinforth's worried faces peered down at her. She sat then stood and wobbled on licorice-stick legs.

"Here!" Watson, who had helped Werner Steinforth carry her to the doctor's, tried to push her back onto the couch.

Doc Neimark's voice boomed, "You can't leave, Mae Ella!"

"I most certainly can. You cannot keep me here against my will. I want to go home. Now!"

She kept insisting on going home until she got her way.

It was all she could think of. Getting home to Johnny and being alone to think. It was snowing when they left the doctor's. Mr. Brady drove like a madman. They just made it home before the soft snowfall turned into a driving blizzard. The storm lasted four days, dumping eleven inches on the first day and fifteen inches two days later.

Those four days, until Father Fitz arrived, were the worst she'd ever experienced, but even before Father Fitz told her, Mae knew in her heart the newspaper story was a lie. "It simply isn't true!" Mrs. Weltes thought she was crazy. Pacing, while the storm roared unabated outside, Mae kept saying. "It's not true, Mrs. Weltes. I would know if it were true. Seriously! I know it's crazy, but I would know."

"If you say so, dear . . ."

"I do. I just know."

Father Fitz finally arrived. "I came as soon as the roads were passable, Mae."

Even before Father Fitz had shaken out his coat and Mrs. Weltes had hung it, Mae pounced on him. "Father, I don't believe a word of it. Now you tell me the truth."

"You're right. He's not dead. I was supposed to tell you that before you saw the paper. Faith! I couldn't get here!" He rubbed her hand. "There was a wake in Oberlin Falls then the snow . . . I'm so sorry that you had these days of heartache."

"It's all right, Father." Mae breathed a sigh and sat down. "I knew. Really. I just knew." Mae heard Mrs.

Weltes say Thank God. Then the door to her room closed. She and the priest were alone.

"The thing is, everybody is supposed to think Sean is dead." Sighing stentoriously, he prepared a cigarette. "Sean made me swear not to tell ye the whole of it before it happened. He didn't want ye to get yer hopes up. Actually, I was supposed to talk ye into an annulment." Father Fitz paced, smoking up a storm. "I agreed because I told meself 'tis nae tellin' a lie if I just . . . But, then 'tis a lie by intent. There's no gettin' around it. He'll have to kill me when he finds out, but I canno' do it."

For a long minute, Mae covered her face with her hands. Then she asked, "What are you talking about and what doesn't he want me to know?"

"Because the ploy might not work. The whole thing could have been botched right from the beginning. Or, afterward, the mob might not buy it even if it did go without a hitch. Or, someone could tip them off months later." He shook his head. "Believe me, Sean's got a hundred reasons why it could go wrong. Mostly his belief in his own bad luck! I told him if any one could pull it off . . ."

Mae waved her hand like wiping a blackboard. "Wait! Start from the beginning. Pull what off?"

"The way I understand it, there was a man named Cavanaugh who was a cop gone bad. He was the one who told the mob that Sean was a plant and almost got Sean killed the night he was getting the information for the feds. Anyway, this guy Cavanaugh had been feeding the mob information from the inside for years. Much as Hanson disliked doing so, they agreed to not prosecute Cavanaugh if he turned evidence secretly and took part in a phony assassination. Cavanaugh supposedly shot Sean when he was coming out of the courthouse. Then Cavanaugh was supposedly shot by one of Hanson's men. Both of them, Cavanaugh and Sean, were publicly pronounced dead but secretly were hustled out of town." Father Fitz stubbed out one cigarette and immediately prepared another one. "So far, Hanson says the mob has gone for it. At least that was the last information I received. God works in mysterious ways but I canno' understand why He would give us a blizzard to contend with along with everything else. I was going to get out here and tell you the plan the same day you saw the paper. You were never supposed to go through what you did."

"It's all right, Father, I never believed he was dead. But I'll admit it was a shock." She poured coffee with a trembling hand. "Why would Sean want an annulment, then."

"Because he doesn't know when or if he can ever come back."

"But if the mob . . ."

Father Fitz laid his hand on hers. "Unless Sean is absolutely certain there is no risk to either you or the boy, he will nae return. He swore that to me, Mae, before he left. Much as ye must know he loves ye, he would nae take a chance with ye or yer bairn's life."

Mae wailed. "When . . . When will he know though? Will it ever be safe?"

Father Fitz stood, patting her back. He shrugged. "I canno' lie to ye either. I dinna know what it will take to convince him to come. His mind was set."

"Where is he?"

"I haven't a clue." He held up his hand, scout's honor. "He dinno' even trust Hanson's organization—probably with good reason—as far as getting messages to him direct. Even Hanson has to go through a certain pub in New York. He said the only reason

I'm to use the contact is to send the annulment papers or if 'tis a case of life or death."

"Flaherty's!"

Father Fitz was surprised "How on earth would ye know about Flaherty's?"

"Never mind!" She sniffed, wiping her eyes. "I must write him. Will you send a letter to that place for me?"

"Yes, I'll send it, but you know Sean. No matter what ye say, yer not goin' to budge him. His mind was set . . ."

"I know. I know! And when his mind is set . . . God, I thought the Germans were supposed to be the stubborn race. Just please send a message to him."

Mae got out one sheet of buff-colored vellum paper out of Granny's chest, a pen and ink. Without a second's pause, she dipped the pen and began to write: *"My husband, Sean. We miss you terribly. I love you. I'm sorry I said what I did. You know I didn't mean it. Come home this minute. Or else." Your loving wife, Mae. P.S. No annulment."*

Days passed. It was hard to keep her spirits up but she was most heartened the day Hanson's men left.

"You'll be fine now, ma'am." The-man-who-showed-too-much-gum-when-he-smiled said. "There'll be no further trouble. Not here at least."

"Thank you, Mr. ah . . ."

"Higgins."

"Yes. Mr. Higgins."

She never could keep their names straight because she'd had so little contact with them. They stayed someplace in town when they weren't "on duty" and took their meals there too. They would descend on the farm platoonlike in three shifts, two men each shift. Apparently assigned certain places, the most visible one was the sentry on cemetery hill. Silhouetted against the gray sky, rifle cradled and city-style coat flapping, he looked like a crow waiting to scavenge. She would bet Granny's sapphire earrings that every man jack of Hanson's men had received one of Sean's vampire-lip, eyelash-counting talks before he left.

Mae sat back, content to wait. She had faith. He'd be back soon now. But more days passed. Weeks. A month. Two months then six.

Sean! Where are you?

Canada

He should have felt right at home. A waterfront town. Narrow, mean streets with filthy gutters, dark alleys and squalid buildings. Pimps and prostitutes. Perverts and punks. The smell of things rotting—fish, animals, souls.

He hated it! Gaunt and hollow-eyed from constant pain, he rarely slept. Instead he prowled the streets and was soon patrolling a regular beat, not unlike a cop.

People noticed. They talked. He could feel their eyes and hear their whispers.

"Look at him." Two men stood in a bar, looking out at the street. "See how big he is? See how he's draggin' that one leg?" The man who spoke claimed to have done some bounty work. "I know I've heard about him somewheres."

His companion tossed off a shot of rotgut. "From what I've heard, I'd leave that fella be if I was you."

The would-be bounty hunter snorted. "Well, you ain't me. Which is why you're drinking rotgut and I ain't." He watched the man through the smoke-grimed window. "No. That man's wanted someplace by somebody. Trick is to find out who wants him and how bad."

Down the street a ways, two whores stood in a doorway spotlit by a bare bulb. "Biggest man I've ever seen," said the henna-haired one, watching the man pass.

Her friend giggled. "Wonder if he's that big all over."

"Only one way to find out, sugar," said the first whore as she followed the man with sly eyes.

He carried a thick crooked staff and used it freely, to lather two thugs intent on relieving him of his money, on a man about to rape a child and on a robber backing out of a bar with the till. More people noticed. And talked.

"Crippled up or no," they said, "I ain't never seen nobody fight like that."

Word spread.

The man knew but didn't seem to give a damn. It was almost as if he was saying "Here I am, arseholes. Come and get it."

It had been an early, wet spring. Pussy willows bloomed in March. Red squirrels chased each other across the icy yard and Mae saw the first bald eagle two days before St. Pat's.

She dreamt of Sean nightly. Vivid dreams that woke her, sometimes with feelings of panic, sometimes with longing, often with a thick heat between her legs. *Sean! Where are you?*

Mae wanted to slow time's passage. It seemed to

her that the more time that went by, the less the
chance there was of Sean's returning. Why hadn't he
at least contacted them?

Summer was early that year too. The sumac's green
grapelike clusters turned red. Mushrooms in the forest
got tops big as pie plates.

She bought granite grave markers for Granny and
Granddad and for Uncle Ed, his wife and two girls.
She had the two workers put up a picket fence around
their plot, then she transplanted wildflowers from the
woods. Columbine, fiddlehead ferns, trillium, Dutch-
man's breeches, ladyslippers. Later, when the prairie
flowers were in bloom she added downy gentian and
yellow violet, goldenrod, and aster.

Finally it was a year and still no Sean!
Sean!

Twenty

Mae hooked the wire loop over the fence post, then took up the picnic basket and Johnny's hand. It had rained overnight and the air was still heavy with moisture. Dew beaded on pine needles and clung to spider webs.

They followed the narrow path to the river through eastern hemlock, white pine and yellow birch. The sound of singing birds filled the air. She had marked her calendar, as she did every morning. One year, six months, four days.

"No, Jack," she said when the child wanted to pick a fragile columbine hovering on the south side of its protector oak. "It will die if we pick it now. We'll stop for it on the way home."

When they reached the river, she spread the blanket under an elm. They fished for a time then swam. Then, propped by her arms, Mae lay on the river bank with her legs in the water. Johnny stood on a bar a few feet away. Naked, with his sturdy, dimpled legs slightly apart, he was contemplating a rock he'd just picked off the sandy river bottom.

Mae grinned. She could read him like a dime novel. Narrow-eyed, he glanced at her and debated. He was strongly considering popping the rock in his mouth. She hid another grin and, looking stern, shook her head. While he weighed the merits of tasting the rock against a sure scolding, there was only the sound of water lapping against rocks, the strident cry of a couple of crows.

In profile, swaybacked and knees locked, Johnny's stomach stuck out like a woman's in her eighth month. Mae shook her head again. "What a terrible physique you're getting, Johnny!"

At the sound of her voice, he turned toward her too quickly, lost his footing and sat hard. After making sure she had observed his ungraceful plop, he opened his mouth and howled. The crows took flight.

"Jack!" Mae smiled at him, shaking her head. "You're not hurt, Jack!"

He continued, beet-faced, for a full minute then abruptly snapped his mouth shut.

"Come over here." She coaxed him, moving her knees up and down, rippling the water enticingly. "Come over here and do like Mommy, Jack."

He watched her for a couple of seconds. "No!" he said emphatically then dropped the rock and crawled to her. Lifting him, she set him next to her and for a while, side by side, they moved their legs in unison. He splashed her. She squealed. He giggled. They repeated the process in reverse. Soon she pressed a finger on his shoulder and watched the indentation turn from pink to white. "I think you're getting too much sun. Let's put on your shirt."

"No!" He crawled off with surprising speed.

Nowadays Johnny's response to every thing was the same: No. "I'll sure be glad when we're over this stage." She waded out of the water to the blanket. She waved at a bee that was hovering over their picnic basket, found his shirt and held it up to him. "Here, Jack. Come over here a minute. You can stay in the water if you wear your shirt."

"No!"

"Johnny!"

The baby giggled and slapped water.

"You've been in the water so long, your buns are shriveled." When she brought his shirt to him, he lifted his arms readily but said, "No!"

Shaking her head again, Mae went back to the blanket. She wasn't in the mood to force compliance. She would allow him a few more minutes of play. She washed their plates and the two forks in the river then packed them in the bottom of the basket. The remains of their picnic—one drumstick and a breast and two hardboiled eggs, she rewrapped and laid on top of the utensils. She bit into a juicy tart apple. "Come out now, Jack and have your nap."

"No!"

It was unusually hot for June. The humid air was so heavy it seemed to induce drowsiness when inhaled. Even the trees were somnolent. Wisps of cottony clouds hung unmoving in the powder blue sky. She took a cup and walked to the river. She pulled the earthenware jug of lemonade out of the river, uncapped it and poured a glass.

"Want some lemonade, Jack?"

"No," he said, yet held out his hand, opening and closing his fist.

She went back to the blanket. "Say 'yes, please' and you can have some lemonade."

"No!"

She clenched her teeth. She was far too lax with Johnny but Mrs. Weltes was worse, catering to the child's every whim. Oftentimes Mae had come close to saying something but was afraid of offending the woman. Having no one else, Mrs. Weltes had taken to mothering Jack and Mae with equal fervor.

Mrs. Weltes stayed over as often as not, either to spell Mae when Johnny was ill or because the weather

was bad. Mae was glad of her company. She slept in
Uncle Ed's old room, which had been converted for
that use with the addition of a new bow-front dresser
and a mirror, and a larger bed with a new headboard.
Last winter, with a fire in the hearth and the tap of
sleet on the windows, Mrs. Weltes and Mae had finished the tree-of-life quilt. Mae had put it on her bed,
where it looked lovely. They baked together once a
week and had shared the work of putting up preserves
last fall. Some nights they tatted or one mended while
the other read from the latest issue of *Vanity Fair* or
the *Saturday Evening Post*.

Mrs. Weltes was comforting to Mae like a well-
worn robe, and she said she felt the same. Many times
she'd told Mae how lonely she had been over at her
farm after her husband died and how pleased she was
with their arrangement.

On the occasions when Mrs. Weltes stayed over,
the two hired hands, Brady and Olness, took their
meals with them, but they slept at the Weltes farm.
Olness had replaced the man hired right after Sean
left. Brady had been there from the beginning.

Brady—his first name was Douglas but Mae thought
of him only as Brady—looked at her now with longing
in his soft, soulful eyes. He was a quiet man, hardworking and unassuming. And he was infatuated with
her. With any encouragement on her part he would say
or do something about it. She took care not to give him
cause.

"Johnny, come over here." He'd stopped crying but
glared at her stubbornly.

Her son was as unpredictable as Minnesota weather
in the springtime. One day he would be sunny, warm
and sweet. On the next he would turn mean, nasty
and thoroughly unpleasant.

He needed a man, Mae decided. A father. Someone

he could watch and emulate. Someone who would intuitively know how to deal with him. He needed Sean.

And Johnny's not the only one, she thought ruefully.

Sean, she knew, would be appalled at her laxity and Jack's unruly defiance. He would place a wide palm where it would make the best impression.

Goaded into action by her mental image, Mae called the child once more and when he ignored her, she scooped him up and swatted his rear. Against loud protestations, she stood him on the blanket and toweled him dry. After he had a long, slurping drink of lemonade, Mae made him lie down. He did so but only after she had threatened another spanking. Less than five minutes later, he had turned onto his side and was fast sleep.

"Thank goodness!" she mumbled.

She waited for several minutes, until she was sure he was sleeping soundly then she hitched her skirts up between her legs and waded into the water. She moved slowly upstream, staying close to the bank. The cool river water felt wonderful, for the midafternoon sun was blazing. Moisture beaded under her hair and dewed her forehead.

A whirring noise drew her attention upward to where a blue heron flew. Landing on the same sandbar where she and Johnny had been sitting earlier, the heron folded his wide wings then took measured steps to the end of the bar. Between each step he paused and swung his black crested head from side to side like a monarch acknowledging his subjects. At the very tip of the bar, he stopped and lifted one leg. Then pointing his beak at the water, he commenced fishing.

Poor heron, she thought. He must have been watching them from one of the pines lining the bluffs, patiently waiting for them to quit playing in his fishing hole.

Mae turned and continued in the opposite direction. Every so often, she checked on the heron, who was as motionless as a picture in an Audubon book. And Johnny was likewise.

She bent, scooped up some water and threw it on her face, letting some dribble inside her partially open bodice. When she bent for another handful, a loud splash near the bank startled her. She stared beneath a rippling, ever widening circle on the river's surface and saw a brown and white striped turtle swimming a few feet beneath the surface.

How quick and agile they are in the water, she thought, compared to their ponderous movements on land. She waded closer to the bank. Next to a flat rock—perfect for turtle sunning—was a clump of white and violet trillium. If it hadn't been for the turtle, she would have missed the fragile three-leafed flowers. "Oh! How pretty!" Since a patch of poison ivy grew right next to the wildflower, she cautiously picked a bouquet.

She craned her neck to see Johnny then checked the heron. Neither appeared to have moved a muscle so she waded on.

Just around the bend was a black raspberry patch. Mae had been gathering raspberries there for years. Granny and she used to go together every summer. The only way you could get to the berries was by water. Granny said she'd never have discovered the patch if it hadn't been for the Indians.

"I remember vell because I vas eight month vid child," Granny told her. "Helmut send me from field. 'No vork!' he said. I tried to argue but Helmut could be real bossy. 'I vant turkey fish' he said."

"Turkey fish, Granny?" Mae had asked. "What kind is that?"

"Von time ven ve ver fishing Helmut catch big sand pike. I fix like turkey. Put bread und sausage und onion inside und bake vid butter und tart apple."

"Stuffed, Granny. Stuffed fish."

"Dat's it!" Granny had pointed at her. "Stuffed turkey fish. Anyvay, Helmut said vas best fish ever had. So. Since I vas too fat and lazy to argue, I go to river to catch Helmut big fish.

"Vel, Liebchen, so much rain dat year! Fishing place vas under two foot vater.

"So. I think big fish are in deep vater. I valk along bank und look for spot to drop line off bluff. I kom round bend und dere, standing in deep vater are three Indian girls. Dey laff, talk den they all look at me. I look. Dey look. One girl, younger even den me, Liebchen, vas just as big vid baby.

"So. I smile. She smile. Ve stand so for a time den she pat her . . . how you say dis, Liebchen?" Granny rubbed her stomach.

"Tummy?"

"Yes. So. She pat her tummy und point at me. I roll my eyes up to sky like so den pat my tummy too.

"I think de Indian girls not kill your granny. So I vent vays avay vere I could still see und I throw my line in. I dig worms, Liebchen, you know . . . shady place by barn?"

Mae nodded. Granny had shown her that good nightcrawler spot years ago.

"In von minute had bite but it vas perch. Too small. I throw back. Pretty soon I get nice bass. Not big enough to turkey but nice. I take my stick vid braided yarn and put fish in vater. Ven I look up, Indian girl smile und nod at me again.

"So. Ve must hav been like so for two hours before de Indian girls go. Other two girls go cross to other side. One girl stood und smile at me. I wave. She wave. She pat tummy again. I nod und do same. She point at bank und den she go too. Ven I go to vhere she point dere is little place dug in dirt vhere girl leave berries for me."

"That was really nice of her, Granny."

"Yes."

"And did you get a big fish for dinner?"

"Yes but first I fall asleep by vater. I vake up ven I hear Helmut kom for me. He hollering, Ilse! Ilse! Ride Jocko like crazy man. I pretend to be sleep und not hear herd of elegants."

"Elephants, Granny."

"Vatever. I haf eyes closed but I know Helmut is looking down at me. He say 'Vel, Jocko, nothing here but dumb garter snake. Try to swallow ostrich egg.' "

Granny laughed. Mae too.

"What did you say?"

"I say maybe tummy look like egg but you like . . . how you say dese, Liebchen?" Granny pointed to her chest.

"Bosums, Granny?"

"Yes. I say 'But you like my bigger bosoms vell enough.' " Granny laughed. Mae didn't, not sure of the joke.

"So then you caught the big fish."

"No. Den Helmut vant to go swim. Den he make me go in vater und den he vant to play vid my big . . ." Granny smiled a small smile and stopped. She sighed. "O, Liebchen."

"What? What then, Granny?"

"Ven we do home Helmut get his turkey fish und fresh berries for dessert but his supper vas very late, Liebchen. Very late."

* * *

Granny said she never saw the Indian girl again. Not many months later the Chippewa were herded onto reservations in north central Minnesota. But she said she often wondered about her. Did her baby live? And was it a strong big boy like her Vilhelm?

Mae arrived at the patch and stood on a rock's slick surface. Water swirled around her knees. She shielded her eyes with her hand. "Why, there's more blossoms than I've ever seen." 'Course, it had been a real wet spring that year. Granny'd always said that's what it takes for the best berries. "A real wet spring, Granny."

With two fingers, she gingerly lifted a long, heavily blossom-laden spear that hung out over the river. The white blossoms disguised razor-sharp thorns, some of which were an inch long.

About the middle of August, this very spot will be a black raspberry lover's heaven, Mae thought. And she sure knew a black raspberry lover . . .

Before she could stop herself, she started thinking about black raspberry cobbler with fresh cream being Sean's favorite dessert. And about Sean. Oh, Sean! *Where are you?* Her sad thoughts dimmed the very sun.

They'd had no word in months. Not even Father Fitz. Hanson, the government man, said he knew nothing. He hadn't even bothered to reply to Mae's last letter.

Father Fitz was optimistic. He still came for dinner at least once a week in spite of the fact that the renovations were finished and there was no real reason for his presence other than the solace he brought Mae.

Since the new year, even the priest had become

less hopeful. "The time has come for ye to decide, Mae. Do ye want to live alone all yer life?"

That question had been asked more than three months ago and she was no nearer to knowing the answer today than she was then.

The one thing that had always remained constant was her faith in Sean. That belief never wavered. If any man alive could extricate himself, the Irishman was that man. She said as much to Father Fitz often "Sean will think of a way." Bolstering her spirits, she said the same to herself daily. And hope surged anew. For a week, two or five months, her convictions had stayed solid. But lately doubt intruded, like smoke seeping under a closed door. She believed in Sean's love for her. She knew how much he wanted to be with her but she also knew he was a man of granite resolve. If he thought, by his presence, he would cause harm to her or Jack, she knew she'd never see him again.

"How can he find out if the mob goes for the sham?" Father Fitz had asked. "Sean can't hardly write them and ask if they believe he's dead, now can he? No, he can't," Father had had to answer himself. "So, he must wait for a sign."

She slid off the rock and waded back toward the heron and Johnny. A chipmunk rustled the brush along the bank, his caramel-striped body flashing between clumps of marshy grass.

She sat on the blanket and listened to Johnny, who was snoring softly. In repose, he looked positively angelic. The tree allowed dappled light through its heavy umbrella of leaves, offering partial respite from the sunshine. She folded an edge of the blanket over the baby's bare legs anyway.

She lay back, rested her head in the crook of one arm and crossed her ankles. The stone in her ring poked into the back of her neck. She sat up and turned it to the side of her finger then lay back in the same position.

Mae made a conscious effort not to dwell on her memories—doing so only caused her anguish—but she was never successful for long. So many things made her think of Sean. Her sapphire ring. Blackberries. The sunshine. Snow. A tenor. Father Fitz's brogue. It was like the day when she had burned all her fingers on her right hand. Everything she tried to do that day had reminded her of the hurt.

There you go again, Mae Ella. Feeling sorry for yourself.

The leaves above looked smeared, as if viewed through a rain-streaked window. She took her handkerchief out of her pocket, sat up and blew her nose. The crane started. He refolded his wings and looked down his long beak at her.

All right, she snapped silently, she'd done some backsliding. But she had a right to know. Was he alive? Maybe he'd been hit by a trolley trying to cross the street! Her vivid imagination took over and ran rampant. She started thinking of all the accidents that could befall him.

Maybe he didn't want to come back anymore! Maybe he no longer loved her. Maybe he hadn't really been in love with her ever!

"No." She rocked her head back and forth on her arm. "Remember to trust, Mae Ella." Hadn't he told her repeatedly that she was everything he had ever wanted? No one could pretend that much emotion.

Yes but that was then and this is now. Hadn't he also promised that he would never leave her?

She closed her eyes and a tear slid out.

Sean had never lied to her. She had to keep that one thought in mind. Every time she'd doubted him, she'd been proven woefully wrong. Not that she needed Moira's latest letter to shore up her belief but it was just another example of how doubt had undermined her resolve. She conjured up the letter. She knew it by heart.

Deerest Mae: I tak pin in hand but can only rite a quik note as we are hafing kumpany in haff an hour. Tim is standin over me and tellin me hurry already. But I no yu wood want to no this.

Jist two days ago a famou [this was drawn through] rich doktor's son on the north side komited sewicide. He hung hisself. They diskovered a note an in it the rich doktor's son [he was traning to be a doktor too] confesed to killing Peter! Yes. Innyway, wot hapened waz he waz gell jea [both drawn through] inveyous of Peter's friendship with Thiro! Yu rember Thiro, don yu?

I was so serprised when this kaim out . . .

Tim is about to find a fite, maiking me rush but I better go.

I wish we kud see each other agin. Little Katie is a tearor too and axe jist like you said Jack duz!

I lov yu. Yur frind Moira.

P.S. Plez escuse my slopey hand writin.

Mae sat up, blew her nose and wiped her eyes. She would wait and she would have faith. She lay down again. Only she didn't know what she would do if he never came back. "Die, I guess," she whispered, "oh, Sean, without you I'll just die of a broken heart."

Twenty-one

Sean knelt with one knee to the ground, his right leg stuck out at a ninety-degree angle. He automatically massaged his thigh. A lethal shillelagh, knurled and scarred, lay on the ground beside him. His companion, old Sandy, had already abandoned him and gone down the path to the water's edge. After a long slurping drink, he lay down in the cool water, hind legs splayed. He appeared to be looking up at Sean. His tail made a little slapping noise in the water.

Sean stared at the pastoral scene below him, fighting an unmanly need to bury his face in both hands and bawl like a baby! How many times had he imagined this moment? A thousand times, at least.

Mae slept on her side, her head pillowed on her arm. Barefooted and with her skirts tucked up, her slender ankles and pale, shapely calves were exposed. Two or three buttons on her bodice were undone. Some curls had escaped from her braid to blow lightly around her face. Her lips were slightly parted, her cheeks either heat-flushed or sunburned.

He spared a quick glance at the boy and smiled. Arms outflung, the boy lay on his back beside her.

God, but the lad had grown like a bad habit!

Sean heard a splash and looked up in time to see a blue heron swallow a green and yellow striped perch. A fishing pole and battered straw hat lay on the bank a few feet away.

His greedy gaze returned to the gel. Neve' would he tire o' lookin' a' her. At last! After all these months! He was home!

Home, he smiled again, as ordered. He had reread her letter until the paper crumbled. "Come home this minute," the note had read. He particularly liked the "Or else" part.

"Sassy little nit! I canno' wait to get me hands on ye!"

By rote, he reached into his shirt pocket for his cheroots then shook his head. Three months now it was since he had given up the filthy weed and he still reached in his pocket ten times a day. Quitting the twenty-year habit had been . . . difficult.

'Twas nae somethin' a man couldn't handle, mind ye, but 'twas nae stroll in the heather either!

Sitting in that shabby rooming house in Toronto and miserable to the bone anyway, he had figured— why not go the limit? And he told himself, when he got home (no' *if* mind ye, but *when*) Mae would approve. She'd mentioned once that she didn't think it was good for him. "I don't want you to die before your time," she had said.

Come to think of it, neither did he.

He had plenty of time to think in Toronto. To decide what he wanted out of life.

He decided that when he died he wanted to be older than sin. He wanted his hair to be gray and his boots to be off. He wanted to be laid out in the front parlor and he wanted a bunch of people—his children and grandchildren—grieving for him.

And he wanted to die before that woman on the blanket.

It seemed a small thin' to ask. Yet there in Toronto, it seemed impossible. 'Twould require a miracle.

So he had prayed. Aye. The McGloin! Harder than a sinner who knows his death date in advance. He figured it couldn't hurt. And maybe, just maybe mind ye, it would help.

Three days ago, it'd happened. A messenger arrived from Hanson. Spinelli, in prison in upstate New York, had been garroted in his cell. The same night, at a ritzy uptown joint, three of his top men had been gunned down before they were able to finish their lobster fra Diablo. Hanson gave credit for the hits to a rival "family."

'Twas the answer to all of Sean's prayers because now none of the other major families cared a rat's arse about the Irishman. Matter of fact, as instrumental as he had been in breaking Spinelli's power hold on the waterfront, he was probably on their Christmas list! Since the minute he received the message, he had been traveling night and day.

Which reminded him—he rubbed the hard stubble on his jaw. Bloody Hell! He should have stopped at Einar's and cleaned up first. He had considered stopping before he rented a horse at the livery but his rationalization for not doing so was that the town busybody would ask a hundred questions and he wasn't ready to go into any lengthy explanations. Truth was, he did not want any further delays in getting to Mae.

Still, rubbing his hand over his jaw again, now he wished he'd taken a half an hour. He raised his arm, ducked his head and sniffed. Nae bad.

He took a deep breath. Well, he thought silently, this is it.

Picking up the shillelagh and using it as a lever, he stood.

He brushed off the seat of his pants and his thighs, front and back.

He searched his pockets. "Bloody hell!" He searched them again. "A foin bloody time to lose me comb!" He finger combed his hair twice.

He turned up his collar and folded his sleeves back another roll.

He ran his tongue over his teeth and a finger under both sides of his 'stache.

He grinned and rolled his shoulders. And started down the hill.

Epilogue

Sean and Mae had three more children, all boys. Between their second son, Liam, and their third, Helmut, they lost a baby girl to diphtheria. Her name was Heather.

Seven years after their last son was born and when they thought they would have no other children, they had another girl. They named her Ilse.

A few days shy of his eighty-first birthday, Sean died in his sleep. His boots, of course, were on the closet floor. Mae was at his side.

Sean McGloin's wake lasted two days. The sprawling farmhouse—twenty-eight rooms by then—was packed with mourners. The funeral Mass, at which Sean's grandson and namesake sang like an angel, was the best attended in anyone's memory.

Mae followed within the year. No one was surprised; they were that close. Although at the end her eyesight was very poor, mentally she was sharp as a tack and twice as shiny.

Their descendants live and prosper in Otter Tail.

Dear Reader,

I'm a pushover for a larger-than-life-sized hero. For instance, I was watching a movie recently in which the male lead tore across the screen, scooped up two flintlocks and fired on the run (with unerring accuracy, of course). Three bad guys keeled over! The cynic sitting next to me said, "Oh, yeah, right! Did you see that?"

I pumped my arm, fist clinched, and replied, "Yessss!"

Here's to the heroes of the world, real and imaginary—long may they reign!

Best,

Wynema McGowan

If you liked *The Irishman,* you'll love Wynema's next book, *Catchin' Heck.* Watch for it in 1996, from Pinnacle and Denise Little Presents. I'm giving you just a little taste of it here—it's priceless!

Denise Little

Prologue

The Northern Pacific Railway had been losing paying customers like an aging whore. Now, within minutes of the end of the line, only a solitary traveler remained.

The conductor ran the front of each shoe down his pant leg and knuckled his moustache. *Why, a person could hardly believe that girl had come all the way from New York City. Not to look at her, sitting so rigidly erect and all.* He cleared his throat and waited until she lifted her eyes. Pretty as a summer's day, he thought. "Two Sisters is comin' up, miss."

"Thank you." Cicely Heckt checked her lapel watch. "My stars! We're almost ten hours late."

"Yes, ma'am, I know but . . ." He shrugged apologetically. "Who would've figured on snow this time of year?"

Cicely smoothed her broadcloth skirt. She wasn't complaining . . . Well, actually, she was. Instead of arriving at a respectable hour she would arrive at eleven o'clock at night and she had no place to stay.

Once again, she anxiously peered through the grimy window at a windswept land that gleamed with eerie incandescence. The ice-sheathed train was paralleling a winterbourne stream. Suddenly it lurched around a curve and rattled onto a trestle bridge. As it exited, the train's kerosene beacon transfixed two foraging deer. They stood like stone statues for a minute and then bounded for the treeline. The countryside was as still as death once more.

It was the most desolate, lonely-looking land she'd ever envisioned. Taking a ragged breath, she whispered, "Welcome to the edge of nowhere, Sissy Heck."

Some might call Two Sisters, Minnesota the edge of nowhere. In reality, it was on the edge of Lake Superior, south of the Ontario border and north of Duluth, which was the nearest town. Although geographically isolated, it was not so far off the beaten track that booted feet were not finding their way to it. Plenty of them; the entire area was enjoying an extended period of prosperity and rapid expansion. In short, it was a boom town. But make no mistake, it was as rough as they get. Card dealers and whores were in as much demand as carpenters and masons. Maybe more so. As they say, Two Sisters was a town with hair on it.

Sissy Heck arrived during a late spring storm on April 28, 1881. It was a Friday night and as usual, every room in town was taken. But of course, she couldn't have known that then.

Leaving the tiny depot behind, she headed off toward the lights. She didn't get ten feet before her high-topped kidskin shoes were so caked with mud it felt as if she were lifting bags of sand. As she made her way along the deserted street she could hear muted conversations and laughter, the tinny sound of a poorly tuned piano, someone's frantic flailing on a fiddle. Snow was slowly falling, smudging the light bestowed by the tar barrel flare on the corner. She paused in front of one of the buildings to switch her heavy bag from one hand to the other. Two hand-lettered signs were

propped in the window: Buddy's Cafe and Help
Wanted. As she watched, the lanterns within were being
extinguished. All but one in the back. She stepped off
the boardwalk and into the alley.

Anyone with two good eyes in their head could see
that Sissy Heck was going to wreak all sorts of havoc
in a female-sparse town like Two Sisters, but one of
Joe Willie Everett's problems on that following morning was that he didn't have two good eyes in his head.
During a fight the previous night, his left eye had
been the only thing between Walter "Hog" Hammond's fist and Duluth. Or, at least, that's the way it
had felt to Joe Willie at the time.

As he entered Buddy's Cafe, he was gripping his
hat and walking scrunched. The former due to the icy
wind off the lake; the latter due to the bootheel which
had so recently reposed between his short ribs.

Sissy Heck heard the front door open. Anxious to
be bright and on the spot she told her new employer,
"I'll get it," and tore into the eating area. There she
saw a big person wearing a sheepskin-lined coat and
a Western-style hat. Of the man's face she glimpsed
only a whisker-rough jaw. It was square as a miter.

With a grunt the man sat at the round table positioned in front of the window. He unbuttoned his coat
and then removed his hat and tossed it on a nearby
chair. He had a full head of streaky brown hair. Un-
cut. Uncombed. Wild. Through Sissy's mind flashed
the memory of a spring day long ago.

She and her mother had finished their shopping and
were strolling down Fifth Avenue when a ruffian—he
looked not unlike this man—came walking along from
the opposite direction. The man had a horseshoe-
shaped moustache and three guns tucked in his belt.

As he drew near, he lifted his hat and shook free a ragged tangle of hair.

My stars! Sissy thought. Do you suppose he could be Wild Bill Hickok? She was fascinated!

Her mother most definitely was not. "A lady," she admonished as she marched her on by the man, "does not acknowledge a person like that."

True to her expectations, the man removed his coat and dismayed her with the sight of a foot-long skinning knife and two black-barreled guns stuck into his belt. She shuddered but, reminding herself how much she needed this job, she forced herself to take a step closer. "Would you care for coffee, sir?" she asked.

Joe Willie heard the voice. It was soft and soothing, like the wind's song through the pines. Definitely not the owner, Buddy Targen, whose Norwegian accent was thick enough to float one of the iron barges anchored in the harbor. He turned his head slightly in order to see the table better—yes, it was his usual table at Buddy's Cafe—and then he looked up.

Sissy saw a one-eyed, grotesquely distorted face with blown-up, rubbery-looking lips. She saw herself as she'd appeared on a certain morning three months ago.

Joe Willie was thunderstruck as well. He saw a young woman with a small face that was pale as paint and paralyzed with shock. Her brown eyes were large, liquid, and blank as a shot deer. She gasped. Her lips rolled back and then her eyes did likewise and she collapsed at his feet, a crumpled thing. He looked down at her for a heartbeat then bellowed, "Buddy!"

From the kitchen, "Hvat is it?"

"Get t'hell out here!"

"Hvat?" The proprietress skidded in and grabbed her heart. "Oh, my goodness!" she exclaimed. (Except it sounded more like "Oh, may gewdness!")

Joe Willie pointed. "Who t'hell's that?"

"My new help"

"Where'd she come from?"

"From the kitchen."

"No, I mean . . ." The girl moaned, lifted her head slightly and threw up on Joe Willie's boot. "Aw crap!" He leapt up, raking the chair across the wood floor.

"Joe Willie! Watch your language!"

"Damnit, Buddy! She just urped on my boot!"

"Oh, you've had worse than that on your boot."

The door opened and Dr. Conor O'Malley entered. Joe Willie waved him over. "Hey, good timing, Doc. C'mon over here 'n' take a look."

"No, no! Not on the floor. Let's put her in the back."

Joe Willie picked the girl up, noted that she seemed to weigh less than his coat, and he carried her into the small room off the kitchen.

He laid the girl down on the bed. On the chair next to her was a doeskin case with a mother of pearl top. Inside was a soft bit of something peachy colored. Without thinking, Joe Willie stretched a hand out to it. Damn thing leapt up and snagged itself on his finger!

"Thought you had more sense than that," Buddy informed him as she moved a fancy leather suitcase that opened into two parts like a book.

Joe Willie had finally succeeded in freeing his finger and jammed both hands into his hip pockets. He gestured with his chin at the girl. "So what about her? Where'd she come from?"

"Just a minute . . . let me dampen this rag first."

From a pitcher on the table she poured water on a folded cloth then slapped it on the girl's forehead like a pancake on a griddle.

"Gut. Now, where was I? Oh, yah. Like I said, my

last girl quit, but I was so busy I didn't have time to do a thing about it until . . . oh, it must've been ten o'clock. Well, I'd no sooner set a Help Wanted sign in the window when there came a tap-tap on the back door and . . . there she was. Dressed as you see her an' totin' that fancy suitcase there. I forget what you call them."

"A portmanteau," the doctor replied as he lifted one of the girl's eyelids.

"Yah! One of them. Anyway, she said she was hungry an' was looking for a place to stay. I made her a sandwich an' a cup of tea an' we got to talking. I told her there wasn't a room in town what with the new hotel not done yet an' it being a Friday night. She said she was lookin' for work. One thing led to another . . ."

The girl regained consciousness and jerked upright. "There, there, miss," Doc O'Malley said, patting her shoulder. "I was just taking your pulse."

She pulled away. "Oh, no. Please. I'm . . ." She looked around, saw Joe Willie again and blanched. ". . . fine."

"Good God!" the doctor said when he looked square at Joe Willie for the first time. "What on earth happened to you?"

"Hog Hammond's what happened to me. Him an' Mart Braun an' some other fella jumped me last night in the alley back of the Wind Fall. One of 'em was carryin' a damned log. Cracked me a good one with it an' then landed about twenty punches apiece before I could get fired up and get my feet under me . . ."

"You look like something for sale at the meat counter," Buddy said.

The doctor asked, "Were you unarmed?"

His deputy, Jim Horse, had asked him basically the same thing. "Why t'hell didn't you use your gun?"

The answer was that he liked besting a man—or three men—with his fists. For the pure sake of doing it. He was good at it, too. "No, I wasn't unarmed," he replied testily. There came a mouselike squeak and everyone looked at the girl, who was staring at Joe Willie and shivering like a froze dog.

"Better save it," muttered the doctor out of the side of his mouth.

"You just asked me . . ."

"Wait out front a minute. I'll take a look at . . ."

"You just tend little Miss Hightone there." Over his shoulder Joe Willie gave her a hard one-eyed glare. "I reckon I'll live."

With the slam of the door, Sissy pushed herself up and smoothed her hair. Realization was setting in. Her first day at her first job and she threw up on her first customer. "Oh, God." She covered her face with her hands.

Buddy rescued a peach-colored dressing gown which was about to meet the floor and then pushed the doctor from the room. "Let's give the poor girl a minute." In a short time she returned alone. "All right now, Mrs. Heck?"

"Sissy, please. Yes. Oh, Mrs. Targen, I can't tell you how sorry I am! It was just such a shock . . ."

Buddy shook her head and said, "I just got a good . . ."

Sissy had to pay careful attention when Mrs. Targen spoke. It sounded like she said, "I yust got a gut lewk at Yoe Villie myself. Shocked a tew, yew bet."

"Why did someone do that to him?" A lump had formed in her throat or she might have cried, *Why did someone do that to me?*

"Why?" Mrs. Targen looked bewildered a minute. "Well, I suppose it had something to do with his job. He's the sheriff."

"The sheriff?" Sissy watched her bustle around, straightening this, neatening that.

"Yah. And a pretty darn good one too. Little rough maybe, but you should've seen Two Sisters before he came. All the stabbings and shootings and . . ." She looked at the girl, noted her lack of color and said, "I hope this don't turn you off on the job!"

"Turn me off on the yob? I mean, job? No, of course not. I'm amazed this hasn't turned you off on me. I can't believe you'd keep me on after I . . . after I . . . Oh!" Her face disappeared into her hands again.

"You bet I will! Why, I know a good thing when I see one."

And so will you! Watch for Catchin' Heck, *by Wynema McGowan.*

FOR THE VERY BEST IN ROMANCE—
DENISE LITTLE PRESENTS!

AMBER, SING SOFTLY   (0038, $4.9
by Joan Elliott Pickart

Astonished to find a wounded gun-slinger on her doorste
Amber Prescott can't decide whether to take him in or p
him out of his misery. Since this lonely frontierswoma
can't deny her longing to have a man of her own, sh
nurses him back to health, while savoring the glorious po
sibilities of the situation. But what Amber doesn't realize
that this strong, handsome man is full of surprises!

A DEEPER MAGIC   (0039, $4.9
by Jillian Hunter

From the moment wealthy Margaret Rose and struggli
physician Ian MacNeill meet, they are swept away in an a
venture that takes them from the haunted land of Abe
deen to a primitive, faraway island—and into a world
danger and irresistible desire. Amid the clash of ancie
magic and new science Margaret and Ian find themselv
falling helplessly in love.

SWEET AMY JANE   (0050, $4.9
by Anna Eberhardt

Her horoscope warned her she'd be dealing with the wro
sort of man. And private eye Amy Jane Chadwick w
used to dealing with the wrong kind of man, due to h
profession. But nothing prepared her for the gorgeous
handsome Max, a former professional athlete who is bei
stalked by an obsessive fan. And from the moment th
meet, sparks fly and danger follows!

MORE THAN MAGIC   (0049, $4.9
by Olga Bicos

This classic romance is a thrilling tale of two adventure
who set out for the wilds of the Arizona territory in th
year 1878. Seeking treasure, an archaeologist and an a
tronomer find the greatest prize of all—love.

*Available wherever paperbacks are sold, or order direct from t
Publisher. Send cover price plus 50¢ per copy for mailing a
handling to Penguin USA, P.O. Box 999, c/o Dept. 171(
Bergenfield, NJ 07621. Residents of New York and Tenness
must include sales tax. DO NOT SEND CASH.*